WEATHERING THE STORM

Linda Kay Silva

Publishing
Company

San Diego, California

Cover Design by Hummingbird Graphics
Book Design and Typesetting by Paradigm Publishing
Copy Editing by Andrea L.T. Peterson

Printed in the United States on acid-free paper
First Edition

Library of Congress Catalog Card Number: 93-87209
ISBN 1-882587-02-2

Dedication

Without good characters, there can be no story.

This book is dedicated to two characters who live in my heart as well as my head. To Delta and Connie, for laughing with me, for sharing my days, for inspiring me to look beyond myself, and most importantly, for allowing all three of us to grow.

Being a writer means spending a great deal of time in my head. It means conversing with the muses, chatting with the various being in my subconscious, and transporting my spirit to whatever realm my fictional characters happen to be. It is an odd profession few truly understand. But for those who have tried and been slightly successful, I wish to offer these thanks:

GINA: The Wonder Twin. Through it all, we still managed to laugh, to dance, and to stay the best of friends. To me, you will always be a fairy princess.

CHLOÉ: In the "gardens and gardens of lesbians," you are truly the most remarkable flower of them all. Thank you for being a part of my dream.

JENNIFER: For giving me the chance to watch and grow. You are even more amazing than I envisioned all those years ago.

NICKY: Because thousands of miles can't diminish the love and adoration I feel for you.

VICKI: For giving me such a great job. I've learned more from you in one year than a decade worth of college. Thanks just isn't enough.

KATHLEEN D.: For believing in me enough to take a chance. You're the best!

HOPPER: Hands down, pal, you're the most fun a girl can have!

MY MOM: For always being there. I love you.

SPECIAL THANKS TO:

ALI: Thucydides said, "The secret of Happiness is Freedom, and the secret of Freedom, Courage." Thank you for possessing the Courage to find me and the Freedom to love me.

1

"I am truly sorry that it has to end this way for you, Delta Stevens. I admire your courage and your guts to confront us by yourself, but this little party is over." Rubin turned to the man called Dice and said, "Take her to where we dropped that kid off and finish her there. Meet us at—" Rubin hesitated before writing something down on a notepad. "We'll be here," he said as he handed the paper to Dice.

Dice took the piece of paper before grinning menacingly at Delta. "You're a dream come true, little lady. You don't have any idea how many nights I laid on that lousy bunk dreamin' of getting even with the cops who let that fuckin' mutt tear my fingers off. I musta done something real good for you to end up right in my lap."

Delta sneered at him. His breath was foul, his body odor rank, and he was the epitome of a disgusting slob. But worse than his appearance, was his demeanor. Dice had a score to settle and settling it meant taking Delta down.

Delta nodded at his two-fingered hand. "It's a shame the dog didn't rip your throat out as well. Poor dog probably gagged on your rancid flesh."

"You fucking bitch," Dice growled, raising his hand to hit her.

But before he could swing, Delta grabbed his wrist and yanked him to her. "You may be able to kill me you sick piece of shit, but I'll see you in hell before I become your punching bag."

Enraged, Dice rammed the butt of the Uzi into Delta's left cheekbone. "I oughta kill you right now."

"That's enough, Dice," Rubin ordered. "Don't you see, she's just trying to get to you?"

Dice looked over at Rubin and slowly lowered the gun.

"Now, get her out of here and erase any evidence of her presence here. When you're through, meet us like we planned."

Dabbing the blood off her cheek, Delta shook her head slowly. "I thought you were smarter than this, Rubin. If I disappear, every cop in the country will be after you."

Rubin shrugged. "From what I've seen so far, I'm not impressed. Now, get her out of here.

Dice leered into Delta's face. "Can we have some fun with her? She did cost me three fingers and a hell of a time in the joint."

"I don't care what you do as long as she can't be found."

On her way out the door, Delta turned to Rubin. "You're going to burn, Rubin. I swear to God, you're going down."

Rubin shook his head. "I'm afraid you're the only one 'going down,' Stevens. It's a shame, really. I hate wasting a good looking woman."

Sticking the Uzi into the small of her back, Dice walked Delta to the car and pushed her into the back seat. Then he reached into the glove compartment and pulled out a pair of handcuffs. "Revenge is grand, ain't it?" Dice said to Jake, who grinned. Reaching over the back seat, Dice slammed the cuffs on Delta's wrists.

"Some of your personal sex toys, Dice? I doubt you could get a woman to sleep with you voluntarily."

His answer was a stinging slap across the face. "Bitch."

Delta grinned and ignored her throbbing cheek. "Is that the best you can do, you little dickweed."

"Why you stupid bi—" Dice yelled, backhanding her again. "You don't even know who you're messin' with."

"Hey," Jake's voice boomed in a low baritone. "Chill out, Dice. You're making a fool of yourself. Wait until we get her out of the city before you start that crap."

Dice held his raised hand in the air for a second before lowering it to Delta's right breast. "Yeah. Okay. I get it. You think you're a tough bitch, don't you? You'd rather I beat the shit out of you than have my own fun. Yeah. I get it."

Delta visibly cringed under his touch. "You're a sick piece of filth, you fingerless bastard. You get your dick anywhere near me and I swear, I'll tear it off."

Dice lifted his hand and slapped Delta again. "Shut up!"

"Cool it, Dice," Jake bellowed again. "I mean it, man. It's too hard to drive with you acting like a maniac. Wait until we get there, 'cause you're starting to piss me off."

Delta grinned into Dice's face and whispered, "And I wouldn't piss him off, Dice, because he's way more of a man than you'll ever hope to be and if he wants me, I'd rather have him." Delta was desperate. If she could divide their attention, if she could get them arguing between themselves, she might have a chance to snatch Dice's weapon from him. It was the only chance she'd have, and it was a slim one at best.

Grabbing her right breast again, Dice moved his face right up to Delta's, "Oh, we're both gonna have some fun with you, little lady."

In a flash, Delta reared her head back and bashed her forehead into his. A sickening crack resounded through the car as their heads collided. Delta had seen her best friend, Connie, do that once, and it worked.

"Goddamn whore!" Dice cried, grabbing his bleeding forehead. Delta had smacked him hard enough to cut his forehead open. "Pull over!"

Jake did not.

"I said pull over!"

"You ain't giving the orders here, Dice." Jake looked into the rearview mirror and grinned. "I told you to let her alone until we get there. Now look what you've done."

"Damn you, Jake—"

"Chill out little man, 'cause if I pull this car over, it'll be to kick your ass. Now just sit there and shut up."

Dice opened his mouth to respond, but said nothing. Instead, he pressed his two-fingered hand against his forehead while poking the muzzle of the Uzi into Delta's ribs.

The rest of the ride was uneventful, as Jake winded and twisted his way through the darkness to the very outskirts of the city. Delta's mind raced with options. Even if she did get her hands on the Uzi, killing them both before they could get to her would take a miracle.

Maybe, Delta thought despondently as the car snaked its way through the night, maybe she had finally run out of miracles.

"This is far enough," Dice said. "We can take her fifty yards or so out, have some fun, and then have her suck on my gun before going nighty-night. How does that sound, Amazon Queen?"

"He really does have short men's complex, doesn't he, Jake?"

Jake looked into the mirror and smiled.

"Shut up!" Dice yelled.

Jake pulled the car off the road and turned to them both. "Look, Dice, take her out and do what you gotta do, but your mouth is beginning to get on my nerves. Call me when you're done."

Dice returned a smile. "Don't you want to play, Jake?"

Jake shrugged. "No way, man. I seen what women look like when you get through with 'em. No thanks." He pulled out a cigarette and lit it.

"Put that thing out, you idiot. You want someone to see?"

Jake pulled a long drag. "I know my job, Dice. We haven't seen a car in over fifteen minutes. Relax. There's no one out here but us chickens." Jake laughed as though he had just thought that one up.

Dice nodded and jammed the gun into Delta's back. "When you hear my gun, come running and we'll finish the job."

Jake nodded and leaned against the car.

Delta took one step and felt her knees go weak. She would have to find a way to use her legs to get to Dice, or it was over for her. Right here, right now, her life would end, and no one would ever know what became of her. The thought sent shivers down her spine.

Ten yards.

Twenty yards.

Forty yards more and Dice pushed her in the back and told her to turn around.

Delta turned, very slowly. She could barely see Dice standing in front of her. The darkness was so thick, it was nearly palatable. Only light from the half-moon illuminated the ridge standing in the distance and the vast flatlands on the opposite side. Delta finally recognized where they had brought her to die; they were in the perfect place to bury a dead body—the Anza Borrega Desert.

Delta weighed her only option. She knew she'd have a chance if she allowed him to get on top of her. Even then, her chances of overpowering him with her hands handcuffed were wafer-thin.

"You let that fuckin' mutt tear my fingers off," Dice said, unbuckling his belt with one hand. "You just stood by and watched him have me for lunch."

"It couldn't be helped. You went for the gun, Dice. The dog did her job."

Dice stepped closer. He was about five feet away. "Oh yeah? And did you do your job by just standing there watching her sink her teeth into my skin over and over again?"

Delta didn't respond. She was trying to formulate a plan. Maybe a leg sweep once his pants fell to his ankles. She'd seen Connie do it once in a demonstration. Maybe...

Connie. She was probably out of her head with worry by now, combing the city for Delta this very minute; cursing herself for letting Delta take such a risk, cursing everybody else because she couldn't find her. Couldn't and wouldn't. Not unless...

"On your knees, bitch."

Delta shook her head. "Not a chance. You want to get off, do it yourself. I imagine that's the only way you get any these days anyway."

Dice stepped closer. "You trying to make me mad or something?"

Delta remained standing. "If you're gonna kill me, you're going to have to do it while I'm on my feet. I will not get on my knees for the likes of you."

Dice aimed the Uzi at Delta's knees. "If I blow your kneecaps out, then you'll be on your knees, won't you?"

"Dice, if you shoot me anywhere with that, I'll bleed to death before you have a chance to have any fun at all."

"Then get on your knees."

"Eat shit."

Dice took one more step forward. If he was two feet closer, Delta would have a chance at the gun. But he was still too far away.

"Then take your clothes off."

"You first. Or is your dick like your brain? Tiny and laughable."

Even in the murky night, Delta could see Dice glaring at her. "As a matter-of-fact," he said, dropping his pants to his ankles, "I got one of the biggest peters women have ever seen."

Delta didn't even look at it. Instead, her eyes remained glued to his gun.

"And you're gonna suck on it if it's the last thing you do." He chuckled. "It probably will be the last thing you do." Raising the gun to her face, Dice motioned for her to step forward. "Come to papa and make his dream come true."

Dream? This was no dream. This was a nightmare. Death, she didn't mind. Torture was also semi-acceptable. But rape, forced oral copulation, and sodomy? Delta cringed at the thought. Her worst nightmares were coming to pass. If she didn't do something about it, she would live out the reality of her worst nightmare.

Nightmare. This had all started because of the nightmares; the recurring images of her bloody failures that visited her nightly. Even now, as she stared down the barrel of the Uzi, those nightmares came flooding back to her. She remembered them as clearly as if they had been real. Over and over, the scars from the Zuckerman caper were ripped open at night, when she tried to close her eyes and forget. Each night, it started with a stifling darkness, as if someone had put a large hand over her mouth to keep her from breathing. Shafts of light filtered through tiny windows too high up to see through, and the sound of rats skittering across metal beams filled the air.

How many times would her subconscious relive the nightmarish realities she had faced on the job? How many nights did she wake up in a cold sweat, still feeling the fear, the adrenaline rush, the overpowering emotions of a memory she wore like an apendectomy scar? More often than she dare count, she saw herself gingerly stepping around a burning chair, following the barrel of her .357 Magnum as it sliced through the inky darkness. With a sharp shudder, she involuntarily remembered her last nightmare. She remembered the nightmare and the chain of events that led her to this desert, to this moment...

"I know you're in here," Delta stated sharply, wrapping her left index finger around the trigger. "I've killed before, you piece of shit, and I'll do it again if you don't leave her alone." Delta waited for a response she knew would never come.

They were alone.

He had planned it that way and would play out his revenge until the bitter end.

Creeping through the murk, Delta was careful to avoid the rays of light dancing across the cement floor. She had been in this position before; she hadn't been a victim then, and she wasn't about to be one now.

"Delta," came a low, gravelly voice from a distance. "You know you can't stop me. No matter how hard you try, I will always beat you."

Delta's heart raced and she wiped the tiny beads of sweat off of her upper lip. The heat was unbearable and the fire that had consumed the chair suddenly swept up the drapes as well.

Drapes in a warehouse? Delta wondered, shrugging off the incongruency.

"Show yourself, you coward. Come out and face me and leave the girl alone."

A maniacal laugh reverberated through the room. "You want her?"

"You know I do."

"Then you can have her. Now and forever."

Suddenly, a body swung down from the metal beam and jerked to a halt five feet from the ground.

"No!" Delta screamed, seeing the girl's body suspended by a thick rope tied securely around her neck. Her head hung lazily to one side, and her eyes...

Those eyes. Those empty, lifeless eyes that stared at Delta, accusing her, berating her, reminding her of what a failure she had been.

Those eyes. How much longer would they haunt her?

Before Delta could move, maggots started worming their way out of the empty sockets, making their way toward the girl's nose. Several fell off as they unsuccessfully inched down her pale cheek.

"It's your fault, Delta. You took the law into your own hands and look what happened. Look!"

Delta dropped her gun and covered her ears. "No!"

"Yes, Delta. You know it's true. She's dead because of you. Dead and gone, and now she is plant food in the cemetery. How does it feel to know you're responsible. Or is it your irresponsibility, hmm?"

Delta pressed her hands to her ears, but she couldn't keep from hearing his words.

"Look at her Delta."

Instead she squeezed her eyes shut.

"Look at her! Or are you afraid?"

With her hands still covering her ears and her eyes tightly shut, Delta could swear she was feeling her heart pounding against her chest. She did not want to look. She didn't want to not look, either.

"Delta...she's okay, really. Just see for yourself. I was just playing a trick on you." The voice seemed distorted and Delta opened an eye to see why. She immediately regretted doing so. Swinging back and forth, as if someone had pushed her, was the little girl, laughing as maggots fell from her face onto the floor.

"No!" Delta cried out. "No! No! No!"

"Delta..."

"Get away from me!" Delta pushed away mysterious hands reaching out of nowhere to touch her.

"Delta, honey, wake up. You're having another nightmare. Wake up."

Delta sat straight up and looked around, still half asleep. Sweat ran down her back and her hands trembled when she reached up to wipe her perspiring forehead.

"Come here, baby," Megan said, gently pulling Delta to her. "You're okay, now. You're with me."

As the remaining sleepy fog lifted from Delta's consciousness, she snuggled close to Megan's breasts, afraid that even they might not be real.

"Same nightmare, sweetheart?"

Delta nodded, trying to slow her breathing. "Close enough."

Every night, for the past two weeks, Delta had experienced the same nightmare like some ghoulish broken record. Over and over again, a little girl named Helen died and had maggots crawling from her eyes. Always, Delta could only stand by helplessly while a voice pierced through the night mocking her. And always, she had awakened sweating, shaking, and wondering if and when it would ever end.

"They're the same, but getting worse. They feel more real to me each time." Delta pressed her cheek against Megan's chest. "I can't stop it."

Gently rocking Delta, Megan kissed her perspiring temple and held her tightly. "Shh. You just close your eyes now and think of you and me walking along the beach, okay?"

Nodding, Delta already felt her eyelids getting heavier. "Don't let go of me, Meg."

Running a well-manicured hand through Delta's sweaty curls, Megan kissed her again. "Not in a million years, my love."

Feeling her head rise and fall to the rhythm of Megan's breathing, Delta closed her eyes and almost instantly fell back to sleep, unaware of the true nightmares which were about to confront her own reality head-on.

2

It had been a full two weeks of suspension when Delta finally opened the door to the new captain's office for her first interview. Two weeks of gardening, suntanning, book reading, and soap opera watching and she had had enough. It seemed like everywhere she turned, whether it was books, television, or music, she saw Helen's little face—the face of a little girl who died at the hands of a madman who had absolutely no regard for human life. Delta had failed to save Helen from Elson Zuckerman's evil clutches, and it had haunted her every night for fourteen days straight. When it wasn't plaguing her during the night, it was running through her days with reckless abandon tormenting her psyche. She couldn't seem to escape the guilt, the frustration, and worst of all, the knowledge that she had failed to save a little girl from the hands of the devil himself.

She had failed Helen, and it felt as if her punishment for that failure would never end.

The only thing Delta had to look forward to was getting back to work. She loved the streets of her beat; the action, the pace, the night-to-night variety of calls she responded to. She enjoyed helping kids get home just as much as she enjoyed busting dope pushers, burglars, muggers, and thieves. But what she enjoyed most was knowing that she was the best there was. Still, even her best wasn't good enough to save Helen.

Knocking on the door to the captain's office, Delta waited for him to call her in.

"Come on in Delta," Captain John Henry said, motioning for her to enter.

She slipped in and closed the door quietly before sitting on one of the large leather chairs across from the captain's large oak desk. She hated the captain's office. It reminded her of the many principal's offices she had been sent to as a kid. It wasn't that she was a troublemaker or a poor student—quite the contrary. Because Delta found schoolwork to be easy, she was always doing things that eventually got her in trouble. How many lectures had she had as a kid on the importance of following the rules?

Delta sighed loudly. Some things never changed.

Captain Henry closed the large file he'd been reading and leaned across the desk. "Enjoy your time off?"

Delta shrugged. If this was his opening line, she was in trouble. "Not particularly. I enjoy my job."

Leaning away from her now, Captain Henry eased back among the shadows of the dark room. What was it with captains, other bosses, and principals who kept their offices like bear lairs?

"So I've heard. It appears you enjoy it so much, you do it even when you're not on duty."

Delta tensed. Her first meeting with the captain and already, she felt attacked. "If you've read the Zuckerman report, sir, you'll see that my off-duty activities saved hundreds of lives."

Captain Henry smiled. "Oh, I've read the report, Delta. A number of times. It also appears that this isn't the first time Internal Affairs has investigated you for off-duty activities."

Delta felt the heat rise in her neck. "No, sir, it isn't. But I've learned a lot and I'm sure I'm a better cop for it."

Captain Henry regarded her through a pair of twinkling blue eyes. He didn't appear to be baiting her; he was feeling her out more than anything else. "I'm sure you are. But your choice of words is interesting. You say you've learned a lot, but your lessons come when you've acted on your own and not under departmental guidelines—is that correct?"

Delta thought about this a moment before nodding. "I suppose so."

"They say," Captain Henry said, leaning forward again, "that those who can learn can also teach. What do you think?"

Delta frowned. What kind of question was that? "I don't know, sir. Some of my college professors were pretty poor teachers."

This seemed to throw him back. "Uh huh. Well, Delta, as your new captain, I've been given the job of deciding how to handle my officers when they're investigated by IA. I've gone through your files with a fine-tooth comb and I believe that some changes are in order if you are to continue working for this department."

The hair on the back of Delta's neck rose. "Changes, sir? What kind of changes?"

Leaning even closer, Captain Henry smiled. "I have decided to take you off of your regular beat and assign you a Field Training Officer position starting immediately."

"Training Patrol?"

"That's right."

"You've got to be kidding."

"Do I look like I'm kidding?"

Delta tried not to glare across the spacious desk at the new captain. Captain John Henry, who sat with his thick arms folded across his weightlifter's chest, reminded Delta of a wooden sailor figure carved roughly out of driftwood. He had Popeye's arms, a strong jawbone, and grayish eyes that said he was a take-charge kind of captain. All he lacked to complete the picture was Popeye's corncob pipe perched beneath his salt and pepper moustache and a tattoo of an anchor on his arm.

"Come on, Captain, anything but TP I'm no teacher. I wouldn't have the first clue how to be an FTO. Besides, what about Jan? She's my partn—"

"Not anymore. Like I said, thing are changing and as of this moment, Jan Bowers has a new partner, a new beat, and a new attitude. I suggest you adopt her approach." Unfolding his muscular arms, the captain leaned slowly and purposefully across the desk. The keen scent of his Old Spice cologne wafted into the air. "Field Training Officers are handpicked, Delta. I picked you. It's that simple."

Delta sighed in exasperation. He did not look like a man who understood compromises or creative bending of the rules. "A rookie will only slow me down, sir."

Captain Henry grinned, his moustache dancing slightly with the movement. "Has it ever occurred to you that slowing down is precisely what you need?"

Delta shook her head. "No, sir. I like the heat."

Captain Henry's old sailor grin widened. "So I've seen. From what I understand, you've been pretty busy lately experiencing that heat; and from all sides."

Delta winced inside. She knew what he was referring to and where he was going with this, and she didn't have a defense or any fancy words to get her out of it. She had gone out on a limb to save Connie and hundreds of others from Elson's sick game of revenge, and now, Internal Affairs was on the other side of that limb holding a saw in their collective hands. "I suppose you could say that, sir."

"I suppose I could say a great deal. You seem to have your hand in cookie jars that aren't even in your house."

Delta cocked her head in question. "Captain, I'd appreciate it if you'd cut to the chase. I don't do well with analogies and metaphors. My suspension is up tomorrow and I'm here because you asked me. Just why did you want to see me?" Delta held his gray eyes with hers.

Captain Henry retained her gaze for a moment before shifting his eyes back to the thick folder laying beneath his arms. "I wanted to see you because of this," he answered, tapping the folder with his stubby finger. Slowly pulling his large frame from the chair and moving over beside Delta, Captain Henry handed the folder to her. "I'm trying to keep a damn good cop from spending the rest of the year, if not the rest of her career, behind a desk."

Delta glanced down at the folder sitting in her lap. It suddenly felt like it weighed 100 pounds. "This is about the Zuckerman case, isn't it? You agree with IA that I could have saved him from falling from that building."

"What I think," Captain Henry said quietly, "is that you're a very fine officer who has made a lot of questionable judgement calls. I don't have to tell you that Internal Affairs has had a field day with some of those decisions."

Inhaling through her nose, Delta sat up straight and locked eyes with him again. "The chief's commendations mean nothing to you, sir?"

Pulling on his moustache, Captain Henry shook his head. "A commendation may be a nice thing to have under your belt, but as your superior officer, I see things in a little different light."

Delta stared hard into his eyes. The color seemed to vacillate between gray and blue. "And what light is that?"

Standing, Captain Henry leaned against the desk and folded his arms again. "Delta, have you taken a good look at this overstuffed personnel file lately?"

Delta briefly glanced down at it and shook her head.

"Well I have. I've been over every inch of your file, and you know what I found?"

Gritting her teeth, Delta shrugged. If he was going to blast her, she wished he would just do it and let her get the hell out of there. The walls were closing in around her and he seemed to be growing larger with every sentence. She didn't need this hassle. After Internal Affairs finished with her about the Zuckerman case, she promised herself to try to keep her nose as far away from trouble as she possibly could. Now, even before the game had begun, she was being benched.

"I am well aware of the contents of my file and the questions raised by IA, sir. The way I see it, it's my job to make certain decisions on the street and it's their job to question them. I did, they did, and it's done."

"Oh, it is?"

"Isn't it?"

Captain Henry picked the file up from Delta's lap and leafed through it. "I found four incidents where you ignored proper procedure, where you and your partner broke regulations, skirted the rules, and, most disconcerting of all, you ignored orders when you felt they didn't apply to you. I've read lengthy reports detailing accounts of you killing one suspect in a warehouse, and shooting the legs out from another suspect who also happened to be a cop. I've read about one man falling ten stories to his death while you stood by, apparently within arms' reach of him. I've read a file filled with both commendations and yellow slips, praises and reprimands—"

"Excuse me, sir, but is there a point to all this?"

Closing the file and setting it back on his desk, Captain Henry paced over to the window that overlooked the bustling station. "As a matter-of-fact, there is." Without turning back around, he continued. "There isn't a cop in California who hasn't heard of your exploits and heroics. I've spoken to officers who have worked with you, and you receive nothing but the highest marks from your colleagues. I've done some digging into your background and discovered that, regardless of the stains and medals in your file, you are considered one of the greatest assets in this department. You are what many of the young guys aspire to be."

"But?"

Captain Henry grinned. "But I'm afraid your reputation as a vigilante who too easily turns her back on departmental rules precedes you."

Delta nodded. She knew well her reputation across town and in other departments, and she was proud of it. In six years, she had had her share of major busts and convictions. Sometimes she played it straight, but more often than not, she found her way around the overly-restrictive departmental rules that hampered other cops from completing the job. She felt cops were required to follow rules that didn't apply to criminals, and those very rules tied the hands of law enforcement officers and kept them from doing their job well. Yes, she broke regulations, but she liked to think of it as creative problem-solving.

Unfortunately, it didn't appear as if Captain Henry was going to see it her way. "Like you said, Captain, I get the job done."

Turning to face her, Captain Henry still had a smirk on his face. For a moment, he just stood there, grinning and shaking his head. "You are just as she said you would be."

This caught Delta off guard, and her left eyebrow raised in question. "She?"

"District Attorney Pendleton. Hers was the first phone call I received when I sat behind this desk. It appears she keeps herself abreast of your career moves."

Delta did not respond. Alexandria Pendleton had been indirectly involved with the Zuckerman case. She had needed an arrest, and Delta gave her one—well, almost gave her one, if he hadn't fallen. If Alexandria had called the captain on Delta's behalf it could only mean that she had been forewarned about Delta's impending transfer and was using her considerable clout to keep it from happening.

"The DA said she'd heard that I was inquiring about the personnel I was taking over and thought I might like her input. Your name came first. It appears she has a great deal of confidence in you and asked me to reconsider IA's recommendation to remove you from the streets for awhile."

Delta did not move. She knew IA would use her as an example of what happens when you don't follow the rules, but she never imagined they would actually take her off the streets.

"Delta, I'm no fool. The DA called because you saved her ass by coming up with the suspect who killed that little girl. You made her and the whole department look sweet on that one. Yes, a man died. But the taxpayers just see that as a fitting end. No court costs, no prison expenditures. You gave them what they wanted; a dead suspect. I saw the polls right after that and the DA's reelection chances are looking pretty good because of it. It would take a miracle for Wainwright to beat her now. It's obvious she feels she owes you, so she made a call on your behalf."

"And?" Delta wanted this conversation to end. If he was going to take her off the street or put her on Training Patrol, then just do it.

"And, given your record, I have considered a lot of things. While I can't just ignore IA's recommendation to take you off the streets, I also can't sit a good cop with an arrest record like yours behind a desk. It was Pendleton's idea to put you on TP."

"I'll be sure to thank her," Delta replied sarcastically.

Captain Henry picked at his moustache. "She and I both know you're far too valuable on the streets to stick behind a desk pushing paper around. However," he paused for emphasis, "IA demands some action and I can't ignore the fact that there are so many 'incidents' in your file. I want those to stop. Period. End of the line. My officers will follow the regulations or they'll work for someone else. This place is under my command now, and I will see to it that it runs smoothly."

Delta slowly rose from the chair and rammed her fists into her pocket. "And you think making an example of me will allow you to do that?"

Captain Henry rose and moved over to sit on the corner of his desk. Delta wondered if they were playing some kind of chess game where one body changes position and the other counters.

"Rest assured, Delta," the captain said, smiling, "I am not using you as an example. I am doing what I believe is best for this department, not to mention, what I think is the right thing for you. It's either a rookie or a desk. One keeps you on the street, the other is pushing paper. I don't think the latter is something you'd enjoy very much."

Delta clenched her fists tighter in her pockets. How was it that she had helped end the string of killings by a psychopath, yet, because she didn't do it "by the book," she was suffering the consequences instead of receiving praise? God, the politics of this job made her crazy sometimes.

Captain Henry continued. "I want you working for me, Delta. Make no mistake about that. But to do that, you have to do things my way and that means you need to mellow some."

Mellow. The word banged like a brass drum off her temples. Cheese mellowed. Wine mellowed. Cops who mellowed lost their edge. It was that edge that made Delta so good and kept her alive. Without it, being on the street would be like facing a machine gun armed with a water pistol.

"Mellow, sir?" Delta asked, trying to maintain some calm in her voice. "You're putting me on TP to mellow me?"

Smoothing his moustache again, the captain nodded. "That's right. I've given it a lot of thought and I believe that teaching a rookie to do things the proper way will reinforce those policies and procedures you seem to frequently forget."

Licking her lips, Delta chose her next words carefully. "I haven't forgotten anything, sir. I admit I bend the rules every now and then, but only when they keep me from doing my job."

Grinning and shaking his head, the captain's eyes sparkled a bluish tint. "Damn it, Delta, you even admit it." Moving back behind his desk, he folded his hands together and rested his chin on them. "I've heard plenty about you, Delta Stevens, right down to your nickname 'Storm.' But nothing could have prepared me for your brash honesty."

Delta shrugged, but remained silent.

"You amaze me. Your butt's on the line here, and yet, you admit to breaking the rules. I don't know whether to respect the hell out of you or kick your ass right outta here."

"I think my record speaks for itself, sir. Good, bad, or indifferent, if we followed every rule, we'd never catch anybody. And anyone who says she can is a lying fool."

Captain Henry studied Delta for a moment before responding. "Our job is to follow the rules and bust those who don't. Surely, you don't stand there justifying your rather obvious attempts at vigilantism."

Delta shrugged again and dug her fists even deeper into her pockets. She felt hemmed in and didn't know how to get out. "Not all the time. Sometimes, the regs limit my ability to do the job well. Tell me you haven't broken procedure in order to bust some scumbag, Captain."

"My actions aren't in question here."

"And mine are?"

"In a way, yes." Lowering his hands, the captain fixed his eyes hard on Delta's. "You were an athlete in college, is that right?"

Delta nodded, puzzled by the non sequitur. "I was, yes."

"Then you should understand the concept of teamwork. Police work is a team enterprise, Delta, and if you're going to have a place on my team, you'll play by the rules. I will not have any of my officers hot-dogging it out there."

Delta bristled at the implication that that was what she was doing. "I do not 'hot-dog' it out there, sir. Ask anyone."

"I don't need to. You don't seem to understand that it isn't your past exploits that concern me. It's your future—a future, I might add, that is hanging by a thread. My job, what we are discussing right now, is whether or not we can fit you into my program. I want you to be on the field and not sitting on the bench. But if you're going to play, then it must be by the rules, both the department's and mine. The choice is yours."

Inhaling slowly, Delta pulled her hands from her pockets and sat on the edge of the chair. As much as she hated the idea of carting a rookie around, she hated the thought of being stuck behind a desk even more. Like eating and sleeping, Delta thrived on the action on her beat. She needed the thrill of the chase and the pump of adrenaline that comes from bringing down a pusher or a wife beater. That was why she became a cop in the first place. She loved the action—the ten minutes of a shift when the air becomes so thick she can't breathe, when her heart pounds so hard it's all she can hear, when she battles her own fears and trepidation in order to succeed. And it wasn't just the excitement, the power, that gave her a rush. Delta loved helping people who needed her assistance. She liked the feeling of knowing she helped a child escape an abusive parent, or a rape victim watch her captor being sentenced. She loved knowing that she was the arm of justice, reaching out to grab those who disregarded the law. There was so much to what she did, she could not imagine her life without it. Delta had spent six fast-paced years on the streets, and if she had to lug around some novice in order to continue doing what she loved doing most, then so be it.

Sucking in her pride and determination, Delta ran her hand through her wavy brown hair. "I want to be on the street, sir. If TP is the only way I can be there, then I don't see that I have much choice."

"Good." Taking the file and scribbling something down in it, Captain Henry slammed it shut. "I was hoping you'd say that. I'd hate to lose a good cop because your pride couldn't handle a reassignment. In the long run, I really think it will do you and the department some good."

Delta shrugged and rose. "Well, I don't know about that, sir, but I do know that I'm ready to get back out on the street. This time off is killing me. If I see one more soap opera, I'm going to sell my TV."

"Then you'll start with your first rookie tomorrow."

"Which beat?"

"I see no reason why you can't stay on your own."

Delta's eyebrows shot up. "My beat isn't exactly the place for a rookie."

This brought a smile to the captain's face as he grabbed the brass doorknob of the office door. "Well, now it's your job to see that he gets ready for beats just like yours, isn't it? If you have any questions, feel free to see me. My door is always open."

Taking the captain's outstretched hand, Delta firmly shook it. "No offense, sir, but I'd prefer a subtle distance between myself and this office. If you know what I mean."

"I understand."

"I'll give it my best, but I can't promise anything. I've never taught anyone anything and I don't even know if I have the patience for it."

"Your best is good enough for me. From what I've heard, you're pretty damned good at just about everything you set your mind to."

Delta nodded. "You heard right on that one."

"Great. Now all we have to do is smooth out some of those edges and we should have a championship team. Take a look at some of the old timers. They've mellowed and they're still excellent cops." Captain Henry patted her on the back. "You'll see. In the long run, you'll be a better cop."

As the door closed securely behind her, Delta shook her head.

Mellow? Delta Storm Stevens mellow?

Maybe. Then again, maybe not.

3

Walking away from the captain's office, Delta felt that she was being watched. It wasn't uncommon for everyone to see her straggling out of a captain's office, but this time, she was the first officer to be called in by the new guy. An inauspicious beginning for Delta, to be sure.

Glancing at the awaiting crowd, Delta grinned and shrugged. "He's a hell of a lot better than Williams ever was."

With that, the room resumed its bustling nature. Everyone was so relieved that Delta had not received a hatchet job on the new captain's very first day that a collective sigh escaped from the room as everyone returned to their duties.

Everyone, that is, except one short, Mexican woman poised at her computer terminal. With prying eyes, she studied Delta's movement across the room and waited with arms folded for Delta to sit down next to her. "I can tell by that look in your eyes it was worse than you thought, huh?"

Lifting her long leg over the back of the chair, Delta sat backwards and rested her chin on the chair back—a habit she picked up during her childhood when her father had her press her gaping front teeth against the chairback. It had been his answer to the "fad" of braces. Somehow, it worked, but Delta was stuck with the habit of turning her chair around backwards whenever she sat down. "Worse is an understatement." Watching her best friend turn the monitor off, Delta sighed. "I don't know what I was expecting. I guess..."

Rising from her chair, the woman gently touched Delta's shoulder. "Come on. Let's talk."

Following her into the bathroom, Delta turned and locked the door. "I feel like such an idiot."

"It wouldn't be the first time. What did he say?"

At five feet nine inches, Delta towered over the diminutive woman. Delta studied her deep brown eyes and knew it was no use trying to disguise the frustration and humiliation boiling beneath the surface. Connie would know. Connie always knew. There was no point in pretending it didn't hurt because what Connie didn't inherently know, she felt, and she would most certainly feel the anguish Delta was experiencing. Good friends were that way sometimes.

Best friends were that way all of the time. At least, Connie Rivera was. She knew Delta better than Delta knew herself. This made sliding anything past Connie a real challenge, and more often than not, Delta just coughed up the truth.

"You're not going to believe this," Delta began, walking over to the sink and staring at her own reflection in the mirror.

"Try me."

Turning around to face her, Delta tried to avert her eyes from the ones drilling into hers. Consuela Dolores Maria Rivera knew Delta well enough to know when to ask questions and when to just listen. Through their six-year friendship, Connie had done both more times than Delta dared count. She could pry even the deepest, darkest secrets from Delta. Occasionally, Delta would try to hide something from her, but it seldom worked. It was simply too hard to hide anything from this perceptive woman. Connie had an IQ of 160, was fluent in five languages (working on her sixth), held a blackbelt in karate, and could see right through the people she cared about. She certainly could see into Delta's soul, and had on many occasions.

"He's bucking me back to Training Patrol. Training Patrol, Con, can you see it? Me trying to teach some green-eared rookie how to survive the streets?"

Stepping up to Delta, Connie smiled. Two rows of perfect teeth glistened against her smooth caramel complexion. If it weren't for the crow's-feet around her eyes crinkling every time she grinned, she could easily pass for late twenties rather than her late thirties. "First of all, the phrase is wet-behind-the-ears and secondly, not that you've asked my opinion, but I think you'd be a very good FTO."

Delta's jaw dropped. "You've got to be kidding. With all the shit that happens on my beat, I can't afford to stop in the middle of a chase or a bust and teach some rookie how it should be 'properly' handled. We'll both get killed."

The smile on Connie's face softened. "You were a rookie once yourself, Storm."

Connie's nickname for her assuaged Delta's anger. "I know."

"I remember how you were. You'd go storming up to a rabid dog with its leg caught in a trap if you thought it would help make a collar. There was nothing you wouldn't do to make even the smallest bust."

Delta grinned. "Yeah, but—"

"But nothing. You shot out of the academy at the top of your class determined to single-handedly rid the world of all its evils. More times than not, that dog took a big chunk out of your butt that first year. If it hadn't been for Miles Brookman and some very patient FTO's, you'd be hamburger by now."

Delta shrugged, knowing that arguing with Connie was a waste of time.

"You were idealistic and obsessed with fighting crime. But it was those ideals that made you work so hard to do your best. You came out like a bullet from a gun, and sometimes, you were on the mark, Other times, you missed by a mile. Stop me if I'm wrong."

Looking down into Connie's face, Delta couldn't help but shake her head. She had come out of the academy like a car taking a corner on two wheels; so eager to put everything she had learned into practice, she often took shortcuts to make that all important bust. Rules, Penal Codes, policy and procedures were of little interest to her. She was not a theorist, she was a practitioner, and too often, Delta felt the rules were overly prohibitive. So what if she found loopholes or used a little creative problem-solving to yank a crook off the street? As far as Delta was concerned, the laws too often protected the perpetrators, and neither victims nor cops benefitted from the archaic "innocent until proven guilty." Too many times, some creep caught with his pants down standing over a raped woman had walked because of a "technicality." Delta simply knew how to avoid such technicalities and send criminals to prison. If she was going to do her job well, she often had to turn her back on "proper police procedure." If policy allowed a criminal to be set free, then she would do whatever she had to to counterbalance the scales. Beat cops understood that much. Unfortunately, desk officers, the media, and the public did not. They all wanted to believe cops could maneuver under such heavy constraints and still be successful in apprehending criminals.

Delta knew better. And she was willing to take risks to ensure her own successes on the street.

"You might have ended up behind a desk or worse if Miles hadn't straightened you out some. You were a little too idealistic for your own good."

Delta smiled gently at the memory. Yes, Miles, her first and best partner had shown her how to do things the right way. He had taught her how to polish her craft and move around the rules without really breaking them. He taught her all the subtle nuances that made a good cop a great cop. He had shown her the real way cops work the streets and not the textbook ways she'd learned in the academy. Miles had prepared her for almost everything.

Almost.

When he was gunned down, Delta didn't care what regulations she had to break to apprehend his killers. That kind of thinking helped her nail the creeps who blew him away. How could anyone expect her to change now?

"But we're not talking about me as a rookie. We're talking about me having the patience to teach one."

Connie grinned. "Where would we be if every Field Training Officer had thought that way?"

Heaving a loud sigh, Delta flopped down on the worn wooden bench. "But doesn't anyone see? My FTO's wanted to be there, Con. It was their choice. They obviously felt confident in their ability to teach. I'm no teacher, Con, I'm a cop."

"You make it sound like that's all you can do. You'll never know unless you try."

"I've never tried bungie-jumping, but I know I wouldn't like it. Come on, Connie, you know as well as I do that Henry is just trying to get in good with Internal Affairs. No one said he had to follow their recommendation. The choice is his and he's burning me."

Connie folded her arms across her chest. "Captain Henry doesn't strike me as the kind of man who sucks up to other people."

Delta cocked her head. She knew by Connie's tone of voice that her impression was based on some good old fashioned dirt digging. "You've been checking him out?"

Nodding, Connie pulled a slip of computer paper from her pocket and unfolded it. "You think I'd have let you go in there today if I thought he was going to crush you? Oh, Delta Stevens, sometimes you forget the wonders Eddie and I are capable of."

Taking the notes from Connie, Delta suppressed a grin. At first, when she heard that Connie named her computer Eddie, she thought Connie was half a bubble off. It was only after they became friends that Delta realized she was wrong. Connie wasn't half a bubble off...she was a few bubbles shy of level. That was one of the things Delta loved most about her; she was the most eccentric person Delta had ever met. But what Delta admired most about Connie was her ability to crack open any computer and retrieve virtually any piece of information on a microchip. Once, on a dare, someone bet that Connie couldn't access NASA's files to see the physical image of the space shuttle Columbia. After pocketing some $250 worth of bets, she smiled proudly as she pulled the information from the computer. Even Delta had been amazed—amazed and a little nervous about the levels of security Connie had breached. But she did it, and any doubters left as poorer believers. What Connie could do with a computer was of mythic proportions, and more than once, her expertise had saved Delta's life.

"You're something else," Delta said, touching her lightly on the shoulder.

Connie nodded. "Yes, I am. But just what, we may never know."

During the Zuckerman case, when Connie's life was on the line, Delta broke more rules than Evel Knievel broke bones to insure Connie's safety. Connie would do the same if necessary. Hell, she already had. That's what made them such a great team. There was a give-and-take to their relationship and they never kept score. In all of Delta's life, her relationship with Connie had always been the most important one. Delta might disappoint her own lovers, but if Connie ever needed her, Delta was always there. Always.

Scanning the paper, Delta saw a number of commendations for Captain Henry for his strategy and calm under fire.

"Look here. Says he was given a commendation by the mayor when he talked down a hostage-taker. All civilians went unharmed. Not bad."

"I'm telling you, Del, he looks good."

"Yeah, well, he could stroll in here wearing a Purple Heart for all the good that's gonna do me. He may look good on paper, but he's a politician just like the rest of the high mucky-mucks."

Taking back the paper, Connie folded it and slipped it neatly into her chest pocket. "Did he say why he was making this decision?"

"Well, not in so many words. He said he wants me to 'mellow.' Can you believe it? Mellow. What kind of word is that?"

Connie sat next to her on the bench and smiled. "Oh, now I get it. He thinks that having you teach someone how to do it the right way will force you to do the same. Model correct procedure for the student to obtain correct behavioral modification for both."

"Exactly. I think."

Eyebrows furrowed, Connie rubbed her chin. "At the risk of further pissing you off, I'd have to say it's not such a bad idea."

"What?" Delta said incredulously. "Whose side are you on, here?"

"You know I'm on your side. I just don't think you're seeing this as clearly as you might."

"What's there to see? Because of my file, I'm being railroaded into a position I'm probably not qualified or ready for. How much clearer can it be?"

Connie took Delta's hands in hers and squeezed. "Want to know what I honestly think of all this?"

Delta looked down at their hands and ignored someone knocking to come into the bathroom. "If I say I don't want to hear it?"

Connie grinned. "I'll tell you anyway."

"See how you are?"

"How I am, my friend, is extremely supportive of you and your life. Ever since Miles was killed, you've taken it upon yourself to be the law even when you're off duty. Delta, our last escapade put stitches in your leg, had my lover kidnapped, and left me emotionally and physically drained. I woke up in a sweat for a week straight before it was all over. I kept seeing him over and over again. I kept hearing his insane laughter pierce through my sleep. I know how it affected me and I know it touched you as well. Hell, it still does. Give yourself a break. Let someone else take the point for awhile. Let someone else put his ass on the line every night. Take a minute to smell the flowers. You've earned it."

Releasing Connie's hand, Delta slowly rose and walked over to the sink. Yes, the Zuckerman caper nearly cost them their lives and the lives of the women they loved. In the same way she had relived it every day since it happened, Delta painfully remembered a little girl's broken body and saw her cold, dead eyes, staring up at her through the haze of an unwanted memory.

Affected her? She had been afraid to go to sleep at night for fear of having yet another nightmare. Elson Zuckerman may be dead, but he still haunted the living. He had left his share of scars on her; some were physical, most were emotional, but they were scars she would carry with her for the rest of her life.

"I'm not sure I even know how to slow down."

Connie rose and joined her at the sink. "Hasn't counseling helped at all?"

Delta winced. She and Megan went into therapy shortly after the Zuckerman case. She thought they were going in for couples counseling, but when they started to delve into their relationship problems, it became clear that it was Delta's half of the relationship that needed the work.

"Slowing down, mellowing, taking a break—no matter what you call it, it amounts to the same thing: I only know how to go full speed."

Connie reached up and lightly touched Delta's cheek. "Right. And those of us who love you just don't want to see you crash."

"You think I will?"

"I think it's time you really focus on what you and Meg are trying to do in your sessions and use this opportunity to get a handle on both your relationship and your career. If you're not careful, Storm, you may lose both. Then where would that full speed get you?"

Delta nodded. "I hear you."

"Do you? Then hear this. I've never seen you take an assignment you can't handle. You can do this, and you know it. You just need to put your heart into it. Whenever you do that, you're unstoppable."

A grin forced its way to Delta's face. "Flattery isn't your style."

"And quitting before you begin isn't yours."

"Touché."

"Wouldn't it be better than being behind a desk?"

Delta nodded. Anything was better than pushing paper. "Yeah."

"Then give it your best shot. Some rookie is going to be awfully lucky to have *the* Delta Stevens as his or her teacher."

Delta grinned sheepishly. "Thanks."

Touching Delta's shoulder, Connie unlocked the door. "Look, I've got a ton of work to do. Meet me at Harry's after work? If you're still in doubt, we can discuss it more then."

Delta nodded. "Only if we can agree on one thing."

"And that is?"

"I may slow down, I may even take a breather, but I will *never* mellow."

Connie turned and hugged Delta tightly. "Good. I'd hate to have to change your nickname to Sprinkles. Somehow, that just doesn't fit."

Tossing her head back and laughing, Delta nodded. Storm it was, and Storm it would always be.

4

Pulling into Harry's Bar, the newest cop hangout, Delta turned off the truck's engine and laid her head down on the steering wheel. She knew things would be different when she came back after her suspension, but she never imagined just how different. Driving over to Harry's, all Delta could think about was working with someone who would ask too many questions, try too hard to impress her, and generally make a nuisance of himself. She couldn't envision herself explaining to every rookie why the shotgun was always her weapon of choice, why vans were one of her greatest fears, or why she called Connie whenever she needed information that was not readily available on the streets. She couldn't picture herself stepping aside to let some rookie fumble his way through a procedure she could do with her eyes closed. And worst of all, she could not see herself opening up and being honest with someone who was just a temporary partner. It would be like having a stranger in the car every night. The way Delta saw it, temporary partners were like scab laborers; they had no real investment or loyalties and they would be the first to bail out when the heat was on. And she didn't need that.

Thinking back to her last counseling session, Delta shook her head. It seemed as if everyone in her life was asking her to slow down. They all wanted her to have a life outside of the beat. She thought she did, but clearly, she was the only one who thought so. Didn't anyone understand that being a cop wasn't just a job? To Delta, it was a lifestyle. It was a way of being, an attitude, a mindset. What happened on the streets in a night didn't end when the shift ended. The images, the feelings, the sights, smells, and sounds stayed with her long after a crime scene was cleaned up.

And still, everyone wanted her to stand back and watch the action instead of participate in it. The captain wanted her to teach, Connie wanted her to smell the roses, and Megan wanted her to put their relationship first. None of them understood that Delta didn't know how to do any of those things. All she ever wanted to do was be a cop. And once she put that badge on, once she made her first collar, she was hooked. Nothing felt like making a major bust. Nothing matched helping someone find their lost or kidnapped child. Nothing compared to a high-speed chase or busting open a crack house. She loved it more now than she did when she was a rookie, and she was damned good at it.

But at what expense?

After the Zuckerman case, Megan laid down the law: either go to couples' counseling or give up the relationship. After only four sessions, Delta realized that her attitude about her work was the one thing that everyone agreed needed to change. Unless she put her badge away and became Megan's lover at the end of a shift, Megan would leave. Who wouldn't?

Life with a cop wasn't easy. Every night, Delta put her life on the line, and every night, Megan would wonder if Delta was coming home. Cops hung out together, spoke in languages and codes that no one else understood, and shared grotesque and macabre images civilians only saw in the movies. They carried off duty weapons, didn't hesitate to get involved off duty if someone was breaking the law, and carried their badges next to their credit cards. The hours were impossible, the days off erratic, and the overtime increasing. It came as no surprise to Delta that cops had the second highest divorce rate; second only to the entertainment industry. A cop's spouse too often has to settle for emotional, if not physical, crumbs.

And Megan had made it clear that she wasn't about to settle for that.

Heaving an exhausted sigh, Delta opened her billfold and winced. She had forgotten to get cash and was left with only her credit cards.

"Way to go, Storm," she grumbled to herself, hesitating before pulling her gold card from her wallet. One of the first assignments the shrink had given her was to try to feel comfortable leaving the badge in the truck.

"Take your wallet, Delta, but leave the badge. Be just Delta, not Officer Stevens. If a fight breaks out, or a crime is being committed, let the officers on duty take care of it. Be a person first. Can you do that?"

Ugh. Delta hated that question. She remembered fumbling for the right words, for any words, that could possibly convey how naked she felt without the shield. It was who she was. Leaving it behind was like leaving the best part of herself in the truck.

Plucking the credit card from the wallet, Delta closed the billfold and set it on the seat. Why was this so hard?

"Hey, Kimosabe. You going to sit in this truck all night?"

Startled, Delta turned to find Connie's face peering at her through the window.

"Sorry." Taking her jacket from the back, Delta laid it on top of her wallet and her nine millimeter off-duty weapon. She rarely went anywhere in the city without it, and now...

"Del, are you okay?"

Covering up the wallet and the weapon, Delta nodded. "Yeah, I'm fine. It's just...ah, hell, never mind." Jumping from the truck, Delta checked to make sure both doors were locked. She felt like she was leaving a baby in the truck unattended.

Opening the glass and brass door to Harry's Bar, Delta waved to Harry who was tending bar. Harry was a tall, beefy man with thinning red hair and a stomach that betrayed his love of Italian food. He had opened the bar for bikers, but when cops invaded the bar, few bikers stuck around.

Nodding to other cops who were belly-up to the bar, Delta grabbed a small table across from the pool table and waved the waitress over.

The motif of the bar was what attracted so many cops to it in the first place. It was the gangster style of the twenties and thirties. On the far wall were black and white photos of Dillinger, Ma Barker, Bonnie and Clyde, Baby-face Nelson, and assorted notorious criminals who had made their marks on history. There were original newspaper clippings detailing their exploits on one wall, and replicas of some of the weapons they carried on the wall above the bar. Harry had some incredible antiques from the period scattered about the bar, as well as some signs and advertisements he had won in a poker game. Harry used to laugh when he told the story about how he won the bar in a poker game, and to this day, Delta still didn't know if she should believe him. What she did know was that she loved the warm atmosphere of the bar, in spite of the smoke and noise.

"I've been thinking—" Connie started as soon as she sat down.

"Uh oh."

"I've been thinking that the captain is laying this on you so you have a chance to prove yourself to him. He wants you to be a team player; he's obviously heard rumors to the contrary. Look at it this way—you have the unique opportunity to start fresh with a captain who seems willing to give you a clean slate."

"Sounds to me like he's already made up his mind."

Connie shook her head. "I don't think so. I think he's caught in the politics between the chief, the mayor, Internal Affairs, and anyone else who thinks we let Elson fall. He doesn't want to lose you, but he can't come in looking like a patsy, either."

Easing back into her chair, Delta watched a fairly handsome young man bending over in his too-tight jeans as he eyed the cue ball. His opponent, a heavy-set biker with a long, ZZ Top beard leaned on his pool stick and scratched under his armpit. The biker was obviously oblivious to the fact that many of the people in the bar were cops.

"You could be right, but that doesn't make it any easier to swallow. Being tested, as it were, doesn't build a very strong bond between the tester and the testee."

"Maybe not, but I, for one, would like to see you focus more energy on your relationship than on your job. I'm worried about you. Megan's worried about you. You've been so quiet lately."

"I've been on suspension, Con. What's there to be excited about?"

"Exactly. Since the suspension, you've been moping around, piddling your time away. This was your chance to have some fun, lighten up, and enjoy yourself, but instead, you just sat around."

Delta shrugged. "Life's just not as much fun without my work."

Connie nodded. "And that, my friend, is precisely why we're worried."

"You don't think I can do it, do you?"

"I think you can do anything you put your mind to. But I do know you've never put your mind to making your relationship your first priority. You're going to lose her if you don't. And if putting you on TP helps save your relationship, then I am all for it. I'm sorry Del, if that's not what you want to hear, but that's how I feel. I love Megan, too, and I'm not real keen on the thought of you losing her."

Delta flinched. She couldn't stand the thought of losing Megan, either.

"Del, ever since Miles died, you've gone full blast. You tucked your head and ran like the dickens, plowing over everything that stood in your way. You've taken so many risks, it's as if you're trying to make up for his death."

Watching the curly-headed young man grin foolishly as he swiped money off the pool table, Delta shook her head. Laughing in a man's face when you take his money was a surefire way of having your own face rearranged. When the young kid asked the biker and his buddies if they wanted a chance at double or nothing, Delta turned away. He was really asking for trouble.

"Slowing down won't make you lose your edge, Del, if that's what you're worried about."

As the four ball spun into the corner pocket, Delta barely managed a shrug.

"If anything, you need a fresher perspective. Everyone needs to take a step back every once in awhile. It's not a sign of weakness to take a look at the big picture."

In her mind, Delta knew that Connie was right. It was her heart she was having a hard time convincing. "It still feels like I'm giving up patrol to be a meter maid." Hearing another ball slam into a pocket, Delta turned to see the young player smiling arrogantly at the biker and his buddies.

"Will you at least give it a chance? Open your mind up a bit and see this as a way of killing two birds with one stone."

Watching the handsome player sink the eight ball and grab the remainder of the money from the table, Delta heaved a sigh. "Well...I've discovered silver linings in stranger places. I suppose I can give it a try."

Smiling widely, Connie clapped her hands together. "Great. Now, can you be a bit more enthusiastic about it?"

"Enthusiastic? Hell, Connie, it's all I can do to choke it down. Now you want me to do it with a smile on my face?"

Connie nodded. "Yes."

"Forget it. I'll give it my best, but I won't do it with a smile. I'll try my hardest and hope like hell everything turns out okay."

"Just okay?"

Delta nodded. "Hey, anything could happen out there on TP."

Connie's eyes grew larger. "Anything?"

"Sure." With a mischievous grin, Delta ordered another round.

"Now you've really got me worried," Connie said, grinning back at Delta. "Suddenly, you have that look in your eyes."

"What look?"

"The look that spells t-r-o-u-b-l-e."

"Trouble? What kind of trouble could I possibly get into on Training Patrol?"

Rolling her eyes, Connie sighed. "That, my friend, is the $64,000 question."

5

When they finished their drinks and conversation, Delta slowly stood and stretched. "I'd better shove off. I don't want Gina to think that I keep you out too late at night."

Connie laughed. "Sit down. There's one more thing we need to talk about."

"Uh oh. I didn't do it, I swear."

Moving closer to Delta, Connie's laughter melted down into a warm smile. "Relax, Kimo, you're not in trouble."

"Whew. So, what is it?"

Connie inhaled slowly and ran her finger around the rim of her glass. "Gina and I are going to have a baby."

"Excuse me? Did you say baby? As in infant? As in tiny human being?"

Nodding, Connie's grin spread from ear to ear.

"Really? A baby? You're having a baby?"

"Yep."

"Well break out the cigars!" Reaching out to hug Connie, Delta squeezed her tightly.

"Not yet. We've been checking out donors versus sperm banks."

"I'm so excited! This is great news! I'm going to be an aunt! You're going to be a mom! We're going to be parents!"

Connie threw her head back and laughed. "Easy, Tiger. It's too early for a pregnancy test, but it's getting close."

"You'll let us know as soon as the deed is done, right?" The excitement in Delta's voice rose above the crack of the pool balls.

"Yes, of course we will. And when we do, the Dom is on me."

"A pregnancy party? Ohhh, I like the sound of that." Waving the waitress over, Delta ordered two glasses of champagne.

When the champagne arrived, Delta toasted to the health of the not yet conceived child. "To my niece and her moms. May our family always be close and loving and share good times."

Tinking the glasses together, Connie sipped her champagne and nodded. "Hear, hear."

"Have you decided on a donor?"

Connie shook her head. "Gina's done all of the research and we decided it's best if we go to the sperm bank."

"Why is that?"

"We don't want the donor to come back ten years from now because he's decided he wants to play daddy. Too many women have trusted their donor to stay out of the picture, and then, boom, here he is, taking two lesbians to court for custody of the child. No thanks."

Delta nodded thoughtfully. "I see your point."

"Gina's going to have her and I am going to adopt. That way, if anything happens to Gina, God forbid, there's no problem with me keeping the baby."

"I never thought of it like that."

Connie gulped down the rest of her champagne and wiped her mouth with the napkin. "There's lots to consider. We just want to make sure no one can take the baby away from either of us."

Delta watched as the pool hustler swaggered out the door. "Sounds like you've done your homework."

Connie reached out and laid her hand on top of Delta's. "Maybe now the big picture for our families is a little clearer to you. I want you to experience this with me and Gina. That won't happen if you keep pushing the edge. Sometime in our lives, Del, we all have to slow down a little. I want you there when this child enters our lives."

Delta sipped her champagne and nodded before turning her hand up and squeezing Connie's hand.

"10-4, Chief. I think the tuner on my TV just received your signal."

"Good. You're my best friend, Del. Hell, you're more than my best friend. You're my family. I want you there. It's that simple."

Delta finished her champagne as well. "Megan is going to just die when she hears this."

Glancing at her watch, Connie jerked her head toward the door. "Well, you just might die if we stay out any later. Let's keep our beautiful women happy by getting home at a decent hour. God only knows, once you're off suspension, early nights become a fantasy."

Tossing two dollars on the table, Delta stood and waved to Harry, who was pouring a drink.

"Be careful out there, ladies," he said, waving with his free hand.

"Count on it, Harry. Have a good week." Stepping out into the warm night air, Delta waited for Connie to close the door. "That man has built himself a very profitable business."

"He sure has. The guys love all those weapons, don't they? I'm sure it's some phallic thing. You know...the bigger the gun, the greater the fun. Something like that."

Delta made a face. "God, where do you come up with those lines?"

"Where else? Mercenary Magazine. Gotta keep up on the latest weapons and spy paraphernalia."

"You're sick."

"Actually, come to think of it, I think I heard it on Donahue. Or was it Oprah?"

"That's even worse," Delta chuckled putting her arm around Connie's shoulders. "Next thing you know, you'll start seeing a psychic."

"Well, there is this Madame Lat—"

"Don't even."

As they strolled through the parking lot, Delta heard scuffling noises coming from the furthest, darkest corner of the lot. Immediately, her senses came to life and she stopped to get a better bearing on where the noise was coming from.

"Con, do you hear that?"

Connie stopped and listened. As she did, she turned and cocked her head at Delta. "Del—"

Delta held a finger to her lips. "Shh. It's coming from over there."

Connie listened more intently. "Yes, it is. But we aren't. Come on, Del, let it be. You're not on duty. Just walk away and let the big guys in blue take care of it."

But Delta wasn't listening to her. Her head was pointed in the direction of the darkened corner, ears straining at the muffled thumps. Squinting in the half-lit lot, she could make out three, maybe four figures in the shadows, moving like strands of a wind chime, sometimes barely touching, sometimes banging into each other and exploding with sound.

"Con, someone is getting their bell rung over there. We should do something."

"We should?"

Delta nodded.

"Del, there's no chance in me talking you out of this, is there?"

"Nope."

Connie just shook her head. "I didn't think so. Damn. All that counseling dough gone to waste. Come on. Let's get this over with."

Already four strides ahead of Connie, Delta knelt behind a huge dumpster. Now that she was closer, she could see four men involved in what appeared to be a major brawl. The all-too-familiar sounds of fists against stomach and jaw bones mutely echoed through the air, as Delta surveyed the surrounding area.

"Well, Storm?" Connie whispered from over Delta's shoulder. "Do we go in there or are you waiting for your white charger?"

Delta nodded. "You ready?"

Connie held out the hands that made her a master at karate. "I'm always ready. Ready is my middle name. What about you?"

Instinctively, Delta reached to her ankle for her nine millimeter, and winced when she remembered she left it back on the seat of her truck. "Damn."

"Oh, swell," Connie said, shaking her head. "You'll never make heroine status now. I'll bet Robocop never forgets his off-duty weapon in the car."

"Very funny."

"But you're undaunted, aren't you?"

"If you're asking whether I still want to go in, yes, I do."

"Great. I don't have my badge. Do you?"

Delta bowed her head in mock defeat.

"Oh, very good. Very, very good. No badge?"

"No badge."

"Wonderful. I just happen to side with a knight who doesn't have a horse, armor, a sword, or a charge card."

"The latter, I have."

"Swell. You can beat them to death with it."

Delta rose from her crouched position. "Want to stay here?"

Connie grinned. "And miss all the fun? Megan would tan my lovely hide if anything happened to you while I stood by guarding this dumpster."

A wry smile slid across Delta's face. "Then follow me, Chief." Appearing from behind the dumpster like two specters in the moonlight, Delta and Connie emerged to find two of the large beer-bellied pool players holding the young pool hustler, while a third man, the bearded fellow who had just had his wallet cleaned by the youth, stepped up to bury yet another fist in the tight stomach of their captive.

"I think that's enough fun for one night, fellas," Delta said, causing all four men to turn her way. Instantly, she regretted not having her "niner" with her. It would have made a much more impressive sight.

"Looka that, Stockton. Two dames."

The pool player with the beard turned to fully face them. They were a good twenty feet away from Connie and Delta, but she could see they were baked. A little good dope, too much cheap beer, and false bravado was streaming from their pores like the scent of a dead skunk.

"No shit," one of the behemoths noted. "And it looks like they came to join the fun."

"I don't think I care for your brand of a good time," Connie retorted. "Now why don't you just let him go and we'll forget we ever saw you."

The man called Stockton spat a wad of tobacco on the ground and wiped his mouth with the back of his hand. He stood two or three inches over six feet tall and Delta estimated his weight at somewhere close to 200 pounds, maybe 210. He reminded Delta of a California black bear.

"How 'bout we make it so's you really never forget us, eh, baby? You and your Chicana friend, eh?"

Delta cast a look over at Connie, who flinched. Even in the dim light from the parking lot, Delta could see the fire in her eyes and the intensity of her demeanor as she studied and calculated the odds of a successful attack.

"C'mon, Stockton! Let's dump this asswipe and have us some fun with these broads."

For the first time, the hustler spoke through grit teeth. "Leave the ladies alone."

"Ladies?" Stockton mocked. "No lady would have walked over here unless she was wanting some action." Stepping up to the hustler, Stockton punched him in the stomach again. "And we're willin' to oblige 'em."

The adrenaline surge pumped through her body, feeding blood into her muscles and making Delta's five-nine frame expand and harden. She loved this feeling; this ride on the razor's edge. "Oh, we want some action, all right, but not the kind you've got in mind."

"Get outta here," the hustler commanded. "I can take care of myself. Go on now—scoot before they hurt you."

Connie took a step forward. Having witnessed Connie's black belt ability in action on numerous occasions, Delta knew she was preparing herself for an attack. And when it came, it was sure to be swift, brutal, and incapacitating. "Well, it certainly does look like you can take care of yourself, Junior." Connie took a step closer.

Delta watched as Connie's hands opened and closed in fists. Maybe she wouldn't need her niner after all.

Stockton stepped closer to Connie. "How about we take care of you first, Senorita?"

Suddenly, the two men holding the hustler dumped him hard on the ground, and Stockton stepped up to him and kicked him in the stomach. Delta could hear the wind rush out of him as he grabbed his battered body.

"What say we party, girls?"

Connie checked with Delta one last time. The fire had intensified into a bright flashing flame, as Connie shifted into fighting mode. Poised, ready, body tight with anticipation, Connie prepared herself for the inevitable clash with the bear. Connie's hands were registered as lethal. Delta did not worry that they were outnumbered as long as Connie stood by her side with her arms and legs ready.

"Storm?"

Delta slowly grinned. "Let her rip."

Before Stockton could take two steps, Connie whirled backward once, leg flying well above her head, and in one bone crunching second, her heel connected with his salt and pepper beard, snapping his head backward with the rest of his body following. In one loud thud, he landed face first on the gravel below, and there he stayed. The veritable fighting machine took one of them out before the other two could even blink.

"Holy shit, Lyle, you see that?"

Delta stepped next to Connie. The energy surrounding the two of them ignited the air. "Nice shot."

Connie's face was granite. "You going to help or just stand there and watch?"

Before Delta could respond, the man called Lyle stepped forward, a large, ugly scowl drawn across his even uglier face. It was hard to believe this man had ever been an infant in diapers and a crib.

"I dunno howya did that to Stockton, little lady, but it'll be a cold day in Alaska before any fluffball spic bitch takes me down."

Delta glanced sideways at Connie. She'd heard Connie called many things before, but fluffball was a new one.

"Fluffball?" Connie mocked, shaking her head. As she uttered the last syllable, Lyle rushed them. In a flash, Delta's left fist struck the third man in the middle of the throat sending him crashing against a lightpost. From the corner of her eye, Delta saw Connie take one step and dispose of Lyle with a jump kick to his sternum. The blow knocked both wind and spit from the man as he reeled backwards, hitting the pavement hard on his back. He remained there as well.

Connie nodded over to Delta. "Nice move, Storm. A shot to the throat? I'm impressed."

"I had a good teacher." Smiling into Connie's smoldering eyes, Delta rubbed the knuckles on her left hand.

Slowly rising to one knee, the man Delta hit shook his head as if trying to clear a fog.

"Stay down, pal, or I'll turn Fluffball loose on you."

The man looked over at Connie, hesitated a moment, and then immediately lay back down. "Ya don't have to tell me twice."

"Should we call it in?" Connie asked, straightening her hair behind her shoulders.

Delta shook her head. "If pretty boy wants to press charges, then I suppose we'll have to. What do you say, pretty boy?" Delta nudged him with the tip of her shoe.

Laying on the ground, still holding his stomach, pretty boy waved them off. "I think I can handle it now."

Delta laughed. "Right. Well, I hope you handle it better than you were handling it when we got here. Come on, Con, let's get out of here." Turning away, Delta chuckled. Immediately, Connie caught up to her and wheeled her around.

"If you ever tell anyone what he called me, I'll poison your coffee. I'll boil your cats, I'll—"

It took everything Delta had to keep from guffawing in her face.

Fluffball? It just might be worth a cup of hemlock.

6

It had been a longer day than it needed to be. It was bad enough that she was being dumped into Training Patrol, but Delta thought she might have busted a knuckle on her left hand, her shooting hand. Unlike most lefties, who had occasional use of their right hands, Delta was the most left-handed person she knew. Heaving a frustrated sigh, Delta longed to sink into one of Megan's long, loving hugs and hide from the world for a little while. Just the thought of hugging Megan brought a smile to Delta's face and erased some of the tension that had built up during the day.

Opening the door to her house, Delta's shoulders drooped in disappointment as she pulled her key from the knob. No lights on meant Megan had chosen to stay at her place for the evening.

Great, Delta thought, as she felt along the wall for the light switch that was placed too far away from the door. One of the worst days of her life and she was coming home to an empty house.

When the lights flicked on, Delta's shoulders straightened back up and a smile found its way to her face as she caught sight of a long, sensuous body laying on the couch in nothing but a red silk teddy—the one she had bought Megan on Valentine's Day.

"Hi," came Megan's sultry voice.

"Hi, yourself." Closing the door behind her, Delta did not move from the entry hall. She preferred, instead, to take in the vision stretched like a contented cat before her. Megan's long blonde hair cascaded freely down her shoulders, coming to rest at the V of the teddy. Her bare legs crossed at the ankles, Megan slowly moved her right foot up her smooth left leg.

Gulping down her desire, Delta stepped away from the door. "Been waiting long?" she asked, freeing herself from her jacket. Beneath her shirt, she felt her heartbeat quicken as she forgot all about the pain in her left hand and the ache in her pride.

"You look fantastic."

Megan's eyes sparkled. "Why, thank you. You look—"

"Like I've had a rough day?"

"Like you lost your dog."

Moving over to the couch, Delta knelt before Megan and laid her head on her chest. Inhaling through her nose, she smelled roses and violets on Megan's skin. "That's kind of how I feel."

Megan's long fingers wove their way through Delta's waves, sending tingling sensations over her scalp and down the back of her neck. "That bad, huh?"

Nodding, Delta buried her face deeper against Megan's body. "That bad." Delta wrapped her arms around Megan's waist and pulled herself on top of her. Suddenly, the fire she'd felt when she walked in cooled to a simmer, as she nestled against the warm, smooth skin of the woman she loved. "I'm feeling kind of puny."

Megan held her tightly and continued stroking her hair. "Puny? I've never known you to feel puny, my love. Is there anything I can do?"

Delta breathed in Megan's soft scent. She smelled better than any woman had a right to. "Do whatever you think will make me feel better." Feeling the rhythmic rising and falling of Megan's chest, Delta closed her eyes and felt the stress slowly seeping out of her body.

"Let me love you," Megan whispered into Delta's hair.

"It's been a long time since we made love." The rose essence wafted around Delta's nose, teasing her senses and warming her. It had been too long since either of them had had the time or energy for lovemaking. Megan was spending more and more time at the university, hanging around people from her Shakespeare class and going for mochas afterwards. Megan's entire world had opened up since she stopped hooking and she was delighting in every second of it. Not only had she hung up her bed, but she'd found a job working at the university bookstore, where she earned about twenty percent of what she had made as a prostitute.

But along with those changes, came changes in their relationship; suddenly, Megan had other people in her life. Suddenly, she, too, was busy. And while Delta was extremely proud of the adjustments Megan had made, she was deathly afraid of losing her. Delta, wasn't the easiest person in the world to be with; she put in too many hours, worked when she didn't need to, kept the job with her even when she was off duty, and took far too many risks than necessary.

And still, Megan was here.

Slowly helping Delta off with her shirt, Megan kissed and nibbled Delta's tight shoulders. "You're really tense," Megan whispered, expertly undoing the buttons on Delta's jeans.

"I told you. Bad day."

"How about we balance the universe with a good night?" Pulling Delta's jeans off, Megan ran one finger against Delta's underwear before slowly removing them as well.

Laying her head back, Delta closed her eyes. "Mm. I love the sound of that."

"How about the sound of this?" Carefully guiding Delta to the floor, Megan took one of Delta's nipples in her mouth and gently sucked on it—just enough to make the slightest noise.

Delta gulped down her excitement. "Sounds good."

"Just good?" Megan took more of Delta's breast in her mouth and sucked noisily. Then, she slowly slid her hand over Delta's taut stomach until her hand reached the curled patch of brown hair.

Delta shuddered. It had been so long.

Megan's fingers ran through Delta's hair, barely touching Delta's growing hard spot. Moving her mouth off the nipple, Megan kissed Delta's chest and shoulder before tenderly biting the soft curvature where her neck and shoulder meet.

"God...Megan."

"Oh, I see this is a little better than good?" Returning to bite Delta's neck, Megan slowly slid one finger into her. Delta's hips immediately raised, allowing Megan's finger full entry. "You're very wet," Megan murmured, moving her lips to Delta's ear.

But Delta was long past responding verbally. Instead, she let her body do her bidding. Wrapping her arms tightly around Megan, Delta pulled her completely on top of her.

Megan slid easily onto Delta, still keeping her finger inside. For a long moment, she stared down into Delta's face before planting tiny kisses on Delta's cheeks, eyes, and lips. "I love you," Megan said, lightly chewing on Delta's bottom lip. As Delta's hips moved into her, Megan slowly slid her tongue into Delta's parted lips and caressed her eager mouth.

Taking Megan's tongue, Delta pressed her hands harder into Megan's back. She wanted this to end and she didn't want this to end. But the explosion building inside her was nearly unbearable.

"You ready?" Megan asked, again moving her lips over Delta's ear. This brought a spasm of chills to Delta's skin and made Megan smile. She knew every inch of Delta's body and needed no verbal response to know the answer.

Slowly moving her finger in and out, Megan let her tongue travel down the length of Delta's neck before coming to a stop at the rigid nipple begging to be sucked. As Delta's hips rose to meet the fluid movement of Megan's hand, Megan pulled harder on the hard knob until it was perfectly erect.

"Megan..."

With her final plea escaping her mouth, Delta's body exploded in a wave of spasms as she gripped Megan tightly, pressing her face deep into her chest. Wave upon wave of delight rippled through Delta's body, cleansing her, pleasing her, releasing her from the stress and heartache of the day. Her stomach muscles tightened, her legs straightened, and every

fiber in her body cried out in erotic delight. As the surge
ebbed and flowed through her body, Delta was trans-
ported to another place, another dimension. Each muscle in her body expanded and contracted with
satisfaction until she very slowly released her grip on
Megan's body.

Raising her head from Delta's chest, Megan smiled.
"Whew. That was a big one."

Delta barely managed a grin. "It's been awhile."

Megan snuggled up next to Delta and nodded. "Too
long." Kissing the top of Delta's head, Megan hugged
her tightly. "So what's made you feel so little today?"

Delta sighed, grateful for the release of tension.
"Puny."

"What's made my knight feel so 'puny' then?"

Delta explained about being put on Training Patrol
and her meeting with Captain Henry. Then she told
her what Connie had said, and how maybe this was the
kind of break she needed to put her life in perspective.

"Do you want to put your life in perspective?"

Delta raised up on one elbow. "I agreed to counseling, didn't I?"

Megan's eyes smiled. "That's not what I asked."
Tracing her finger along Delta lips, Megan paused for
a second, before tapping Delta's chest. "What does your
heart want to do?"

Laying her head back down on Megan's chest,
Delta thought for a moment before answering. "I want
to keep you, keep my job, keep my sanity. I want to be
the best at my job without sacrificing my relationship
with you. I want us to work." Looking back into
Megan's eyes, Delta very lightly, very gently, kissed
Megan's mouth. "I want us."

Delicately returning the kiss, Megan drew Delta
closer. "That makes two of us."

Delta reached a hand up and lightly laid it on one
of Megan's breasts. Funny thing, she thought, how
comforting breasts were. "It seems I'm having to work
at everything these days. Does it ever get easier?"

Megan laughed. "I wonder that sometimes myself. You know, honey, it's easier to break the law than to obey it."

Delta's eyebrow rose in question. "I've never looked at it that way."

Megan nodded. "How many people drive fifty-five? Do you realize how hard it is to *try* to drive the speed limit? It's a lot harder than just cruising along. You've got to keep watching the speedometer."

Delta studied Megan's mouth. College had matured her so much that she was beginning to sound a lot like Connie. "So what's your point?" Kissing Megan's nose, a sudden urge streaked through her nervous system like a flow of electrical current. She loved this wonderful woman with all of her heart.

"The point is, it's hard for you to do your job when you follow rules. It's hard for me to work so hard at the bookstore and make less money. And it's difficult to make a relationship work without rules." Pulling Delta closer, Megan held her tightly. "Affairs of the heart are never easy. You love your job, you love me, and you love our relationship. All of the things you love most are asking you to work hard and follow the rules. It's no wonder you're feeling puny."

Leaning forward, Delta lightly kissed Megan's lips—softly, as if her lips might break. Moving in the rhythm of two lovers who knew their partner so well, their lips glided across each other's, tongues barely touching—movement that expressed the depth of their love, the strength of their bond. It was a first kiss, the kind you do when you're first going out, the kind that lovers forget about once the fireworks have dimmed. The type that reminds you why you fell in love with each other in the first place. There was no better experience than to be understood by the one she loved and to be embraced in Megan's warmth and understanding. This kiss melded them together like steel. Neither one was a separate entity now, both were a composite of their union, a mixture of each other. Nothing else existed in that long moment, only a bright light that shone from within, bathing the two of them in a shower of intimacy.

As the kiss slowly, quietly, gently melted away, Delta knew that she loved Megan with every ounce of her heart and mind. Gazing into Megan's sapphire eyes, Delta reached up and stroked her cheek with the back of her hand. She had seen Megan's soul, felt the depth of her love for Delta. In that one, prolonged kiss, Delta knew Megan loved her beyond anything else, and all she wanted was that love returned.

"I love you Megan Osbourne."

"I love you right back, Delta Stevens."

Laying her head back on Megan's chest, Delta listened to the rhythmic sound of Megan's heart until her eyelids drooped and her body twitched. "Meg?"

"Yes, sweetheart."

"Thank you."

7

"I assume you thought over my offer and are willing to give it a go?" Captain Henry asked after Delta closed the door to his office.

Standing next to the leather chair opposite his desk, Delta wondered if it was too late to turn back. Instead, she nodded and replied, "I have and I am."

Captain Henry grinned. "Good. I've spoken with the instructors at the academy and I believe I've chosen the best rookie for you."

Delta's eyebrow raised. "Rookie, sir? As in one?" Most Field Training Officers trained several different rookies over the course of a month. This move was one unfamiliar to Delta.

"Oh, don't worry, it has nothing to do with you or your competence. With all of the blasted budget cuts, we don't run TP like we used to." Captain Henry's grin deepened. "Or are you not into reading departmental memos, either?"

Delta snapped her fingers. "That one must have slipped by."

Waving off her rebelliousness, he twirled his moustache in his fingers. "Instead of sending you a bunch of babes in the woods, we'll partner you up with just one."

Delta thought about this for a moment. Maybe this was the silver lining. At least with one partner, she could get used to him, instead of having to retrain him every time he came back from some slovenly officer who never moved his fat butt off his engraved chair at the local donut shop.

"I can go along with that."

"Good. Because we're giving you a fellow that has about as much raw potential as I've ever seen. Kid has guts, smarts, energy, and can shoot the eyes off a fly."

Delta looked out the window but said nothing.

"Delta, I don't blame you for thinking I'm out to get you, but you couldn't be further from the truth. I truly believe this is an excellent way to save your career and keep you on the streets where you belong. In any case, I'm not the villain here."

Delta cast a cold, hard eye at him. She had remained silent long enough. "Sir, can I express just one opinion without feeling like you'll hold it against me?"

Captain Henry smiled, but his pupils shrunk to pinpoints. "I suppose that's only fair."

Placing her hands on the back of the chair, Delta steadied her nerves. "I'm a damn good cop. My arrest record and commendations speak for themselves."

"Agreed."

"But I think this is the biggest crock of shit I've ever experienced and the sooner you get me back on the street with a real partner, the better it will be for all of us."

The practiced smile did not leave the captain's face. "Well, now that that's said and forgotten, I'd like you to meet your next assignment." Opening the door to his office, Captain Henry motioned for Delta to follow. As she stepped out the door, she was surprised to see him leading her to the indoor firing range.

Opening the door, Captain Henry grabbed two ear protectors and handed one to Delta.

"Watch the second one from the left. A real dead-eye. Haven't seen a pure shooter like that since Pete Maravich. His file says he has twenty-ten vision in both eyes, and it shows."

"If he's so good, why isn't he being sent straight to SWAT?"

"He needs to tone down some. He's a little over-eager and carries an attitude with a capital 'A'. He's rough around the edges, but with the correct training, he could be one of the best."

Placing the earphones over her head, Delta followed Captain Henry into the main portion of the range. Three of the twelve lanes were taken by officers wearing the orange headphones and yellow goggles, aiming their various weapons at black silhouetted targets. Even with the earphones on, the crack of the guns reverberated through the room.

The officers' backs toward them, Delta concentrated on the one the captain pointed out to her. She was instantly impressed by the complete lack of movement from his arms and body as he fired. His head never wavered, his four-inch .357 magnum barely kicked in his large hands. Six brisk shots in a row, and he ejected, rammed a speed loader into the chamber and fired off six more rounds, all with the precision and accuracy of a machine. Her silver lining was beginning to look golden.

"Damn," Delta murmured, impressed with both his speed and efficiency.

As the captain took his head gear off, so did Delta. "Wait until you see his scores."

The rookie holstered his weapon and waited for the silhouette to be mechanically reeled in. Not taking his goggles or headphones off, the tall, broad-shouldered young officer snapped his target off the clip and studied the holes carefully.

Walking behind the rookie, Delta leaned over and stared down at the target he was still studying. All twelve shots were within three square inches of each other, many of which were overlapping holes already made. His accuracy was unerring.

"As much as it pains me to say this, Captain, I'm impressed."

Captain Henry nodded. "Carducci, meet your FTO, Delta Stevens. Delta, this is your bucking bronco, Tony Carducci."

Turning around, Tony stripped off his goggles and headphones and offered Delta his hand. But Delta didn't see his extended hand. Instead, she was staring at the bandage covering his left eyebrow and the discoloration surrounding his right eye.

Immediately, Delta withdrew her hand. "No way," Delta said, ignoring Tony's hand. "Not you."

Smiling a crooked smile, Tony lowered his hand and scrutinized Delta's face. "*The* Delta Stevens? You're pairing me with her?"

Delta backed away and shook her head. "I don't think so, Captain. Not a chance. I'll work with anybody but him."

Suddenly realizing when he had seen her last, Tony's lopsided smile grew wider. "You're the one who pulled my ass out of that jam last night!" Well, I'll be damned! Officer Delta Stevens saved my butt. It's a small world, isn't it?"

Resisting the urge to put some more color over his eye, Delta turned her back on him and toward the captain. "Too small. You've got to get me someone else. This will never work."

"I take it you two have met."

Delta heaved a frustrated sigh. The gold lining had clearly been fool's gold. "You could say that. Look, Captain, I said I would do this, but you can't stick me with this...with—"

"Yes? With what?"

"With this jerk!"

Coolly, Tony leaned against the wall, still managing his Huck Finn grin.

The captain, however, wasn't so cool. "I wasn't aware that I'd given you a choice."

"You didn't, Captain, but—"

"But nothing. You will work with Tony Carducci whether you like him or not. This isn't a romance, Stevens, it's a job. And your job is to train this man the best way you can. Do you understand?"

Delta inhaled slowly. She couldn't even stand to look at the rookie standing there with that smug look on his face. "Yes, sir."

"Good, because I don't give a rat's ass what the history is between you two. From here on out, you're on the same side, you got that?"

Both parties nodded. Tony seemed unaltered by Delta's attack of his character and merely shrugged off her insult. "Can we start tonight, Captain?"

Captain Henry looked over at Delta, but she did not return the gaze. "You ready to work tonight, Stevens, or do we find you a nice big desk?"

Delta glared over at Tony Carducci. She hated this. She hated someone else co-opting her choices. And she hated the fact that this particular decision had already been made. "As ready as I'll ever be, I guess."

"Your enthusiasm is overwhelming."

"So is your choice of rookies."

Captain Henry let that one go. "Meet for muster and be sure to have the weekly FTO report on my desk every Monday morning by Oh-nine-hundred sharp."

"Great!" Tony said, snapping to attention. "Come on, partner. Let's go kick some ass." As Tony strolled to the range office, Delta glowered at Captain Henry. Every fiber in her body recoiled against the idea of suffering through ten hours or more with a punk she'd already seen bite off more than he could chew. This wasn't a partnership, it was glorified babysitting.

"You're making a big mistake, sir. That kid is an accident waiting to happen."

A slight grin twitched Captain Henry's moustache. "Well, it's now your job to see to it that it doesn't." Whirling out the door, Captain Henry vanished, leaving Delta to nurse her anger alone.

Watching her new partner strut over and flirt with the data entry clerk, Delta grit her teeth. He was all the things she hated most about some men, rolled into one big chauvinistic, egotistical pig.

"Accident waiting to happen?" Delta uttered to herself. "I'm afraid it already has."

Trying not to slam the door behind her, Delta walked over to Connie and plopped down in the chair.

"I'm afraid to ask," Connie said, glancing over at Tony.

"Can you believe it? Of all the rookies, of all the people in the world, I have to be partnered with that jerk."

"It's bad karma, Del. Even before you became partners, you had to save him from himself. This doesn't bode well at all. What are you going to do?"

Watching Tony maneuver around the clerk, Delta sneered in contempt. She should have let those guys pummel some sense into him. Instead, she saved him just in time to be a headache for her. What luck. What joy. What a drag. "There's not much I can do. The captain was adamant about it."

Connie turned from Eddie. "So, you're stuck with him?"

Delta sighed loudly. "Appears so. It's that, or sitting behind a damned desk all night long."

Connie faked a wince. "Oh, now wouldn't that just be awful?"

"I'm sorry, Con, but I just don't know how you do it. It would drive me crazy to sit here all night."

"That's because you are a doer and I am a thinker. They pay you to do and they pay me to think. It's what we were born into. Knowing this, you're going to have to go out there and do the best you can with what you have."

Delta nodded and rose. "I hate it when you're so damned logical."

"That's what I get paid for." Connie reached out and squeezed Delta's hand. "That, and making sure you stay out of trouble."

"Oh really? And just how successful have you been in that venture?"

Connie's eyes glistened. "I've had better successes."

"I'll bet." Releasing Connie's hand, Delta patted her on the top of the head. "And how successful have you been with yourself on those Elson nightmares?"

"Much better. Gina has been a big help. Once we established that they weren't guilt-induced, they disappeared. He only appears after late night Mexican food or David Lettermen reruns."

"Good for you."

"And yours?"

Delta shrugged. "Every night. It hasn't stopped. Even after two weeks off, I'm exhausted. I haven't had a good night's sleep in a long time." Seeing Tony approach them, Delta inhaled slowly and felt the muscles in her shoulders tighten. Everything about him made her cringe.

"Hey, pard, you ready to roll?"

Delta and Connie exchanged pitiful glances. No cops they knew called their partners, "pard."

Turning to him, Delta smelled the powerful scent of Brut aftershave hovering about him like an invisible cloud. "We'll roll, Carducci, when I tell you we'll roll. I don't know what they're teaching in the academy these days, but here, we muster before we hit the streets. You do know what muster is, don't you?"

Bowing his head, Tony pulled his hands out of his pockets and ran them over his slick black hair. He was as Italian as his name: dark brown eyes set against olive skin and black wavy hair that swirled down the back of his neck. His shoulders were broad and tapered down to a flat stomach and small waist. Delta would never admit it, but he was a handsome young man who had turned many heads in Harry's Bar the other night. Still...

"Cut me some slack here, okay? I'm just a little excited about my first night, that's all." Tony smiled one of his patented grins.

"Well, hose yourself down, because if we're going to do this, we're going to do it right."

"Fine by me. I'll see you at muster then." Turning on his heels, Tony Carducci disappeared into the adjoining room.

"Think you were a little hard on him?"

"You heard him. You saw how he operates. You tell me."

Connie turned back to the monitor and shrugged. "I think you have your work cut out for you. He's definitely going to be a challenge."

Delta looked at the invisible trail left by her new partner. She imagined the trail to be the fumes of his potent cologne. "Thanks. I don't like the idea of going out to the streets with such a loose cannon. The challenge won't be how to train him."

"It won't?"

Delta shook her head and started for the muster room. "Nope. The challenge will be how to keep us both alive."

"Then it's up to us to keep your hunk of manly man on the up-and-up."

Delta turned her head and grinned. "Us?"

Connie nodded. "But of course. You do what you need to do on the streets and I'll dig and see what I can come up with. Trust me on this, Del."

"Why? Another aura?"

Connie laughed. "Something like that."

Before Delta could reply, the door to the muster room opened and Tony stuck his head out. "Muster's about to start. You coming?"

Delta sighed loudly and nodded before turning back to Connie. "The Boy Blunder awaits. Any last minute advice?"

"Yep. Keep him in front of you whenever he has his gun drawn. I hate the thought of finding out he inadvertently blew the back of your head off."

"Nice thought."

Reaching out to Delta, Connie lightly touched her shoulder. "Be careful out there, Storm. He makes me nervous."

"Affirmative." Wheeling around, Delta was surprised to find Tony's head still sticking out the door.

"Did she call you Storm?"

Delta only nodded as she brushed by him through the door.

"Cool. What a great handle. I thought my nickname was bad, but yours is really cool. Well, Storm, let's r—"

Turning on him and finding his height equal to hers, Delta went nose-to-nose with him. "If I ever hear you call me that again, I'll kick you ass. You understand?"

Nodding rapidly, Tony backed away. "Geez, don't get so uptight. I only thou—"

"You thought wrong. Let's get one thing straight, Carducci. We're partners. Not friends, not buddies, not pals. My job is to teach you the streets and your job is to shut your mouth and listen. You got that?"

For a moment, the air was thick with cold anticipation as all eyes focused on the two of them locked in a powerful glare.

"I said, do you understand?"

"I get it," Tony said through a clenched jaw.

"Good. Keep it that way." Turning from him, Delta pushed two desks out of the way and headed to the far corner of the muster room. If familiarity breeds contempt, Delta wondered, then what does contempt breed?

She hoped she didn't have to find out.

8

When they entered muster, the room was abuzz with cops telling jokes, tall tales, and sexual escapades. This was the time when people bonded and shared portions of their private lives. Some officers rarely opened up and stuck only to talking about the details from the previous shifts. It was a time when information was exchanged, personalities were revealed, and humor was applied to a variety of circumstances. It was also the time when they discovered what events transpired on the shifts prior to the one they would be working.

To Delta, muster was a mixture of personal sharing and professional caring. She'd always enjoyed muster because it reminded her of her college days when the locker room was alive and crazy.

Taking a seat next to Carducci, Delta pulled out a notepad to take notes.

"What's that for?" Tony asked, pointing to her clipboard.

Delta sighed. Why anyone would choose to be a teacher was beyond her, and whoever said there was no such thing as a stupid question obviously never taught anyone stupid. "For notes. I like to take notes in case I forget something."

Tony nodded, moving his whole body while doing so. He reminded Delta of a puppy whose body was too big for it. "Cool. Then I guess if you're going to take notes, I don't have to."

Delta wrote the date on the top of the paper before looking up at him. "I suggest you get used to taking your own notes."

Still nodding, like he was listening to a song on a walkman, Tony grinned. "Sure. Can I borrow a piece of paper?"

Sighing even more loudly, Delta pulled a piece out and handed it to him.

"Thanks. Got a pe—"

"Get one yourself," Delta growled as the duty sergeant strolled up to the podium.

"Evening ladies and gents in blue. I hope your day was peaceful because your nights are about to get hairy."

"What else is new?" Steve "Downtown" Brown heckled.

The sergeant glared a warning before continuing. "Two rapes reported this morning on the east side. No ID on either perp. Both women were pretty badly beaten up, so be sure to read Schumann's report."

Several heads nodded and uttered epithets under their breaths. For the next several minutes, the sergeant went over all the burglaries, robberies, and various misdemeanors from the previous shifts. Then, he cleared his throat and leaned forward on the podium. Everyone stopped writing and waited for him to continue.

"As I'm sure you're all aware, C.I.C's are on the rise here in California."

Tony looked over at Delta, but before he could ask, she answered his question in a whisper. "Crimes Involving Children."

"Word has it," the Sergeant continued, "that the sale of pornographic and snuff films have quadrupled in recent weeks. This memo from the Department of Justice was sent to every police department with a fax machine. This, ladies and gentlemen, is some serious business."

Some of the officers whistled. The DOJ wasn't one to hit the panic button and send out memos to every police department in the country. For them to do so, meant that there were some perpetrators out there worthy of very special attention.

"Apparently, kiddie porn isn't enough for the bastards anymore. Now, there's a group of sickos producing snuff films with children and the fellas at DOJ believe the ring is heading our way."

A female officer raised her hand. "Ring, Sarge? Isn't that a bit archaic?"

The sergeant smiled. "The boys in the big house say it isn't mob connected, gang related, or group identified, Lucy, and that's why catching them has been difficult. They suspect a small group of these whackos are headed by a particular individual who has money and connections. Connections, I might add, in Hollywood."

The picture suddenly became clearer.

"This individual has a monopoly on the market because he's producing high-quality snuff films that aren't phony like some of the other ones from the underground."

"And they're headed our way, sir?"

The sergeant nodded. "The feds think our perps are coming to Hollywood looking for investors. Apparently, the feds got close to yanking their chains in New York, but they got away. Their info leads them to believe that L.A. is their next stop. And to get to L.A. from there, they're most likely going to have to go through River Valley first."

"Are the feds actively pursuing them?"

The sarge nodded again. "You bet. And they've made it clear they don't want any intervention. What they do want is prevention, and that's what we're gonna give them. You're all to triple and quadruple your drive-bys of parks, pools, playgrounds, pre-schools, and anywhere else kids under the age of ten might be."

Delta raised her hand. "Sarge, I understand the need for prevention, but not intervention? What's up with that?"

Several officers nodded in agreement.

The sarge shrugged and then winked. "You know how the feds are. They work in mysterious ways of which I am not privy to. They may have bigger fish to fry and don't want us getting in the way of that. But I will tell you, now that you've asked, that the perps travel with their equipment in a camper or van and should be considered armed and dangerous."

"Not as dangerous as I'll be if I catch them," someone said from the back row.

The sergeant closed his folder. "That's just what the feds don't want. If you suspect anyone might be among the men they're looking for, notify command immediately. Any more questions?"

There were none.

"Okay then, this last item concerns all of you. Have any of you seen the science experiment we used to call a refrigerator?"

Everyone chuckled.

"The captain says to clear out your Tupperware or lose it for good. Someone has three week old gefilte fish in a Ziploc bag that is about to burst at the seams. So, *please*, take your lunches home."

Delta capped her pen and made a beeline for the sergeant before he could get out the door. "Sarge, is it possible for us to see the memo?"

Sergeant Kincaid paused and ran a thick hand over his balding head. "Delta, somehow, I'm not surprised that this case would interest you. Don't you think it would be wise if you stayed out of trouble for a little while?"

Delta bowed her head. Sergeant Kincaid had been one of her training instructors in the academy. "I can't help it, Sarge. I lost one kid already and it's tearing me up."

Putting his arm around her, the sergeant smiled warmly. "I warned you about that in the academy, didn't I? Don't try to make up for something you couldn't stop, Delta. It's like a baseball player who keeps striking out because he's trying too hard to get a hit. Don't blame yourself and don't try so hard to make up for Helen's death. You can't change the past, Delta. Let it go."

Nodding, Delta inhaled slowly and walked away.

Let it go? If only she could.

9

I suppose you want to drive," Delta said, tossing Tony the keys.

"I wouldn't mind." Hopping in the car, Tony jammed the key in the ignition and started the engine. "God, don't you love the sound of these babies?"

Delta just shook her head as she reached over and turned the engine off. "You have a list here that needs to be checked before you hit the streets."

Tony turned to her, a puzzled look settling on his face. "A list?"

"It won't do you a damned bit of good to go blasting out of the parking lot with only half your equipment. You have to make sure that everything works, that you have everything you're supposed to have, and that the unit is full of gas."

"Isn't the last guy in the car supposed to fill it?"

Delta cringed. "Yes, that's how it's supposed to be, but you'd be amazed at how many sergeants and lieutenants 'forget' to gas up before they come in."

Tony nodded. He reminded Delta of a horse ready to burst out of the starting blocks. "Okay. So, I check all of this stuff and then we can go?"

Delta handed the clipboard to him. "Yep. I'll look in the trunk, you do the rest."

Tony glanced at the list and started checking items off. When they were through, Tony jumped back in the driver's seat and gripped the wheel like a race car driver. On his hands were black leather gloves with the fingers cut off. "Can we go?"

Delta stared at the gloves. Used to be that the only cops who wore gloves were the ones who liked to crack heads. But now, with the AIDS scare, almost every cop she knew donned the black leather gloves just as they did the bulletproof vests.

"All right, eager beaver, go for it."

As Tony pulled out of the lot, he turned to Delta and flashed his most charming and sincere smile. "You don't really do all that checklist stuff every time, do you?"

Delta couldn't remember the last time she and Jan had done it. It was something that seemed to get interrupted as soon as they were in the car. Too often, she took for granted the necessary items would be where they were supposed to be. But she wasn't supposed to tell a rookie this, was she?

"Get used to it. How would you like to get to a scene and you need a rope to get down a hill to help a victim, and when you open the trunk, it isn't there. How would you explain that to the captain? Or worse, how would you explain it to the family if the victim died because you couldn't get to her?"

As Tony nodded, Delta wondered how long she would be able to last in the car with his overpowering aftershave. Miles had stopped wearing his after Delta told him it gave her a searing headache. But then, that was Miles.

"You can't believe how long I've wanted to do this!" Tony said as they rolled up to a light.

Oh yes, she could. Being a cop was something Delta had always wanted to do. The excitement, the thrill of the action, the feeling of helping people who needed assistance, gave her a reason to get up in the morning. She loved it. She had always loved it. Remembering how her first day felt, she grinned. It was like the carrot and the stick all the way through the academy, and when she finally got on the streets, that carrot tasted better than anything she had ever eaten or would eat.

"What do we do now? Just drive around looking for action?"

"You were at muster. Weren't you listening? Let's cruise by the arcade and check on the kids."

For awhile, they drove in silence—silence Delta was more than happy to have. There would be plenty of time to answer the onslaught of questions he was bound to have, questions she hoped she would have the patience to answer.

Finally, Tony cleared his throat and turned to her. "You don't like me much, do you?"

Delta shrugged. "I don't know, yet. From what I've seen so far, I don't think so."

"Why? What've I done to piss you off so much?"

"For starters, you hustled men who had every right in the world to want to crush your face. Then, when my friend and I intervened to keep them from bashing your pearly-whites down your fool throat, you pull some macho act that, frankly, turned my stomach. And you never even offered your thanks. You tell me how you'd feel?"

As the light changed, so did Tony's expression. "I've been told that I make a good first impression where the ladies are concerned."

Delta visibly cringed. "That's your first problem. I'm not a 'lady.' I'm a cop. I'm your partner, the person who has to trust in your ability to size up situations and make the right choices. I wouldn't say hustling a couple of big bikers was a very bright move. Nor was turning down help when you so obviously needed it."

Tony grinned. "I suppose not. But you can't judge me by a couple of stupid mistakes. You act as if I've done something to you personally."

"Turn left here," Delta said, leaning back and letting a loud sigh escape her lips. "Look, Carducci, it's no secret that I didn't sign up for this assignment. It was thrust on me like hot coals. No offense, but babysitting a rookie isn't exactly my style. I work hard, fast, and live by my gut. My beat isn't a place where someone with training wheels should play."

"You don't think I can do the job?"

"It's not that. This is one hell of a tough beat. If I were a captain, I wouldn't assign an inexperienced cop to it."

"Well I'm supposed to be getting the right training from you so that I *can* be experienced. How can I learn anything if you treat me like some jerk?"

Delta nodded in understanding. "Look, to be honest, you'd be better off asking for a transfer to someone who really wants to be an FTO. I'm a cop, Carducci, not a teacher. I keep saying that, and no one seems to want to hear."

Tony nodded as if he understood.

"Carducci, I work on instinct and gut knowledge. I don't know how to teach those anymore than I could teach you how to have courage. I've had a rough couple of months and the last thing I need right now is to try to bottle my expertise and pour it down the throat of some rookie."

"If it's nothing personal, could you at least give me a chance? I mean, you're no teacher, and I sure as hell am no student. Maybe I'm not like all the other rookies out of the academy. At least give me a chance."

Delta tried not to grin. Of course he was like the others. She remembered her buddies from the academy. And no matter how good they were, they all came out the same: over eager, rambunctious, and idealistic, usually completely unaware of the real and present dangers of the street. She had been where he is and when the harshness of the beat slammed her in the face, her idealism quickly took a backseat to her survivalism. One didn't learn that; one had to simply wait to experience it.

"I don't see that I have much choice, do you?"

Tony shook his head. "Thanks for the confidence."

The hurt in Tony's voice was evident. "Look, I apologize for being so rough on you. But if you'd done what I have, you'd find this assignment patronizing and slightly demeaning."

"That's just it. I do know what you've done. " Tony said, fully smiling. "I've heard of your adventures. The academy is full of stories about you. Everyone knows who Delta Stevens is, man. You're the stuff legends are made of. Can't you just forget what an ass I was the other night and start new right now?"

A sudden warmth wound its way through Delta's hardened exterior, forcing a slight grin on her lips. She could see where his charm might be disarming to women who would notice such traits. He was a little boy in a man's body, who just wanted to be a good cop. She had to give him that much. "All right. If I'm stuck with you, we might as well find a way to get along." Delta tried not to smile, but Tony was sitting there with that silly, proud grin on his face. She couldn't help herself. Okay, so his first impression stunk. If people judged her by her first impression, she'd have no friends.

"Great. What do you want me to call you? I mean, I already know what *not* to call you."

"Just call me Delta. If you ever call me anything I might consider sexist, you're history. Pull that Mister Man crap like you did the other night and I'll do everything in my power to see that you end up in dog pound school. Make any racist, bigoted, sexist, or homophobic remarks and they'll have to surgically remove my baton from your butt. If you can handle that, then I'll agree to a fresh slate."

Tony nodded, as if he was going to be tested on this material. "Okay, Delta. That's cool. I can handle that." Tony let out a monotonic whistle. "Boy, are the guys going to turn green when I tell them who my FTO is. You're all we talked about after the Zuckerman case." Tony's enthusiasm and excitement over her past was slowly melting the cold wall she'd raised. "Did you really climb up ten flights in an elevator shaft with blood pouring out of your leg?"

Putting down her pen and realizing she wasn't going to get any work done until his curiosity subsided, Delta nodded. "My stitches broke open half way up the elevator shaft."

"Holy shit. And you just kept going?"

"I had to. My best friend's life depended on it. It's not as heroic as everyone makes it out to be."

"Heroic? Man, they should have promoted you!" Suddenly, the light in Tony's eyes changed as he slowly turned to Delta. "Now I get it. That's what you're all pissed about, huh? Instead of a promotion, you got me."

Delta shrugged away the all-too-familiar ache. "Something like that. I made a lot of mistakes going in there. People, a child, was caught in the crossfire of Elson's sickness and was killed. You don't make mistakes like that and expect a promotion." Delta tried to ignore the pain searing her chest like a glowing branding iron, but it was no use. She would never get over the pain of seeing Helen's head dangling at an impossible angle, her eyes staring up at the sky. Those eyes would stay with her for the rest of her life, as would the eyes of Helen's mother when she stared down at her child's little lifeless body.

"But you stopped him. So what if you broke a few regs? You should have had a hero's parade."

Delta searched for some neutrality in her voice to hide the agony of remembering. "One doesn't get promoted in law enforcement unless you follow all of the rules and take stupid tests that have absolutely nothing to do with your ability to handle yourself on the streets."

"From what I hear, your ability is pretty amazing." Tony interjected loudly.

Not amazing enough, Delta thought, thinking back to the multitudes of questions Helen's mother angrily hurled at her, questions with no answers—questions Delta would ask herself for the rest of her life. The woman's child was dead. It was no wonder the mother reached out to hurt the one person who could have saved her daughter's life.

Could have. Police work was full of could haves, should haves, might haves, ought to be's. It was this singular "could have" which imbedded itself into Delta's spirit as sharply as Elson's star imbedded itself into her thigh, leaving a scar far deeper than the corporeal one she would carry forever.

"I get the job done, that's all."

"That's all? You've got one of the best conviction records in the department. In report writing, they always used your old reports as examples of how to do it right. There are records in the academy that will never be broken. Man, you're what every rookie wants to be some day."

Delta looked out her window. She hoped that those same rookies never had to hold a dead child in their arms, or feel the helplessness of not being able to prevent her death. She hoped they understood where taking chances would get them. It was so different on the street than in the academy. It was almost unfair to send such unprepared waifs into the dangers of the night.

Closing her briefcase, Delta ran her hand through her hair. If there were some sickos stealing and murdering children, she had an obligation to keep other children from harm; and there were two children in particular whom she had sworn to protect.

"Carducci, there's some personal business I need to take care of. Swing by Pulido Avenue for me and stop when I tell you to."

As they turned onto Pulido, Delta pointed to a white and yellow house on the corner. "That one. I'll only be a minute." Delta leapt from the car when it stopped and jogged up to the door. Raising her hand to knock on the front door, she was surprised when it sprung open and two brunette children stood smiling crookedly at her.

"Mommy, mommy, it's Auntie Delta!" Throwing the door wide open, Colin pushed past his sister and jumped into Delta's arms. Delta was amazed at how much taller they were than the last time she saw them.

"Hey, there, Tiger. How's my best guy?"

"Great! I got a hit yesterday!"

"It was an error," Casey said, hugging Delta around the waist. "The shortstop missed the ball and it went right through his legs."

"Well, at least you're hitting the ball, eh, Tiger?" Squeezing the seven-year-old and feeling the same bond she had shared with his father, Delta kissed Colin's head before setting him back to the ground. "How was your game. Case?"

The little girl shrugged. "Okay, I guess. They still won't let me pitch, but I hit a double the other day." Casey cast a cutting look at Colin. "And it was a *real* hit, too. No error."

"Great. Sounds like camp has helped you both. Where's your mom?"

"Right here."

Looking up, Delta's eyes met Jennifer's. A tenderness washed over her like pulling a down comforter around her ears in the winter. "Hi, Jen," Delta said, rising. "You're looking great."

Jennifer wiped her hands on a towel and tried to hide her blush. "You kids go out back and feed the doves. Auntie Delta will be out to play with you in a minute."

"Do we have to?"

Squatting down so she was eye level to Colin, Delta ran her hand through his thick mane. Every time she saw him, he looked more and more like Miles. "Your mom and I need to talk adult stuff for a minute. I'll be right out when we're done, okay?" Watching both kids skip away, Delta felt her connection with them tighten and strengthen. They were the first children Delta had ever loved, and now that Miles was gone, she loved them even more.

"Come on in," Jennifer said, holding the door open for her.

"You're looking like you're taking good care of yourself these days," Delta said, sitting on a bar stool and watching Jennifer cut carrots.

"I'm getting there. Lord knows it hasn't been easy."

"I know."

Jennifer glanced up from her cutting and grinned. "I've seen that same look on Miles's face, Delta. You're not here for a casual visit with the kids, are you?"

Delta didn't answer.

"I didn't think so. What's going on?"

Delta looked out the window and watched Colin tossing food to the doves. "We have reason to believe there's a kiddie-porn ring in town." Delta waited for

Jennifer to catch her breath before continuing. "I wanted to tell you in person because it's important that you keep a real good eye on the kids."

Jennifer placed her hand on her chest and shook her head. "How horrible."

"Until we catch these bastards, I think you should pick the kids up from school and don't let them play out in the front by themselves. These guys are professionals, Jen. I'll feel better if I know you're taking extra precautions."

"Oh, I will, Del. God knows I will. I'm so glad you told me. Without Miles around..." Jennifer's voice trailed off. "I'm glad someone in the department still cares enough to send out warnings. Thank you, Delta."

For a moment, the room filled with Miles's presence, as it had done so often between them in the past.

"I love those kids, Jen. You know that. Just the thought of some dirtbag...it just makes me sick." Delta stared out the window as the two kids tossed a football back and forth.

"Well, I appreciate your confidence. It's only been recently that I've regained my own."

Delta's eyebrow rose. "Oh?"

"Now stop that, Delta Stevens."

"What's his name, Jen?"

Blushing again, Jennifer went back and continued cutting carrots. "He's a fireman."

Delta groaned. "Not that. Anything but that. What is it with you and guys in uniform?"

Jennifer grinned and tossed a carrot at Delta. "The kids love him."

"Good for them. What's his name?"

Shaking her head, Jennifer poured carrots into the bubbling broth in a pot on the stove. "Uh uh, Officer Stevens. If I tell you his name, you'll run a check on him and send Miles's old pals to make sure I'm well cared for. No thanks. When and if the time comes, you'll meet him. But I won't have you snooping around in your usual overprotective manner."

Delta feigned hurt. "Now, would I do that?"

"Excuse me, but you *have* done that. Or have you forgotten?"

No, Delta hadn't forgotten running the plates on an accountant that Jennifer had dated twice. He had borrowed the car from his brother who had spent time in jail on embezzlement charges, but Delta didn't know the car wasn't his. When the guys at the station got wind of it, they harassed him until he finally dumped Jennifer. It wasn't until after he dumped her that they discovered the truth about the man's name and his innocence in anything remotely related to embezzlement.

But by then, it was too late.

"No, I haven't forgotten."

"Good. Now, it's sweet of you to worry and all, but I'm a big girl capable of choosing my own companions."

Delta couldn't help but smile at Jennifer's strength. "I'm sure of that. But I'm not about to sit back and wonder if the guys you go out with are on the up and up. Not when I have—"

Suddenly, Jennifer broke into laughter. "Oh, Delta Stevens, you're so much like Miles, you make me hurt. Trust me. He's a very nice man who hasn't done anything more than kiss me goodnight. If I need you and your famous white charger, I'll call you. But you have got to let me stand on my own two feet, okay?"

Delta nodded. "Okay. Just know that you and the kids are family to me. Don't blame me for caring as much as I do."

Wiping her hands on the wet towel, Jennifer moved in front of Delta and hugged her. "Of course I don't. You must know how important it is that you love us so much." Pulling away, Jennifer smiled warmly. "You came all the way over here to check on me and the kids, and I love you for it. Delta, in the cop world, you're one big, bad, cop. But the kids and I know differently. You're just one huge marshmallow. I appreciate that about you."

"But?"

"But I'm still not going to tell you his name."

Smiling, Delta nodded. "Okay. You keep his name secret, but you keep those beautiful kids out there safe, you hear me?"

Shaking Delta's hand, Jennifer smiled back. "It's a deal." Wiping her knife off, Jennifer cut the last of the carrots. "Stay for a quick dinner?"

Delta stood and shook her head. "Can't. I'm training a rookie who, for all I know, has fallen asleep in the car."

As Delta opened the door and watched the two children feeding and cooing back at the doves, a picture of Miles flashed through her head. She remembered him standing there at the birdcage, holding Colin up so he could see the first baby birds of the season. She could even hear Colin's tiny voice as he cooed at the mother as she fed the babies.

Glancing back at Jennifer, Delta's eyes were moist.

Jennifer laid her hand on Delta's shoulder. "I know, Del. It happens to me all the time."

Wordlessly, Delta swung open the screen door and stepped into the backyard. As the two children ran toward her, Delta felt a familiar chill run the length of her spine. They were dearer to her than she could ever imagine, and she remembered a vow she had made a long time ago, upon the grave of the only man she had ever really loved.

And now, as she held their precious little bodies in her arms, Delta vowed she would do what she had to to stop the snuff films—not for her own release of guilt, not for her own glory, but for the two little beings she had promised so long ago to protect with her life.

And if that's what it took, then so be it.

"Take good care of your mom for me, okay guys?" Hugging Colin and Casey to her, Delta said her good-byes and squeezed Jennifer tightly before heading out the door. "If you ever, ever need me—"

"I know where to call. Thank you for coming by, Del. Come over for dinner real soon, okay?"

Delta smiled. Suddenly, she felt like crying. After Miles's death, Jennifer and the kids had adopted her and welcomed her into their family. It was this family she would run through brick walls for, and if anyone even remotely threatened it, Delta would do whatever she had to to stop them.

"Will you make my favorite?"

Jennifer nodded. "Liver and onions with lots of crispy bacon. You got it."

Delta's heart warmed even more. "Love you guys."

"We love you, too, Del. Be careful."

With that, she jumped back into the patrol car.

"All done?" Tony asked, starting the engine.

Before she even had a chance to answer, their number was called. "Let's hit it!"

Tony gassed it and squealed down the road. When he came to the intersection, he slowed at the entrance. "Which way?"

"Take a left." Picking up the mike, Delta responded to dispatch and jotted down some note without looking up. "Take the next left," she commanded.

Without hesitating, Tony swung the patrol car to the left and avoided a cat scurrying across the street. "What's the call? I totally missed it."

"There's a 4-15 on North Austin Street. Neighbors heard glass breaking from inside the house. Step on it, will you?" As soon as she said those words, Delta regretted it. In a flash, Tony pushed the accelerator to the floor and peeled down the street.

"Slow down, for God's sake! You trying to get us killed?" Feeling the car slow down a bit, Delta picked up the mike and double checked the address. If it was the house she thought it was, the trouble could be far greater than a domestic quarrel.

"This is S1012, checking on that address for the 4-1-5. Is that 4691?"

"S1012, that's a 10-4. Neighbors say a blue Toyota Corolla is parked in the driveway and that they could hear screaming and crying coming from inside the house."

"10-4. We're two away. Send a back-up unit."

Knuckles white on the steering wheel, Tony Carducci inhaled loudly. "Back-up for a lousy family feud? What for?"

"Okay, Carducci," Delta said, leveling her gaze on the side of his face. "Lesson number two. Never, and I mean *never* underestimate your suspect or the circumstances."

"Yeah, but—"

"But nothing. Do you realize how many cops are killed during domestic violence? Didn't they give you those stats at the academy?"

"Yeah, but—"

"Then you should have them engraved on your mind. Four-fifteens may not seem dangerous, but they are. Period. You approach them just as if you were approaching a burglary in progress. You know why?" Delta didn't wait for him to answer. "Because nine times out of ten, when we step in to keep some asshole from whacking his wife, *she's* the one who turns on us. More wives have shot at or tried to stab cops than you can imagine. I don't intend on being one of the stats you clearly didn't pay attention to."

Tony opened his mouth to respond, but thought better of it.

"Anyway, a little over two years ago, my partner busted the husband at this same address for beating up his wife. She was one of the few women brave enough to press charges against the slime."

"And you think he's back to get her?"

"It's possible. If so, then he's a very dangerous man. Men who come back are violent criminals, Carducci, and will kill you if you give him the chance. Don't."

Tony nodded. "Got it." As he pulled onto North Austin Street, Delta reached for her baton and flashlight. Looking over at Carducci, she saw that he was enjoying the fast pace and the potential for danger. Rookies were so naive.

"Pull over here."

"But this is only 4600."

"Damn it, Carducci, don't question me every time I tell you to do something! Just do it!"

Tony did as he was told and when the car stopped, he immediately threw open the door.

"Get back in here!"

"But aren't we—"

"We're not moving until we have a plan. A plan of action, Carducci, is necessary in every situation. This isn't Hollywood and you're not John Wayne."

Tony waited for more directions.

"You take that side of the house and watch the windows. Don't go to the back. Last time we were here, there were three very large, very mean Rottweilers. I'll have back-up cover the street behind the house. You just make sure he doesn't get around you. Got that?"

Tony nodded.

"Good. Any questions?"

"Nope."

"Then let's go."

As they slowly approached 4689, Delta was out the door before Tony could stop the car. Coming toward them was a woman covered in blood, holding the side of her head.

"Help me!" she cried, running toward Delta. Her eyes wild with panic, the entire side of her head covered with blood, the woman reached a pair of bloody hands toward the car.

"Which way did he go?" Delta asked. The side of the woman's face looked like a coconut that had been bashed open with a baseball bat.

The woman pointed in the direction of Conan Doyle Street. "He's crazy! Do you see what he did to me? Crazy son of a bitch!" Taking her hands from her head, the woman stared down at the blood-soaked palms and shook her head. "He said he'd be back, that bastard! Look what he's done to me!"

Delta looked at the woman's head. "Ma'am, I think we'd better take care of your head—"

"Fuck that!" She cried. "Go after him! I want that asshole jailed for life! I'll press charges again and again if I have to! Don't just stand there gawking at me! Do something!"

Delta nodded and jumped in the patrol car to radio for an ambulance and direct back-up to tend to the woman's head injuries.

"Back-up's here," Tony said, motioning toward the unit that pulled up.

Slamming the mike back in the cradle, Delta pointed to the woman as the two officers hopped out of the car and nodded their understanding of the situation. They would care for her; Delta and Carducci would go after her husband.

"He'll be heading south for the freeway, Carducci. Let's go!"

Tires squealing down North Austin, Carducci slowed as he reached the intersection of North Austin and Conan Doyle.

"What are you waiting for? A traffic light? Go!"

Looking left, then right, Tony turned left onto Conan Doyle as Delta called in the description of the car and the direction she guessed he was heading in. When another unit came on and said they had spotted a car matching the description speeding through an intersection, she flipped on the lights and siren.

"There's a faster way, Carducci! When you come to Poe, go west and then south again to Shelley." Looking at her new partner for the first time since she got in the car, Delta noted the beads of sweat dotting his forehead. She wondered if it was the excitement, the adrenaline, the chase, or the fear, that brought this on and she wished she was driving.

When they came to Poe Street, again, Carducci slowed down, even though there were no cars approaching from either direction.

"Goddamn it, Carducci, move it, will you? We haven't got all night! Once he gets to the freeway, it's a different ballgame!"

Nodding quickly, Tony took a right turn.

"I said west! Turn this thing around and go west!" Delta covered her face with her hands and wanted to switch seats, but she knew it would take more time than they had. Already, they were losing valuable seconds.

"What's the matter with you?" Delta shrieked above the blare of the siren. "Didn't you hear what I said?"

"Yes, damn it, I heard! I'm a little nervous, that's all."

"That's all? A woman has her head bashed in and you're driving like a little old man because *you're* nervous? Get over it Carducci and put the pedal to the floor!"

Suddenly, another unit came on the radio saying they had just picked up the chase heading toward the Crowsy Tunnel.

Delta picked up the mike. "If he goes through the tunnel, he'll be heading for downtown. We'll head him off at Sherwood." Hanging up the mike, Delta told Tony to head north down Esperanza.

"We're out of our beat, aren't we?"

Delta nodded, eyeing the speedometer. She wished he could push it a little harder. At this rate, they were out of the race. "Yeah. Why?"

Tony shrugged. "No reason."

When they approached Esperanza, Tony slowed down once more. Before Delta could stop him, he was flying south down Esperanza.

"What are you doing?" Delta screamed. "I said north! North is that way!" As Delta reached for the mike, a baritone voice boomed across the airwaves.

"S1012, this is Sergeant Rich. We just passed underneath you on Sherwood. We'll assume your position in the pursuit. You can return to your beat."

Snatching up the mike, Delta growled, "This is S1012, we copy." Slamming it back in the holder, Delta felt every fiber in her body burn with anger.

"Pull over."

Tony did as he was told and they switched seats without exchanging a word.

They rode in silence most of the way back, and when they returned to their beat, Delta made a follow-up check at the woman's house. The ambulance door was just closing and the neighbors crowded along the street like vultures waiting for its prey to die.

"Stay here," she ordered, slamming the door after her. She was so incensed that he'd botched the chase, she could barely stand to look at him.

Approaching Officer Firth, who was taking down witness statements, Delta inhaled slowly through her nose and tried to relax.

"You lose him?" Officer Firth asked, lowering his pad.

Delta shrugged. "I wouldn't know."

Firth looked over Delta's shoulder and grinned. "A rookie with bran for brains?"

Delta shrugged again. The heat of embarrassment rising to her cheeks. "Something like that. How are things here?"

Firth shook his head sadly. "If her head had been a baseball, he'd have hit a homerun."

"It was a bat?"

"Apparently so. Took it with him, which is good. If the guys stop him, he's history. He won't see daylight for years."

"How is she?"

Firth glanced over at the ambulance. "She'll be okay. A few stitches here and there ought to help. She's a pretty tough lady."

"I suppose she'd have to be after being his punching bag for years."

"Yeah. It's a shame they let guys like that off the hook so easily. Shoulda kept the bastard locked up for good."

Delta nodded.

"We're square here, Stevens, if you want to take off. She'll be okay."

Okay? The word rang through her head like a cracked bell. No abused woman would ever truly be "okay." Why was that so hard for some men to understand? Just because her head would heal didn't mean her spirit wouldn't feel that blow for the rest of her life.

Okay? How could someone be okay after being beaten by someone who vowed to honor, to protect, and to cherish her?

Shaking her head sadly, Delta looked up from her thoughts and glared through the window at Tony, who was staring straight ahead. Maybe that's why she was so hard on him for blowing the chase; crimes against women moved Delta unlike anything she'd ever experienced. She wanted to be the one to pull that bastard out of the car and read him his rights. She wanted him to know what it felt like to be powerless against a woman. Quite simply, she wanted to be the one to see him go back to jail for a long, long time.

Jerking open the door, Delta dropped angrily into the driver's seat. "Any word?"

Tony looked out the window. "They lost him," he said weakly.

"Shit!" Slamming her fists on the steering wheel, Delta shook her head. "We were that close. That close, damn it!"

Turning from the window, Tony stared down at his hands. "It was my fault. I'm sorry."

The rage bursting inside her, Delta turned on him. "What in the hell were you thinking about? Don't you know north from south or east from west?"

Even with all of the noise outside the vehicle, the inside of their car was sullenly quiet.

"Well? What happened?"

Tony slowly glanced up and allowed only the briefest contact with Delta's eyes before returning his gaze to his hands. "I don't."

Delta leaned forward to hear him better. "You don't what?"

"I don't have a sense of direction. Sometimes, when I'm nervous, I forget."

"You forget?" Delta didn't know whether to laugh or cry. "You forget what?"

"Which is which."

Leaning back in her seat, Delta shook her head. "Oh, that's just great. How in the hell did you ever get through the academy?"

"I told you. It only happens when I get really nervous. I'm sorry."

"Yeah, well, tell that to the lady in the ambulance. Damn it, Carducci, are there any other quirks in your character that I should know about? Any skeletons in your closet that could get us killed? Do I need to go through your file to see if there's anything in there you haven't told me?"

Tony shook his head. "No."

"Are you sure?"

Tony nodded. "Positive." Looking back up at Delta, Tony's eyes revealed his defeat. "You're not going to tell the captain about this, are you?"

Delta could only stare at him while the anger slowly burned itself out. A partner who didn't know directions or couldn't get his bearings was like a blind guide dog—no use to anyone and more of a detriment than the handicap itself.

"Is it something you can work on, or are you cursed with being a directional dunce forever?" Delta's voice was cold and biting. "Be honest with me, Carducci. Our safety's at stake here."

Tony shrugged and moved his eyes away from her penetrating stare. "I'm willing to work on it, but I don't know if I can fix it."

Delta leaned forward, her eyebrows capping a pair of intense green eyes. "That's not what I asked you."

Looking back out the window, Tony sighed loudly. "I don't know. I'd have to work on it during really stressful situations. Believe me, I've practiced and studied and even seen the academy shrink."

"And?"

"And it comes and goes."

Delta eased back. "That's what they're going to be saying about you if we can't straighten you out."

Tony nodded. "I know." Turning to her, his eyes were pleading. "This is your big chance to dump me, Delta. If you tell the captain, it'll be desk duty for me."

Delta stared into his eyes and thought about Tony's words. The right thing for her to do was to tell the captain that he was a deficit on the street. After all, Carducci's "problem" was responsible for losing an attempted murder suspect, and without directional capabilities, he was a hazard to both of them. Maybe if she dumped him now, she could get a partner she could actually work with. Maybe if she unloaded his arrogant self on the captain's doorstep, she'd get a rookie she might even like.

Maybe.

Closing her eyes and inhaling slowly, Delta could see Miles's face. She remembered him telling her once that, "good, bad, or indifferent, your partner is like your spouse. He'll make a lot of mistakes, he'll fuck up at bizarre moments, and he'll piss you off like no one else can, but as long as those things stay between the two of you, they'll get resolved and you'll both be better for it. The last thing you *ever* do is snitch on your partner."

Yes, the right thing for Delta to do was to dump Carducci at the captain's feet, denounce him as the directional boob that he is, and ask for reassignment. That would be the right thing—procedurally.

But the best thing to do was to maintain the integrity of their partnership, blunders and all. The best thing for her to do was to work with him on his inadequacies and help him overcome his nervousness.

As usual, the best thing had nothing to do with the right thing.

Leaning back over, Delta softened her tone of voice. "Let me tell you something, Carducci. When I was first working with Miles—"

"That was your partner who was killed, huh?"

Delta nodded. "Yes." For a moment, memories overwhelmed her. Suddenly, she could smell Miles's new cologne and feel his presence next to her. It happened less frequently than it used to, but at times like this, it was as if his spirit somehow swept through her and touched her soul just to remind her that he would always be there.

"Delta?"

Shaking the memories back to the trunk of her mind, Delta sighed heavily. "I made my fair share of mistakes, Carducci. Hell, I came out of the academy like the Tasmanian Devil whirling around, knocking stuff over left and right, going through everything instead of around it." Delta grinned. "Sometimes, I still do. But through it all, not once did Miles reprove me to our superiors. Not once did he call me on the carpet for pulling a major boner. You know why? Here's lesson number three, Carducci. Miles believed that good cops aren't born, they're made. My job right now is to help make you into one. That's what Miles did for me; and it's what I'm going to try and do for you. As long as you don't endanger lives, as long as you continue to learn and grow, then we'll work through your malfunctions, no matter how quirky they may be. You're my partner, whether I like it or not, and I have my own codes to live by here on the street. One of those is that you never rat on your partner. If you put my life in danger, that's a different story. But for now, we're stuck with each other."

For the first time in an hour, Tony allowed himself the slightest grin. "Thanks, Delta. You won't regret it. I swear you won't."

Starting the engine, Delta drove into the night. "I'd better not. Because if I do, my little Hispanic friend at the computer will kick your balls up into your neck."

Tony nodded. "I'll just bet she could."

Delta turned and smiled. "Could and would."

"Then I'll do my best to keep that from happening."

"You do that, Carducci. You just do that."

10

"S1012, we have a request for a 9-1-0 at 45 Alcott Way. See the woman."

Delta picked up the mike and responded affirmatively. "What's a 9-1-0?" she asked Tony as she slipped the mike back in the cradle.

"You don't know?"

Delta sighed. "Of course I know, you dolt. I want to see if you know."

Tony's forehead furrowed in thought. "Someone requesting assistance?"

"That's a 4-1-0. Try again."

"Oh." Drumming his fingers on the dash, Tony chewed his bottom lip. "A trespasser?"

"Six-zero-three. Carducci, didn't you learn *anything* in the academy?"

Shrugging, Tony surrendered. "I give up."

Delta shook her head. "Are you sure it was the *Police* Academy you went to? A 9-1-0 is someone asking us to check on the well-being of someone else. You know, an elderly neighbor no one has seen in days or something like that."

"Oh, yeah. Now I remember."

Pinching the bridge of her nose, Delta sighed loudly. How had he passed the academy? "Take this left and then a right at the first stop sign. The house is the second from the corner."

Tony looked amazed. "You know that by heart?"

Delta nodded. "After five years, I hope so. I know every inch of this beat as well as those on either side. Believe me, it pays to know."

In two minutes, they arrived at the address where an older woman stood waiting in the driveway. The small black woman dressed in a robe and slippers walked to the edge of the sidewalk when they drove up.

"I'm Officer Stevens," Delta said, getting out of the car. "Are you the woman who called?"

Pushing her glasses back up her nose, the old woman nodded. "Mr. Richardson, my neighbor, reads his papers every morning, just like clockwork. He also puts his garbage out every Wednesday night right after the ten o'clock news."

Delta nodded and motioned for her to continue.

"But his newspapers have been stacking up and when he didn't bring his trash out tonight, I got worried. It's not like him to be so unpredictable."

Delta pulled her pad out and jotted this down.

"Maybe he's on vacation," Tony offered.

The woman made a disgusted noise with her dentures. "For fourteen years, young man, Dudley always told me when he would be away and I'd water his lawn. Fourteen years. I hardly think he went away this time without telling me. No...I think something has happened to him."

Flipping her pad closed, Delta glanced over at Dudley Richardson's house. "We'll be glad to take a look, ma'am."

"Should I wait out here?"

Delta turned back to her and smiled. "Go ahead and go back inside. One of us will come over when we're finished with our investigation."

"Investigation? Oh my." With that, the old lady tightened her robe and scurried back into her house.

Delta walked toward the house and pulled her six-cell flashlight from the holder. When she realized Tony was lagging behind, she turned and peered through the darkness. "Well? What are you waiting for? An invitation?" Opening the gate, Delta shined her flashlight through the garage door window. Other than a washer and aging dryer, the garage was empty. Moving toward the back of the house, Delta shined her flashlight through the sliding glass doors and saw a kitchen and small den. Nothing appeared disturbed. For a moment, she cocked her head to see the amount of dust coating the furniture.

"What?" Tony whispered.

"Dust. Dust will tell you a lot about a crime scene."

"What crime? He's probably on vacation."

Delta straightened up, opened her mouth to respond, and then thought better of it. He'd learn soon enough.

Moving over to the smaller kitchen window, Delta saw that it was cracked open about an inch. Looking through the glass, she didn't see anything but a sink full of dirty dishes. Then, she put her face up to the small opening and sniffed. The stench invaded her nostrils, pushing her violently away from the window.

She knew that smell.

It was the stench, the odor, of death and decay.

"What? What is it?"

Delta pointed to the crack in the window. "Put your nose in there." Tony did and immediately reeled backwards. "Holy shit!"

"That's death, Carducci. Nothing in the world smells like it."

"You mean—"

"Dudley Richardson, or someone else in there is dead. Check the other windows while I call it in."

Thirty-five minutes later, an unmarked homicide vehicle pulled up and out of the passenger side came a Danny DeVito clone.

"I jumped right to it when I heard your call, Stevie." Detective Russ Leonard reached up and patted Delta on the back. He had an annoying habit of invading her personal space. Connie thought it was because he had a crush on Delta. Delta knew it was because he lacked social skills. Judging by his nefarious reputation, Delta believed her view of him was more correct.

"So, you think you gotta stiff?"

Delta nodded.

"We'll see soon enough, won't we?" Leonard issued orders to his men before turning back to Delta. "I'm surprised to find you back on the streets so soon. I thought for sure you'd be sitting pretty behind a desk for awhile."

Delta shrugged. "They needed FTO's."

Leonard laughed. "Like hell they did. It's more like you got friends in high places."

Delta resisted the urge to slap the back of his head. Detective Leonard could get under her skin faster than anyone she knew.

"I'm glad you're back, Stevie. We don't have as many stiffs when you're not around."

"Very funny."

"It's true. I don't know why it is, but people seem to die around you." Then, to Carducci, "Better watch yourself, kid. There's a black cloud hanging over this one."

Tony leaned all the way over to whisper to Leonard. "I'll take my chances."

When Leonard's men got the front door opened, the stench of death rushed out like warm poltergeists.

"Yep. Stevie, you gotta dead one." Pulling a small blue container of Vicks Vaporub from his pocket, Leonard dabbed some under his nose and handed the plastic jar to Delta, who followed suit.

"There," Leonard said, inhaling deeply. "That's more like it. Never leave home without it, Junior," he said to Tony. "Know what I mean?"

Delta gave Tony a look that said don't even bother with a response. Detective Leonard was just a stump of a man—all thick torso with short appendages and no neck. He resembled a cartoon, especially when he pulled one of his unlit cigars from his pocket and clamped down on it. Delta thought he watched too much TV as a kid.

"Everybody ready?" Leonard asked, slapping Tony's shoulder. "Your first stiff?"

Tony nodded.

"An easy intro, kid, really. It's when you get a bloated floater that it takes your breath away. This...well, this won't be too hard unless parts of the corpse are cut off. Then it gets a little rank. Just the other day—"

Delta cleared her throat. "Detective, do you mind not discussing those particular cases with my rookie?"

"*Your* rookie? All of a sudden, you get possessive on me? What gives here?"

Delta made more eye contact with Tony that said to keep his mouth shut. If he understood, he didn't acknowledge, nor did he respond to Leonard. "Just dispense with the gallows humor, Leonard, okay?"

Chuckling to himself, Detective Leonard started through the door.

As they entered the tiny house, the stifling air acted like an invisible barrier pushing against them. Delta knew both by the smell and by her gut that death was still lingering in this house, and she only hoped it wasn't a gruesome sight. Lately, murders had become increasingly vile and ugly. People were doing more horrendous things to victims than simply shooting them. Hell, look at Jeffrey Dahmer and the scads of other cannibals, necropheliacs, and Manson look-alikes arrested after he was.

The thought brought bile to Delta's throat.

"I see they paired you with a man," Leonard said as they walked carefully through the house.

Delta nodded, but said nothing. Talking only made her smell more.

"The smell is awful," Tony finally said.

Leonard approached him from behind. "It ain't like the movies, Junior. So if you're gonna huck up your lunch, do it away from my crime scene, okay?"

Tony nodded as Leonard walked into another room. "Is that guy for real?"

Before Delta could answer, Leonard called from the other room. "Found 'em."

Tony looked at Delta. "Them?"

"Jesus Christmas and Merry New Year," Leonard spat. "What in hell?"

Delta started down the hall and took a right into the first bedroom. "Oh shit, no," she groaned, stopping in the doorway and leaning against it. It suddenly became very hot and the room began to spin.

Laying naked on the bed was the body of a white man, face down on the pillow with half his head blown away. Dried blood and brains splattered the white wall above the bed and the entire pillow looked stiff from caked blood. His left arm dangled off the side of the bed and his right hand clenched a .38.

Leonard skillfully picked his way across the room and motioned for Delta to stop. "You ain't seen it all yet, Stevie. Better suck in some fresh air for this one."

Delta steadied herself and stepped into the room.

"Stevie, I really don't think you wanna see this. Why don't you and Junior go start your reports and leave this for me and my guys?"

Delta cocked her head. She'd never seen Russ Leonard try to shield anyone from anything. "What is it, Leonard?" Moving over to where Leonard was standing, Delta swallowed back her own vomit.

"We don't have a suicide here, Stevie. We got a possible 1-87 as well."

Delta forced herself to join Leonard on the opposite side of the bed, and immediately regretted doing so. Laying on the floor handcuffed to the naked man was a boy about ten years old.

"Oh shit," Delta said, covering her mouth and taking several steps back.

"I told ya. These are the worst." Leonard bent over and inspected something Delta couldn't see.

"Interesting," Leonard mumbled, pulling his notepad out and jotting something down. "I can tell you right now boys and girls, this one is gonna be a twister."

Feeling light-headed and needing fresh air, Delta pushed past Tony and hurried outside.

"You okay?" Tony asked, coming to her side.

Delta bent over and put her hands on her knees, the fetor of death still burning in her nostrils. "I'm...fine. I'm just sick...of finding dead children."

"Is that what it was?"

Delta nodded and inhaled deeply. "Apparently, Dudley Richardson, if that's who it is, was a little more unpredictable than his neighbor could ever imagine."

"What a bummer."

"Yeah. Not a great way to start a night. Who would do that to a kid?"

Leonard stepped outside and lightly touched Delta's arm. "You hangin' in there, Stevie?"

Delta managed a nod. "I don't know how you do it, Leonard. How do you get in that car knowing you may be coming to scenes like this one?"

"Someone's gotta do it. By now, I gotta cast iron stomach. Still...seeing kids...Ah hell, we're all messed up. Come on, Stevie and let's get this place closed off."

Delta and Tony helped cordon off the crime scene and Delta let Tony watch the Crime Unit as they went through their paces. A part of her wanted to get the hell out of there fast, but the part of her that was supposed to be teaching Tony knew he needed to see this aspect of an investigation.

"Leonard," Delta asked, sidling up next to him. "Will you do me a favor and let me know what comes of this?"

Leonard grinned. "You'll never give up your sleuthing ways, will you, Stevie?"

"Not if I can help it, Detective." Reaching out, Delta touched Russ Leonard for the first time since they'd met. "I never realized how tough your job was until today. Having to see shit like that would drive me crazy."

Leonard shrugged and blushed. "Adults, I don't mind, but kids..." Suddenly, Leonard looked hard into Delta's eyes. "Oh, I get it. You think—"

"What I think, Leonard, is that there's been two deaths on my beat and I would really appreciate some follow-up information."

Leonard smiled knowingly. "And I thought I had balls. You're gonna do exactly what we've all been told not to do, aren't you?"

Delta stared at him. "What makes you say that?"

Turning from her, Leonard walked back toward the house. "You could be suspended for a year, Stevie, but nothing can change one simple fact about you."

"And that fact is?"

Turning around, Leonard grinned. "You're a rogue cop, Stevie. Always have been, always will be, and there ain't a soul alive that can hammer that out of you."

"I came by it honestly," she said, hoping none of Leonard's men were listening.

"Yes, Stevie, I'm afraid you did. Miles Brookman taught you well." With that, Detective Russ Leonard lumbered back into the house.

To herself, Delta smiled and said, "Yes, Leonard, he did."

11

Delta sat and stared down at her hands. If she would have known that couples' counseling was going to be so hard, she probably would have bonged it altogether. But, here she was, with a question glaring her in the face and she didn't even know the answer.

"Delta?"

Looking up from her hands, Delta shrugged. "I'm not sure I understand the question."

Amanda Stone smiled her most patient therapist smile. "I asked whether or not you feel you prioritize the important things in your life."

"You mean, have I numbered them in order of importance?"

Amanda nodded. Megan nodded. Everyone seemed to be nodding except Delta. Maybe she was the only one who truly didn't get it. Wasn't counseling supposed to help self-esteem? Instead, all this seemed to do was shake hers.

"Yes. Something like that."

Delta thought for a moment. She wasn't a list-maker. She just cruised through her day doing what needed to be done. "Not really."

"Would you mind trying it?" Amanda leaned toward her, her long black hair dropping forward like a curtain. She was one of those women you could look at and right away peg as a therapist. She had compassionate eyes that said she was sincerely listening and a mouth that let you know when she thought you were trying to bullshit yourself.

Delta shrugged again. "Sure. Why not. What, exactly, am I listing?"

"The important things in your life. Your job, you family, your friends, Megan, material things. Things of that nature."

Delta nodded and reached for Megan's hand. "I love Megan more than anyone I've ever loved."

Amanda smiled and nodded. "Yes, but where does she fit in the scheme of your life?"

"She's the most important part. Is that what you're asking?" Delta felt like she was in a play without a script and they were both reading off of cue cards.

Leaning forward, Amanda's smile softened. "Delta, you're here because you and Megan feel you use work to emotionally distance yourself from people. You both believe you give your energy, your time, your heart to the job. What I want to know is how do all these pieces fit together in your life? Don't say what you think we want to hear or what you think is the right answer. Be honest with yourself; what is the one thing in your life that gets your best energy?"

Delta stared down at the floor. She wanted to say her relationship. But then, that wouldn't be honest and Megan deserved her honesty. Lifting her head, Delta whispered, "My job."

"Your job."

Delta nodded, looking over at Megan with apologetic eyes. Megan squeezed Delta's hand and brought it to her lips. "It's okay, honey. It's no surprise."

"It's no surprise, Delta, but why was it so hard to admit?"

Delta shrugged. "I don't want to hurt Megan."

"That's why we're here, sweetheart. So we learn how not to hurt each other."

"Why do you think admitting that will hurt Megan?" Leaning back, Amanda flipped her hair over her shoulder. Her dark eyes zeroed in on Delta's.

"Because she should be first. Isn't that the way it's supposed to be? Aren't we supposed to put our relationships before everything else?"

Amanda's lips turned up slightly. "'Supposed to' by whose rules? Delta, the last two times we've met, I've gotten the impression that you don't follow rules and conventions very much."

"I don't."

"So why are you trying so hard to follow that rule?"

Looking over at Megan, as if she might help her with an answer, Delta heaved a sigh. "Because I don't want to lose her. Megan means so much to me, but I can't seem to give her more than my career."

"Do you want to?"

Delta nodded. "I do."

"Why do I feel like there's a 'but' hanging in the air?"

Releasing Megan's hand, Delta stared down into her palms. "I guess...I want to, but I don't know how. All my life, all I've ever wanted to be was a cop. Every relationship I've had prior to this one with Megan came second to that."

"Why is that?"

God, Delta hated this. She felt like her soul had been unzipped and that they were poking around inside trying to find out what hurts and what doesn't. "No one ever understood how much I love my job, or why. They'd bitch and moan that I wasn't home enough, that I didn't give them enough when I was home, blah, blah, blah."

"Does Megan do this?"

Delta looked at Megan and smiled warmly. "No. Not yet."

Amanda's eyebrows rose. "So, you anticipate that she will?"

Delta hesitated before answering. "Yes. And who wouldn't? I put in long hours, I risk my life, I eat, sleep, and drink my career. At some point, she'll have to take a look and see if what I give the relationship is enough for her."

Amanda turned to Megan. "And is it?"

For the first time, Megan adjusted her position in the chair. "Delta knows how much I love her. But love isn't really the issue here, is it?"

Amanda smiled the smile Delta was sure all shrinks were graded on in college. "I don't know. Is it?"

Megan blushed. "Love might have brought us here, but it isn't the reason we came."

"Then what is?"

"Right now, there are a lot of changes going on in my life and I wish Delta didn't work so hard so she could help me sort through them all."

"But?"

"But she can't."

"She can't? Why not?"

"Because she puts our relationship on autopilot. Delta stops working on everything but her career, especially when she's working on a major case."

Amanda turned to Delta. "How do you see this, Delta?"

Delta shrugged. "It's true. When I've got something really hot happening, I forget about everything else in my life."

"Including your relationship?"

Delta nodded.

"And I take it you don't want to do that anymore."

Reaching over for Megan's hand, Delta bit her lower lip. "I've never given someone all of me. I guess I've been afraid of giving me up and then being stomped on."

"Like you've saved some of yourself for reserve."

Delta leaned forward. "Exactly. I hold back in all situations except the job. Megan is the first woman I've been with who's been willing to help me learn how to be a better partner because, in all honesty, I don't know how to give any more than I already give."

"I see. But you do want to give more?"

Nodding, Delta pulled Megan closer. "Yes, I do. She is an incredible woman, Amanda, and I really, really love her. She deserves my best."

"And you don't believe you are giving that to her?"

Delta slowly shook her head. "You heard her. She needs me right now and I'm not even sure I can be there for her."

"Do you want to be?"

"I think so."

"You're not sure?"

Heaving a loud sigh, Delta rubbed her eyes. "Change isn't easy for me."

Nodding while she jotted a few notes down, Amanda studied the two of them for a moment before speaking. "Desire to change is only the first step. You must know, in your heart, that you're capable of change. Willing and able, like Megan said last week, are two entirely different things. I'm going to leave you with this question, and I don't want you to talk about it, Delta, I just want you to think about it."

Delta nodded. "Okay."

"Let's say love was in the shape of a golden key. If that key was sinking and so was your badge, and you could dive in to save only one, which would it be, and why?"

Inhaling deeply, Delta nodded. "Okay. Anything else?"

"Yes. Megan, you have needs which aren't being met. I want you to focus on meeting them yourself. That will take some of the pressure off of Delta."

Megan nodded.

"It seems you both love each other so much that it should be able to carry you through. Well, I hate to burst any bubbles, but it won't. Love isn't enough. You obviously know this, or you wouldn't be here."

Both Megan and Delta nodded.

"So, it's time to start visualizing, start thinking about what needs to happen to make change, and what each of you will do if the change doesn't happen or isn't enough of a change. How does that sound?"

"Scary," Megan answered.

Amanda grinned. "It is. Any kind of change is scary, but relationship changes are the most frightening. As long as both of you continue to communicate and work toward a common goal, you should be okay."

Okay. There was that word again.

Okay. Delta didn't want to be okay. She wanted to be better than okay. Her relationship with Megan was too important to just be okay.

Rising from the chair, Delta didn't hear what Amanda was saying to Megan. She was too busy thinking about a key and a badge slowly sinking from her grasp in a pool of calm water.

She didn't have a clue which one she would save.

12

Delta awoke to the annoying ringing of the phone. She hated being awakened this way; it always made her heart beat fast.

"Hello?"

"Stevie? It's Leonard. You wanted me to call if we found anything out about our alleged murder-suicide."

Delta sat up and changed ears with the phone. "I'm listening."

"Right from the get-go this didn't appear right. Too many inconsistencies for the naked eye, but the lab boys cleared it up pretty damn fast."

"Inconsistencies, like what?"

"Ballistics shows that both the boy and Richardson, the adult male victim, were shot by the same .38. But the autopsy on the boy revealed a millimeter hole and a two-centimeter ring of tattooing, which could only mean that the boy was shot at a distance of approximately four feet."

Delta waited to see where Leonard was going with this.

"If the boy and Richardson were handcuffed together at the time of the first shooting, Richardson was not the one to squeeze the trigger."

A chill swept through Delta. "Are you saying there was a third party?"

"Most definitely. We ran a trace metal test and no gunpowder residue was found on Richardson's hands. He didn't shoot the gun at all."

"Is that what you were looking at?"

Leonard chuckled. "I was looking at the way he was clutching the gun. His finger wasn't on the trigger. With suicide shots like that, the victim usually grasps the gun harder. He did, but his finger wasn't in the saddle."

"So, someone else shot him."

"Yep. Someone out there wants us to think Richardson shot the boy and then himself, but that's not what happened. I'd bet my dinner on it. Someone was in that house with them and set the whole scene in motion."

"Interesting choice of words," Delta muttered.

"Don't try to snow me, Stevie. I know what you're after and I know why. Hell, more than anybody, I know why."

Delta held her breath and waited.

"And that's why I'm calling. If you're gonna do what I think it is you're doing, I want you armed with the right info."

Releasing her breath into the phone, Delta nodded. "Thanks, Leonard. I appreciate it more than you know. Did the lab find anything else?"

The line was suspiciously silent.

"Leonard?"

"Look, Stevie, I know you're a feminist and all, but I'm not real comfortable describing what went down prior to the shooting. Suffice it to say, there was some weird shit going down between Richardson and the boy."

"Thanks for your concern, but I'm a big girl and I need to know what kind of lunatics are running around my beat."

"We're not talking lunatics, Stevie. These jokers are way out there."

"Leonard—"

"Alright, but you gotta keep a lid on this, Stevie. I've already been in the shit-house once because of you."

"I'll keep everything quiet till you give the word."

"All right then. The boy, on whom, by the way, we still have no ID, had been sodomized by Richardson and someone else. Richardson had semen traces in his stomach and had handcuff marks on both wrists."

"Richardson was a pedophile?"

"A kiddie-lover. Yep. At least, he was right before he got whacked."

"What about the neighbors?"

"No one saw a thing."

"Time of death?"

"They'd been dead a couple of days."

Delta rolled over and wrote everything on the pad she kept by her bed. "Anything else?"

"Yeah. We found a bunch of porno videos behind the bookshelf in the bedroom. They were rented from Kempt's Porn Palace on Esplanade."

"Any with kids?"

"All."

Chills swept over Delta's entire body. "You think it's them?"

"Can't be sure yet. It sure doesn't look as professional as that memo made these characters sound. Pretty sloppy, as a matter-of-fact. According to their MO, the bad boy ring leaves little evidence behind. Usually, they destroy entire buildings. Something went sour on 'em."

"Wonder what happened."

"Oh, I know what happened. Dear old Mrs. Lanning next door is what happened. Apparently, she had been nosing around the place. My guess is she made them nervous so they got out of there before she could ID anyone."

"So she didn't see anything?"

"Nope. They're very good. I tell ya, Stevie, they didn't leave much, but what they did leave could give us a lead."

Us? Delta smiled. It would seem that some of her alleged vigilantism had rubbed off on the irrascible detective. "I'll check my sources, Leonard, and give you a call if I come up with anything."

"Do that. Oh, and do us both a favor and call me at home. The last time we got mixed up together, I ended up losing a week's pay."

Delta nodded. "Gotcha. Keep in touch."

"You, too. And try to stay out of trouble."

Hanging up the phone, Delta wrote down a few notes before picking the receiver up once more and pressing the first number of her autodial. "Con, it's me. Wake up. We've got some work to do."

13

When Delta walked into Connie's house without knocking, as she usually did, she smelled the welcome aroma of freshly brewed coffee. She loved Connie and Gina's cozy home and the warmth it exuded. She knew she would come to love it even more when there was a child running about.

"If you're still in the sack, finish it up and get on out here!" Delta yelled down the hall before walking into the kitchen to find Gina holding two cups of coffee.

"You're too late," Gina said, grinning. "Quickdraw MacGraw struck again." Handing Delta her Phantom of the Opera mug, Gina stood on tiptoe to kiss Delta's cheek. "Gotta run, Sugar. You two behave, you hear?"

"Now why is it everyone feels compelled to say something like that to me?"

Opening the front door, Gina laughed. "You're kidding, right?" And with that, she whisked out the door.

"Did you run my girlfriend off again?" Connie asked, taking Delta's cup from her and sipping the steaming coffee.

"I guess so."

After fixing herself a cup, Connie plopped in front of her computer and waited patiently for it to finish beeping, clicking and whirring at her. "Okay, what have we got so far?"

"Not much. No ID on the kid, but he looks Hispanic and—"

Connie turned from the computer and frowned. "Why is it that everyone assumes that a caramel-colored person with dark hair is Hispanic?"

"I said he *looks* Hispanic. He could be Greek for all I know."

Connie harrumphed and returned her attention to the computer. "What else?"

"The guy rented videos from Kempt's Porn Palace."

"There's a good start. I'll access their files for all of the movies Richardson rented in the past year. We can then see if they were produced by the same company or companies."

"For what purpose?"

Connie sipped her coffee before answering. "You have to remember, Delta, that our suspects are in town looking for the big score. They're motivated by money. We don't know what connection, if any, Richardson had with them, but we do know he was into video excitement, and they are into video production. I'll wager Mr. Deceased Richardson is a star in one of the up-and-coming snuff flicks. So, we'll check and see what kind of movies he rented and if there's any correlation with the way he was found."

Delta shook her head. "Geez, you're good."

Connie shrugged the compliment off. "I get paid to think, so here I am...thinking."

Delta grinned. God, she loved Connie Rivera. "What next?"

"You hit the streets and see what you can find out about Kempt's. It's a little shithole next to a dive bar, but they have some very interesting clients. Kempt's has been around for nearly twenty years. You don't stay in that kind of business unless your customers have lots of dough."

"So, I hit the streets and see what I can find, Leonard will pursue his normal line of investigation, and you'll pirate whatever you need from the computers."

Connie nodded and clicked the mouse twice before turning to Delta. "You know why Leonard's helping, don't you?"

Delta shook her head.

"He's involved for the same reasons we are; he feels as responsible for Helen's death as we do. I heard him talking to one of the guys the other day, and you can believe me when I say that her death has really affected him. He thinks if only he would have, could have, might have, etcetera."

Nodding in slow understanding, Delta sighed. "He's not such a bad guy after all."

"No, he's not. He truly cares. Russ Leonard is a 'go by the book' kind of guy. The fact that he's out of bounds should tell you something. This is a big, big deal."

Indeed, it was. Delta had despised Russ Leonard for his narrow views during the Zuckerman case, and when they needed his help most, he refused because what she and Connie wanted done wasn't "correct procedure." Shortly after he turned them down, Helen was killed, her blood staining everyone's hands who had worked on the case, including one hard-headed detective.

And now, here he was, offering to help Delta do what no one was supposed to be doing.

No one, that it, except the feds, and no one had heard from them since the sergeant read the memo.

"I'll hit the streets with my little Italian Albatross tonight and see what I dig up."

"Good. In the meantime, I have a few other places Eddie needs to visit before I root around in Kempt's computer basement."

Finishing her coffee, Delta started for the door. "We'll connect again tonight."

"You got it. Oh, and Del?"

"Yeah?"

"Stay out of trouble."

14

Getting into the patrol car, Delta thought back to the scared little family that adopted her after Miles died, and when her friendship with Jennifer grew deeper. Understanding each other's need to share stories about the man they both loved gave them a bond that lasted well after the wounds had finally healed. When Jennifer discovered that men were interested in her, it was Delta who convinced her that it was okay to start dating again. It was Delta who stood by her through that first date and reassured her that it was what Miles would have wanted. after all, when Delta had been given a new partner, it was Jennifer who stood by her as she and Jan got to know each other. When it was time for Jennifer to start living again, it was Delta who held her hand and promised to stay by her regardless of who she saw or what she did. Life was for the living, and while they both would forever carry the memories of Miles Brookman, it was time they both moved beyond the past.

When Jennifer finally stepped away from Miles's shadow, it was Delta who babysat for the two children who called her "Aunt." Delta loved those kids. Both of them had Miles's gentle disposition and zany sense of humor. They loved to hear stories about their father, and Delta was only too happy to share what she knew about the man they had only known for a short while. Their personalities were composites of the man Delta would have given her life for, and nothing short of death would prevent her from seeing that no harm ever came to either of them.

It was a promise she'd made at Miles's gravesite, and she intended to keep for the rest of her life.

"Hey, Delta, you okay?" Tony asked, slowing down as they passed a convenience store.

Inhaling slowly, Delta shrugged. "I had a hard time sleeping last night, that's all."

"This kiddie case?"

Delta nodded.

"You gotta be pretty whacked out to do shit like that."

Turning so she faced him, Delta looked hard at the side of Tony's face. "Definately whacked out. I'm all for First Amendment rights, but you've gone way over the line when you start exploiting kids. Way over the line."

"Did you see the faces on the guys at the scene who have kids?" Tony asked.

Delta nodded. "I can't imagine how they must feel. You're right. Children used to be the one thing we held dear. Now, they're at a greater risk than ever. Remember when you could just hop on your bike and ride over to the park to play basketball with your friends?"

Tony nodded, a grin slowly forming on his lips. "Yeah, and when everyone on your block would go trick-or-treating together and you didn't have to worry about razors in apples or drugs in the candy?"

"And you could play kick-the-can until midnight because your parents felt safe leaving you out on the streets?"

Tony blew a big breath from his mouth. "Those were the days, eh?"

"Yeah. And now, we've got these assholes in our city, killing children, and we're supposed to sit back and let the FBI take over. Right.

"You've never sat back in the past." The words seem to jump out of Tony's mouth.

Slowly, Delta turned so she faced him. "Look, Carducci, I shot those men because I had to. As much as it may appear, I am not the vigilante the academy stories portray me as. You do what you have to do out here to make sure that your number one objective is accomplished. Did they tell you what that objective is?"

"To make the streets safe?"

Delta smiled a patient smile. She remembered that silly line from her own academy training years ago.

"No, Carducci. Our number one objective out here is to make sure that we both get home safely. No matter what happens out here, no matter how many damn rules and regs you have to break, you remember that that's our greatest priority. We may have to hurt people to make it happen, but that's part of the job. We're not sacrificial lambs, Carducci, even if the tax-payers think they own us. You got that?"

Tony nodded. "Gotcha. And that's what you were doing when you shot those guys?"

"Exactly. And no matter what else you hear, that's the only reason I pulled the trigger. And I'd do it all over again if I thought it meant the difference between driving myself home and being carried away in an ambulance. There's nothing heroic about self-preser-vation, Carducci. And make no mistake about it, that's exactly what it was."

Tony nodded. "I got it."

Delta slowly turned and pushed her face closer to his. "Do you? And do you understand that sometimes that means breaking the rules? Because if our lives are ever at risk, I don't care how many rules and regs you've got to break, I want you to break them. Do you understand that?"

"I hear you loud and clear."

Delta backed down a bit. "Good. And I'll deny saying that if you ever try to burn me with it. We're partners, Carducci, and after your own hide, my safety comes next. We take care of each other, no matter what it takes."

Tony nodded. "I read you, Delta. Honest, I do."

"Anything you want to say before we drop this conversation?"

Tony shook his head. "You amaze the hell out of me, that's all."

"Well, stop being amazed and just assure me that you'll do what it takes to keep us alive."

Tony nodded vigorously. "Don't you worry, Delta Stevens. Breaking rules is my second favorite activity." Turning to smile at Delta, Tony shook his head like a little boy. "There's only one thing those academy stories didn't exaggerrate on."

"What's that?"

"What a tough woman you really are. You don't mess around, do you?"

Delta shook her head. "Not out here."

"Not at all is more like it. You and your friend really kicked ass outside the bar that night. You two meant business. I...I never really thanked you. I suppose it's the macho Italian in me, but I can't say I've ever been rescued by a woman before."

Suppressing a smile, Delta faced the front again and watched two prostitutes slink through the crosswalk. "Oh, so that's the reason for your cavalier, albeit reckless, attitude?"

"I come from a very traditional Italian family, where the man is the strong one. The man makes the decisions and the woman's place is to maintain his castle. I've never been one to rely on a woman for much of anything."

"Except sex?" the words escaped Delta's mouth before she could stop them.

"That's not what I meant. It's a cultural thing. My mama spent her life in the kitchen and my two older sisters got married right out of high school. My family is Old World and it's sort of in my blood. I won't apologize for it, Delta, but I do try to keep up with the times. I've ticked enough women off to know the Old World attitude ain't happening. That kind of shit isn't going to get me through the door, let alone in the sack."

Delta shook her head. "You mean you're *aware* of your disgusting macho behavior?"

Tony shrugged, but did not take his eyes off the road. "Yeah. I try to control it, but my father had a big influence on me. 'Son,' he'd say just before I went out on a date, 'just don't get her pregnant.' That was my only worry. Forget her feelings, forget she has a mind; after all, he treated Mama like she was some kind of servant. 'Get me a beer, get me my dinner. Stop that kid from crying.' It wasn't until I moved out of the house that I realized most women in this country refuse to be treated the way he treated my mother. But by then, I had already learned a lot of stupid things."

Delta didn't know what to say. Suddenly, she realized she had judged the book too soon. Tony Carducci, the macho man, was merely a facade hiding the real man his father would be ashamed of. He was a victim of the backwards, archaic social standards, and probably just recently realized that most women didn't want to be bashed over the head and dragged out of a room by their hair.

"So, you're not as big of a chauvanistic asshole as you appear?"

Tony grinned. "Not always. I have my moments. But when you grow up in a neighborhood full of other tougher Italians, you develop a tough exterior real quick."

"You mean there's hope?" Delta smiled and patted his hairy arm.

Tony grinned. "Sort of. But cut me some slack in the female department. I may know how to woo them, but it's a new thing to have to work with one."

"Have to?" Delta goaded.

"Ah, man, you never let up, do you? I didn't mean it that way."

Laughing, Delta shook her head and rolled down the window. It was a beautiful Indian Summer night. "If you're going to 'have to' work with me, Carducci, you've got to get one thing straight."

Tony groaned. "And that is?"

"Try to remember to put your machismo in your locker before you hit the streets."

Tony nodded. "I'll try. But I can't make any promises. I'm not very good at those, either."

Delta smiled warmly at him. "Somehow, Carducci, I'm not surprised."

15

Delta looked forward to lunch with Alexandria all day. There was something about the District Attorney's calm assertiveness that drew Delta to her. Something about her kept Delta on edge, kept her guessing from one minute to the next. She was a woman who took chances, who put faith in other people, who rose to every challenge like a champion. When Connie's life was in danger, when they were thrust in the middle of a serial killer bent on destroying not only Connie's life, but many others as well, Alexandria risked her own career to support Delta and Connie's efforts to bring him in. There were few people in Delta's life who garnered as much respect, but Alexandria Pendleton was one of them.

Looking up from her coffee, Delta watched the tall, slender woman stride into the restaurant carrying a briefcase in one hand and a silk jacket in the other. Tossing her long auburn hair over her shoulder, Alexandria casually leaned over to the hostess and whispered something to her. When the hostess glanced up, she grabbed a menu and started toward Delta's table.

"Alex," Delta said, greeting her with a tender hug Delta saved only for her closest friends. "It's been too long." Pulling away, Delta motioned for her to sit down.

Laying her briefcase on the seat next to hers, Alexandria ordered a glass of white zinfandel before turning to Delta.

"Are you angry with me?"

Delta grinned warmly. "Because of this TP thing?"

Alexandria nodded. "I didn't know what else to do." Looking straight into Delta's eyes, Alexandria's gray-green eyes penetrated Delta's. "I knew how much it would kill you to be behind a desk. I did everything I could, but my hands were tied."

For as long as they'd known each other, Alexandria had always played it straight with Delta. No matter what the situation called for, Delta could count on Alexandria to dispense with unneeded particulars and cut to the chase . It was Alexandria who gave Delta the time she needed to find Elson Zuckerman. It was Alexandria who fulfilled her promise to put Miles's murderers away for life. She was one of the few people Delta trusted implicitly, and if Alexandria Pendleton said her hands were tied, then Delta believed her.

"No, I'm not angry, Alex. When Captain Henry said it was your suggestion, I knew you were trying to keep my career alive."

Drawing in a long breath, Alexandria sighed. "Internal Affairs went over every inch of your file. They pulled things out of there that would make you dizzy."

"Were they looking for anything in particular?"

Alexandria shrugged. "My personal opinion is that they were looking for a reason to hang the lesbian out to dry. You know how narrow-minded IA can be."

"So, you think my sexual orientation had something to do with it?"

"Something, but not everything. IA sees you as a vigilante and turned everything in your file around to make it appear as if that's exactly what you are. When I heard what they intended to do, I stepped in."

"But their minds were already made up?"

"Not exactly. It was a pretty touchy situation. The chief didn't want to look stupid by punishing someone the media has labelled a heroine, yet he and the captain felt obligated to hear I.A's conclusions. They also felt they needed to send a message to other officers that vigilantism won't be tolerated. Your transfer to TP is their message."

Delta ran her fingers through her hair. It was all so damned political. All she wanted to do was get criminals off the streets. But the system protected the suspect and hounded the victim. And if she thought independently of the system, she would have to pay a high price, regardless of how successful her deviations might have been. Bureaucratic bullshit is what prevented the wheels of justice from turning.

"I'm glad I'm still on the streets, Alex. Thanks."

"Oh, don't thank me, Delta. You wouldn't have been in this mess if I hadn't asked you for a favor. You came through for me. Returning the favor was the least I could do. I only wish I could have done more."

"Hey, I'm on my beat, aren't I? That's the most important thing to me."

"I'm glad you see it that way. When I didn't hear from you, I thought the worst. I wanted to do the best by you, Delta. You deserve it."

"And you did. Thanks."

Alexandria leaned away from the table and draped her arm across the back of the chair. "You know, I may be DA, but I'm a rookie when it comes to knowing what makes you cops tick. I was nervous as hell coming over here."

Gazing into Alexandria's eyes, Delta admired the fire and passion she held for justice. Alexandria was a fighter, a winner, a woman complete with steel nerves. If she was nervous to see Delta, it sure as hell wasn't because of the Training Patrol issue.

When the waitress came over, they both ordered and waited for the waitress to refill their glasses before continuing.

"I've worked with you long enough, Alex, to know that you didn't just call me to lunch to make sure I wasn't angry with you. You could have done that over the phone. What's up?"

Running her index finger around the rim of her wine glass, Alexandria could not stifle her grin. "You're a rogue detective, Delta Stevens. I am not supposed to be so easily read. You sure you don't want to come work for me as a special investigator to the DA?"

Delta grinned. "No thanks, Alex. I'm just a beat cop. Now, are you going to tell me the real reason for this lunch?"

Alexandria lowered her voice to a whisper and leaned forward. "I think you already know."

Delta nodded and leaned closer to her. Their faces were inches apart. "The kiddie-porn flicks?" Delta knew she had a direct hit even as the final word escaped her lips.

Alexandria stared into her wine glass. "This is a highly sensitive matter, Delta. I don't need to tell you that the FBI are creeping all over the place, and the community is scared to death. You can do a lot and get away with it, but start messing with people's children, and the public wants an arrest yesterday."

Delta waited for more. She knew Alexandria well enough to know there was more than just public opinion at stake here.

"Many of the school buses in the west district were emptier than usual because parents chose to drive their kids to school. They're afraid their children will be next."

Trying to push away the memory of Helen's parents when they identified her little body, Delta focused on Alexandria's eyes. They were grayer now, as they always got when she was making a point. "Can't blame them, can you? Kidnapping children is one thing, but torturing and murdering them is incomprehensible. If I had kids..." Delta thought back to Jennifer's kids. "I'd drive them to the front door of school." Sitting more erect in her chair, Delta sighed. "I've held a dead child in my arms, Alex. I see Helen's little face in nightmares every single night. I'd give anything to be able to erase what happened to her."

Alexandria cocked her head to the side. "Anything?"

Delta nodded. Here it comes—the real reason Alexandria wanted to see her.

"You know the feds have created a task force to deal with this situation." Alexandria lowered her tone even more.

"I didn't know, but I could have figured."

"The problem is that they've got guys on it who don't know the streets as well as you do. If there's anyone who knows the streets and has connections, it's you."

Leaning back again, Delta calmly replied, "Then put me on the task force."

"I tried. No go."

Delta shook her head. "Stubborn assholes. They're going to let politics stand in the way of catching these creeps."

Alexandria shook her head. "Not if we can help it."

Delta's left eyebrow rose in its characteristic question mark. "We? Why, counselor, I believe you have something up those sleeves of yours. Could it possibly be Mr. Wainwright?"

Color quickly rose to Alexandria's cheeks and she turned away. As she slowly turned back, her eyes were more green than gray and sharp like a tiger's. "It's no secret that Wainwright has the backing of the monied conservatives."

Delta nodded. The whole picture was unveiled.

"The conservatives want a man in power, and they'd back just about anyone with a dick."

Delta suppressed a grin. Alexandria rarely swore. "And?"

"And I've worked too hard to lose this because of some assbackward politicians who think a man would have a higher conviction rate than I do."

"Your conviction rate is excellent."

"Tell that to the boys."

"And you think that trying this case will cement closed the lid on Wainwright's campaign?"

Alexandria nodded. "It isn't just a matter of politics, Delta. Wainwright will make cuts we can't afford to have happen. He's more of a politician than he is a lawyer. This city needs me to stay in office, but, if we can't come up with suspects who are ravaging children, he'll use that against me and I won't stand a chance. He's a dirty player and he'll use anything he can against me."

"Just what is it you think I can do? If your hands are tied, mine are handcuffed, Alex."

"Let me pass any information I get from the task force on to you. Delta, you have connections the mob dreams of having. If the perps are out there, if they're on our turf, I know you'll find them before the feds. They're too caught up in all the gadgets and BS to be any real help. I need this case."

Delta looked hard at her. Alexandria Pendleton knew exactly what she was asking of Delta. Already on thin ice, she was asking Delta to skate out to the middle of it to save her career. It would be an awful lot to ask someone who wasn't used to being on thin ice.

But Delta was used to it.

"I know I'm asking a great deal of you, Delta, but I guarantee I'll make it worth your while. I still have a few power markers to call in if I need to."

Delta waved her off. "I don't do favors for my friends with the hope of being repaid. If you need help, you know you can always count on me. That's just how I am."

Alexandria smiled softly, her eyes suddenly yielding to a warmth Delta had rarely seen. "Thank you. You're a great friend."

Delta smiled back. "Yes, I am."

"Megan is one very lucky woman."

Delta watched as Alexandria's eyes misted over with a different kind of intensity, one she had never seen. "You know I'll do whatever I can, Alex. "

Reaching across the table, Alexandria touched Delta's hand. "That's one thing I've always appreciated about you, my friend."

Locking eyes with Alexandria, Delta felt the heat from her hand swim up her arm and spread across her chest. Slowly pulling away, Delta grinned sheepishly. "I'll give it my best."

"That's precisely what I'm counting on."

16

Delta looked at her watch for the fifteenth time in as many minutes. Megan was already an hour late from her study session and Delta had to be at work in an hour. For a panicky moment, Delta thought that this was a sign that they were in way more trouble than she imagined. They seldom had time together, and the few minutes they had planned on spending alone were ticking quickly away.

Since Miles's death, time had a greater significance in Delta's life. When she held the body of her partner in her arms and watched his blood flow across the dark pavement, Delta knew her life would never be the same. Time, her life, her loves, her relationships meant more to her. That fateful night had changed her. The problem was that Megan had changed too.

Going to school full time had opened Megan's eyes to a new and incredible world. She discovered a love of literature and, of all things, law. She had changed her major from business to business law and was considering going to law school. Suddenly, Megan had new friends, a new job, a new life, and new excitement that comes along with it all. One night, when Megan had just returned from a play, she was wildly gesticulating about the characters and the scenes and the music, and suddenly, Delta realized that Megan's world was changing so rapidly, she couldn't keep up. When Megan announced that she felt as if she had just awoken from a ten year coma, Delta suddenly became very scared.

Slowly at first, Megan became more and more interested in the university and all of the riches it afforded her. Before they knew it, they really were just two ships occassionally sending messages to each other. They weren't even passing in the night any more.

The worst part was, Delta understood what it was in her own life that often took her away from Megan, and she was working on that. But, like Miles's and Helen's deaths, Delta felt incapable of keeping Megan from growing away from her. The powerlessness she felt at the hands of death was beginning to overwhelm her own life. Delta Stevens could save a hotel full of people and shoot the stem off the apple, but she could not stop her relationship from running the course it was on, even if she did choose the key.

That damned analogy was beginning to eat away at her. Of course she would choose to save the key.

Wouldn't she?

Checking her watch again, Delta started when the phone abruptly rang. She knew what this ring meant. She'd heard it too many times in the recent past to ignore it.

"Hello?"

"Are you mad?" It was Megan.

"Not really," Delta lied. "More worried than anything else."

"I'm so sorry, but Dr. Rosenbaum was giving an exclusive reading from his new novel just for faculty, and he invited me to come along. I'm sorry I didn't call, but you don't just get up and walk out of a reading. It's really rude."

"I'm sure. How is good ol' Doc Rosenbaum?"

"He's fine. Delta, are you okay? You sound funny. You are mad, aren't you?"

"No, Hon, I'm not mad. Just concerned."

"Well, I'm okay and I'm on my way home."

Delta gripped the phone hard. "That's not what I meant."

"I know, but I don't think we should talk about it over the phone."

"Well, I have to go to work. How about dinner tomorrow or the next night? Just the two of us. We can talk, or not talk. But let's try to spend some time together."

"I'd like that." Megan's tone softened.

"Good. So would I."

"Del?"

"Yeah?"

"We're going to be okay. You have to believe that."

Sighing, Delta looked at her own reflection in the mirror. "I'll try. See you in the morning." Hanging the phone up, Delta continued to stare at herself in the mirror. Suddenly, she felt as if she wasn't the one who had the choice to make. Maybe it was Megan's key sinking in the water and Delta was just standing by to see what she chose. Maybe they had spent so much time worrying about Delta's job that nobody was paying much attention to what was happening to Megan.

And maybe, Delta thought as she lay her head on the table, Megan's key and my key had already sunk to the bottom.

17

Sitting next to Connie, Delta ran her hand through her hair. She was beginning to feel old and it bothered her. Suddenly, when she looked in the mirror, she saw two deep green eyes with a wizened look about them and worry lines running across her forehead like the Grand Canyon. And it was no wonder. Ever since she had busted the guys who killed Miles, her every move was examined with scrutiny. She felt like a microbe under a microscope and couldn't shake the feeling that she was always being watched. Now, with a volatile rookie in her hands, her lover, her shrink, and her friends gauging her every choice, it was as if the entire world was watching to see if someone could tame this wild bronco.

And Delta was beginning to wonder about it herself.

"How'd it go?" Connie asked, turning from Eddie and pressing the screen saver button.

Delta shrugged. "We didn't see each other. She kinda had other plans."

Connie looked out at Delta with one eye. "Uh oh."

"It's no biggie. She's just enjoying school, that's all." Delta leaned across the desk and saw a list of city names in Arizona. "You been working hard?"

Connie slid the paper toward Delta. "Is there any other way? The problem I'm having is sorting the leads from the nonleads. Our guys don't leave many clues, and the ones they do leave are circumstantial at best."

"What about the task force?"

Connie shook her head. "Word has it, they're willing to forfeit the little fish for the shark."

"Damn it."

"Yeah, my sentiments exactly. I want you to consider what getting in their way might cost you. We're not talking about a piddly little city P.D. here, Delta. We're talking about G-men, and they carry a lot of weight."

Delta shrugged. "So does my guilt. Thanks for the concern, Chief, but I want this bust."

Turning back to the computer, Connie punched in a few numbers. "I figured you'd say that. I have a few angles I need Eddie to assess, and after I run them, I'll let you know what I come up with. But Del," Connie swiveled around in her chair and laid her hand on Delta's shoulder. "You mess this up, and IA won't have a choice but to pull you."

Delta nodded, keeping her eyes on Connie's. "Chief, if I mess this one up, then I'll let them." Looking around and then checking her watch, Delta wondered where her student was. "Junior must have slept in."

Connie grimaced. "Ugh. You sound just like Leonard."

Delta laughed. "That little guy has a way of growing on you."

"Right. Like mold on cheese. Anyway, Tony already came in and told me to tell you he'd be waiting by the patrol car. He mumbled something about checking the unit out before you hit the road. It sounds like he's trying to get on your good side."

Delta smiled. "At least he's learned *something* since we've been on the street. For a minute there, I was beginning to wonder if he didn't have some major learning disabilities."

"We'll know soon enough, won't we?"

Grabbing her gear, Delta tapped her finger on the list of names and looked at Connie with questioning eyes.

"This is some info I pulled from the feds' system." Lowering her voice, Connie turned back to the screen and pretended to work. "The perps came from either Arizona or New Mexico, I'm not sure which. It's possible they may have Arizona plates, which would fit in around here in the summer time."

"They might have stolen a California vehicle when they got here."

Connie nodded. "Maybe. My guess is they have some pretty elaborate equipment that they keep either in a van or motor home, or someplace confined. The feds have a video of the suspects' work. Don't ask me how they got it, but it's Code Green—for private consumption only. Leonard's been trying to get his hands on it, but they're not buying. I'm seeing it later."

"How do you rate?"

"Captain Henry called me in and asked if I wouldn't mind viewing it. As the department's think tank, I suspect they simply want my take. Maybe it's in Spanish or French or something. I don't know. But I'll fill you in on all the disgusting details later."

"Great. Beep me when you have something." Moving toward the glass doors, Delta started to push them open, when Connie called her back.

"Del, nobody wants this collar more than you and I. But you've got to be careful. I mean it this time. Don't mess around with the feds."

Smiling, Delta cupped Connie under the chin. "You got it." Whirling back around, Delta shoved open the glass doors and headed for the parking lot.

Mess with the feds? They'd better hope they don't mess with her. Federal agents or not, they weren't going to stop her from continuing with this investigation. Rounding the corner, Delta found Tony and another officer battling away at each other like two ants on an ant hill. In the scuffling and scraping, they were locked in combat like two wrestlers, each trying to get a better grip on the other.

"What in the hell is going on here?" Delta asked, standing back in time to avoid Tony's errant swing at the other cop.

When the other cop stopped in mid-swing and looked over at Delta, Tony grabbed him in a headlock and bent him in half.

"God, Carducci, haven't you caused enough trouble already?" Delta asked, shaking her head. "Whatever you boys are fighting about should be done on your time, not mine. Goddamn it! Let him go."

The officer struggled to free himself from Tony's large bicep, but Tony treated him like a slight nuisance and tightened his grip.

"You heard her. Let go of me!" the officer growled, his voice rasping against the force pressed against his neck.

"Damn it, Carducci, are you *trying* to get yourself tossed out of the department? I said let him go."

Angrily shaking his head, Tony wiped his bloody lip with the back of his free hand. "No way. Not until he apologizes."

Bending over so she could see the red face of the other officer, Delta shook her head. "Apologizes? For what?"

Tony squeezed his neck harder. "Tell her."

Glancing back up at Tony, Delta's eyebrows knitted together. "Tell me what?"

"Apologize, Miller." Tony's voice was low and cold.

Straightening back up, Delta jammed her hands on her hips. "What is this about?"

"Miller?" Tony wheeled Miller's head around so that he was as close to facing Delta as possible.

"All right, all right," Miller wheezed. "Just let go. You're hurting my neck."

"I'll hurt more than just your neck if you don't apologize nicely to my partner." Letting Miller go, Tony folded his arms across his chest like a father waiting for his son to explain how the car got dented. Miller, a man who stood a shade over five-seven, was no match for the larger, stronger rookie, who stood glowering at him like some dime store totem pole.

Bowing his head, Miller rubbed his left jaw as he approached Delta. "Look, Stevens, I said something about you to Carducci and I'm really sorry for it."

Now, Delta folded her arms as well and she and Tony stood like bookends towering over the shorter officer. "What could you possibly have said that would piss Carducci off so much?" Delta had an inkling, but she wanted Miller to own up to it.

Looking away from her piercing eyes, Miller shook his head. "I'd rather not say."

Tony suddenly took a step toward him. "If you had the balls to say it to me, at least have them to say it to my partner's face."

Delta tried not to grin at Tony's constant use of the word "partner." Clearly, he took the idea of a partnership seriously. Ah, she thought, a strength in his character she could appreciate.

"Well, Miller? It appears as if you owe me some kind of apology for saying—"

Clearing his throat, Miller inhaled deeply and glared at Tony before eventually spitting out, "I said you were a..."

Tony moved a little closer to him.

"...a pussy-eating dyke." His voice was barely audible, and Delta had to strain to catch every syllable.

"And what else?" Tony growled.

"And I'm sorry, Stevens. I shoulda kept my mouth shut."

Delta nodded, feeling bitter that she had to work with someone so close-minded and puny. "Yes, you should have."

"Can we just forget I said anything?" Miller stuck his hand out to Delta, who only looked at it with disdain.

"Sure. I think I'll also forget that you are a homo sapien. You know what that translates as? Of course you don't. It means, 'man who thinks.'" Delta inhaled through flared nostrils. "I should have let Carducci twist your little pencil neck like the rotten twig it is. Get the hell out of my face before I let him."

Picking his hat up off the ground, Miller quickly scurried away.

"Son of a bitch," Tony muttered, straightening his own uniform.

Walking over to him, Delta slapped him in the shoulder. "And what's the matter with you? You can't go around beating people up who say things you don't like. For God's sake, Carducci, do you have to act like such a Neanderthal?"

Buttoning his collar button, Tony shrugged. "I can take a shot at someone who thinks they can spread rumors about my partner just because she's a better cop than he'll ever be. Miller's an asshole who obviously doesn't have anything better to do with his time than run around gossiping like a little old lady."

Delta simply shook her head. He was so frustratingly naive. He envisioned himself as her champion, as the partner who would waylay anyone who said a bad word about her. And she knew she couldn't just let this go. If he was going to jump into every bit of gossip with both feet, he at least deserved to know the truth about the person he was defending.

"Carducci, I appreciate you defending my honor, but there's something you should know."

Nodding, Tony waited.

"What Miller told you is not a rumor."

Tony leaned toward her as if he hadn't heard her correctly. "What?"

Delta grinned. He looked as if she had just slapped him across the face with a dead fish. "I said, it is not a rumor. I am exactly what he said I was. Well...maybe not in such gross terms."

Tony opened his mouth to say something, but nothing came out. For a moment, he stared at her, as if trying to understand a foreign language. After a thick moment of silence, his only words were, "You are?"

Delta nodded. "I am. Although his wording was more vulgar than I prefer, the sentiment is the same. I am a lesbian."

Tony just stared at her. A tense silence hung heavily in the air as they waited to see who would be the first to break it.

Finally, Tony cleared his throat and quietly said, "So...let me get this straight. What you're saying is...that you're gay."

"If that's an easier term for you than lesbian, yes, I am."

Shaking and scratching his head, Tony's face showed utter confusion. Finally, he looked up at Delta and grinned. "You sure had me fooled."

Brushing a smudge off his shirt, Delta started toward the unit. "Fooled? How so?"

"I don't really know how to explain it. It's just...you look...so normal."

The word made Delta cringe. "Just what does 'normal' look like, Carducci?"

Tony shrugged again and Delta knew by the pinkening of his cheeks that he was straining to find the right words. So far, he had been unsuccessful.

"Well...I don't really know. I mean, I watch the news. I've seen lesbians and stuff before, but I never thought—"

"That you'd actually work with one?"

Tony bowed his head. "Something like that. I also thought..."

"Yes?"

"Well, that you all looked alike."

Delta smiled. "Oh, I see. You thought we all looked like truck drivers with flannel shirts, big leather belts, chewing tobacco in our mouths, and sporting traditionally male haircuts."

The pink turned to red.

Bull's-eye.

"You can be honest, Carducci. You did, didn't you? You probably also thought we all hate men and run around with hairy armpits and no bras." Delta paused and glanced down at her chest. "Not that it wouldn't be nice not to have to underwire every day."

The red in Tony's face deepened. "Well...I..."

Delta smiled gently at him as a signal that her words, though potentially harsh sounding, were not intended to put him on the defensive. She had done that too many times as a young, almost militant lesbian, who didn't care that stretching her wings often meant poking someone else in the eye. "Come on,

Carducci, it's the nineties. Just like the rest of the world, we come in all shapes and sizes. The day of wearing green on Thursdays is over. Besides, don't you think you'd be hard pressed to find anyone in California who could define 'normal?'" Delta waited, but she could tell that Tony was still chewing on her first questions. "Carducci, lesbians don't—"

"Shh," Tony said, putting a finger to his lips and looking around quickly to see if anyone was within earshot. "You want people to find out?"

Delta smiled and shook her head. "Most of them already know. It's no secret."

Tony's eyes grew wide like a child who just found out Santa doesn't exist. "It isn't?"

Opening the car door, Delta got in and waited for him to fold his long legs in and close the door before continuing. "People keep things secret when they are ashamed or afraid. I'm not. I came out a long time ago because the secret was eating me up inside and making me pretend to be someone I'm not. When I came out to Miles, I knew it was the right thing to do."

"Because you knew he wouldn't let anyone fuck with you?"

"That and the fact that I was tired of the charade. Pretending to be straight takes so damn much energy. After awhile, it feels like one big game to see how long you can keep people guessing. I just got tired of it."

"But what about all the assholes like Miller, who give you a bad time about it and say shit behind your back?"

"Well, you already said it. He's an asshole. He'd have some knife to stab in my back if I were a straight woman and not interested in him. Jerks are naturally like that. I learned long ago not to waste my breath or my fists on someone that narrow-minded. Some people can open their minds, some can't. I don't choose to spend time trying to pry open the minds of those who can't. It's simple. Besides, I don't parade my sexuality around. If I did, the brass would make soup out of me."

"Don't the other guys...you know...guys like Miller...don't they give you a bad time?"

Delta shook her head. "Look, after shooting the legs out from under another cop, nobody messes with me now, unless they're just stupid."

"Like Miller."

"Yeah. Like Miller."

As they pulled out of the lot, Delta sensed Tony mulling over her words. She waited in relative silence while he sorted through this new information. She didn't care whether he accepted this revelation or not. It would simply be harder to get along during his TP training if he harbored any resentment or hostility. That was the problem about coming out to new partners. Reactions were always unpredictable and, often, the news created tension between partners. Unfortunately, having Tony Carducci for a partner was tension enough.

Finally, when Tony spoke, his voice was softer and quieter than she had ever heard.

"Delta?"

"Yeah?"

"I've been thinking it over. About this...gay thing and all."

"And?"

"And I don't really care who you sleep with. It's just..."

"What?"

"Well, to be honest, I've never known a gay woman before."

Delta grinned at his choice of words. "Lesbian, Carducci. We're called lesbians. It won't kill you to say the word."

Tony swallowed loudly and stared out his side of the window. "I know. It's just that I've never known any...lesbians before...I mean, maybe I have."

"More than likely you have and just didn't know it."

Tony nodded, his face a mixture of consternation and puzzlement. "I guess, the hard part is that I know you think I'm some kind of chauvanist pig and all, and now I don't know what not to say. I try to keep my mouth shut but, damn it, Delta, this is really new to me."

Glancing at him, Delta reached over and patted his shoulder. For all of his overflowing machismo, Tony Carducci did have a heart. Sure, he was naive and had an overabundance of testosterone, but at least he cared enough to ask questions. At least the man inside the body wanted to know how to be, how to coexist with someone far different than he had ever known. And this little bit of insight shed more light on Tony's character than anything else Delta had seen so far. Hope poked its head around the corner.

"Look, Carducci, say whatever you'd normally say, unless it's derisive or discriminatory. If you were working with an African-American, you wouldn't make stupid Black jokes, would you?"

"No way."

"Then give me the same respect you would anyone else. It's not a disease. While you certainly don't have to walk on eggshells around me, I don't want you attacking me, either. Treat me like you did before you knew and we'll get along just fine, okay?"

Tony stared straight ahead and nodded. "I think I can handle that."

"Good."

For the next ten minutes, the only sound in the patrol car was the crackling of the radio. Delta was glad that Tony chose to think to himself instead of trying to make polite conversation or small talk. She had to admit that he had taken the news better than she thought he would. He had, after all, listened with an ear that showed a gentle concern for their working relationship. Unlike many of the other men she had told, Tony had not made any lurid comments about "watching" or what was it like sexually. His first concern was for their partnership, and she liked that.

What she liked even more was discovering that there really was a soul beneath all that mousse and cologne. Looking over at Tony, Delta smiled and he turned and smiled back. Something had broken between them. It was like a ray of sun breaking through the clouds after a storm.

"Thanks for sticking up for me, anyway, Carducci. I appreciate it."

Tony shrugged and looked away, the pink reappearing on his cheeks. "Wasn't anything. I didn't do it because I think being gay is disgusting or anything like that. I did it because you're my partner and no one can just rip on my partner when I'm around and expect to walk away without some teeth missing."

Delta hid her grin. Playground politics were at work here, and she knew there was no use in trying to talk him out of twenty-something years of male socialization. "Well, thanks, anyway. It means something when someone sticks up for you, know what I mean?"

Tony nodded. "I may not know the streets very well yet, Delta, but I do know a little bit about people. And I know that you're good people regardless of who you sleep with. You're good people and you're a damned good cop. Who gives a shit about the rest?"

Delta shrugged, letting the grin slip out just a little bit. "More people than you might imagine."

"Well, not me. What you do on your own time is none of my business. And vice versa."

"Agreed."

As the car silently slipped through the streets like a snake slithering through the jungle floor, Delta thought about her other coming out experiences. If there was one thing she had learned, it was to resist predicting how someone was going to react to the news. She had had husbands of best friends toss her out of the house. She had watched her sister-in-law move the baby into another room, and she had seen people she barely knew welcome her into their families with open arms. She couldn't have predicted that Tony would have been okay with her.

"You're really being a trooper about this, Carducci. It isn't an easy thing for some men to get used to."

Tony turned in his seat to fully face her. The pupils in his eyes were dilated and his eyebrows formed a crown as they knitted together. "I may be a lot of things, Delta, but stupid isn't one of them. I wouldn't trade being taught by you for anything in this world. I wouldn't give a damn if you slept with donkeys. Teach me what I need to know out here. The rest isn't any of my business."

"No, it isn't. But being a lesbian isn't about sleeping with women. We have relationships, commitments, unions. We're couples in every sense of the word."

"As long as you don't steal my action, know what I mean?" Tony forced a grin and shrugged. "Letting a lady get away to another guy is one thing, but I don't know how I'd feel if we were both hitting on the same woman and she walked away with you. Nothing personal, but I don't think I'd handle that very well."

Delta shook her head. "Trust me, Carducci, you and I will never compete for the same woman."

Tony shrugged. "I guess not, huh?"

"Besides, I'm..." Delta hesitated. What was she? Committed? Separated? Alone? "In a relationship."

Tony looked sideways at her. "No kidding? You don't look like the domestic type to me."

Delta laughed. "I don't?"

"Nope. You look like someone who likes playing the field."

"Well, I'm not. I like being monogamous."

"Really? Good for you."

Delta patted his arm. "You know, Carducci, you're okay. Stick with me, and the rest will follow soon enough."

Tony stared at Delta and squinted. "The rest?"

"Of your humanity training. I'm going to make an open-minded human being out of you yet."

Just then, their number came up on the radio and Delta motioned for Tony to take the call. Watching him speak into the mike, Delta warmed inside. It had been a long, long time since a man had defended her honor. It had been just as long since she had felt comfortable with a man as a partner. Tony's willingness to jump to her defense spoke volumes about his level of integrity and his understanding of the importance of partnerships.

"Ready to roll?" Tony asked, turning on the lights and sirens.

Delta nodded. "I'm ready, Partner."

18

The night continued without incident or further discussion of Delta's sexuality. It appeared as if Tony was at least able to accept the initial phase of her coming out to him. That was a big plus in his favor. It also meant he was capable of separating the person from the badge, and that was equally important. It was a lesson many rookies didn't learn until it was too late.

Delta wondered if she had ever learned it at all.

"Delta?"

"Yeah?"

"Thanks for leveling with me about this...lesbian thing. I've been sitting here thinking about it and it must have taken a lot of guts to open up to a guy you don't like very much."

Delta flicked her high beams at a slow moving car and shook her head as she whizzed past it. "It has nothing to do with liking you, Carducci. If you can't trust your partner, no matter how different you are from each other, then you're in trouble."

"You trust me?"

Delta thought about this before answering. "Yeah, Carducci, I do. I wouldn't get into the car every night with you if I didn't."

"What about my stupid mistakes?"

"Mistakes are only stupid when someone gets hurt by them. Besides, you're allowed a few mistakes."

"As long as they're not too stupid?"

"Exactly."

"Did you make stupid mistakes?"

Delta winced inside at the memory of the biggest mistake she had ever made. Every day since Miles had died, she looked at the shotgun in the unit and wondered what her life would be like now if she had had it the night they stopped that van.

"Yeah, Carducci, I have."

Delta peered through the night, looking for any sign of her best street connection. After cruising past the pool hall, the pizza joint, and the liquor store on the corner, she finally pulled up to two prostitutes standing on the corner.

"What are you doing?" Tony asked as Delta rolled down her window. "Listen and learn, Carducci." Then to the women, "Hey gals, long time, no see."

"Delta!" the tall black woman in the red wig shouted as she ran over to the window. Her left pump nearly got wedged into the sidewalk and she practically stumbled into the car. "Hey, Sugar. You take our best gal and disappear into Never Never Land? Where you been?"

Delta grinned. Candy was one of Delta's favorite prostitutes. "Getting into all sorts of trouble."

"And where's Megan? Where you been keeping her, girlfriend?"

"Off the streets, that's for sure."

"Hey, girl," the short white woman said as she moseyed up to the car. "What's shakin'?" Leaning over, the woman saw Tony and winked. "Mm Mm, but your partners just get better and better looking."

Delta looked over at Tony, who blushed. "All looks, girls, and no money."

Both women laughed. Then Candy leaned in closer. "Whatcha need, Sugar?"

"I'm looking for Julio, and I haven't found him in the usual places."

The woman with the wig smiled. She had perfectly straight teeth. "Try Chuckie's. Julio's been hanging there a lot."

"Chuckie's Steak House?"

"Mm Hm. And that'll cost you, Sweet thing." Candy pushed her hand through the window and held her palm up.

Delta looked down into her hand and grinned. "Bill me."

"I'll take your handsome partner for payment," Candy said, winking at Tony and rolling her tongue over her thick lips.

Delta shook her head. "You don't want him. He's an amateur."

"Oh, Sugar, that's just how I like them."

All three woman laughed. "Now you get outta here, girl, before you ruin our action."

As Delta drove away, Tony cleared his throat. "Uh, Delta? What was that all about, and why didn't we bust them? They were obviously hookers."

Delta couldn't help but smile. He was so young. "No, Carducci, they were prostitutes, and I don't bust prostitutes."

"Why not?"

"It's a victimless crime. And if there ever is a victim, it's usually one of the girls. Women have the right to do what they want with their own bodies."

"But what about diseases and stuff?"

Delta shrugged. "Hell, we should legalize it, tax it, and pull this country out of debt. With AIDS spreading the way it is, legalization and registration of all prostitutes may be one of the safest ways to go."

"I doubt a lot of the guys would agree with you on that one."

Running her hand through her hair, Delta nodded. "Probably not. I wish we cops were a little more progressive, but cops don't like change. Do you know how long it took police departments to go from the nightstick to the PR24?"

Tony nodded. "A long time."

"Right. Because cops, like most people, detest change. And even though the PR24 is harder to master than the straight baton, with the handle, you can do so much more with it." Pulling into Chuckie's parking lot, Delta looked around for Julio. "Damn him. I hate when he does things like this." Opening the door, Delta told Tony to wait in the car.

"Wait?"

"Yeah, wait. Julio doesn't like other cops very much. I won't be long."

When she opened the door to the steak house, Delta stopped in her tracks when she saw Julio behind the counter flipping burgers.

"Julio?"

Turning to see her, Julio shook his head and cut his eyes over to a door that said "Employees Only."

Delta got the hint and followed him through the door.

"Whatcha doin', man? Tryin' to get me fired?"

"Fired? You work here?"

Julio closed the door behind Delta and led her back to the storeroom. "Yeah, I work here. Wussamatter? Think Julio too stupid to get a job?"

Delta shook her head. "Not at all. " It was the first time in three years that Delta had ever seen Julio not baked out of his mind. "I'm just...surprised, that's all."

"Yeah, well, if my boss sees me talkin' to you, he may think I done somethin' wrong, know what I mean?"

"I wouldn't have come if it wasn't important."

"So, now that you found me, wussup?"

Delta felt like she was talking to a stranger. Julio had never been straight during any of their previous encounters. As a member of the Crips, Julio had been a dope man, always making sure the gang had plenty of party goods. One day, when Julio's girlfriend was facing a possible gang rape by rival gang members, Delta and Miles had saved her. This had earned Delta his eternal loyalty, a gift she heartily accepted.

"What have you heard about snuff flicks lately, Julio?"

Julio bowed his head and scuffed his shoe on the ground. "Man, I was hopin' it was anything but that, Officer Stevens."

"Why?"

"Killin' kids is a mean business, man. Gangs don't do it, the mob don't do it, man, nobody who isn't loco does."

"Well, Julio, someone is doing it, and I need help finding out who."

Julio shook his head before peering around the corner. "Word has it some dude from Venezuela or Brazil is in town looking for green. Guy goes by the name of...oh shit, man... what was it? Papa, or Poppy, or something like that. No one knows what he looks like, but his main man is a tall skinny dude who been askin' about buyers and shit."

"What else?"

Julio thought for a second before answering. "Chit has it he lookin' for dark meat, if you get my drift."

"African-Americans?"

"Naw. Not that dark."

Delta nodded. "He's been looking for Hispanic kids?"

Julio nodded. "Something like that. Guess the dude is here to show his goods to the locals, you know, to make 'em hungry for more. That's all I know, Officer Stevens. Nobody wants to mess with these guys."

"Because of the kids?"

"Naw. 'Cause the feds are after them."

This surprised Delta. How had word already leaked out that the feds were in town? "How do you know?"

Julio shook his head. "You know the deal, Officer. I tell you stuff, but I ain't gotta tell you where I got it."

Delta nodded. "Sorry."

"Look, man, you better go. I don't want no trouble. I need this job."

"You do? Since when?"

Julio bowed his head again. "Since my ol' lady's knocked up."

Delta stopped. "You're having a baby?"

Julio looked up at her and grinned sheepishly. "Yep." Pushing past Delta, Julio retied his apron. "I want you to nail those fuckers, Officer Stevens, before my baby comes. I mean, you wouldn't want to see someone who fucked with my family."

Patting Julio on the back, Delta started out the door. "That's the plan, Julio."

"Funny how having a baby changes how you see things."

"Even funnier how things change when you're not high."

Julio grinned, displaying the cap on his front tooth. "Yeah. That, too."

"Thanks, Julio. And good luck with your bambino."

"Ah, man, don't start with all that fatherhood shit. Being a father ain't gonna change my ways, Officer."

Delta patted him on the back. "Talk to me in nine months, *amigo,* and we'll see if you're singing the same tune."

With that, Julio headed back behind the counter. "I also heard you gotta airhead for a partner. You watch your ass out there, Officer Stevens. Even good cops get killed."

"I'll do that." Stepping out the door, Delta inhaled the smell of freshly cooked hamburgers. Julio had a job and was going to be a father. Maybe there was hope yet.

19

"You sure have some weird connections, Delta," Tony said when they pulled out of the driveway. The night felt like a stranger peeking through their windows as they told dispatch they were back on the air.

Delta glanced out the window for one more look at Julio as he snatched the order from the little silver spinner. "Weird is in the eyes of the beholder, Carducci. That kid is my eyes and ears on the street. He's more valuable than five undercover cops. Julio always knows what's going down and he gave me another piece to the puzzle. Pull over so I can call Connie and let her know what I found out." Jumping out of the car, Delta raced to the phone, called Connie, and was surprised to get Connie's voicemail. She left a brief message about Papa's or Poppy's name and told her she'd tell her the rest later. When Delta returned to the car, Tony was staring out the window.

"You okay?" She asked, lightly touching his arm.

Tony shrugged, but did not look at her. "When I was a kid, one of my friends was kidnapped from our neighborhood. Her name was Anya and she was only ten. I remember how the panic and fear gripped the adults as they searched everywhere for her."

"Did she ever turn up?"

Tony shook his head. "Never."

"I can't imagine anything worse than having your child snatched. Some people never know what happens to their children. I think that's the worst."

"I'd rather know."

Delta turned as she slowed to a stop. "Know what?"

"That my kid was dead. I'd rather know the truth than to spend my life wondering if he was still alive, hurt, or being mistreated. Man, that's a torture no one should have to go through."

Delta listened carefully to Tony's words as she measured the weight of the plans she was tossing about in her head—plans that might get them both into a lot of trouble.

But trouble was a part of Delta's life she had come to expect. She knew, from the age of thirteen, that controversy followed her everywhere and that rebelliousness was simply a glitch in her character. That was one of the reasons police work was for her. It kept her balanced between her rebellious nature and the rules of life—rules she too often disregarded, rules she was contemplating disregarding at this very moment.

Staring out the window, Delta thought back to the days when she had just graduated from the academy. She remembered how the streets came to life at night. There was an underbelly to the night that threatened to consume those who didn't understand this world of darkness. The beings who walked the dreary, dark, and dangerous streets at night seemed to dance with the shadows, as the moon glared down, threatening to unfold the secrets of the night dwellers. In the cold, bleak landscape, the sounds of crickets and screeching tires intermingled like two songs playing simultaneously. Nothing was as it appeared during the night hours; a cry in the darkness could just be a cat or someone singing—or it could be someone screaming for help. Only the veteran of the streets could tell the difference. As the darkness covered the city, a different world emerged. It was the antithesis of daylights' beings in three-piece suits who strode with confidence down these very streets. This darkness, this heavy cover settling over the city, was why Delta loved her job. It was what made her want to save the world from itself. Yes, she came out of the academy with her ideals flying out of her pockets like loose change. She wanted to be an impact player, a person who could make a difference in the lives of people tossed aside like an unmatched sock. Being a cop was the best way she knew of to make that difference. And she had made a difference. So far, apart from her individual successes on her beat, she had saved a police department from ruin and a hotel full of people from being killed. She had made an impact.

She wanted to do it again.

Only now, she would be risking the wrath of a captain who had put her on TP in an effort to save her already tenuous position in the department. Delta had been a rogue cop and a hero all in one night. She had been placed on TP to teach, to learn, and to remember all the rules she had bypassed over the last couple of years.

But what good was teaching, learning, and remembering, if the people she had sworn to protect were being victimized? What good was she as a teacher if her student never experienced success? What the hell good was she if she followed the damn rules yet seldom made the major busts?

Turning around to Carducci, Delta inhaled, blew out a breath and pulled the car over.

"What's the matter?" Tony asked when they came to a stop. "Want me to drive?"

Shaking her head, Delta licked her lips and turned the radio down. "Carducci, I want you to listen carefully to me because I am only going to say this once, okay?"

Nodding, Tony's face was a mixture of secrecy and excitement.

"My job is to teach you the streets, right?"

"Right."

"And so far, I've done that, haven't I?"

Tony nodded. "Yep."

Delta smiled. "I'm glad. But we have a little problem here."

Tony's face fell. "Did I do something wrong?"

"Oh, no, Carducci. This isn't about anything you've done wrong."

Visibly relieved, Tony relaxed. "Whew. For a minute there—"

"You're doing fine. Well...with a few minor incidences, but that's not the problem."

"Then what is it?"

"A long time ago, I promised a friend I would do whatever I could to keep his children safe. As we speak, children are being hunted out here and the feds are getting so bogged down in red tape, they'll never find them. Government guys usually have far different agendas than the rest of us. They're always looking for the big score; they always play for keeps. Look at the Waco fiasco. They had a chance to save lives, but instead, they botched things up royally. They failed because they went for the whole pie. In the process, little slices of that pie—children—were killed."

Tony nodded, his face changing from apprehension to comprehension.

"Look, I'm going to be totally honest with you. I've been put on ice here on TP. My job is to train you to the best of my ability. But I'm a cop, Carducci, not a teacher. And when I see crimes against the people on my beat, it's my job to go after them, regardless of my title. I don't give a shit about 'the big picture' or 'the big fish.' My job is to arrest people who victimize other people. And FBI be damned, that's what I'm going to do. Are you following me?"

Tony nodded. "Loud and clear. You want to go after the porn ring."

Delta nodded once. "I can't sit back and play teacher while children are being whisked away practically out from underneath my nose. If that's the way the captain and everybody else wants this played, they can have my badge, because it isn't worth the metal it's made of."

Fiddling with his pen, Tony looked up and locked his eyes onto Delta's. "So you want to know if I'm with you. Is that it?"

Nodding, Delta tore her eyes from his and stared out the window. "I know it's asking a lot. You're just a rookie and you have a lot to lose."

Drawing circles with his pen, Tony did not respond.

"I might be able to do this on my own time, but that reduces the amount of time I have to work on it. I'll understand if you don't want to have any part in it. Hell, I'll even help you get transfered to another FTO if you want."

Inhaling slowly, Tony stared out the window as well. "I didn't become a cop to sit on the sidelines while someone else played my position. If you want help with this, Delta, then count me in."

Looking back at Tony, Delta shook her head. "You're taking a big, big risk by doing this. If we're caught nosing around, I'm history and you're...well, I don't really know what they'd do, but it wouldn't be good."

Tony shrugged. "I don't know either, but anything's better than just sitting on our hands. I trust your instincts, Delta. And if you think we have a shot at nailing these bastards, then let's go for it."

The pressure in Delta's chest eased a bit as she pulled back into the thin traffic of the night. "I promised Miles I'd make the corner of the world his children lived in a safer place. Well, that corner's being violated, Carducci, and I couldn't live with myself if I didn't do something about it. Sometimes principals overrule practicality."

Tony smiled. "I'll remember that."

"Good. And while you're at it, remember that when all is said and done, it doesn't really matter how you catch a criminal as long as you get the job done."

"I will, boss." Smiling his big toothy grin, Tony turned the radio back up.

Glancing over at him, Delta wondered if including him was the right thing to do.

"Carducci?"

"Yeah?"

"If this leaves this car, both our careers are ruined."

Tony turned and offered her a smile she hadn't seen on his face before.

"Delta, you may think I'm a jerk and that I'm young and a bit stupid, but there's one thing I want to do more than anything else in the world."

"And that is?"

"To solve a major case with you. If we do that, I can write my own ticket anywhere I want. That's what I really want and if you're gonna let me in on this, then let's do it."

Delta opened her mouth to respond, but didn't really know what to say. She had her copilot, she had her map, and she had Connie.The race was on and Delta knew where her first pit stop would be.

20

"Storm, you're playing with fire. You know that, don't you?"

Swinging the chair around so she could sit backwards, Delta grinned. "I like it hot."

Punching a few buttons on the keyboard, Connie called up some files. "That's what worries me. Including Tony in this scares the hell out of me. But I know better than to try to stop you. What's done is done."

"Good. What do you have so far?"

"Apparently, our suspects have traveled through the southern half of the U.S. on their way here. There have been snatchings from Oklahoma, Texas, New Mexico, and Arizona, as well. We've been able to tie those kidnappings together by witnesses who say the kids were snatched by the same tall, skinny guy. His MO is he steals a car first, cruises around playground and park areas, does a drive by, and then makes the grab."

"Not very elaborate."

Connie shook her head. "Doesn't need to be. Once they make the snatch, we figure they meet up with another car, probably a van, hide the kid, dump the stolen vehicle, and then they're long gone."

"Any pattern to the kinds of cars they steal?"

Working the computer like a massage therapist, Connie called up more information. "Great question. I wondered that myself a few hours ago." Studying the file, Connie nodded. "Our thin man has a prediliction for Camaros and Mustangs. Oh, and one Trans Am. Three were red, but the Trans Am was yellow."

"Easy to hot wire."

"Yep."

"What else?"

"Eddie's having a hard time getting into the fed's system. What we've gotten so far comes from a favor I called in and from my own research."

Delta wrote down a few notes and waited for Connie's fingers to stop flying over the keyboard. "The fed's little task force believes that the guy who does the snatching is just a flunkie. They think the video man is an ex-con who was in for kidnapping or child molestation, or something of that nature. They're going back the last ten years in their files to cross index every felon who's out on parole."

"That's a lot of work."

"A lot of useless footwork." Turning from the computer, Connie rubbed her red eyes. "There are two keys to catching these guys before they leave town. One is in the stolen vehicle pattern, and the other is infiltration of the ring."

Delta considered this for a moment. "That's an interesting angle. Do we have enough information to be able to do that?"

Connie nodded. "Just about."

"And what about the stolen vehicles?"

"The cars are the only tangible pattern we've come up with. Our thin man likes fast, red ones. He probably doesn't even realize he's carved out a pattern for himself. It's one of those simple things that usually gets crooks arrested."

Delta nodded and watched Connie work on the computer. "I like the idea of getting someone on the inside. Do you think the feds have anyone in there?"

Connie laughed and started punching more info into the computer. "I hardly think so. I saw two of them talking to the captain earlier and they're just chasing their tails. The problem I see with the feds is that they all look like agents. Like someone cut them with a cookie cutter; there isn't one of them who wouldn't be spotted before they could even get out of the car."

Delta nodded. They did all have that Clint Eastwood look about them. Even in the nineties, few women held top government positions, and the FBI was no exception. It was, unfortunately, still a 'good old boys' organization.

"Besides, even if they did manage to slide someone in, they're hunting a different animal than we are."

"Because they aren't satisfied with catching the thin man."

Connie shook her head. "Nope, they're not. They want Mr. Big."

Delta's eyes sparkled. "If they're not gonna go after him, then—"

"We are. And I think the best way to do it is a two-pronged approach."

Her adrenaline surging, Delta leaned closer. She knew Connie would formulate a plan. It was only a matter of time. "Prong number one?"

Connie smiled. "We have a beautiful Camaro in the compound—cherry red, fast. And Smith says we can have it for a week."

Delta's eyes lit up. "It's worth a shot, don't you think?"

Another cop strode past them and Connie pushed a button for the screen saver to appear.

"I can rig the computer to say that Officer so-and-so needs to inspect the vehicle for a couple of days. Do you think one is enough?"

"Got any others?"

Returning to the screen, Connie pulled up a menu of cars held in the compound. "We have a blue '65 Mustang, but nothing else that compares to that red Camaro."

"Then skip it. How long can you get it for?"

"A week, tops."

Delta shrugged. "Can you get a bug for it?"

Nodding, Connie picked up the phone.

Delta checked her watch. It was after two in the morning. "Isn't it a bit late to call someone?"

"Nah. Electronic wizards rarely ever sleep. Putting her mouth on the receiver, Connie spoke into it. "Sal? It's Connie Rivera. How's our project coming along?" Connie made her hand like a duck and moved it in a talking motion. "Yeah, I need that wireless tap we spoke about earlier. No, I need a stronger one than that. Let's say with a range of up to ten miles with a motion detector. You can? Great. No, I'll be over later this morning to pick it up. I'll also pick up that business card." Connie listened for a moment. "It's hooked up just to the machine, right? Excellent. You're a gem. I'll tell her you send your love, yes. Thanks a bunch, Sal." Hanging up the phone, Connie turned to Delta and smiled. "Done. Sal's a great connection. The tap will act as a homing device with a range of up to ten miles. It will begin beeping as soon as there's movement. I'll get you the radio receiver and a transmitter as well."

"What will it do?"

"When the Camaro starts to move, the beeper sounds. When your vehicle starts moving, you look at the little picture and it will show you a green flashing dot, which is the stolen vehicle, and a red flashing dot, which is your vehicle. That way, you know where you are in relation to the stolen vehicle. It's all laid out in a grid system. Sal showed it to me once. Pretty incredible stuff."

Delta shook her head. She was constantly amazed at technological advances. "Wow."

Connie nodded and grinned. "It's a better way of tailing a suspect minimizing the chance of being spotted. The feds have something like it, but Sal's is mostly military stuff."

Delta held up a hand to stop her. "I don't want to know."

"Oh, yeah. Anyway, I'll get it from Sal. You'll just keep the receiver with you at all times and you'll know when the car is grabbed."

"Okay. Prong number two."

Connie pushed the screen saver button before scooting closer to Delta. "What we're dealing with here are pedophiles. Last night, I read Krueger's *Analysis of the Behavioural Patterns and Conditions of Pedophilia.*"

"Certainly not the best bedtime reading," Delta said coldly.

"No, but I learned a great deal. Pedophiles enjoy correspondence and contact with other people like themselves. As if their sickness is some kind of a social club. What we need to do is become part of the local club."

Delta shuddered. "That's such a gross thought."

"Yes, it is. But it's also our best strategy. I've located the name of a fellow who organizes the local meetings and get-togethers."

"Get-togethers? These people actually meet?"

"Yep. They even have their own newsletter. Believe it or not, the guy who runs the meetings out of Kempt's Porn Palace is the vice president of the River Valley Baseball Program." Connie grinned. "I got that little gem from one of the guys working the kiddie-crime unit."

"Okay, so the VP of the baseball program may be our first contact."

"Right. The feds are watching him closely, but they don't think he knows anything. He's just the head of the Rene Guyon Society."

Delta hadn't heard the name before. "Rene Guyon?"

Connie paused while a clerk set a file on her desk. "It's a group for pedophiles who like to engage in sex with younger children. Their motto is 'sex before eight or else it's too late.'"

Delta's stomach heaved slightly. "Sick."

"No kidding. They have a newsletter outlining upcoming events. There's a membership of more than 1,000 people countrywide, and the Los Angeles and surrounding communities crowd meets tomorrow night."

"Tomorrow night? Can we be ready by tomorrow night?"

"We have to be. Apparently, this meeting wasn't on the agenda or in the newsletter, so it could be a meeting to inquire about investors." Connie shuffled through some three-by-five cards and plucked one from the deck. "My source thinks they may even be previewing one of the videos."

"Where?"

"That was the only thing he didn't know. It's the secrecy that makes me think we're onto something big. That, and the fact that this meeting was called in such a hurry."

"So now what? This doesn't do us any good if we don't know where they're going to be."

"I've covered that as well. What you need to do is go undercover to Kempt's and ask for Fibber."

"Fibber?"

Connie sighed. "Yeah. As in Fibber McGee and Molly. Pedophiles also tend to use nicknames from children's shows."

"Okay, I go to Kempt's and ask for Fibber. What's going to make him tell me?"

"Oh, ye of little faith. Hand Fibber a $100 bill folded around your membership card and ask him what's shaking."

"You're kidding."

Connie's eyes narrowed. "Do I look like I'm kidding? Del, these people have to be extremely careful. Do you have any idea what inmates *do* to pedophiles in jail?"

Chills ran down Delta's arms. "Where do I get my membership card?"

"One's being made as we speak. It has a seal of some sort, so it's taking a little while to duplicate one, but you'll have it before you go. It says you're from out of state, in case Fibber or anyone else wants to know why they haven't seen you at any of the local meetings."

Delta inhaled a deep breath. "Thomas Jefferson would commit suicide if he were alive to see how we use his constitution."

Connie smirked. "Indeed."

"Anything else?"

"Yeah. When you get to the place where the meeting is being held, you knock on the door and say that you hear they have some good pie."

"Pie?"

"Yeah. It stands for Pedophile Information Exchange. It's actually based out of London and has branches here in the States. Anyway, that should get you through the door. After that, the rest is up to you."

"You my back-up?"

Connie nodded. "Wouldn't have it any other way. Just remember, no matter how disgusted you might get, these aren't the people we want. Just view them as stepping stones."

"Will I have cash with me in there?"

"No. That's too obvious. Remember, these people still retain their freedom because they are discreet. Just make some inquiries, watch the video, and leave the business card I'm picking up from Sal."

"Business card? For what?"

"You're going fishing tomorrow night and we need the little fishes to have some place to call if they take the bait. Sal has a phone line that's just hooked up to an answering machine. The machine is then attached to her beeper. The moment the phone rings, her beeper goes off and she can get the message the second it's recorded."

"Amazing. Do I get to meet this woman?"

Connie grinned. "Soon. You'll like her. She is one of a kind."

"Then it's all set. I drop some hints, we wait for them to pick up the bait, and then—"

"And then we have to be very careful. If they bite, we won't be dealing with pedophiles any longer. We'll be dealing with kidnappers and murderers."

Delta thought about Helen, and about Casey and Colin. It wasn't pedophiles she was after, though she promised herself to make herself more aware of crimes against children. No, she wanted the killers. She wanted the people for whom there was no hiding behind the First Amendment. "Don't worry, Chief. I won't blow it."

"Great. Just don't push it. Kiddie porn cases take a long time to unfold. Time is on our side because the porno ring must know how close the feds are and will want to make a quick buck and an even quicker escape."

Reaching out, Delta laid her hand on Connie's wrist. "Chief, does *anything* ever escape you? This is incredible work in such a short time."

Connie laid her other hand on top of Delta's. "I saw that look in your eyes the moment you knew they were coming our way. I knew you'd go after them. I just didn't want you going off half-cocked, that's all. Besides, I'm the brightest woman we know. It wasn't that hard."

"I only hope my performance can match yours."

Connie's eyes narrowed. "Oh, it had better. My only foe was the computer and time. Your enemy will be men with guns and bloodstained hands. You have to be better than good."

"Right. Anything else?"

"Yeah. When's the last time you talked to your girlfriend?"

Delta sighed. She hated it when Connie came at her from out of the blue. "Well, I was hoping—"

"Hoping won't do it." Picking up the phone again, Connie dialed and handed the receiver to Delta. "Tell her you're on your way over."

Taking the phone from Connie, Delta sighed again. When Megan answered the phone, her voice was sleepy. "Hello?"

"Hi, babe, it's me."

"Are you okay?"

"I'm fine. I'm sorry to wake you up, but I was wondering if you'd like me to come over." Delta could hear Megan wrestling with the covers.

"I have a test in the morning, Del, or I'd love to."

"What about after? Want to have lunch?"

"Um, well, Elizabeth and Terry want to go shopping for some clothes for their exchange trip. They're going to Costa Rica."

Delta frowned. Who in the hell were Elizabeth and Terry, and why were they going to Costa Rica? Had Megan mentioned this once and Delta hadn't listened?

Suddenly, Delta felt very out of touch. "Sounds like fun. Where did you meet these women again?"

"Meet them? Delta, they're in my Intro to Law class, remember? I told you all about them and the exchange trip they're going on this summer. Don't you remember?"

Delta didn't. "Oh, yeah, I forgot. It's late, that's all."

Megan yawned into the phone. "Del? Is there something wrong?"

Wrong? Megan was hanging around women Delta had never met, she was going off shopping and frolicking and who knows what, and Delta didn't even remember hearing their names before. Wrong? Usually, Megan would cancel any lunch date in order to spend time with Delta. Was the honeymoon over so soon?

"Uh, no, there's nothing wrong."

Connie frowned at Delta and prodded her with a pointy finger to the shoulder.

"It's just that I feel a little disconnected from you. It seems like you've been so wrapped up in your friends at school that we haven't had much time together."

"Then let's spend some time together."

"Great. Can we do lunch or dinner tomorrow night?"

"Oh, I can't. Paige has the lead in the musical and we're all going out to dinner before the curtain opens."

Paige? Who in the hell was she?

"Okay. You tell me the night."

"How about Wednesday night? I get off at 9:00, but we can go out after."

"I can't. I have a class in Crime Scene Preservation. It's over at 10:00 and then I have to go to work. I'm off Thursday night. What about then?"

"Hmm. That doesn't work for me. The animation festival is in town and a bunch of us from my paralegal class are going." Megan paused and sighed. "It doesn't appear as if we're going to see each other anytime soon."

"Then let's make it Friday night. Just the two of us."

Megan yawned again. "Sounds great. Keep your calendar clear, okay?"

"You, too."

"Sure thing."

The line was silent for a moment and Delta wondered if Megan was still on the other end. "Meg?"

"Yeah?"

"I love you."

"I know. I'm beat, honey. Can we talk later?"

"Yeah. Sure. Later. Goodnight."

Click.

Delta slowly replaced the phone in the cradle. "Looks like I'm free until Friday night."

"Del—"

"Save it, Chief. I'm all talked out. I have seventy-two hours to myself and I'm going to use every second I can to find these assholes and bring them in."

Connie frowned, but said nothing.

"I'm going to Kempt's tomorrow and we'll set this whole action rolling."

"Don't you make a move without me, Storm."

Delta forced a smile. "Wouldn't dream of it."

"Good. Now get out of here and let me finish my work."

Rising, Delta headed for the door.

"Del?"

Delta stopped, but for some reason, didn't turn around.

"She has to do what she has to do. You know that, don't you?"

Slowly turning around, Delta nodded. "That makes two of us, doesn't it?"

21

"How do I look?"

Connie stepped back and jammed her hands on her hips. "Gee, I don't know. What is a pervert supposed to look like?"

Delta studied herself in the mirror. She looked appropriately wealthy, yet subdued enough to be believable. Believability was the key. They had to get them to take the bait now, or they would never piece this mess together.

"Got some money?"

Connie nodded. "Yeah, but don't use it unless you have to. Flashing too much dough is a dead give away."

Delta turned and stared at Connie. "Mind using a different cliche—perhaps one without the word 'dead?'" Delta adjusted her skirt and flicked off some lint. "God, how do women wear these blasted things? They're so uncomfortable." Pulling up the slack in her nylons, Delta shook her head. "And these are the worst. I'll just bet some man invented them."

"Del, I don't think I have ever heard you whine as much as you have tonight. It's only for a few hours."

"A few hours? Some women wear them *all day*. I couldn't do it. If I had to wear a dress to be a cop, I don't think I could do it."

Connie just shook her head.

"And how do you keep the crotch from sagging? It feels like I'm wearing diapers."

"Keep your legs together," Connie said, handing Delta a wad of $100 bills. "Hell, how should I know? I only own one dress and it's a sun dress."

"Well, next time, let's use that one, 'cause these nylons suck."

Grabbing the rest of their things, Connie pulled Delta out the door.

Twenty minutes later, Connie pulled into the parking lot behind Kempt's Porn Palace. "You okay?"

Delta inhaled slowly to steady her nerves. "I am. I can't say the same for my nylons."

Pulling out a small notepad, Connie flipped it open and scanned it quickly. "Okay, the guy at the counter with the reddish hair is Fibber. There should be a second guy called Philip. Apparently, Phil doesn't know anything. All set?"

Delta pulled her nylons up one last time. "Yep."

"Here's your membership card. It's not a fake, like I thought. So if they call that chapter's president and ask if you exist, you really do."

"I'm impressed. You've got some pretty incredible connections, you know that?"

Connie nodded. "All to keep you safer, my dear. Del, please be careful in there. I don't need to tell you how dangerous these kind can be. Don't get cocky."

"Cocky? Me? I don't know what you're talking about. I thought I was 'mellowing.'"

Connie couldn't stop her grin. "Play it safe, Storm."

Delta saluted her. "Will do, boss." Opening the door, Delta stepped unsurely on her high heels. "It's a wonder podiatrists don't make the FDA put health warnings on pumps. These are horrible. They're the perfect compliment to the equally hazardous nylon droop."

Connie ignored her. "I'll drive around to the front so I can have a good view of the front door. If anything gets weird—"

"I'll holler." Delta checked to make sure the tiny microphone attached to the back of her necklace was still there. It was the smallest mike she'd ever seen.

"Be careful, Del. I mean it."

Delta winked and walked around the corner and into the store.

Kempt's Porn Palace reminded Delta of a maggot's nest—dark, creepy corners where even creepier people writhed from one aisle to the next, avoiding eye contact with the other maggots. Occasionally, there was heavy breathing in the video section, as a handful of men previewed the latest, hottest porn flicks. Of the dozen or so people in the store, Delta was one of two women. It was for that reason she and Connie believed no one would suspect her as a plant. Delta had to smile inwardly when her presence obviously made some men uncomfortable, like the first female reporter in the NFL lockeroom.

Delta casually browsed through the video section, staying far away from men who carried their hands in their pockets. She felt like a hen walking through a foxhole, as men peered out from under magazines, books, and video machines at her long legs.

After ten minutes of idle browsing, Delta strolled over to the front counter where Fibber sat reading a *Voyeur* magazine.

"Can I help you?" Fibber asked, not removing his eyes from the magazine. He rhythmically popped his gum as he switched it from one side of his mouth to the other.

Delta glanced around quickly before sliding the folded $100 bill on the counter. Only one corner peeked out from under her palm. "How you doing this evening, Fibber."

At the mention of his name, the clerk glanced up. "Not bad."

"Good. I was hoping that I might make it better."

Fibber's gaze followed Delta's until he saw the money on the counter. "You have my attention."

Delta smiled. "Good. Look, I'm new in town and a friend of mine just told me that there was a special screening of some videos that I ought to see. I was told you'd know where the previews are being shown."

Fibber looked up from the money and studied Delta for a moment. "You interested in renting them?"

Leaning across the counter, Delta grinned in his face. "Not that it's any of your business, Fib, but no, I'm not. I'm much more interested in purchasing some pie."

This changed Fibber's demeanor immediately. "Oh," he said, straightening up and finally putting the magazine down. "I see." Looking all around, Fibber slid his hand across the counter until it met Delta's. Delta released the bill and the membership card.

"One minute." In a flash, Fibber escaped around the corner and out of Delta's sight. For a second, Delta wondered if she'd blown it. Then, before she knew it, Fibber was back and slid the membership card back to Delta.

"Can't be too careful," Fibber said, smiling a crooked smile.

"No, one can't." Delta tucked the card in the only pocket in the dress. From the same pocket she withdrew a business card with just a phone number. "This is where I can be reached. It's a machine, but I check it every hour."

Fibber nodded. "What kind of pie are we talking about here?"

Delta smiled. "Sorry, Fib, but you're just the middle man. Just tell your boss that I'm a very wealthy woman. I could enhance his business dramatically." With that, Delta turned on her pump heel and whisked out the door.

"Outstanding," Connie said, when Delta closed the car door. "You reeled him in like a pro. I could tell just by watching him. Hook, line, and proverbial sinker."

Delta agreed. "We should be getting a call shortly. I don't know where you got that membership card, but I think it saved the day."

"No kidding." Connie looked over at Delta, who writhed in her seat. "What are you doing?"

"Getting these damned nylons off," Delta said as she wriggled and squirmed in her seat.

Connie jerked her head in the direction of a pick-up parked two cars away. "That's not all you're getting off."

Looking up at the man in the truck, Delta cringed. "Yuck. That's sick. Take me home so I can shower. I feel so...so..."

"Dirty?" Starting the engine, Connie laughed. "No desire to try the straight world? Just think, you could have your pick of any manly man in that place."

Delta shuddered and made a sour face. "I'd rather eat elephant shit."

22

Pacing back and forth, Delta glanced at the phone every other minute. It had been two hours since they'd left Kempt's, and still no call from Sal. It was driving her crazy.

Just as she was beginning to bite her third nail off, she heard Megan's key slip in the lock. Megan stood at the door with her purse under her arm, her long hair blowing to one side, and a drop dead aqua silk jumpsuit on.

"Hi." Standing back so Megan could enter, Delta inhaled Megan's Opium perfume as it followed her through the door.

"Hi, yourself." Megan set her purse on the table and turned to kiss Delta lightly on the mouth.

"I thought you had a luncheon or something like that?"

Megan nodded and pulled Delta to the couch. "I did. I just cut it short because I think we need to talk." Megan lightly touched Delta's cheek with her finger-tips. "I know I've been so busy carrying on with my new friends, I haven't even made time for us."

Delta shrugged and glanced over at the phone. Why did she choose this time to have this talk? "We're both busy, Meg. That happens in relationships. I'm happy for you that you have new friends and new interests."

"Exactly: *for* me, not *with* me. Delta, you and I are traveling in opposite directions. I don't even feel as if we're on the same path. I have a life at the university that you know nothing about."

Delta inhaled deeply. "Like Elizabeth and Sherry?"

"That's Terry, and yes, like them. This morning, I was sitting in the student union having coffee, and I realized that I'm not giving this relationship 100 percent, either. All this time, I've been pointing the finger at you, and here I am, zipping around doing hundreds of things without you."

"But you enjoy doing them." Delta was having a hard time concentrating on this conversation. What would she do if the phone rang? Answer it? Put Megan on hold? Suddenly, she could see that golden key sinking quickly to the ocean floor.

"Yes, I do. I'm enjoying life more than I ever have."

Gazing into Megan's face, something in Delta's throat tightened. "There's another agenda here, Megan, I can see it in your eyes. So why don't we skip the preface. You want out?"

Megan took both of Delta's hands in her own. "Not at all."

"Then what?"

"I just think that maybe we both need some time away. Maybe each of us needs to examine her life apart from the other and see if we have what it really takes to do this relationship justice."

Delta's jaw clinched and she folded her arms across her chest. "I can do that without being apart from you. Damn it, Meg, I love you."

"And I love you. But Amanda is right. Love isn't enough. And neither of us are putting enough time or energy into maintaining our relationship. We're going through the motions, that's all."

Delta couldn't disagree with that, no matter how much it hurt to hear it—and boy, did it hurt. "So, now what?"

Megan reached down with one hand and pulled something out of her purse. "I've been giving you a hard time about your job. Well, I've been no better, honey. I dove into my school work and my new life at the university, and I haven't paused long enough to see where I'm going. Well, this morning, I realized that I haven't exactly been a shining partner, either. I haven't given you everything you need. And you know why?"

Delta shook her head. She felt about five years old.

"Because I haven't given *me* everything I need. I've spent the last eight years pleasing everyone but myself. Then, I get into this relationship and I'm still trying to please you. Well I can't make anyone happy until I take care of me."

"What needs are you talking about?"

"My need to grow. My need to experience the world without feeling like I have to ask permission."

"I've never—"

"I know you haven't. You've never done anything but be supportive. And I love you so much for that. But, Del, there are things I want to do that you can't do with me because of your job. That's nobody's fault. It's just the way it is."

Delta tilted her head to the side, puzzled. "What is it you want to do?"

Megan handed Delta the university's brochure for traveling abroad. "I want to go on that exchange with Liz and Terry."

Delta stared at the pamphlet as if it might bite her. "You want to go to Costa Rica? Don't you think leaving the country to find yourself is a little extreme?"

Megan laid the pamphlet next to Delta. "I want to travel, Delta. I want to see the world and see what I've been missing all these years. You had a chance to do that. I never have, but now I do. Now I can kill two birds with one stone by taking classes and doing an internship in Costa Rica. I can travel and go to school at the same time."

Delta felt dizzy. In one instant, Megan had managed to bring her world crashing down around her. "You...want...to...go...to...Costa Rica?"

Megan nodded. "It's just for the quarter. Three months, that's all."

"That's all?" Delta rose from the couch and paced over to where one of the cats was laying. "Three months? Megan, three months is forever! You want to travel to the boondocks for three months without me?"

"Can you go?"

"You know I can't."

"Exactly. You can't doesn't mean that I can't. Honey, I really want to go. And it might just be the best thing for us."

"Us?" Delta mocked laughter. "Us? There is no us if you just flit on down to Central America for three months. You've got to be kidding."

"I'm not," Megan said quietly. "I want to go. I need to go."

"Then go!" Delta grabbed the door knob, swung the door open and gestured for Megan to leave.

Slowly rising, Megan walked over to the door, gently closed it, and turned to take Delta in her arms. "I'm not leaving you, Delta."

Clutching Megan tightly, Delta buried her head in Megan's neck. "It feels like it."

"Well, I'm not. I'm doing something I've always wanted to do. It doesn't mean the end of us."

"It sure feels that way."

Kissing Delta's cheek, Megan gazed deeply into Delta's eyes. "You want to bust your rear end to catch crooks, and I want to experience a side of life I've only dreamt about. Right now, those two things are mutually exclusive. So, let's stop beating our heads together and just do what it is we both need to do."

Delta tore her eyes away and glanced over at the quiet phone. The bottom line was that Megan was right. There were things they each wanted and needed to do which didn't include the other and no amount of words and no expensive therapy could change that.

"You want me to send you off to Costa Rica with a smile on my face?"

Megan grinned. "You don't have to smile. Actually, a few tears and 'I'll miss you' would really make me happy."

Returning to the couch, Delta picked up the flyer about Costa Rica and glanced at it. "Seems to me," she said, handing the flyer to Megan, "that you get the better end of the deal. You get to sunbathe on the Caribbean, and I get to run around with pushers, pimps, and perverts. Somehow, that doesn't seem quite fair."

"I'll bring back plenty of goodies." Threading her arms around Delta's waist, Megan nuzzled the back of her neck.

"There's only one goody I want, and that's you." Turning in Megan's arms, Delta kissed her long and passionately.

"Mmm. How about me with a golden tan?"

Delta smiled. "When do you leave?"

"I met with Professor McVeigh this morning to see if there were any openings."

"And?"

"If I want to go on the same trip as Liz and Terry, I'll have to leave in six days."

Six days? Delta's heart sank. "So soon? It doesn't give me any time to get used to the idea of you being gone."

"Would you ever get used to it?"

Delta grinned. Megan knew her so well. "No."

"I didn't think so. Look, I'll be attending a university full time for the first month, then I get a part-time internship for the second month, and the third month I work full-time at the internship. It's perfect for me."

"And what kind of internship are you looking at? Banana picking? I mean, isn't Costa Rica a third world country?"

Megan's face softened. "That's what the rest of the world thinks, but no, they're not. It's a beautiful country with friendly people and an excellent university."

"So what's your internship about then?"

"Paralegal."

Delta was taken aback. How much of Megan's life had she really missed these last few months? "Paralegal?"

Megan nodded. "After spending all those crazy hours with you and Connie, I've decided to try my hand at law. What did you think I was taking all those law and poli-sci classes for?"

"Paralegal, eh?"

"Has a nice ring to it, don't you think? Megan Osbourne, paralegal par excellance." Snuggling into Delta's arms, Megan sighed heavily. "I'm coming back, you know. I don't want you to think that I'm leaving for good. You can't get rid of me that easily."

Holding her closer, Delta kissed her forehead. "Wouldn't ever want to."

Turning in Delta's arms, Megan's face was a mask of seriousness. "You mean that?"

"Megan, I have loved you since the first moment we met. Believe it or not, I really do understand what's going on with you. I wish you didn't have to go thousands of miles away to do it, but if that's what you have to do, then I'll be as supportive as I can."

"You won't regret it."

Delta's smile faded. "I hope not. I don't know what I'd do without you."

"Do you know what you'd do with a new and improved me?" Megan kissed Delta's chin, cheek, and neck.

"I think I could figure something out." Lowering her mouth to Megan's, Delta tasted every bit of her she could. "I love you, Megan Osbourne."

"And I love you, my beautiful Storm."

23

"She's going where?"

"Costa Rica." Pulling her seat belt over her lap, Delta shrugged. "I should have seen it coming, but I guess I've been too wrapped up in my job."

Reaching across the car and patting Delta's leg, Connie gave her a sympathetic smile. "It was bound to happen, Del. At least Megan is smart enough to catch it now instead of five years down the road when you're really invested."

"Yeah, I guess so. It doesn't make it hurt any less." Staring out the window, Delta tried to ignore the ache in her heart.

"She's doing the right thing, you'll see. When Megan comes home, she'll be ready for your relationship. She will have sown some wild oats and gotten that out of her system."

"Well, it's that sowing part that bothers me." Just the thought of Megan with another woman or, god help her, a man, made Delta's stomach turn.

"Don't second-guess her on this, Del, or it will drive you crazy."

"It already is."

"Then accept it and let it go. Be grateful she was straight with you. Not many people would be so honest. She obviously trusts you enough to handle this. Give her the same respect."

Turning from the window, Delta squinted at Connie. "Do you always have to be right about everything?"

Connie grinned. "That's how I maintain my genius status. Besides, you might stop coming to me for advice if I was ever wrong."

Delta's grin matched Connie's. "I wasn't aware I had asked you for advice."

"Sure you did. In a roundabout way. But seriously, Del, you're going to be okay. It's not like she's leaving you alone. Gina and I will make sure you behave, brush your teeth, and eat well."

"Thanks. I feel better already." Shaking her head at Connie, Delta felt lighter than she had since Megan had told her. "You never cease to amaze me."

"That's what Gina says after sex. I'm something, aren't I?"

Tossing her head back and laughing, Delta didn't even try to respond. When Connie got like this, the best thing to do was to not egg her on.

"So where are we going now? I thought we needed to stay by the phones."

"We're going right to the source. I thought we'd pick up the Camaro and give you a chance to meet Sal."

"Where did you say you know this Sal person from?"

Connie shrugged. "Here and there. Mostly from my pals in the military."

"The military?"

Connie nodded. "I worked with some people from the Marines when I was at MIT."

"The Marines? Your friend Sal is in the Marines?"

Pulling into a driveway of a house that looked like it belonged on the front page of *Better Homes and Gardens* Connie turned the motor off. "Sal wasn't in the Marines. Her father was."

In a flash, a small, wiry little boy peeked out from behind the six-foot gate, wearing a camouflaged baseball cap with matching fatigues.

"Sal!" Connie cried, sweeping the little boy off his feet. Upon closer inspection, Delta realized that this little boy with the short brown hair poking out from underneath the cap was, in fact, a woman.

"Sal, I want you to meet—"

"Storm," Sal said, reaching her hand out and grasping Delta's firmly in it. "Connie's told me so much about you. It's great to finally meet you in person."

"Same here." Bowing her head, Delta surveyed the petite woman who was wearing lace up black army boots. She stood a shadow over five feet tall and kept tucking her hair behind her ears. She looked like a little boy wearing his father's clothes.

"No call yet, huh?" Delta asked.

Sal shook her head. "Nope. I'm sure they're checking you out."

"What about the real woman who belongs to that membership card?"

Sal smiled and her freckles seemed to jump around on her face. "Not to worry. Everything will check out just fine."

"How about the transmitter?" Connie asked.

Sal jerked her head toward the garage. "Slipped her in like a glove. You have a ten mile radius, it will flash when the vehicle is moving and stay on when the vehicle comes to a stop." Sal pulled something from her pocket and handed it to Connie, who showed it to Delta. "Keep this with you. It will beep when the vehicle starts moving. After that beep, it will flash until the vehicle comes to a stop. It will beep once again when the vehicle starts again."

"So it beeps after the car starts from a stop light or something?"

Sal nodded. Delta noticed a pack of freckles living on her nose and two very thin lips resting beneath a cute button nose. Right away, Delta liked this midget of a woman.

"Your receiver will show you where you are in relation to the flashing green light. Each quadrant of the grid is half a mile, so you can gauge where you are accordingly. Any questions?"

Connie nodded. "Were you able to make any other connections for us?"

Sal grinned. Her two front teeth crossed over each other and a single dimple showed in her right cheek. "We hit the jackpot. I contacted Josh to see what he could come up with. We landed four more."

"Red ones?"

Sal nodded vigorously. "Red ones."

Connie turned to Delta to explain. "I didn't think one car was enough to lure our perp from his hiding place. So Sal located four more red Camaros."

"With transmitters?"

Sal nodded. "Of course."

Delta thought about the logistics of having five cars tapped and waiting to be stolen. "Where are these cars now?"

Sal shot a questioning glance over to Connie, who shook her head. "You haven't told her?"

"Not yet."

"Told me what?"

"Sal has arranged to have the Camaros placed in certain high crime locations."

Delta's eyebrow rose again. "What do you mean, 'placed?'"

Sal strode forward and looked up into Delta's face. "You want to catch a mouse, you should probably set more than one mousetrap, right? Well, I sent the boys out with the cars and had a van round them all up. Simple."

Simple? While she was muddling around with her relationship woes, Connie had clearly been doing all the hard work. "What 'boys?'"

"Sal has some Vietnam Vet friends who do some work for her occassionally."

Delta cocked her head in question. "Work? What sort of work do you do?"

Sal shrugged and grinned mischieviously. "A little of this, a little of that. The boys are my...partners. And they sure came in handy." Moving away from Delta, Sal adjusted her cap and started for the garage door. "We didn't move it, just like you asked, Connie." Lifting the door, Sal unveiled one of the most beautiful cars Delta had ever seen. It was a cherry red Camaro with the license plate FAST on it. It shone like it was wet, and there was enough chrome on it to make it look like it was wearing jewelry.

"It's a beaut, isn't it?"

Delta nodded as she stared at her own reflection in the chrome bumper. "If this car doesn't interest a thief, I don't know what will."

"I'll bet she purrs when her motor's running."

"I'd take that bet." Tossing Connie the keys, Sal reached in the car and pointed to where the transmitter was. "I put her inside so we don't have to worry about water or bad weather, or anything like that."

"Good." Connie took her keys from her pocket and tossed them to Delta. "I'll follow you. I think we should take it to the Latino part of town. Maybe leave it at Kennedy Park."

Delta nodded. "If they're after darker kids, that's the best place for it." Looking down at Connie's keys, Delta sighed. "I won't even ask why you get to drive the cool car."

Connie's teeth sparkled as she grinned. "You do great work, Sal. Remind me of that when I return the favor."

Adjusting her cap once more, Sal nodded. "You'll get my bill soon enough." Turning back to the gate, Sal nodded in Delta's direction. "Some day, I'd really like to sit down and have a beer and trade war stories with you, Delta Stevens."

Delta grinned. "I'd like that. And thanks."

"No problema. I'll call as soon as the phone comes to life. We'll get those pricks. Don't you worry. I gotta run now, gals, I'm waiting for some of my other irons in the fire to start glowing." Winking at Connie, Sal disappeared behind the gate.

"She's an interesting duck," Delta whispered to Connie.

"Yes, yes she is."

"You've never spoken about her. How come?"

"Sal's a very private person. I respect her privacy."

Delta put her arm around Connie and patted her shoulder. "You're a great friend."

"Yes, I am. Now let's get this car out so our sicko snatcher can fall in love with her."

"Con?"

"Yeah?"

"It's about the other cars. That was a great idea."

Shrugging, Connie gingerly sat in the Camaro. "One of the vets owns a car dealership. These guys are more than willing to help Sal out."

"Can I ask why?"

Staring the engine and listening to it hum, Connie nodded before closing the door and rolling the window down. "Her father saved their lives in Da Nang."

"What happened to him?"

"After he had saved the four guys, he went back for one more and had his throat slit by one of the booby traps the Congs had set."

Delta clutched her chest. "How awful."

"No, Del, the awful part was that the Cong jumped all over him, cut his head off and waved it in the air. Those four young men watched their hero destroyed right in front of their eyes. According to Sal, that was when they decided that no matter what happened, if they got out of there alive, they would see to it that Sal and her brothers were taken care of. They've been taking care of her ever since."

Delta slowly shook her head. "What a story."

"Isn't it, though? It's one of those Vietnam stories that should have made it to TV. It really shows how deep that kind of love and respect goes."

"I like her."

Connie grinned. "I know. Sal's not hard to like." Slowly backing the Camaro out of the garage, Connie held her hand out for Delta. "All our pieces are in place, Del. Now, it's their move."

Nodding, Delta headed for Connie's car. If they could pull this off—if they could get into that meeting or come up with the man who was abducting the kids—no one would touch them.

No one. Not Captain John Henry. Not the chief. Not even the feds.

Smiling, Delta drove off.

24

It was 9:30 that night when Delta's phone finally rang. She jumped to it and grabbed it off the cradle before it could completely finish its first ring.

"Yeah?"

"It's Sal. They took the bait."

Delta's heart raced. "What's the line?"

"*That* part isn't so good. The guy who left the message wants you to go to a phone booth on first and Hamilton and bring the money with you."

Delta didn't like the sound of that. Carrying a lot of money could be asking for trouble. "When?"

"Midnight."

"Tonight?"

"Yep."

"Anything else?"

"He said to wait for a call in the phone booth and he'd give you more instructions then."

Delta nodded and reached over to click the television off. "Got it."

"Is there anything else I can do for you, Delta?"

"You've been a real gem, Sal, but now it's up to me and Con. Thanks."

"Roger. Good luck, Delta."

Depressing the button, Delta dialed Connie and told her it was going down.

"They obviously checked you out first," Connie said flatly. "Will we wire you up?"

Delta shook her head. "That's too risky. If they're this cautious, you know they'll pat me down. They might even run a metal detector across me."

"I don't like it."

"Neither do I, but Con, we're this close. If I get in there, we have a good chance of stopping these guys. This is the break we've been waiting for."

Connie sighed loudly into the phone. "I know that Del, but it doesn't mean I have to like it."

"Relax. I'll take one of the transmitters and use your car. That way, you'll at least be able to follow."

"Great idea. I'd feel much more comfortable doing that. What about back-up?"

"I'll call Carducci."

"You've got to be kidding. Why him?"

"He wants in on it. He's willing to put it on the line to make the collar. Besides, we might need him. He's a sharpshooter, remember? If anything slides sideways, Carducci can start blowing people to smithereens."

"Good point."

"I'll need the rest of the money and an athletic bag."

"Don't you want a briefcase?"

"Nope. Too formal. Too suggestive of a setup." Delta doodled dollar signs on a piece of paper.

"Anything else? Is there anything we're missing?"

Delta thought for a moment before answering. "I don't think so. We have about two hours before showtime, so if you think of anything we need, just yell."

"Delta—"

"Don't worry so much, Con. I'll have you and the transmitter, and Carducci and his rifle, and me and my wits. Everything will be fine. See you in an hour." Hanging up the phone, Delta went over to her closet and fished out one of Megan's dresses.

This is it, Delta thought as she hastily threw on the uncomfortable dress. This was what she had been waiting for.

25

At two minutes to midnight, Delta drove right up to the phone booth and got out, taking the maroon athletic bag with her. Once in the phone booth, she had only a ten second wait before the phone rang.

Obviously, they were watching her.

"Yes?" She said, placing the phone to her ear.

"I'm sure you understand the need for us to be cautious, Ms. Anderson. We're in a very risky business and we must be careful."

"Of course. I understand completely."

"Good. I see you brought the money."

Delta did not look around, but it was clear why they had chosen this particular phone booth. There were high rises on all four corners, allowing the caller complete anonymity as well as a perfect aerial view of the phone booth.

These guys were better than she thought. She would not underestimate them again.

"This is only half of what I'd like to invest. As you can imagine," Delta said, using a voice she never knew she had, "people in my positon cannot be too cautious, either."

"I appreciate your discretion, Ms. Anderson, and I certainly do understand."

"You'll receive the other half once I am convinced that this is a first class operation. I will not invest my money with amateurs."

The man chuckled. "Amateurs get caught. You can rest assured that this is a five-star organization. We do quality work and we already have more than 1,000 orders for the next video. At one hundred dollars a pop, you don't need a calculator to figure out how much advance money presales have brought us."

Delta nodded. "Very lucrative."

"Quite. Now, you should see a blue Honda Accord pulling up to the curb. The driver will bring you to an undisclosed destination where you'll have a chance to preview our film and to work out the necessary arrangements."

Delta glanced out of the booth and watched as the Accord pulled to a stop. Her stomach felt like it was going to jump into her throat. Unarmed and untapped, if Delta got into that car, she would be completely alone. Because Connie was going to follow using the transmitter, she had parked on a parallel street and wouldn't even see Delta getting into the Honda.

Great.

"Again, I apologize for the excessive caution, but it is in order."

Delta swallowed hard. "I understand. My partners will be grateful."

"Your partners?"

"Of course. There are three of us interested in profiting from this investment."

"I see. And you were picked to make the transaction?"

Delta nodded. "I am the best business woman of the bunch. My partners make a lot of money. It's my job to invest it for them. So you see, they will be quite happy to know how discreet and professional your operation's been so far."

"Good. I don't wish to frighten you, but our business...well...it wouldn't do for you to be a cop or to be followed by one, now would it?"

Delta laughed. "Perish the thought." Watching the driver step from the car, Delta tried to remain calm. She saw no other alternative but to go through with the ruse; if she tried backing out now, they might become suspicious.

"Martinez has a metal detector to run over you and the athletic bag. Again, just a precaution."

The large man, Martinez, looked like an ex-wrestler for *Big Time* wrestling. His shoulders were so broad, he would have to turn sideways to get into the phone booth. His forearms were bigger than Delta's thighs. In his large hand he held a device shaped like a lint brush. Delta managed a grin as he approached the phone booth.

"Once Martinez is through, he will accompany you to the next destination, where we will be able to conduct our business in a more secure environment. And you can be sure that all of this will be well worth it. Investing with us is a sure bet."

Delta nodded and wondered where the caller was calling from. "That's what I'm counting on."

"Good. We'll see you shortly."

Hearing the click of the phone, Delta hung up and stepped from the booth. The man-monster did not smile or even move a facial muscle as he ran the detector over her.

"Been doing this long?" Delta asked when he turned the detector off.

Martinez didn't answer, but solemnly opened the car door for her.

"I'm sorry, Chuckles, I didn't realize you were the strong, silent type." As Delta ducked her head into the car, she peered in the side mirror to see if she could catch a glimpse of Connie's car. When she didn't see anything, Delta leaned over, buckled her seat belt and swallowed the trepidation rapidly rising inside her.

When Martinez got in the driver's side, the Honda dipped considerably from his immense weight. Delta guessed him to be close to 300 very solid pounds.

"Where to, Martinez?" Delta asked, rolling her window down. For a brief flash, she considered bailing out of the car and running like hell, but decided against it. If the caller could see her well enough to know she had an athletic bag, what prevented him from having a rifle pointed right at her head?

"What's that?" Delta asked, turning toward Martinez. "You must have been mumbling. I asked where we're headed."

"You'll see," Martinez grunted, pulling away from the curb.

Looking out the rearview mirror, Delta sighed.

Goodbye, Con, she thought, as they entered the freeway. Don't wait up.

26

The drive only took fifteen minutes. They arrived at a Super Seven Motel on the outskirts of the city. The location didn't surprise Delta; the motel sat across from two different freeway on-ramps with a winding frontage road with numerous turnouts. It was a mile before the freeway ran into one of the busiest and most confusing interchanges on the L.A. freeway. It was no wonder they hadn't been caught; they were smart about where they met and how many escape routes they would have.

"Room nineteen." Martinez grunted. "Knock twice."

"Thanks for the ride, Mr. Happy," Delta quipped as she dragged the athletic bag with her. "It's been loads of fun, really. I hope we have a chance to chat again real soon." As she walked toward the hotel, Delta scanned the near empty parking lot and the surrounding terrain. It was dark, quiet, and much too foreboding. She knew if she made one mistake, if she tipped her hand just once, she would not leave this motel alive.

When she came to room nineteen, she knocked twice, and waited. When the door finally opened, a tall, thin man with a receding hairline stood in the doorway. He was wearing jeans, a white t-shirt, and a suit jacket. He looked like a throwback of the old *Miami Vice* fashion *faux pax* of the early eighties.

"Ms. Anderson?" someone from the room said.

"Yes." Delta grinned at the thin man as if she were enjoying this whole transaction. Underneath her forced facade were drenched armpits, a rapidly beating heart, and trembling knees. Stepping into the room, Delta knew she was in way over her head. The problem was, there was nothing she could do about it.

"Are you going to let her in or are you going to stand there barricading the door?"

The thin man leaned out the door and looked around. When Martinez nodded once to him, the skinny guy stepped out of the way to let Delta pass.

Delta stepped into the tiny, mildewy room. It was dark and dank, like any cheap, sleazy motel, with brown wallpaper that curled at the top and cigarette burns on the table's edges. The bedspread was worn and tired and appeared to have come from a Sear's catalog during the early seventies. If it wasn't for the twenty-seven inch television set and VCR, the room and its occupants were anachronisms.

"Have a seat," the thin man said, gesturing at a chair that looked like it had been bought at a flea market.

Delta glanced at the worn upholstery. "No thank you. I prefer doing business standing. Will I be dealing with Poppy tonight?"

The thin man shook his head. "Poppy don't make no deals."

Before Delta could ask another question, the battered bathroom door opened and a dark haired man in his mid-forties came out drying his hands on a towel.

"Ms. Anderson," he said, tossing the towel on the counter before extending his hand to Delta. "I'm Rubin. I'm so glad we have the chance to do business together."

Delta took his hand, which wasn't completely dry and shook it firmly. It had been his voice on the other end of the phone and Delta couldn't tell if he was Spanish, Middle Eastern, or neither. "My pleasure."

"Thank you for being such a good sport about our security measures, but Poppy is very conservative when it comes to business matters." His face was fleshy like a man who drank too much, and his stomach was distended as well. He wore a three-piece, charcoal colored suit and a college class ring on his right hand. Clearly the man with the power and the money, Rubin bore all the markings of the lead man. Turning from

Delta, he addressed the thin man. "Offer our guest something to drink, will you?"

Delta held up her hand. "Nothing for me, thank you."

"Very well." With a nod of his head, Rubin sent the thin man over to the television set, where he stood awaiting further directions. "Very efficient of you to bring cash."

Delta glanced over at the athletic bag and nodded. "We believe in expediting matters. We didn't want you leaving town before we had a chance to talk. And, well, let's be frank here. Money talks."

Rubin stepped closer to Delta and smiled. "I like your style. It would please me greatly to do business with you."

"And my partners."

"Of course. And your partners. But I don't mind saying, Poppy doesn't care for silent partners."

Delta shrugged. "They have a lot to lose. They have even more to contribute to your operation. Silence is golden, Rubin, and in their case, silver and platinum as well."

The smile on Rubin's face grew. "Oh, I do think we're going to get along quite well." Stepping away from her, Rubin sat on one of the beaten chairs and lit a cigarette. "Smoke?"

"No, thank you. But if you don't mind, I have an early engagement in the morning and would appreciate it if we could get down to business."

Drawing deeply on the cigarette, Rubin nodded. "As you wish." Then, to the thin man, one more jerk of the head, and the thin man pushed a video tape into the recorder.

"Our filming is done with some of the best video equipment on the market today," Rubin began in a salesman tone of voice. "No more crappy amateur super eight pictures that are all grainy and distorted. We use only the highest quality film. I'm sure you'll agree when you take a look at it that our videos have the best picture, the best sound, and the best plotting of anything on the market. That's what makes this such an exciting business. Because of our high standards, we'll be the number one distributor of this genre across the country. So you see," he said, turning to catch Delta's gaze full on, "your investment could possibly net you a return of more than ten times your original investment, and in a very short period of time."

Delta nodded and turned to the television. God, she didn't want to see this video. It was one thing to act like a business woman cutting a deal. It was quite another to watch snuff pornography and act like she enjoyed it. If she wasn't careful, she could very well tip her hand right here.

Just before the movie started, someone knocked twice on the door and the thin man answered. At the door stood a young man in his early twenties, holding something in his hands. But it wasn't what he was carrying that caught Delta's attention—it was his left hand. His left hand had only two fingers and he was scarred all the way up to his elbow.

Turning quickly away, Delta fiddled with the zipper on the athletic bag. She was in big trouble now. The newcomer, who was whispering to the thin guy hadn't yet noticed her. But if he did, she was sunk. He was one of the first busts Delta had made as a rookie. But that wasn't why he would remember her. No, he would remember how he lost his fingers to a K-9 dog when he reached for his gun during a raid. The dog had bounded across the room and tore into him the moment he moved. The cop partnered with the dog was patting another suspect down, and Delta didn't know what to do. So, she did nothing.

When the dog was through mauling him, his hand and arm were pretty ripped up. That was the first time Delta had heard the phrase "creative report writing." She and the other officers agreed afterward that he lost his fingers because he wouldn't surrender the gun and the dog made him surrender it. The brass bought it and no one was written up for it. The suspect, however, continued to rant and rave all through his trial that the cops let the dog maul him. The whole incident was filled with ugly memories.

"Ms. Anderson, this is Dice. He's our front man here in River Valley."

Delta slowly turned from the athletic bag. Maybe she looked different now. Maybe his memory was shot from all the speed he'd done during his short life. Maybe...

Swallowing the ball of fear in her throat, Delta raised up and met his gaze. If Dice recognized her, he gave no immediate indication. Instead, he reached out and shook Delta's hand.

"Have we met before?" Dice asked, releasing Delta's hand.

Play it cool, Delta thought. Hold his gaze. Don't be afraid. "I go to special screenings in the city and in Hollywood. Perhaps we've met there."

Dice frowned. "Yeah. Maybe." Handing the video to the thin man, Dice moved over to the other worn chair next to Rubin.

"We've missed the beginning," Rubin said to the thin man. "Rewind it so Ms. Anderson can see it from the start." To Delta. "High resolution, outstanding sound bites, enthralling plots, and of course, its authenticity, make it easily the best on the market today. It won't be long before we'll be expanding our market internationally."

Delta nodded, but kept her gaze on the TV. She could feel Dice's penetrating gaze at the side of her face as he tried to figure out where he had seen her. She knew he was trying to retrieve her face from his scratchy memory banks.

"The American consumers are no longer willing to sit through those cheesy, cheap celluloid films made famous in the sixties and early seventies. There's a huge demand for quality projects and we believe we have the means to supply that demand. Take a look and see for yourself."

Delta didn't want to look. She wanted to get the hell out of that room before someone figured out who she was. With no weapon, no back-up, and an ex-con trying very hard to place her face, Delta knew she only had minutes to get out before she was completely at risk.

As the video started, Dice leaned over to Rubin and whispered something in his ear.

This is it, Delta thought, her heart racing and her palms sweating. She'd been made. Did she bolt for the door? No, she'd never make it. Did she just deny she was a cop? No, they'd believe Dice. The bathroom. Maybe she could excuse herself to the bathroom. God, she felt trapped.

Before she had a chance to act, Rubin put the VCR on pause. "Dice just informed me, Ms. Anderson, that Poppy has requested a meeting with you. Apparently, he is very interested in your investment and would like to handle it personally."

Delta studied Rubin's face and knew he was lying. Dice had remembered.

"Don't even think about it, Officer," Dice said, pointing an Uzi he seemed to produce from nowhere. How had she missed it?

Delta cut her eyes to the door, but the thin man had already slipped in front of it. He, too, had his gun trained on her.

Rubin slowly rose from his chair, his expression bitter. "A pity you weren't on the up-and-up. It could have been fun working with you."

Delta shrugged. She had to think fast or she was as good as dead. "Kill me and you'll be signing your own death warrants."

Rubin smiled. "A bold try, Officer—"

"Stevens. Delta Stevens."

"Officer Stevens. But don't insult my considerable intelligence by bluffing. There is no back-up waiting for you. We've seen to it that you aren't wired, and there's little chance of anyone in this motel hearing you if you scream. So I suggest you cooperate and make it easier on yourself."

Delta looked over at Dice, who glared harshly at her. Pure hatred flowed from his eyes like laser beams.

"I been dreamin' about meeting you again for a long time, bitch. Now, my dream is gonna be your worst nightmare."

Nightmare? This was no nightmare. This was a moment when Delta would discover whether she had used up all her miracles. Standing in the desert, with a madman threatening to violate her body before destroying her, Delta realized that her worst nightmare was about to burst through the plane of reality, and she was going to have to face it alone. What had began as an attempt to right the scales after Helen's death had turned into a bad dream, only Megan wasn't there to wake her up.

No one was there. Delta had made the ultimate gamble and it looked as though that gamble was going to transform into the supreme sacrifice. If she was going to buy it here in the desert, she was not going alone. Raising her foot in the air to attempt a leg sweep, Delta stopped in midair when something incredible happened. In the click of a second hand, Dice's chest exploded, spewing blood and flesh fragments onto Delta's face. The look on his face was one of incredulity. Someone had blown his guts out and he took one step backward before dropping to his knees and falling face first in the sand. Dead.

Without so much as a moment's hesitation, Delta pushed him aside and grabbed the Uzi with both hands.

"Asshole," Delta muttered, as she reached into his back pocket and pulled out his wallet. Every piece of evidence she could gather would be important if she could stay manage to alive. Whoever had blown a six-inch hole in Dice was still somewhere in the desert.

The car, Delta thought, Martinez was still waiting at the car. She carefully picked her way across the desert so that she would approach the car from the opposite direction. If she could kill Martinez and get the keys to the car, she was home free.

Free.

God, she was so close. Maybe she hadn't run out of miracles after all.

Moving from shadow to shadow, until she was about thirty yards from the car, Delta slowly inched her way forward. Still leaning against the car, his cigarette now extinguished, stood Martinez, head bowed as if he'd fallen asleep.

Odd, Delta thought. Had Martinez killed Dice and then come back to the car?

Slowly, quietly inching her way still closer, Delta dropped to a soldier's crawl to eliminate her silhouette. From where she was, it didn't appear as if Martinez had been the one who shot Dice. Martinez's gun was nowhere to be seen, and he just stood there, not looking out at the desert or even smoking a cigarette. By the angle of his head, Delta thought he might be reading something. If he didn't kill Dice, hadn't he at least heard the shot?

Suddenly, Delta shivered. Someone else was in the desert with her, someone who wanted all three of them dead. No witnesses, no bodies, nothing. Maybe she wasn't as free as she thought she was.

Picking up a rock, Delta tossed it close to the car and waited for Martinez's reaction. When he didn't move, Delta crawled closer. Something wasn't right.

Ten feet from the car, Delta squinted through the night and finally saw the reason for Martinez's lack of response: someone had slit his throat from ear to ear and from chin to sternum. His head hung on by the vertebrae alone. Whoever had killed him was a natural killer. And they were probably looking for her right now.

Looking around from her position in the sand, Delta decided to chance it. She needed to get the hell out of there and she'd have to have a car to do that. Sliding foward, she crawled underneath the car and pulled Martinez's body down into the sand.

Methodically checking all of his pockets, Delta searched his bloodied clothing for the keys.

Maybe they're still in the car, Delta thought, wondering whether she should risk coming out from under the car. After all, she did have the Uzi. If she could just get in the car and—

"Looking for these?" came a voice even deeper than Martinez's. Delta looked out from under the car and saw a pair of army boots. The car keys landed silently in the sand right between the pair of size twelve shoes. "Don't shoot, Delta. It's us." From nowhere came the tiny voice of a woman.

A woman? Looking again at the army huge army boots, the picture became very clear. "Sal?"

Abruptly, a small face lowered to Delta's and smiled at her. "In the flesh. You gonna come out now?" Then the face disappeared. "Josh, help her out from there, will you?"

A pair of large hands reached underneath the car and pulled Delta out. She was still gripping the Uzi.

"It is you! Thank God. What the hell are you doing here?"

Sal reached into her pocket and pulled out a pair of keys to unlock the handcuffs Dice had put on Delta earlier. "You want to go get the Jeep, Josh? We need to get out of here in case they sent anyone else to check up on those two bozos."

Josh nodded and took off into the darkness.

"Jeep? Sal, what's going on? How did you know where to find me?"

Running her small hand over the bump on Delta's forehead, Sal smiled softly. "All in good time. Right now, we have to finish this business." When Josh pulled up in the Jeep, Sal took Delta's arm and pulled her from the Honda to the Jeep before handing the Honda keys to Josh. "Both bodies."

Josh nodded and picked up Martinez's corpse as easily as if he were picking up Sal.

Delta was suddenly exhausted, and the events happening around her seemed to be happening in fast motion. "Sal, I don't understand."

Getting in the Jeep, Sal reached into the glove compartment and pulled out an ice pack. "Here," she said, bashing it against the dash. "Put this on your forehead."

Delta did as she was told and waited in silence as the Honda returned from the direction of Dice's body and started up the ridge. Sal started the Jeep's engine and followed.

"We had nothing else to do, and Connie thought you might need more back-up than just her and Tony."

"Back-up? You and Josh were my back-up?"

Sal nodded, pulling out a pack of gum and offering a piece to Delta. Suddenly, there was a loud explosion, and Delta realized that the Honda had gone end-over-end off the edge of the ridge in a mass of flames.

Sal stopped the Jeep and peered over the edge. "It'll take the boys in blue a long time to figure out what happened to those creeps." Sal pulled the car up a bit and waited for Josh to come running back.

"All taken care of, boss. Two crispy critters in the trunk of a burned out Honda. The car went right into the gulley. Could be days, maybe even weeks, before anyone finds them."

Sal grinned. "Great."

"Sal..." Delta said, gingerly placing the ice pack on her forehead. Her whole face hurt. "Would you mind filling me in? Just how is it that you followed us without any transmitting devices?"

Josh hopped in the backseat and handed something to Delta. They appeared to be square binoculars. "Take a peek through these babies."

When Delta brought them to her eyes, everything in the desert was illuminated. She could easily see the road, cacti, and even a rodent scurrying across the dunes.

"Incredible. But that doesn't explain—"

"It's a night scope. It actually lets you see in the dark. We were able to follow you from quite a distance on this shitty road without having to turn our headlights on."

Delta lowered the scope from her sore face and shook her head. "Did you follow me to the motel?"

"Actually, we got lucky on that one. Connie wanted us to stay out of sight, like she did, but Josh and I decided that our fatigues looked too obvious for anyone to be concerned about us. No one would ever believe that two people dressed in jungle fatigues would be tailing them."

Delta looked at them both. Sal was right. "Good point."

"So Josh and I moved closer. Good thing, too, because we just barely caught you getting into that Honda."

Delta lightly touched her burning forehead. A small egg shape protruded from below her hairline. She imagined her face was one large bruise. "And Connie? Where is she?"

"We radioed to her what was going down and she arrived at the motel only seconds after we did. Connie sent us after you while she and Tony registered in the room next to the bad guys."

"She sent you?" For a moment, Delta felt hurt that Connie didn't come after her herself.

"Yep. She made it clear your life was in our hands and told us to do whatever we had to do to protect you. She mentioned something about gathering evidence while the place was still hot. Or something like that."

"And all this time I thought she'd be frantic."

"I'm sure she was. When they escorted you out, Tony started out of the hotel room, and Connie pulled him back in. She and Tony were going to see if they could listen in and find out where they were going next."

"Why didn't Connie tell me about you two?"

"It was a last minute detail. Actually, she came to me for the night scope, and Josh and I volunteered to help out. Delta, Josh was a point man in 'Nam. You know, the guy who went first to set off traps and spot snipers." Sal beamed with pride. "He's very good. A couple of white-collar crooks could never beat him. Connie made the right choice."

Delta reached across and touched Sal's arm. "Thank God she did. I thought I was history back there."

Sal grinned. "Naw. Connie knows how to look after her own. You're family to her, Delta, and family takes care of each other, huh, Josh?"

Josh nodded.

"So what happened once we left the motel?"

"We followed you out here, drove up to the ridge and put that asswipe who was going to kill you in the sights. End of story."

Josh proudly held out an AK-47 assault rifle with a folding metal stock. By the looks of it, it was probably one he had used in Vietnam. "Josh shot him?"

Sal shook her head. "Nope. I did."

Delta was stunned. "You?"

Sal nodded. "Josh had to take the big guy out first. I was to wait until his cigarette went out and then take out that other prick. Pretty good piece of shooting if I say so myself. Daddy would have been proud. He took me to the range all the time before he shipped out. Looks like all those years of practice finally paid off." Sal adjusted her cap. "Guess it was my turn to save a life. Dad would be proud."

Delta was shocked. This petite woman wearing army fatigues had saved her life by calmly squeezing a powerful round through the chest of a man she didn't even know. "Sal, I don't know what to say."

"Don't say anything," Josh said, touching Delta's shoulder. "Like Sal told ya, family takes care of each other."

Delta leaned back, letting exhaustion roll over her like a small wave. She had come, she thought, millimeters from dying, yet she was plucked from death's grasp by two people who hardly knew her. The thought made her dizzy. Or was that from the bump on her head?

"Sisterhood is powerful," Sal said, glancing in the mirror at Josh.

"Yeah," Josh said, spreading a blanket over Delta's lap. "Just like brotherhood."

Closing her eyes, Delta leaned her head back on the headrest and fought the fatigue creeping through her body. As images of the night flashed before her, Delta inhaled slowly and released the last of her fear.

"It wouldn't have been right," she said through sleepy lips.

"What wouldn't have been right?" Sal asked as she drove over the winding road.

"For me to die in the desert."

Sal nodded. "Because it wasn't your time?"

Delta grinned. "No. Because I'll be damned if I'm going to die wearing a goddamn dress."

27

When Delta, Sal, and Josh finished telling their tale to Connie, she pulled Delta to her and hugged her tighter than she ever had. "Thank the goddesses you're okay."

"Okay? Have you taken a close look at my face? Megan will go ballistic when she sees it."

"Megan will just be happy to have you home in one piece. I certainly am."

Delta looked into Connie's eyes and smiled. Her face ached and she had a pounding headache, but she was alive. "I owe my life to you, Chief. If you hadn't thought everything through..." Delta stopped and shuddered. Just the idea of Dice's hand on her gave her the chills.

"It's okay, Storm," Connie whispered, running her hand through Delta's hair. "The edge was just a little sharper this time. You might have thought you were going off half-cocked, but that's not something I'd ever let you do. You're too important to me."

Tony, who returned from the kitchen holding a beer, nodded. "Shit, Delta, you guys are a two-person police department."

Connie shook her head. "Tonight, it took all five of us."

Sal and Josh each held up a beer. "Hear, hear. To success."

"To success."

After everyone except Delta took a drink, Tony sat on the couch next to Connie and Delta. "You were real cool, Delta. Man, when that guy had that Uzi in your back, I thought I was going to piss in my pants."

Delta chuckled. "You and me both. But enough about me. What did you get? Anything good?"

Connie nodded. "They're almost finished with their current filming. The kid you found at Richardson's wasn't supposed to get whacked, so they're looking for another kid to finish 'production.'"

"They're not bolting out of town?"

"Not yet. But then they didn't know their pals would never return."

Tony sipped his beer and nodded. "I've never seen two people move out as quickly as those guys did. In five minutes, they had the TV, the video, everything out of that motel room and were in the wind."

"Did you get anything from the room? Prints, anything like that?"

Connie nodded and walked over to her briefcase. "We got two good sets of prints, but let me tell you, Del, these guys are pros. They wiped down everything. I mean everything. Well...almost everything."

"Yeah, man, Connie lifted the first set of prints from the inside door of the medicine cabinet."

Delta smiled at her. "Now who's the pro?"

"Well, the second set was much harder. I got it from underneath the arm of the chair. Those aren't real good, but they'll do. We should have something back on them within the hour."

"Excellent. What else?"

Connie put the prints back and pulled out a stenographer's notebook. "The reason the feds have had such a hard time tracing the kidnapped kids is because all but one of them were stolen off of reservations."

Delta perked up at this new evidence. "Indian reservations?" She suddenly remembered Connie's remark about everyone thinking dark-skinned children were Hispanic.

"A little girl was abducted from a Pueblo reservation in northwest New Mexico just a few days ago. Apparently, the family didn't know she was missing because she was supposed to be staying with her grandmother."

"A few days ago? That means she could still be here."

Everyone nodded in unison. "Let's hope so. As soon as I heard Rubin mention 'the Chiricahua boy,' I understood exactly what their game plan has been." Sipping her beer before continuing, Connie walked over to Eddie and flipped off her computer screen saver button. "When we got back, I ran a check on all the kids reported missing from specific geographic locations. Look what I came up with." Ripping a piece of paper from the printer, Connie handed it to Delta.

At first, it just looked like a map of the United States. As she looked closer, Delta saw there were dark and light patches sprinkled throughout the North and Southwest, and red dots scattered about randomly. "What's this?"

"That," Connie said, sitting next to her, "Is a map showing where five of our missing children were snatched from. See these lighter areas? Those show the cultural areas of certain tribes. The darker areas are actual reservations."

Delta counted twelve red dots within the darker shaded sections. Five dots were from areas in Montana, Wyoming, and Idaho, while the remainder were scattered through Utah, New Mexico, and Arizona. "A dozen kids have been kidnapped off reservations in the last two months? Why hasn't anyone done anything? What the hell have the feds been doing?"

"You can't blame everything on them, Del. They didn't know the kids were Native Americans."

"But they should have known. How could they not know this?"

Taking the paper from Delta, Connie set it on the coffee table. "Easy, Kimo. You need to understand something about the Native American mentality. There is no love lost between the federal government and these people. Even if the feds came in to help, the distrust is so deep, I'm not sure it will ever be repaired. The Indians on a reservation have their own government, their own police, their own ways of handling things. I'll bet most of these children went unreported for days before the reservation police called in help.

Even then, they probably only got help from the local authorities. That's the way it is; that's the way it's always been."

Sal sucked her teeth and finished off her beer. "How sad."

Connie continued. "It's been that way since the very beginning. Obviously, Rubin and his friends knew this and capitalized on it. They snatched kids from people who would wait an eternity before asking for outside help. As much as I hate to admit it, it's a great plan."

"Why hasn't anyone put it all together?" Josh asked.

"Keeping track of the goings-on on reservations isn't easy. There's a lot of crime, a high rate of alcoholism, and truancy rates are very high. Add to this the lack of communication with state officials, and there you have it. It's an ugly situation ripe for someone to come in and take advantage of."

"And that's what they've done."

"Right. And it probably wasn't that hard. Think about it. Rubin is darker skinned. He could fit in very easily on a reservation."

Delta cast a sideways glance at Connie.

"No, Del, I'd bet everything I own he isn't a Native American, but he's obviously been successful passing as one."

Delta nodded. "If only we could get a bead on who Rubin or Poppy are."

Connie smiled broadly. "I found a notepad in the hotel room and I'm sure someone had written something on the top page before tearing it off. The guys at the lab should be able to tell us just what was on it within an hour."

Delta shook her head. "You're amazing."

"Not really. I figured I better come up with some excellent clues or risk you pouting forever because I didn't come after you."

Delta blushed. "It was a good call, Con. We need evidence. Josh and Sal handled my end with such a level of expertise that it makes my head spin."

"I was hoping you'd see it that way. Tony and I heard them discussing something about getting rid of anything that might come back to haunt them. Your intrusion has them running scared, Del, and desperate people do desperate things. I think we can expect them to make a major move within forty-eight hours."

"What kind of move?"

"They're not here just to get money, Del. They have a product to deliver, and as yet, it isn't finished. No product equals no money, so they're now in a bind to produce."

Delta rose off the couch so fast, she got dizzy. "That means some of those kids may still be alive."

"Exactly. And we have less than forty-eight hours to find them."

"But how? They could be anywhere."

Connie looked over at Tony and they grinned. "Tony and I found out one of the reasons why they steal red Camaros."

Delta waited. "Why?"

"Because that's the name of the film they're shooting. Remember the classic movie we saw as kids called the *Red Balloon*?"

Delta nodded. "It was about that little boy who had a red balloon and the other kids..." Delta raised her hand to her mouth.

"Right. Well, Rubin's boss is making a movie called *Red Camaro*. They use the stolen cars in the movie."

Delta reached over and took Connie's hand. "We're getting closer, aren't we?"

Connie grinned. "I believe so."

"So, now what?"

"Now, we wait to see what the guys at the lab come up with."

"And then?"

"And then, it's showtime."

28

Delta fished around her drawers for the one shirt she knew Megan really liked. In a few days, Megan would be headed for Central America to put her life in order. Away from the daily grind at the bookstore, away from the throng of idiot college boys hitting on her, Megan might find whatever it was she was looking for. It would be good for her, Delta attempted to assure herself, not really believing it.

The day had crawled by, with more than twenty calls to and from Connie about additional information Eddie had picked up. They were zeroing in and Delta was getting high on the excitement. She owed Rubin and the thin man a few bruises.

Bruises. Gina had come over earlier in the day to apply makeup to some of the bluer bruises Delta now wore. She didn't want to upset Megan before she went on her trip; it would only make her worry more than usual. No, Megan deserved to go off and do her own thing without wondering whether or not Delta was being dragged out to the desert to give some asshole head before he plugged her full of lead.

Right.

Plucking up a turquoise polo shirt Megan had bought her, Delta held it up to her chest and smiled. They had had so much fun the first time they went clothes shopping together. In Neiman-Marcus, Megan handed Delta this shirt and Delta, as was her custom, looked at the price tag first.

"Eighty dollars?" she had practically yelled. "Eighty dollars for a shirt? You've got to be kidding."

The next thing she knew, she was being hustled into the changing rooms with a hand clamped over her mouth. She knew by the Opium perfume whose hand it was.

"Would you mind not embarrassing me?" Megan said in mock anger.

"Embarrassing you? It's those people out there who should be embarrassed! Eighty dollars for a stupid shirt. Hmph."

Half an hour later, Delta walked out with $880 worth of clothes she was sure she could have gotten for less anywhere else.

Ah, those were the days when life wasn't so complicated.

Tossing the shirt over her head, Delta surveyed herself in the mirror. She, too had changed since they had met nearly two years ago. Megan had brought to her black and white world an unexpected freshness of grays and a rainbow of colors. Megan was the first really honest person Delta had ever been with, and Megan had taught her how to relax and enjoy life in front of the badge. Face it, Delta thought, Megan's taught me a lot, period.

The ringing phone pulled her away from her thoughts and Delta belly flopped on the bed to answer it.

"It's your lucky day!" she said happily. "This is not an answering machine!"

"Aren't we in a good mood?" It was Connie.

"Yes, I am. I'm finally having a well-deserved date with my lover."

"That's right. Then I won't keep you long. We're batting 500 in the fingerprint department."

Delta rolled over and grabbed her pen. "Shoot."

"Rubin's real name is Elliot De La Cruz, and he's a big time hustler from Chicago."

"Chicago?"

"He's wanted for practically every major deviant law on the books. Apparently, he's been in Mexico for the last five years and has resurfaced as the right-hand man of this Poppy fellow."

"Nothing on him yet?"

"Zilch. We won't get him until we bag at least a medium-size fish. The guy whose wallet you took is

D.H. Trindell, AKA Dice or the Dice Man. He got his tag because of the way he sliced and diced up other inmates in the slammer."

"Nice guy. What about the other set?"

"Nothing so far. They're not the greatest, so it'll take a little time for the computer to sort through."

Delta jotted all this down.

"I have some buddies on the Navajo reservation who helped me get information on the kids snatched from the Southwest reservations."

"And?"

"And the little boy found at Richardson's belongs to the Chiricahua tribe in Arizona. I told him where the child is and what happened to him, and my friend, Two Fist, promised to call in all of his markers to help us locate the families of the missing kids."

"Damn good work, Connie."

"Thanks. Now enough is enough, okay? There's nothing more to be accomplished tonight, so try to have some fun. You go out with Megan and give her your best. And yes, that's an order."

Delta smiled. "I'm going, I'm going. Say 'hi' to Gina and send her my love." Hanging up the phone, Delta sighed. She might have a good time, but she wouldn't stop thinking about the men she was after—not until they were behind bars. Grabbing the receiver for the decoy cars from her nightstand, Delta put it in her pocket and headed out the door.

29

Pulling on her high tops, Delta tugged at the laces one more time before looking at the finished product in the mirror. Megan would approve of the "little tomboy" look Delta so perfectly achieved. Wearing the turquoise polo shirt, 501 button-down jeans, high tops, and her brown leather bomber jacket, Delta decided she much preferred that term over "the big dyke look" which Sandy, her ex, had called it. Either way, it was a more comfortable choice of both clothes and words.

Pulling out of the driveway, she set the receiver on the seat of the truck. It never ceased to amaze her how many electronic gizmos Connie could pull out of a hat. She had connections even the CIA would envy.

Checking the receiver, Delta sighed. She wondered if she didn't have some sort of secret wish to get kicked out of the department. How many more times could she skirt the rules and bend the letter of the law before someone came down on her for good? Rolling her window down, she also wondered how so many cops could continue to work in a system that continually failed everyone except the criminal. There were criminal rights advocates and there were rules that law enforcement officers had to follow that crooks didn't. Over and over again, vile human beings were allowed to roam the streets because the system was set up to protect "the innocent." In Delta's world, the innocent meant women and children; it meant those who did nothing more than be at the wrong place at the wrong time. The innocent didn't mean the pusher, the pimp, or the pornographic prince. But they were the ones who knew how to beat the system at its own game. They *knew* the law was on their side. And because they knew it, because it was so obvious that the law supports crooks instead of victims, they are able to stoop even lower and victimize children.

Children like Helen, who had simply gotten in the way of a lunatic bent on destroying Connie, children like the ones who were snatched every day in this country. It was clear to Delta that if children were increasingly becoming victims in this warped society, then the rules needed to change. And if no one else would change them, Delta Stevens would.

Pulling into Harry's parking lot, Delta wasn't at all surprised to find it crowded. Recently, Harry had mounted shrapnel from a Patriot missile from what was then called "The Gulf War," and a lot of new faces showed up to look at his find.

The thought of traveling across town to see something that had devasted people's homes and possibly killed innocent people made Delta shake her head sadly. She didn't want to think about such sadness tonight. No, tonight, she wanted to be with Megan. She wanted to hear what Megan was feeling and really listen to her needs. Tonight, Megan was going to get 100 percent of Delta Stevens.

Delta grabbed the receiver and stuck it in her jacket pocket before locking the truck and heading toward the bar. It was a cool night and she was glad she hadn't thrown her favorite jacket away when Sandy asked her to.

Opening the door, Delta squinted through the darkness and toward the area of the bar where she and Megan usually sat. Instead of finding Megan sitting by herself, Delta was unpleasantly surprised to find Tony sitting with her and leaning far too close to her.

"Damn him," Delta growled, stepping away from the door. She knew Tony well enough to know he was probably wearing his "aren't I handsome" face complete with his disgustingly grotesque Mr. Macho Charm. For a moment, Delta wanted to go over and rip that stupid smile off his face and cram it down his throat. She wanted to grab him by the hair and—

Then Delta remembered. Tony didn't know that Megan was her lover. He didn't know that she wasn't the slight bit interested in him or any other man in the bar. He didn't really know squat.

Upon further inspection, Delta noticed the look of utter contempt on Megan's face as she tried to move away from him. Like so many men Delta had met, he was completely ignorant of any messages Megan might have been sending. Because of his inability to read anything other than the lump in his pants, Tony had failed to notice the fact that Megan was not laughing, she was not smiling, she was not flirting, and she appeared utterly bored. Still, Tony was undaunted, and Delta had seen enough.

Strolling over to the table, she held her finger to her lips when Megan caught sight of her.

"Hey, Carducci," Delta offered, patting him jovially on the back.

Tony barely looked up. "Uh, hi, Delta."

"Fancy meeting you here on our night off. Is this your girlfriend?" Delta tried not to grin at Megan, who managed to keep a poker face. Delta would remember that if they ever played cards against each other.

Leaning closer to Delta, Tony whispered over his shoulder, "Beat it, Delta. Your cramping my style."

Moving closer to him, Delta whispered back, "Don't worry. You don't have any."

Straightening up, Tony cleared his throat while giving Delta obvious facial signs that she was getting in his way. "I forgot my manners," he said, turning his most charming smile on for Megan. "It's rude of me not to introduce my partner. This is Delta. And Delta, this gorgeous creature is Prudence."

It took every ounce of energy Delta had to keep from busting a gut on that one.

Reaching her hand out, Delta took Megan's warmly in hers and fought back the guffaw begging to be released. "Prudence? What a lovely name."

Megan held Delta's hand a moment too long and batted her eyelashes. "Why, thank you. Delta is an interesting name, as well."

Sitting across from Megan, Delta held her sapphire eyes in hers. They were both enjoying Tony's discomfort a bit too much. "It's the fourth letter of the Greek alphabet. My grandparents were Greek fishermen."

Megan scooted closer and continued gazing at Delta. Unsure of what to do, Tony put his arm around the back of Megan's chair.

"So, you're Greek?" Megan purred, not taking her eyes off Delta.

Delta grinned, more at Tony's uneasiness than at Megan's question.

"Well, Delta, I'm sure you have things to do, so we won't keep you," Tony said, casting his eyes at the door.

Taking Delta's hand in hers, Megan squeezed it. "I think I'd like to keep her."

At this, Tony practically jumped out of the booth. "What the hell? Man, come on, Delta, I saw her first!"

"Finders, keepers, Carducci? Aren't you a little old for that?" Rising from the chair, Delta motioned for Tony to sit back down.

Pulling Delta aside, Tony mumbled his apologies to Megan before taking Delta on. "Remember when we had that talk about you being..."

"A lesbian?" Delta practically yelled the word.

"Keep your voice down! Man, you're really blowing it for me."

"You're assuming you have a chance."

"Well, I did, until you came along!"

Turning from Tony, Delta gave a tiny wave to Megan, who waved back. "Forget about it, Carducci, she's way out of your league."

"Oh, and I suppose she's in yours?"

Smiling, Delta nodded. "I hope so. She's my lover."

Tony opened his mouth but silent air was the only thing that came out.

"Lover, Carducci, as in partner, mate, spouse, girlfriend. You know."

"You're shitting me," he muttered, staring at Megan as if she were a mannequin who had just sprung to life.

Delta shook her head. "Nope."

Scooting across the booth, Megan joined them and held her hand out for Tony. "I'm Megan."

Reaching into his pocket, Tony pulled out some dollars and slammed them on the table. "You don't...she doesn't...oh, fuck it," he said, jamming his fists in his pockets. "What's a guy got to do these days to see if a broad is just a damn broad?"

Delta clamped down on her jaw and stepped closer to him. "I'm sure you'd like to rephrase that, Carducci. We might have had a little fun at your expense, but that doesn't mean you have to act like an asshole."

"Del, it's okay," Megan interjected.

Delta held her hand up. "No, hon, it isn't. He didn't need to insult you."

"Insult her? Get off it, Delta, you pull a gag like that on me and expect me to play nicely?"

"Precisely."

"Well forget it. You get all pissed off at me for just doing what guys do—"

"And what's that, Carducci? Act like big dicks with tiny little heads?"

"Jesus! Cut the feminist crap, man. It was an honest mistake. This isn't a gay bar, you know."

Suddenly, Harry called out to them. "Hey, you two, take it outside."

"What do you know about guys, anyway, Delta?" Stepping past the table, Tony headed for the door. "You're always so damn busy putting us down, you wouldn't know a decent guy if he ran over you."

"You're right!" Delta yelled, starting after him. "It's been a few years since I met one! Aren't they on the endangered species list? I'll let you know if I find another one in this decade."

Standing at the door, Tony whirled around. "Look, we can't all be like your sainted Miles Brookman, but you're going to miss out on a lot of good people if you keep that female superiority shit up!"

Delta felt the blood drain from her face. "Don't you dare talk about Miles Brookman! You're not fit to clean his gun!"

"Man, you're crazy! I'm outta here." Shoving the door open, Tony stomped out.

Megan rose. "Del, please let it go. He didn't mean any harm. Besides, we're the ones—"

But Delta had stopped listening. Storming through the bar, Delta brushed off any hands that tried to stop her. Maybe it was the stress, maybe it was the fear, and maybe it was her horrible experience at the hands of Dice, but Delta had lost it. She had gone over the edge and wanted to strike out at any man who invaded her space.

At this moment, Tony Carducci was that man.

"Look, Carducci," she said, as she ran to catch up to him. "I don't have to sleep with men to know what big pricks they can be."

"Maybe not, but you haven't even given me half the chance I deserve because I have one! Man, don't you see? What you're doing to me in the name of feminism is every bit as shitty as what straights do to you."

"What in the hell would you know about bias, Carducci? You're a white man. You have all power."

Tony shook his head and picked up a rock to throw at a parking sign. He missed. "Man, Delta, what do you want from me? Perfection? I'm doing the best I can here just to understand that my partner is a lesbian. I've never known a lesbian before. How the hell was I supposed to know she was your...your..."

"Lover, Carducci. That beautiful woman in there is my lover. She's not a broad, she's not a dame, she's a woman. And you were treating her like she was the main entree when I walked in. Women are people, Carducci, not meals, not delicacies, but people."

"Right. And she's a beautiful woman, Delta. Everyone in that place wanted a shot at her. Why should I be any different?"

Delta took two steps away from him. Then, she picked up a rock and threw it at the parking sign. She hit it. "You got me on that one. Why should you? Why not act like all the other assholes? She's my lover, Carducci, and you were all over her like a cheap suit."

"How was I suppose to know? Instruct me, oh Training Patrol Guru, how the hell I was supposed to know she was gay? By the way she sipped her drink? By the way she sat? I'm not a fucking mind reader, Delta!"

"No one's asking you to be, Carducci! All I'm asking is for a little decency training. Not all women enjoy being pawed, Carducci. And just because a woman is good looking doesn't mean she wants assholes groping her."

Shaking his head, Tony started walking away. "You got a hot poker up your ass, and I sure as hell don't have to stay around while you yank it out and try to shove it up mine. I'm sorry about what happened to you out in the desert, but it had nothing to do with me."

Delta started her retort, but Tony continued. "Whatever your beef is, it isn't with me."

Before Tony could take another step, the receiver went off. Both Delta and Tony stopped yelling and stopped moving. "That's our car!" Delta cried, grabbing the receiver from her pocket. "Tony, call it in! I'm going after them."

"But—"

Delta waved him off. "There's no time! Just go!" Sprinting in the direction of Harry's parking lot, Delta was stopped by the sound of Megan's voice.

"Delta!"

Caught between possibly busting the perps and saving her personal life, Delta turned around and waited. On one side stood Megan, their rocky relationship, and their life together. On the other, was her career, her sense of duty, and the lives of others.

It was not an easy choice. But she made it anyway.

"I'll be right back, I promise!" Jumping into the cab of her truck, Delta squealed out of the parking lot in chase of a blinking green light. Glancing at the receiver, Delta realized it wasn't far from where she was, and in less than a minute, she was only four cars behind a bright red Camaro with dealer plates.

"Bingo!" she said, tightening her grip on the steering wheel. Somewhere in her gut, she knew the thin man was behind the wheel of that car. It was the same electric energy that grabbed her instincts during the Zuckerman case. This was it.

Trying to follow as inconspicuously as possible, Delta let three more cars ahead of her. She had the receiver and that was all she needed to keep a safe distance. Driving on for two more minutes, Delta wiped her upper lip with the back of her hand.

"Where are those units?" she mumbled, looking at her watch. She had been following this guy for almost five minutes now and there were no black and whites in sight. Surely, someone was out there looking for a bright red Camaro with dealer plates?

When the Camaro took a series of turns, Delta knew he was simply trying to establish that he hadn't been tailed. Ah, Delta grinned to herself, the beauty of high-tech police work.

The next time she stopped, Delta allowed a little more distance between the Camero and her truck. As she waited, a black and white rolled through the intersection, oblivious to her waving hands in the cab of the truck.

"Damn it! " she cried, beating the steering wheel with her fists. "What's the matter with those guys?"

Suddenly, the green light was no longer flashing and Delta watched and waited to see if it was going to blink again. After waiting what felt like hours, it was clear that the Camaro had arrived at its destination. In a moment, she slowly rounded the corner and saw the Camaro pull into a garage.

"Come on, guys, where are you?" When the garage door came to a close, Delta pulled over seven houses away, jammed her gun in the back of her pants, and quietly clicked the door closed. Looking up and down the street, Delta wondered where everyone was. Something was desperately wrong.

Opening the passenger side door, Delta pulled her ankle holster out from under the seat, pushed the nine-millimeter into it, and made her way across the shadowy front lawns that stretched like a darkened football field before her. In the sparse glow of the city night, Delta heard every cricket, every blade of grass crunch beneath her feet, and every dog within a mile barking to the twilight hours. By the time she reached the house where the Camaro was safely behind the garage door, a white, unmarked van pulled into the driveway. The van had no plates and bore no markings other than a dent in the right fender. From her vantage point behind the acacias, Delta watched as the garage door opened, allowing the van to pull in while three dark figures walked casually out.

Flattening herself against the house, Delta held her breath. One of the figures, a man with a foreign accent, was gesticulating wildly while the other two—the thin man and Rubin—tried to calm him down.

Crouching behind a bush, Delta looked up and realized she was next to an open window. She guessed it was probably the kitchen. Slowly raising up, she slipped her fingers against the window and opened it a little more before sliding back down behind the bush. From somewhere inside, she could hear the television booming loudly. She guessed there were four, maybe five men. If three of them were outside, at least one, maybe two would be inside. Checking the house out from her concealed position, Delta cursed when she discovered that it was a two-story house.

Gazing back down at her watch, Delta sighed. It was pretty clear no unit would be showing up. For whatever reason, she was on her own here. She'd be flying solo. She'd have to rely on her own best judgment. She lived for these kinds of choices. This was the razor's edge she had spent her career balancing on. At times like these her fate rested on her own shoulders. *This* was what pumped her up and gave her a natural high. *This* was why she so loved the streets and their dangers.

One slip and it would be over for her and any children inside. One wrong move might sentence herself and others to death.

Inching closer, Delta listened to the heated conversation among the three men.

"I told you he was stupid enough to be dangerous."

"It's not a problem, man. Relax."

"Relax?" the thin man said. The feds are all over town, that bitch cop must have done something to Martinez and Dice, and we got a bunch a kids we gotta waste. Man, this has really gone sour. I say we bail."

"Bail?" Rubin's calm voice said evenly. "We've only delivered half of what the man ordered."

"So what? I'm not about to go to jail for some screw-loose dude, even if he is rich."

"What about the brats?"

"Leave them."

"No way! We busted our asses to get those Indian pups. Now you're telling me we aren't going to use 'em?"

The thin man raised his voice. "I don't give a shit what the man wants! I'm not spending time behind bars for him or nobody else. I been there, man, and I ain't going back."

A fourth man joined them. "Cool it, will you? I just talked with Poppy and he agrees we gotta jet. He's got another line on a real high roller in 'Frisco and he wants us to lay low while he makes the arrangements."

"So what are we supposed to do with the kids while we're laying low?"

"Poppy says he wants everything destroyed. He wants us to gut this whole house and everything in it. He thinks bringing the brats along is too risky, so they're staying here. Able is drugging the kids right now. We'll leave them here. Kirk, come help me detonate this place."

Delta had heard enough. The razor's edge just got sharper and she knew that the fate of the children rested on her next decision—a decision that could mean the end of her career, if not her life. But then, weren't the two synonymous?

Slowly standing, Delta peeked in the window and saw two men hurrying about, placing explosives and gasoline-soaked rags all about the house. Running through a mental list of choices she had, Delta looked around before sprinting in between houses to the house next door.

"Who's there?" A gruff voice asked after Delta pressed the doorbell.

"The police," Delta pushed out in a loud whisper. "I need to use your phone."

"Oh yeah? How do I know it's really the police?"

"Look through the hole. I'll show you my badge." Delta waited, feeling her heart banging.

"People make fake badges all the time, you know."

Frustrated and losing time she couldn't afford to waste, Delta pulled her gun from her holster and pointed it at the peephole. "That may be true, sir, but does this look fake to you? This is an emergency. Open the damn door before I blow it off its hinges and arrest you for obstructing justice."

In a blink, the door was open and Delta rushed past the man. "I need your phone."

"Over there," he grunted, following her into the kitchen. "What's going on?"

Picking the phone up, Delta rang Connie's desk. She picked it up on half a ring.

"Where the hell are you?" Connie asked as soon as she picked up the phone. "We've been looking all over the place for you. Are you okay?"

"I'm fine. Listen, the perps are at 683 West Tennyson and they're getting ready to bust out of there. They're going to blow the house up."

"West Tennyson? Are you sure? Carducci said you headed east. We've got units all over the place down there."

"Well, send them west. Send firetrucks and paramedics also. There's a number of children who've been—" before Delta could finish, she heard a huge explosion followed by a secondary explosion."

"Del? What the hell—"

"I gotta go, Con. Get those cars here ASAP!" Dropping the phone, Delta rushed out the door.

In the violet of the night, the house next door was ablaze with orange and glowing yellows from the garage and the kitchen windows. Black smoke twisted menacingly up to become one with the darkness as the flames greedily licked at the shingles on the roof. The van was gone and Delta couldn't remember if she had mentioned it to Connie or not.

"Lord, help me," Delta uttered as she ran to the fiery house. The heat from the garage made it impossible to approach from the front so Delta scooted to the back of the house to check there.

After trying one locked door, Delta realized she was wasting lifesaving seconds looking for an easy way in. Picking up a piece of firewood, and noting the irony, Delta tossed it through the window. Immediately, a whoosh of hot air hit her in the face so hard, it felt like it singed her eyebrows.

Inhaling deeply, Delta zipped up her bomber jacket and tried to ignore the fear clawing at her courage. Then, as if an afterthought, Delta jammed her weapon back in her ankle holster.

"You've got to go in, Storm," Delta said to herself as she felt the searing heat bow out the window. From outside, she could see the flames devouring curtains in the family room. Like a living tornado, the flames jumped from one piece of furniture to another, engulfing everything in its path.

Inhaling one more time, Delta picked up another piece of firewood and knocked the remaining glass away before climbing through it and into the orange inferno.

Inside, the heat was stifling. Besides the curtains and furniture, the rug was on fire and things not yet been touched by the fiery tentacles were beginning to melt. Running into the kitchen, Delta wet a towel and wrapped it around her head like a turban. As she turned toward the animated flames, her anxiety grabbed her, immobilizing her for a moment. Thoughts of what the angry fire could do to her burned her mind like a glowing brand. When she was a child sick with fever, she had had nightmares about burning alive. She would wake up drenched with sweat and kicking at the covers. Those nightmares had seemed so vivid and real. And now, those nightmares had sprung to life.

Then, as suddenly as they came, the nightmare images flowed from her mind only to be replaced by her second greatest nightmare: A child with blonde hair was on the floor of a carnival ride with her dead eyes staring up at the heavens. It was an image that had haunted her more than any other in her adult life.

"Come on, Storm. This is your big chance." Taking another step toward the fire, Delta pulled her shirt up around her nose and prepared to take the stairs. "Come on, Con, don't let me down now." Delta inhaled, held her breath, and ran through the three-foot wall of flames blocking the stairs. Bounding up the stairs two at a time, and oblivious to her burning pant leg and the fiery fingers caressing her ankles, Delta wondered if she should have left her gun outside.

As she reached the top of the steps, she rolled and slapped at the fire burning her jeans.

She yelped when she looked down at her singed jacket and her already-starting-to-soften tennis shoes. It was far hotter inside than she had imagined.

On her feet again, Delta watched the fire creeping up the bannister as it reached toward the ceiling. It would be only minutes before the fire would consume the house and everything in it. The heat was already unbearable, and the blue-gray smoke filled the upper half of the house like a demonic genie.

Her eyes watering and stinging from the smoke, Delta wiped them with the edge of her now nearly-dried towel. "Hello? Can anyone hear me?" Delta felt the first closed door she came to. It was scorching to the touch. "Hello?" she yelled, coughing as soon as she inhaled a lung full of smoke. "I won't hurt you! I'm here to help!" Kicking the hot door in, Delta saw nothing but a column of flames. "Where are you?" Holding her forearm above her forehead, she peered inside at the burning room and knew, if anyone was in there, they were dead.

Approaching the second door, Delta felt it as well. It was warm, but not as hot as the one before. Kicking it in, she found two children about five years old on the burning bed. Both boys were dark-skinned with black hair, and they were wearing jeans and white t-shirts. The fire was only four feet from their heads, and already, Delta could see heat blisters on their arms.

"God, no," Delta said as she ran over to the bed and tore both children from it. Their bodies hung like limp sacks of corn meal as their arms flopped over her shoulders. Immediately, the bed burst into flames and the room instantly became an inferno.

Sliding open the door to a short balcony, Delta set the boys against the railing and ran back in. The fire, like an oil spill, spread rapidly through the house as if chasing her.

Moving past the bathroom, which was the only open door upstairs, Delta peeked at the balcony and knew she had less than a minute before the heat became unbearable and she would have to leave any children she had not yet found.

Coming to the third and final door, Delta didn't need to feel it to know the fire raged on the other side. Nonetheless, she smashed the door open and was immediately thrown backward by a large whooshing force that blew out of the room and knocked her across the hall.

"Shit, shit shit!" Delta yelled, rolling over and beating at the fire on her jeans. The arm she slapped with was also covered in flames and she managed to put it out by using the towel from her head. Surveying her clothes, Delta reached up and felt her face. From what she could tell, her eyebrows were gone and she suffered some kind of burn on her cheek.

Knowing she could not enter that room and that anyone in there would be dead, Delta decided to try the closets in the two rooms she did have access to. The first closet had telltale signs of arson, as rags, turpentine, and other flammable containers were strewn carelessly about. When Delta opened the second closet, she almost missed the little girl who must have managed to crawl into a corner before the full affect of the drugs took place. Delta knelt down and cradled the girl in her arms. The girl's eyelashes fluttered for just an instant, as if she was still trying to fight off the drugs.

"Hang in there, baby," Delta whispered, setting the girl on the balcony with the boys. Peering through the night, she wondered where the guys were; her hopes bolstered slightly by the distant sound of fire engines.

Turning back into the house, Delta was face-to-face with a wall of flames. Inhaling her last clean breath of air, she plunged through the flames and stepped into the bathroom to check it out.

At first, she saw nothing. Then, her gaze traveled over the bathtub, and Delta saw her. All she saw was black, tangled hair until she peered through the smoke and saw that the little bundle in the bathtub was another child. Without hesitating, Delta pulled her from the tub and set her on the balcony with the others.

Delta knew she would not be able to reenter the house. She had a short time before the entire house would be a huge bonfire. She had no choice but to drop the kids into the bushes below and hope the branches broke the fall—and nothing else. Hell, kids could recover from broken bones, but fire? That was another story.

Delta couldn't see the hedges very clearly, but it appeared as if all but one of the kids could safely land on them. She would have to take one of the kids with her.

Grabbing the littlest girl by her wrists, Delta swung her back and forth, gaining enough momentum to swing her out and over the hedges. When she was almost perpendicular to Delta, she let her go and watched as her lifeless body turned half a turn and landed in the middle of the hedges. To Delta's surprise, they supported the girl's weight.

She did the same with the two boys, but as the last boy crunched into the hedges, the balcony started to give way and Delta barely managed to get back inside with the little girl from the bathroom before the gutter came crashing down.

Hearing sirens in the distance gave Delta the renewed courage she needed to make her way through her adversary. She was not alone. If only she could beat the flames below. If only she were a little faster. If only...

Delta stopped herself. She had faced her own death once this week, and survived. Now, she was responsible for the life of a little girl, if there was still life. There wasn't time to see if the little girl was dead or alive; the heat was so unbearably hot and the smoke so thick and intense, Delta knew she had only seconds before both overtook her.

Opening her jacket up, Delta wrapped the immobile child close to her. Like a ragdoll, her little legs hung from underneath Delta's leather jacket.

"I got you, honey," Delta whispered as she zipped the jacket halfway up. From the top of the stairs, Delta could barely see through the haze of smoke scratching the back of her throat and nostrils. But she could see enough to know that all of her escape routes were choked off by the seven-foot wall of flames tickling the ceiling. One look down the stairs told her that the entire lower level was an inescapable inferno. Every piece of furniture was being consumed by the ravenous flames; the walls were now three-dimensional with flames moving and dancing on them as if they were alive. The fiery whips controlled everything, and Delta knew if they were going to make it out alive, they would have to go through them.

Taking the girl back to the bathroom and coughing so hard she thought a lung was coming up, Delta stepped into the shower and soaked both of them before resoaking the towel and wrapping it around her own head and face. Then, she moved to the top of the steps once more and stared down at the growing wall of flames. Her eyes burned from the smoke, and her lungs heaved in and out trying to pull fresh air through the towel. If the fire was a thing of its own design, then the heat it exuded was unlike anything Delta had ever faced. It was an invisible barrier pushing her backwards. The flames, alive as they stretched and reached for her at the top of the stairs, dared her to try to get past them. Suddenly, in a wild flash of panic, Delta understood why she had been so afraid of fire as a child. Fire was an enemy that carried with it a wide range of arsenal. As it raged about devouring everything it touched, it sent out heat and smoke to melt and penetrate those yet untouched by the flaming arms. It was as alive as any suspect she had ever taken down, except that it had no conscious; it didn't care that a little girl's life was at stake. She could not reason with this enemy.

"Not this time," Delta growled through tears that ran down her burning eyes. This time, she would not fail.

Tucking the little girl deeper inside her jacket, Delta glanced down at her melting tennis shoes. Her face, her hands, her entire body felt as though she were inside an oven. Frantically searching for the best route, Delta noticed the large plate glass window next to the front door. The front door was encased in flames, and Delta knew from experience, that the knob would melt her palm if she even touched it.

Glancing quickly around, it became clear to her that the only way out was through the window. If she could gather enough steam behind her, she could make it through that window, the fire be damned.

"This is it," she said, inhaling one last time, and feeling the burn in her lungs. This was the sharpest point of the razor's edge and if she was wrong, she would never dance on it again. As she prepared for one final charge down the stairs, her final thoughts were of Megan and Connie and all of the things she hadn't done with her life.

"I'm sorry, Megan," Delta whispered, zipping her jacket up all the way. Whether she would live to admit it or not, Delta had chosen her badge. The key, she realized, had probably already sunk. "Damn it." And with that, Delta bolted down the flaming stairs two steps at a time.

All around her, the flames voraciously grabbed at her as she forced her way through the hellfire and suffocating heat. Like a science-fiction movie, the invisible shield of heat tried to push her back up the stairs and into the arms of the eagerly awaiting flames. Like a strong headwind, it pushed against her.

Nearing the bottom of the stairs, Delta knew she needed enough momentum to propel herself—and the child—through the thick glass, or else she stood a good chance of breaking her neck or shoulder. With one step to go, Delta used every fiber in every muscle to hurl herself toward the window. In a leap that defied the law of gravity, Delta jumped headfirst toward the window, rolling slightly in the air and allowing her shoulder to take the brunt of the powerful impact. As her shoulder and head collided with the glass, the heat, which followed so closely behind her, violently shoved her through the window and continued to harass her as she landed with a heavy thud on the ground below.

"Put those flames out!" Someone called from what seemed to Delta to be another planet.

Suddenly, someone was beating her and trying to roll her over. The heat, the flames, must have followed her, and like leeches, stubbornly clung to her jacket and jeans.

"Roll her over, damn it! Her back is on fire!"

Someone kept trying to move her, but Delta reached a burnt hand out and managed to knock them away from her. Whether she was fighting the fire or the hands that grabbed at her, she did not know.

Nothing was clear to her now, except the burning of her clothes and her lungs gagging from smoke inhalation.

"She won't let go!"

One arm held the bundle under her jacket, while the other flapped around, hitting, pushing, slapping anything and anybody who came near. To Delta's ringing head, buzzing ears, and aching body, the fire was now personified and was eating away at her.

"Hey, what's she got in that jacket?" Someone else asked. The words were slow and laborious, and very distorted. She knew she was ready to visit the Land of the Unconscious, and struggled to keep some sense of what was happening to her.

"Shit, Chief, I think it's a kid!"

"A what?"

Through clenched and watery eyes, Delta saw the black edges of unconsciousness silently overtake her.

"A kid. She's holding a kid."

"Well, get it away from her! Hey! Move that hose to the other side!"

With grays turning to black, Delta knew she was about to succumb entirely to the throbbing of the impact. If only she could pry her swollen eyes open and see what was happening; but the smoke, the heat, the intense pain made everything an incredible blur. Suddenly, her body was no longer solid or tangible to her. She was floating on a cloud, aware that she was about to become lost in another world. The noises about her melded together and almost sounded like soft melodies. She had even relinquished whatever it was she had been holding onto. Funny...she couldn't remember....

"...on his way."

"...Get that stretcher over here, now! I swear to God, you people are moving in slow motion tonight!"

"...gasoline, sir..."

"...explosives..."

"...and she's alive as well..."

As the last vestiges of her consciousness faded away, Delta strained to hear the one person she knew could penetrate through her foggy haze. It was no surprise when she finally heard that voice ring through the cacaphony of blurred sounds tripping violently through her head.

"Storm, it's me. You hold on, you hear me? You just hold the fuck on."

"Con?" Delta choked out, before immediately giving in to a coughing spasm. Her chest felt as if a thick, steel band surrounded it, and squeezed every time she tried to breath.

"Shh, Storm, don't talk. The paramedics need to check you out. You've got to stop fighting them, okay?"

If Delta answered, she wasn't aware of it. All she could feel was her body being lifted and something wet flowing over her face. And as the paramedics worked over her, Delta wondered how much longer it would be before she stopped fighting and just let herself fade to black. It reminded her of not wanting to throw up—fighting to keep the vomit from coming up. Maybe she was afraid to let go. Maybe if she did, she would never wake up. Maybe her arms and legs had burnt off or were cut to shreds. Maybe she could hear the fire laughing at her as she was overcome with increasing pain.

Maybe...

Maybe it was no coincidence that the only image in her mind's eye was that of a golden key sitting at the bottom of an ocean.

And just as she was losing the battle to stay awake, Delta heard one more voice close to her ear. It was not the one she had expected.

"Delta? It's me, Carducci. Oh, man, say something."

Swallowing the dry sandy desert her throat had become, Delta reached for the last words she could speak before letting the black unconsciousness sweep her away: "It was west, you dumbass. West."

30

Trying to open her eyes, Delta thought they had been glued shut. Every muscle in her body ached and her face felt puffy and swollen. For a minute, she had forgotten what had brought her here. Then, as her memory cleared and her mind fought off the remnants of drugs, she remembered fighting her way through the inferno with a little girl in tow.

A little girl?

It was all coming back to her now: the porno ring, Dice's maniacal grin, the kidnappings, the red Camaro, the burning house that threatened her life even more than Zuckerman had.

"She's waking up," came Connie's voice softly. Hadn't Connie been there when Delta catapulted through the window? Didn't somebody push or pull her through the fire? The events were a jumbled blur through her throbbing head, and she knew it was useless to try to put them together just now.

Now. What time was now? How long had she been in that hospital room sleeping under painkillers and watchful eyes of nurses? Time, space, sequence, were all out of whack for her. The only comfort was the fact that Connie was near. Near enough, in fact, to be holding Delta's hand.

"Del, sweetheart, it's Megan. Can you hear me?"

The words sounded like they were being spoken through a cardboard tube. Swallowing the one tiny drop of saliva she could muster, Delta opted for nodding until she could find her voice. Inhaling slowly, she felt the pain in her chest from inhaling hot air and poisonous smoke.

"You're in the hospital and you're going to be okay. Do you understand?"

Why was Megan talking to her like she was an idiot, Delta wondered? Her eyes were closed and her body ached, but she wasn't a moron. Nodding, Delta worked on lubricating her parched throat.

"Are you in any pain, honey? Can I get you anything?"

It was so good to hear Megan's voice, worried and scared as it was. She wondered how long Megan had been in the hospital; how long had she sat there waiting for Delta to come to?

"Wa-ter?" Delta forced out. Then, she could hear Megan pouring some in a plastic cup before guiding it to Delta's hand.

Sipping the cool, comforting water, Delta rested her head on her pillow and sighed. The water calmed the aching, scratching sensation she'd felt since waking up.

"Anything else?"

Delta nodded. "The little...kids," she rasped, her throat feeling like someone had rammed a flaming sword down it.

"They're fine, sweetheart. You saved their lives."

"All?"

"Yes, my love, all."

Nodding, Delta raised her head and tried again to pry her eyes open. At first, everything was blurry, and the glare from the flourescent lights reflecting off of the harsh hospital walls hurt her already painful eyes. Somehow, the pain faded when she looked at the faces of the two most important women in her world sitting on opposite sides of her bed, both looking like they hadn't slept in weeks—neither, she knew, would have been willing to leave her bedside.

As Delta focused on Megan's tender eyes, she closed her own and sighed. "I lied," Delta said, opening her eyes and gently pulling Megan to her. The voice was not her own. It was harsh and husky, like that of someone who had been smoking for fifty years. Even those two simple words burned. "I said I'd be right back. I'm sorry."

"Oh, Delta." Tenderly wrapping her arms around Delta, Megan buried her face in Delta's neck. "You have nothing to be sorry for, my love."

Stroking Megan's hair with one bandaged hand, Delta glanced over at Connie, who forced a grin. Connie looked more scared than Delta had ever seen her. Had she been that close to death?

"I..." reaching for the cup of water, Delta sipped it before continuing. "I scared you and left you at Harry's. I'm sorry."

Raising her head so she was nose-to-nose with Delta, Megan sniffed back her tears. Years of love and laughter flowed between them like the fluid flowing through the IV into Delta's arm. "You always scare me, silly. If you apologized every time you did it, that's all you'd ever have time to say."

Delta grinned. It made her head pound more. "Yeah, but this time I cut it a little too close."

Megan nodded. "Yes, you did."

Reaching her free hand over to Connie, Delta took Connie's hand in her own and gazed for a long time into the quiet brown eyes staring down at her. She had scared Connie, too.

"I'm okay, Chief," Delta said, gently squeezing with her gauzed hand.

"Yeah? Well, a few hours ago, you came too close to looking like a crispy critter."

Delta nodded. "I don't think I ever want to be that hot again."

"I'll second that."

"I'm okay, Con."

"Well, Storm, okay seems to be your trademark these days." Taking Delta's wrapped hand between both of hers, Connie held it like one would a baby bird. "If you were bucking for hero status, you're there."

"That's not quite what I had in mind."

Connie grinned. "I know. How are you really feeling?"

Throat and eyes burning, muscles aching, head throbbing, and hands scorched, Delta had never felt worse. "Like a half-cooked shishkebob." Running her hand through Megan's silky hair, Delta suddenly noticed the bandage covering her right hand and immediately felt her face and head and found more gauze. "The real question is, how am I *really?*"

Megan touched Delta's face and smiled warmly. "You're the bravest woman I've ever met, that's how you are."

Delta shot a look over to Connie, who nodded. "Physically, you're fine. Other than a few strands of singed hair, and some second degree burns on your legs and arms, you can consider yourself one lucky woman."

Delta inspected her body. "That's it? It feels like I spent the night inside a microwave."

Connie nodded. "I'll bet. Your jacket kept you from being fried alive."

"Then why am I hooked up to the bottles?"

"Dehydration. The heat from the fire dried you like a fossil. It was a lot hotter in there than you think."

Delta sighed. "I don't want to know how hot it was. Believe me, it was hot enough."

Megan brought Delta's hand to her lips and kissed it. "But you made it out okay and that's the important thing. You saved lives, my love. Precious little lives."

"Then, you're not angry?"

"Angry?" Megan scowled. "About what?"

"About dinner. I really bailed on you when it—"

Megan placed her fingers over Delta's mouth. "As always, Delta Stevens, you were as unpredictable as the shifting wind. And, as usual, you did what you thought was best under the circumstances. And, as usual, it paid off. How could I be angry with someone who risked her life to save children she didn't even know?"

"But we had so much to talk about."

"Yes, and we'll still have that talk. But for now, I just want you to rest and relax and know that I'm right here." Megan tapped Delta's chest with a manicured finger. "And I always will be."

Like some kind of shaman medicine, Megan's words touched her spirit and radiated through her body, easing the aches and pains from her ordeal. If her heart was okay, her body would follow.

"I...needed to hear that."

Megan grinned gently and set Delta's hand down. "I know. But right now, we need to focus on getting you out of here."

Nodding, Delta ran her hand through her hair. "Right. Tell me about the kids."

"The children are a little shaky from the combination of drugs and smoke inhalation, but otherwise, they're fine. I would imagine you'll become quite a folk hero on the reservation."

Delta tried to smile, but her face didn't seem to want to cooperate. Suddenly, she remembered the Camaro. "Sal..."

"Don't worry about Sal. Josh said it was insured and he was more than happy to help."

"But we didn't catch anybody, did we?"

Connie shook her head. "No, we didn't, but you saved lives, Delta. That's all that matters, and it's something Sal and her buddies understand all too well."

Delta looked thoughtfully at her hands. "I've seen them in action, Con. You have remarkable taste in friends."

Connie brought one of Delta's hands to her lips and gently kissed it. "Yes, I do. So don't sweat it. You were great."

Looking up from her burnt hands, Delta's eyes narrowed. "Maybe. Does the captain think so, or did I nail down the lid to my own coffin?"

Connie shrugged. "Beats me. I've been too worried about you to care less what the almighty captain thinks. But don't you worry."

"Besides," Megan added, "you're a headlines grabber, my love. Look." Holding the Los Angeles Times up for Delta to see, Megan beamed proudly. Off Duty Cop Saves Kidnapped Children from Fiery Death. The subtitle to the headline read, <u>Officer Delta Stevens of River Valley P.D. Saves the Day.</u> "The *River Valley Reader* ran the story on the front page."

Delta bowed her head and grinned. She knew there were others at work this very minute trying to keep her butt out of the sling for this one. Looking up at Connie, Delta's left eyebrow rose in question. "Did Alex get that headline run?"

Connie nodded. "I think so. She called and told me she would do whatever she could to keep you out of trouble on this. You know she'd never let you go down without a fight."

Delta smiled. This time, her face worked. "No, she wouldn't."

Clearing her throat, Connie bent over, kissed Delta's forehead, and started for the door. "I'll give you two some time alone and see just how long we can keep the wolves at bay." Opening the door, Connie hesitated a moment. "Storm?"

"Yeah?"

"I'm glad you're okay. I don't know what I'd do without you."

"Cheer up, Chief. You're never going to have to find out."

Watching Connie disappear out the door, Delta told Megan, "She's my best friend."

"Yes, she is. And she just about drove herself mad with worry."

Delta reached for Megan's hand. "I'm glad you were here with her."

"Well, someone had to be strong, and it didn't look like it was going to be her. Actually," Megan lightly touched Delta's gauzed hand, "taking care of Connie forced me to be braver than I would have been."

"Good. I wouldn't want you to be so worried."

"Honey, I worry all the time, you know that."

"Yeah. I guess I do some pretty crazy things."

"Yes, you do. And I love you anyway."

"Enough to understand why I left you at Harry's?"

"Yes."

"Enough to believe me when I say that I support your decision to go on the internship?"

Megan leaned back. "Don't be ridiculous. How can you even think of letting me go at a time like this? You really are crazy. Maybe that bump on your head scrambled your brains."

"Meg—"

"No." Abruptly standing, Megan stepped away from the bed. "I won't hear any more. I'm not going and that's final."

"Meg, look. I'm a little charred around the edges, but I'll be back to work before the weekend. I'm fine. Really I am."

"Delta Stevens, you can be so pigheaded."

"Pigheaded? I thought I was being supportive and understanding."

Standing with her hands on her hips, Megan shook her head in exasperation. "If you weren't sitting there like a piece of over-cooked meat, I'd put another knot on your forehead. God, even in a hospital, you can be such as ass."

Delta smiled. "Then that must mean I'm okay."

"The hell you are. You're just a bigger pain in the butt, that's all."

"Maybe, but I'm your pain in the butt."

That did it. Fighting a battle she knew she couldn't win, Megan smiled. "We'll talk about it later." Bending over and kissing Delta's forehead, Megan lightly brushed her lips across Delta's. "Right now, I want you to get some rest." Tenderly kissing Delta's lips, Megan paused over the large bandage on Delta's eyebrow before gently laying her lips on the gauze. Hugging Megan gingerly, Delta realized she was exhausted and light-headed. "If the captain's out there, you better send him in. I'm getting a little tired."

"You sure you want to see him now?"

Delta nodded and leaned back against her pillows. "Better now than later. I just want to get it over with."

"Do you think Alexandria was able to help?"

Grinning and feeling the last of the painkiller wearing off, Delta nodded. "You can bet she's the one responsible for the front page story."

"Well, she owed it to you, didn't she?" Turning around, Megan blew Delta a kiss. "You've got five minutes with your precious captain, and that's it. If he doesn't say what he needs to say in that time, tough shit. If you won't take care of yourself, then I'm going to. You got that?"

Delta smiled as she saluted. Her head was throbbing and her eyes were beginning to hurt again. "Five minutes. After that, I promise to rest."

"Good." Walking back and kissing Delta on the lips, Megan held her breath. "I do love you so."

"I know. Me too." Watching Megan stride out the door, Delta thought how good it was to be alive, no matter how shitty she felt. And boy, did she feel shitty.

31

"Was Lady Luck with me or what?" Lifting the covers Delta surveyed her bandaged legs. Her shins were wrapped in the same kind of white gauzy material as her hands, but other than that, she could detect no major injuries. Reaching her hand up to her head, she carefully felt the egg-shaped bump protruding from her forehead, another injury inflicted by that nasty plate glass window. In the middle of the bump sat a huge chasm-like gash about three inches long stitched together with what felt like wire.

"Great. Now I have just the perfect accessory to wear with the scar on my thigh." Running her fingers down her thigh to the place where Elson Zuckerman had imbedded a Chinese throwing star, Delta involuntarily winced. At thirty years old, her body resembled Joe Namath's knees.

As Delta finished her checklist of injuries, there was a light knock on the door, followed by the head of Captain Henry.

"Your friend says you're ready to see us now?"

Delta straightened. "Us?"

"The chief came as soon as he heard. Feel up to it?"

Delta nodded, feeling slightly uncomfortable that the chief was choosing this opportunity to ding her. "Why not? Come on in."

Lumbering through the door like a sailor walking into a hair salon, Captain Henry stood stiffly at the door and waited for Police Chief Walker to enter. Delta had met the thin and balding chief on a couple of occasions, none of which were worth remembering. Politically, he was too closely allied to the mayor to be of any real service to his officers, but Delta appreciated the fact that he gave his female officers the same respect he gave to his men. Secretly, she and Connie both thought he might be gay, but they'd never jeopardize their careers by vocalizing those thoughts. He was here, and right now, she had to deal with whatever he had to say.

"Captain. Chief Walker." Delta nodded her head at the two as they stood on either side of the bed like a pair of stone bookends. The captain was still in uniform but Chief Walker was wearing a gray sweat suit with a torn front pocket. It was the first time Delta had seen him in casual clothes. She wondered if he had been jogging before coming to the hospital.

"Officer Stevens. It's been awhile, hasn't it?"

"Yes, Chief, it has." Now she remembered. Their last two meetings were the result of "questionable actions on the part of a law enforcement officer out of the line of duty," or so read the final report. It did not surprise her that he was here with her now, not just because one of his officers had been hurt in the line of duty, but because it was exceptionally good PR to make a statement to the press from the hospital where the wounded cop was recovering. Delta was astute enough politically to recognize a PR ploy when she saw one.

Nonetheless, that PR might be the one thing that kept her neck from the guillotine. In fact, Delta was counting on that.

"How are you feeling?" The chief asked, stuffing his hands into the pockets of his sweats.

"I'm fine, sir, really. I should be back at work in a day or two."

"Excellent."

"Yes, and speaking of excellent," Captain Henry added, "You've done one hell of a fine job saving those kids. The department is proud of you."

"Thank you. I hate to be rude, Captain, but I'm feeling a little light-headed and wish you'd say whatever it is you have to say."

Chief Walker shook his head. "You never change, do you, Stevens?"

"It doesn't appear so, sir. "

The captain and chief exchanged glances and nodded to each other before calling a secretary in to take the report. While Delta hadn't been surprised that the two men were in her room, she was surprised that they actually brought a secretary with them. They must think Delta had more information than she actually had.

After the secretary settled in, Delta spent ten minutes telling her story. She told everything except the fact that the Camaro and the bug had been planted, that she had seen two men killed in the desert, and that they had been on the case since its inception. Basically, she told them nothing.

"Let me get this straight, Stevens," The chief said, eyeing Captain Henry suspiciously. "You and Rivera put two-and-two together about the children being Indians—"

"Native Americans, sir."

"Whatever. And then you discover there is some kind of stolen vehicle pattern, so out of the blue you decide to chase after a red Camaro that zips right in front of you?"

Delta nodded. "That's about it. It was a hunch, sir. Nothing more, nothing less."

"I see."

The secretary glanced up from her pad and grinned slightly at Delta.

"I have great hunches," Delta said, shrugging.

"So it would seem." Captain Henry paced over to the window and stared out. Delta could hear it coming like a Mack truck down a gravel road. "Is that the only suspicion you and Rivera have regarding this case?"

Delta nodded.

Returning to the bed, Captain Henry pulled a chair up and leaned close to Delta. "Stevens, there are three federal agents outside who don't believe that. They don't believe that you just decided to jump into your car and race after a red Camaro. They don't believe that you and your partner just happened to end up at the same bar on your night off, and they sure as hell don't believe that you aren't witholding information from them. Do you get my meaning?"

Delta nodded, not taking her eyes off Henry's. "Yes, sir, I do."

"Then if you know what's good for you, you'll come clean with me and the chief so we can pad the way a bit for you. You have an awful lot to answer for."

Delta shrugged and looked over at the secretary. "There's nothing more to tell, Captain. Carducci and I did just happen to end up at Harry's. I did just happen to chase after the Camaro, and I just happened to hear their conversation about burning the house down."

"Then why did you call Rivera and not dispatch?"

"Carducci should have already called dispatch, so I called Connie to make sure all bases were covered. I mean, I couldn't figure out why no one had arrived yet. I didn't have time to call them and find out why, so I called the one person I knew wouldn't let me down."

"So you're saying Carducci let you down?"

Delta shook her head and immediately regretted doing so. It felt as if her brain cells rattled against her skull. "Not at all. I'm saying I needed back-up and I called the one person who would make sure I got it."

Captain Henry nodded. "I see."

Suddenly, the chief spoke up. "Your 'hunches' sure do put you in the spotlight, Stevens. You certainly have the makings of a hero."

"A heroine, sir, and thank you, but I just do what my gut tells me to."

The chief reached out and took Delta's hand. The darts he threw at Captain Henry with his eyes did not go unnoticed. "Well, you keep listening to your gut, Officer. We need more cops like you, Stevens. You had a tough choice to make and it seems you made the right one. You saved children's lives, Stevens, and there isn't a soul in this city who gives much of a damn about how you did it. Congratulations on a job well done. You're a wonderful asset to your department."

Feeling her head spin, Delta closed her eyes for a second and saw images of the fire leaping up around her. "I'm just glad we're all okay. Connie says the kids are doing fine."

"Yes, doing quite well, considering the circumstances. Some of the families flew in from the reservations and the feds have a pack of investigators already on their way to the Southwest. They expect to dig up some data that will help lead to the arrest of these scumbags. You should be proud."

Delta smiled weakly. A pounding had begun in her head. "Actually, I'm just exhausted. Can we wrap this up?"

The chief nodded and cleared his throat. "You know, I suppose you'll warrant a commendation for this."

Delta shrugged. A commendation to her was just another note in her already towering file. What she wanted was to be left alone. "Thanks, sir, but all I want is to work the streets."

Glancing back at the captain, the chief nodded. "We'll see what can be arranged. For now, just rest knowing that we've picked up on your lead and are following through."

"What about the feds?"

Captain Henry's moustache rose as he smiled. "Don't worry about them. I made it clear that if they needed anything from you, they were to go through me first. I think they're a little peeved that you outdid them."

"And I am still outdoing them sir. If they've gone to the Southwest looking for 'clues,' they're dumber than I thought. Our guys are still here in River Valley, not in the Southwest." Delta closed her eyes and leaned back against the pillow. "But thanks for buffering for me, Captain. I really don't need any more run-ins with Internal Affairs."

"Consider it done. And don't rush back to work. You get all the rest you can and soak up all the attention you're going to get from the media and your fans. You've earned it."

Opening her eyes, Delta was surprised by the captain's honest display of emotion. It was the first really kind thing he'd said to her. "Thanks. Right now, all I want is to rest."

"Done." Lightly touching Delta's arm, Captain Henry rose and joined Chief Walker at the door. "You're a damn good cop, Delta Stevens. I may not believe a single thing you said in here just now, but you do know how to get the job done."

"Thank you, sir." Closing her eyes again, Delta waited until she heard the door close before picking up the phone and dialing.

"This is Delta Stevens...yeah, I'll hold." Delta waited less than ten seconds before the line clicked over. "Hi, Alex, it's me. I just called to say thanks."

32

The sound of the door closing quietly woke her with a start. Cracking open her eyes, Delta looked up to find Alexandria Pendleton standing uncomfortably at the foot of her bed. She was wearing a peach blouse with a teal skirt. She looked wonderful.

"Hello there, Counselor," Delta said, struggling through the ache in her body to sit up.

"You're quite the heroine, aren't you?"

Delta shrugged. "You win some, you lose some. This time, I won."

"And it was that important to you, wasn't it? Winning, I mean." Alexandria crossed her arms over her chest, towering over Delta. She did not look happy.

"No, Alex, what was important was saving the lives of those kids." Delta shifted in the bed. "I failed to do that once and it's been haunting me ever since. Besides, isn't this what you wanted? Didn't you want to shine over Wainwright? What's with you, anyway?"

Alexandria turned away and rummaged through her purse. "I've tried not to care," she answered, not looking up from whatever held her attention inside the purse. "I've seen what lengths you'll go to get the job done, and I can't seem to stop caring about you."

Delta was beginning to get it. "Is that so awful?"

"It is," Alexandria looked up from her purse, "When you go off half-cocked against wackos. Delta, you could have been killed. And now look at you..."

Delta held one hand out for Alexandria and pulled her over to the side of the bed. "I'm not here because of you, Alex. Trust me when I say that."

"How can I, Delta? Have you taken a good look at yourself? Every bump and every scar on your body, I am, in some part, responsible for."

Delta blushed. "No, and I don't have to look at myself to know I've done a damn good job. Alex, ever since Helen was killed, I've been carrying this huge ball of guilt. I've seen her dead eyes in my dreams. I've seen Helen's little face so often, I thought I'd gone crazy. So you're right—I have tried to balance the scales a bit. And you know what? I'm glad. I'm glad because people like you trust me enough to tell me to go for it. I did and I won. We won. These aches in my body are all part of the game. Be happy we are all alive."

Alexandria sat on the bed and held Delta's hand. "I am. It's just..."

Pulling Alexandria to her, Delta hugged her tightly. "You care about me. As much as it's against whatever creed you signed in blood, you do care about me. And I'm glad, Alex. I'm really glad you do. Because I care about you, too."

Raising her head from Delta's shoulder, Alexandria fixed her hair and smiled warmly into Delta's face. "I think you've shown me that enough times, Delta Stevens, don't you?"

"This thick head of mine learned something the other day, Alex, and I want to share it with you. Family comes through for each other. It doesn't have to be your biological family, either. We're family, and because we are, you feel comfortable asking me to take risks. And because we are, you save my charred hide by going to the press with the story. That's what family does for each other, Alex. That's what we're all about. Don't apologize for it. Accept it and be happy you have people who care about you as much as Connie and I do."

Alexandria slowly stood up, but continued to hold Delta's hand. "You amaze me, Delta Stevens. I thought I was supposed to come in here and cheer you up. Instead..."

There was something about the look in her eyes, about the worry lines running across her forehead, that sent warning signals through Delta's body. At first, she thought she was misreading them, but a closer look into Alexandria's eyes told Delta everything she needed to know.

Alexandria Pendleton cared too much.

As if sensing Delta's thoughts, Alexandria walked over to the same window that had attracted Captain Henry's attention. "If you want off of TP, I think it can be arranged now.

"I'll think about it. Right now, I just want to see the guys follow through on any leads the feds might have to catch those bastards."

Alexandria blew out a long sigh. "Watching those federal guys work makes me understand why you cut corners."

This made Delta smile. "Isn't that the truth? They're so wrapped up in procedure and protocol and doing everything by the book, it's amazing they arrest anyone at all. Connie tells me they're even going to the Southwest. Good going, guys, but didn't we just prove to you that our suspects are right here?"

"The feds want the guy at the top."

"Right. At the expense of how many other lives?"

Stepping closer to the bed, Alexandria stared down at Delta for a long time before speaking again. "I'm really proud of you, you know."

"I know."

"Do you? Do you have you any idea, Delta Stevens, what it means to me to have someone like you working in this city? I come to you for a favor and you literally put your neck on the line to deliver. You're amazing. But best of all," Alexandria's eyes softened, "you're a truly great friend."

Delta saw the same look in Alexandria's eyes that she'd seen earlier. "I'll do in a pinch. Hey, I see you're using the press to beef this up."

"Oh, I am. We've been meeting with them all morning. The public loves a hero, and we've just given them one.

"I didn't do it alone, Alex—"

Alexandria held up a hand for her to stop. "Del, if you think I'm going to give a shred of credit to your bumbling boob of a partner, then you really do need a doctor to examine your head. He nearly cost you your life."

"Not so fast, Counselor. Tony called it in like I asked him to. Everything was happening so quickly, I'm sure he just got confused."

"Well, I don't care if he was confused or not. That man shouldn't be on the streets if he doesn't know straight up from a duck." Alexandria's voice rose slightly, but she caught herself. "You just say the word, and he's out of there. I'll make sure of it even if I have to do it myself."

Delta shook her head. "I can't make any decisions right now, Alex. My head hurts so much, it's all I can do to decide whether I want red or green jello for breakfast."

"I'm sorry, Del, have I tired you out?"

"No, not really. I just don't want to see anybody slamming Carducci, that's all. The poor guy is probably feeling really shitty about this whole thing."

A surprised expression fell over Alexandria's face. "You mean, you haven't seen him since the fire?"

Delta shook her head. "No. Why?"

Walking over to the door, Alexandria peered out the tiny square window before answering Delta's question. "He hasn't left the waiting room since they brought you in here."

"What?" Delta pulled herself up higher in the bed. "You're kidding."

Alexandria shook her head. "Connie tried to get him to go home and get some sleep, but he wouldn't budge. He's just been sitting there, staring at the floor."

"Why hasn't he come in to see me?"

"Embarrassed, probably. He knows how close you came to not making it out of that house alive. How would you feel?"

Delta thought for a moment. "Alex, would you mind calling him in here for me?"

"You sure you're up to seeing him?"

"He needs to see me. He needs to know that I'm okay."

Shaking her head, Alexandria walked back over to the bed and held Delta's hand once more. "You're one of a kind, Delta Stevens. You know that, don't you?"

"Yeah, well, when we find out what kind, look out."

Smiling, Alexandria held onto her hand a second longer before starting for the door. "Get yourself some rest, okay?"

"Will do. And Alex, thanks for stopping by. It means a lot to me."

"My friends mean a great deal to me, Delta. Take care."

Watching the door close behind Alex, Delta heaved a sigh that seemed to bounce off the bright walls and land against her forehead. She must have misjudged her jump and hit the glass with most of her head instead of her shoulder; she was getting tired of the pounding headache.

Hearing the slow squeak of the door, Delta glanced up. Poking his head in first, Tony leaned halfway in. "The DA said you wanted to see me."

Poor guy, Delta thought. He was miserable and uncomfortable, and he didn't even know where to put all the feelings he'd felt since the night of the fire.

"Get your butt in here, Carducci," Delta said, waving him in.

Cautiously entering the room, as if he were in a china shop with very narrow walkways, Tony stood straight with his hands at his sides. His eyes were big saucers that took in the room like a child might a haunted house.

"Have a seat."

In two big strides, Tony was at the chair. He sat down heavily upon it. He was still wearing the clothes he'd been wearing at Harry's. "How're you feeling?"

"Better than last night. My head is still vibrating from hitting the window, but other than that, I'm fine."

Staring down at his clasped hands, Tony nodded, but said nothing.

"Carducci, it wasn't your fault. I would have gone into that house whether there was back-up or not. You have to believe that."

"But there could have been back-up if I wasn't such a fuck-up."

Delta leaned forward. "Look, you can sit there and kick yourself for making a mistake, or you can look at the outcome and know that it all worked out. Remember what I said about getting the job done? Well, we did."

"You did. I nearly got you killed."

"The fire nearly killed me, Carducci, not you. Look at me."

Raising his head slowly, Tony looked at Delta with tears in his eyes. She knew he had seen his career as a cop go up in the same flames that almost took her life.

"Carducci, the end justified the means. Stop dwelling on the mistakes. That won't get you anywhere."

"That's just it, Delta, my career won't be going anywhere after this. I blew it big time. You should see what the papers are saying about the asswipe who called in the wrong directions."

"I don't care what the papers say. All I care about is the fact that a bunch of kids have the chance to grow up. Damn, Carducci, that's something to be proud of."

Tony looked back down at his hands. "They'll probably take you off TP now."

"Probably."

"You deserve that much, Delta. What you did...well...it was great. I only want the best for you."

"Me, too. And I hope the best for you. Right now, that means going home, getting cleaned up, and bringing me something for breakfast that doesn't look or taste like plastic. Will you do that for me?"

Tony's head jerked up and the gloom in his eyes was immediately replaced by a flicker of excitement. "You bet. What would you like?"

"Everything. Eggs, pancakes, sausage, toast, coffee, the whole ball of bacon. But be careful. Don't let

Nurse Ratchet see you. She thinks the world's most perfect food is lime jello."

Rising, Tony fumbled in his pockets for his keys. "Anything else?"

"How about a newspaper?"

"You got it. I'll be back in a flash."

"Oh, and Carducci?"

"Yeah?"

"Take a shower." Delta grinned. He reminded her of a puppy that just wanted to do the right thing but didn't quite know how to do it.

"Gotcha. I'll be back with the best breakfast this side of the Mississippi." And with that, he flew out the door, leaving Delta wondering about their tenuous future.

33

That evening, Delta arrived home to find it blanketed with flowers and gifts from the guys at the station. Closing the door behind them, Megan escorted her to the couch and ordered her to sit down and stay there for the remainder of the evening.

"I mean it, Delta. I don't want you getting up for anything. For once in your stubborn life, let someone take care of you."

Fluffing up a pillow, Delta did as she was told. "It feels good to be home," she said.

"Connie said she'd be right over after she finishes up a few things at work. Gina sends her love and says she'll see you tomorrow. The phone has been ringing off the damned hook. I didn't realize so many people cared about you."

Delta grinned. "What can I say?"

"You can start by telling me who all of these women are." Megan grinned back as she handed Delta a list of women who had called.

"Looks like my date list from my little black book," she said, winking. "Actually, it's just the dispatch crew, the clerks, the secretaries, other cops, and detectives. All of the women I work with."

"Hmph. I suppose I should pay more attention to the women you come in contact with, huh?"

Patting the couch, Delta made room for Megan. "The only woman I want you paying attention to is me."

Snuggling up next to Delta, Megan was careful to avoid touching her wounds. "That's an easy request."

"Good, because the next request might not be."

Raising up so she was eye to eye with Delta, Megan waited. "Oh?"

"Meg, I know this fire thing came up at a bad time and all—"

"I thought we had already discussed this. There's no reason to apologize."

"I'm not apologizing. I'm trying to tell you that I want you to go to Costa Rica as you planned."

Megan's expression didn't change. "Excuse me?"

"Honey, I want you to go. I've thought long and hard about it and I think you're right."

"You're sure?"

"Meg, I'm not going to die. I'm not going to fall apart. Staying here under such ridiculous pretense is only going to prolong the inevitable."

"And what's that?"

"That you need to go find out who the new Megan Osbourne really is. My accident doesn't change that fact."

"Did you bake your brain while you were in that house?" Megan teased, dropping a kiss on Delta's cheek.

"No. But when death stares you in the face, you suddenly realize how short life is. I don't want to take anything from your life, sweetheart. I want to add to it. If you need to explore your life away from me, then I understand. Well, at least, I'm beginning to."

Lightly touching Delta's lips with her fingertips, Megan sighed. "You don't think the timing is bad?"

"I think the timing is just right. I want to be a good partner to you, Megan. I love you so much I just want to do right by you. You've been so supportive of me, I think it's time I returned the favor."

Megan lowered her mouth to Delta's. She kissed her tenderly for a long time. It was a kiss that said "I'll love you for the rest of my life." It was a kiss that told Delta she had made the right decision.

"I love you, Delta Stevens."

"Then, you'll go?"

Looking deep into Delta's emerald eyes, Megan nodded. "I'll go. I'll go because I have to, because I need to. Because I want to come back to you knowing beyond a shadow of a doubt that here is where I want to be—that you are who I want to spend the rest of my life with."

Kissing Megan's chin, Delta hugged her. "If going will tell you that, then go. But damn you, Megan, you had better come back ready to live with me, ready to love me, ready to...marry me."

Megan quickly pulled away. "What did you say?"

"I said, marry me."

For a moment, Megan didn't know what to say. "Are you serious?"

Delta nodded. "I want to have a union with you, Megan. I mean, when you're sure that I'm the one you want and this is the life you choose."

"A union?" A small smile crept onto her mouth. "You mean with a preacher and everything?"

"Everything. Will you? I mean, when you get back, will you give me an answer?"

Throwing her arms around Delta, Megan squeezed her so tightly, it hurt. "Yes, I'll give you an answer." Kissing Delta hard, Megan abruptly rose. "You never cease to amaze me, Delta Stevens."

"I hope I never stop."

Suddenly, the front door opened, and there stood Connie with her hands full of newspapers. "I thought maybe your scrapbook wasn't full yet."

Delta grinned and smelled the wonderful aroma of Megan's freshly brewed coffee. "Come on in. Want a cup of coffee?"

"This late? No thanks. It'll keep me up for hours."

"I thought that was the plan."

"The plan," Megan said, returning to the front room, "is for you to get some rest. Right, Connie?"

Shrugging at Delta, Connie sat down. "You mean after I tell her what I've found out?" The rebellious twinkle in Connie's eyes gave her away.

Turning on her heel, Megan shook her head as she walked back into the kitchen. "You're both incorrigible—beyond hope."

Looking at Connie, Delta shrugged. "Beyond hope?"

"You heard her." Connie grinned.

"Well, would you mind being the best woman of an incorrigible cop who's completely beyond hope?"

"Get outta here."

Delta grinned. "You and Gina had one. I think it's time for Megan and me to make a formal commitment to each other."

Connie jumped to her feet and started dancing a little dance. "You're going to get married! Can we make it a Navajo ceremony? I know, how about a dual ceremony. One for the blessing of the baby by Changing Woman, and the other, a marriage ceremony. It'll be great!"

Delta looked at Connie as if she'd gone nuts. "Right. And who's going to marry us? Shaman Lady and Goofy Two Steps?"

Connie stopped her little dance and jammed her hands on her hips. "You can have such a teeny tiny little mind sometimes."

"Perhaps because it's been smashed up against my skull twice in one week."

"Well, I don't care. I'm going to ask Megan if she would mind having a dual ceremony."

"She hasn't said yes to any ceremony, yet."

"Ah, then we shall pray to the White Shell Woman while she is gone that Megan sees that her true path lies with you."

Delta couldn't help but laugh. "What the hell has gotten into you? Locoweed?"

Connie tried to hide her grin, but was unsuccessful. "Okay, I've been reading a book about the Navajo tradition, and I'm a little pumped for the baby. Gina is being inseminated today."

Delta's mouth opened but nothing came out. "Excuse me? Did you say—"

Connie's grin brightened. "After everything you've been through, we decided not to wait. Life's too short, Kimo, to hem and haw around, so we sat down last night and decided that we wanted a Native American child."

"I...I don't know what to say."

"The Native American heritage is dying a slow death, Delta. Keeping the bloodline alive is a gift Gina and I can give back to the Indian nation. It's the very least I can do."

"Is the father full-blooded?"

Connie nodded. "I brought his picture."

Delta sat up so quickly, it hurt her. "No kidding?"

"I knew you'd ask. Here." Handing Delta the picture, Connie beamed. "I think he's beautiful."

Taking the wallet-size picture, Delta carefully studied it. The man looking back at her had deep brown eyes on either side of a strong nose. What stood out most were the dimples in his cheeks and his flawless smile. Connie was right. He was beautiful.

"Whoa. I suppose my niece will end up being the next Gerber baby, then. He's gorgeous."

Taking the picture back, Connie studied it a moment. "Yes, he is. Now do you understand why I'm a little fired up?"

"I'm so happy for you, Chief."

"Happy enough to have a double ceremony?"

Megan came out of the kitchen with two cups of coffee. "Yes, Connie, if Delta and I decide that a union is what we want, then I would be honored to have a double ceremony."

"I'm glad one of you has the sense the goddesses gave you."

Delta merely shook her head. "Consuela Rivera, if my head wasn't pounding before you got here, it sure is now."

Connie started reaching into her pocket. "Wait. I was just reading about the ancient Hopi herb for headaches...."

34

When Delta walked into the station the next day she received a hearty and sincere round of applause from her colleagues. Cops seldom show much open emotion, and it deeply touched her that they would stop what they were doing and acknowledge her return.

"Thanks, guys," Delta said, feeling both proud and slightly embarrassed by the commotion.

"Hey, Stevens!" One very large officer named Erwin called out. "When I grow up, I want to be just like you!" Everyone laughed and there was the usual cliched comebacks about Erwin growing more than he already had.

"You frame that leather jacket," another officer said. "The paramedics said it saved your life."

Nodding, Delta stopped when a clerk threw her arms around her and hugged her tightly. "I have two kids of my own, Delta. What you did...it makes me so proud."

"Makes us all proud, you hotdog!" another voice chimed in.

"Thanks, really. But you're making a fuss for nothing. You'd all have done the same."

"That's right," Connie said, emerging from behind her desk. "You guys act like she's a heroine or something. Sheesh. If you don't stop now, we won't be able to get her big head through the door."

Again, the crowd snickered.

"You done good, Delta."

Grinning sheepishly, Delta shrugged. "I was taught by the best. What can I say?"

Suddenly, a young officer with a crew cut stepped forward and shook Delta's hand. "I'm proud to say I work with you, Delta, and I'd be really proud if you were ever my partner."

"Hey, speaking of partners, where the hell is *wrong-way* Carducci, anyhow?"

Suddenly, the grins turned into scowls, and Delta felt the tension flowing through the room.

"Maybe," another cop offered, "since your tail was cooking in the fire, his ass is in hot water."

"Serves him right."

"Yeah. Man, if he were *my* partner—"

Looking around the room, Delta saw the grim, frowning faces of her colleagues. It was one thing to make a mistake; it was another matter entirely when a cop almost bites it because of another cop's error. Forgiveness didn't come easily to this group, and Delta knew that Tony had probably taken a verbal beating for his blunder the night of the rescue.

"Come on, guys, lighten up," Delta admonished.

"Lighten up? Stevens, you gotta be crazy. If he were my partner, he wouldn't be after a fuck-up like that."

"Dougherty's right. That rookie nearly got you deep fried. As it is, he still got you sent to the hospital. That didn't need to happen, Stevens, and you know it."

"Look, we were off duty, Carducci had had a drink or two. Nobody expected that we'd have to think so damned fast on our feet. He made a mistake. What do you expect? Perfection?"

"We'd expect him to know his left from his right," Came a deep voice from the corner. "Or his right from his left. Or up from down...or...."

"Admit it, Stevens, he almost got you flame broiled like a Whopper. We all know it. Don't try to protect him, man. He fucked up royally and I, for one, don't care to work with someone that stupid."

"Ditto!"

Connie stepped over to Delta and gently laid her hand on Delta's shoulder. "Give it a rest, you guys. She's back one minute, and the next, you're giving her shit. Ease up, okay?"

"We're not on her, Rivera. It's her dim-witted rookie, AKA The Cop Who Couldn't Find His Ass With Both Hands."

As a few officers chortled at Tony's new moniker, the door slowly opened and Tony walked in looking like a man who had just bet everything he owned on a lame pony. Instantly, the laughing subsided and everyone ducked their heads and went back to work.

Lowering his head, aware that the whole room had just been talking about him, Tony headed for the locker room.

"Hey, Carducci, wait up." Brushing past a few of the back slappers, Delta reached him in three of her long strides.

Slowly looking up, Tony forced a small grin. "How you feeling?"

"I'm fine. Really." If anyone had bet Delta that she'd see the likes of Tony Carducci cowed, she would have bet a month's pay that it would never happen. And she would have lost. Standing before her now was a beaten man, a rookie who had probably taken a lot more abuse in the last two days than the verbal sputterings she had just witnessed. Delta knew what bastards the Internal Affairs cretins could be, and she knew by Tony's hang-dog appearance that they hadn't been kind.

"Delta, I know I let you dow—"

Suddenly, the captain's door opened and Captain Henry appeared, hands on his hips, wearing something between a frown and a scowl on his weather-beaten face. "Stevens, when you're done signing autographs, I want to see you in my office."

Frustrated by his timing, Delta patted Tony on the back before heading for the captain's office. "We'll talk later. In the meantime, don't let the guys get to you."

"Yeah. Sure."

Following Henry back into his office, Delta knew what was coming. She knew, and she had prepared herself.

Moving his great frame around to his side of the desk, Captain Henry clicked his little lamp off. "It seems you find yourself in the limelight once again."

Delta couldn't tell by his demeanor whether that was a good thing or not. "If I had my choice, sir, I wouldn't be."

"Don't get me wrong, Delta," the captain said, opening the file laying on his desk. Delta hadn't noticed it when she sat down, but she knew exactly what it was. "You have, again, brought this department some very positive media attention. What you did, how you risked your life, is stuff the media loves writing about and the public adores reading."

Delta watched Henry move in his seat like a panther paces back and forth at the zoo. She had no idea where he was going with this, but wherever it was, it was making him very uncomfortable.

"It seems," he continued, "that no matter where you're assigned, you always seem to end up in the thick of things."

Delta started to respond, but thought better of it. She wanted to see where this was going before she tried to back out.

"Saving those kids has sure made us look good in a year when police brutality claims the headlines."

"Thank you, sir." Now she was really baffled. Just what was he trying to say? "Captain, just where, exactly, is this conversation heading? You seem at a loss for words."

"That's just it, Stevens, I am." Leaning across the desk, Henry's eyes narrowed. "Where do we put you now? The department is going to look real bad if we keep you on Training Patrol after this. Already, the papers want to know why you're there now. *The Trib* is actually speculating that you're being punished for your role in the Zuckerman death."

Delta's eyebrow rose. "Aren't I?"

Slamming his fist on the desk, Captain Henry caught himself and walked over to the window. "Damn it, Delta, you're not making this easy for me."

"Captain, I'm not exactly sure what *this* is."

Folding his arms across his chest, Henry stood there staring at her. "You and I know that it wasn't luck that made you follow that Camaro. I don't know how you did it, but somehow, you managed to weasel your way onto this case."

"But—"

"Let me finish. Right now, how you knew, how long you've been collecting evidence, and how many regulations you've broken during your investigation are moot points to everybody. And I do mean everybody. Suddenly, you've become the golden girl of the police force and I don't know what the hell to do about it."

A lightbulb flashed. "Oh, I get it now. You want to put me back on the street." Standing up, Delta walked over and looked out the window at the office outside. Department politics bored her. The feds and their bureaucracy annoyed her. The press and their power irked her. It seemed that at every turn, somebody was getting in the way of her doing what she did best: be a cop on the streets. "That's it, isn't it? Put the heroine back where she belongs before we get any more heat from the press, and maybe she won't tear us a new asshole for putting her on Training Patrol in the first place. Is that it?"

"Something like that."

Turning toward him, Delta snarled. "Yeah? Well, the whole thing stinks. I'm not a puppet to be manipulated according to public opinion. You *did* put me on TP to teach me a lesson and to show the others what kind of a captain you'd be if anyone didn't play the game your way. So don't bullshit me or the press into believing otherwise."

"It wasn't like that."

"The hell it wasn't. You used me as an example and now that the media is knocking at your door, you want to take me from the corner you sent me to to save face? Thanks, but no thanks."

"I'm afraid it's a little more complicated than that."

"Is it? Well, I don't care! This is my career we're talking about, Captain, and I don't want to be involved in the political mish-mash of this department. I won't be a pawn to be moved at the whim of the chief or Internal Affairs or even you, for that matter."

"Now wait a minute—"

Delta whirled around. After having some asshole slap her around and put an Uzi to her head, and after nearly burning to death, Delta felt no inclination to be diplomatic. And she didn't give a damn.

"No, you wait a minute. I've done what you asked me to do. I took a rookie to the streets, and we—" Suddenly, Delta stopped. "That's it, isn't it? You're taking Carducci off, aren't you?"

Inhaling slowly, the captain played with his moustache. "He really messed up, Delta. You know that. If someone had told me he had no sense of direction, he would never have been on the streets in the first place."

From somewhere deep inside her, a ball of fire ignited and started moving toward the surface of her subconsciousness. This flaming sphere, this righteous indignation had a name. And that name was Miles Brookman.

"So, that's it? Is that your inspired compromise? Take Carducci off the street and label him a failure so you can slip me right back out there without looking stupid. This makes me sick."

"Jesus Christ, Stevens, give me a break here! He can't give or take directions correctly, he's got an attitude problem and he—"

"Makes the perfect scapegoat. At least have the balls to admit it, Captain."

"Now see here—"

Delta laughed. "Or what? You'll fire me? You want to play petty politics, Captain, then I just joined the game. You can't fire me right now unless you want to look like the biggest dumbass west of the Rockies, so don't wave your finger in my face. If you're going to make a decision about me or Carducci, then at least have the guts to do it above board. If not, then stop wasting my time." Grabbing the door, Delta paused. "I had hoped you were different than the other captains, but you're not."

"Delta, wait."

Delta gently closed the door, but kept her hand on the knob. "What?"

"First of all, I'm not playing games with you. I have to do what's in the best interest of this department. I happen to believe that means you're on the street—"

"And Carducci's behind a desk."

"Damn it, Delta, the man has no sense of direction! I can't allow another one of my officers to be put at risk again because he can't tell north from south or east from west!"

"What about his potential. Are you going to throw that away too, just because he has some directional problems?"

"He has a handicap, Delta, one I should have been made aware of. I think it's best for everyone involved if I take him off TP and find someplace else for the kid to work. That's my decision."

Delta folded her arms across her chest and considered his words. She knew that the best thing to do was to go along with the decision and dump Carducci while she had the chance. Yes, he almost cost her her life, but she had made a bad decision once and didn't she live with the fact that that might have cost Miles his life? Sure, the best thing to do was to agree with the captain, get back to the streets, and forget that her career was now being controlled by the press. The best thing was to simply accept it.

But then, there was the right thing. The right thing, the way she had been taught by Miles, was to stay there and fight for her partner, much as Miles had done on any number of occasions when Delta had broken the rules. The right thing was to return the favor that had been done for her all those years ago and give Carducci a fighting chance to deal with his handicap. The right thing was for Delta to refuse to be dominated by the media, by self-serving players in a game she couldn't stand playing.

The right thing. Delta wasn't used to doing what was right. More often than not, when she had the choice, she chose the best thing—which usually wasn't the right thing. But this time was different. This time, they were talking about the dreams, the career, of a man who didn't want to be anything else but a cop. She knew that by the way he polished his badge in the car when he wasn't driving. She knew it by how well he fired a gun. And she recognized it when she saw the pride on his face whenever he got behind the wheel. Tony Carducci may be a lot of things that Delta didn't care for, but deep inside, the guy was a card-carrying cop. He simply needed someone to give him the chance to show it.

"I don't want a new partner." Delta stated firmly.

"What?" The captain asked incredulously. "You're joking."

"Look, Captain, I, more than anyone, know that Carducci has a lot to learn. But who doesn't? No one comes out of the academy a perfect cop. No one ever becomes a perfect cop. We all have a few wrinkles that need to be ironed out, that's all."

"Not like this one." Scratching his head, Captain Henry looked at Delta a long time before sighing. The sigh seemed to let his stomach out and it rested securely against his belt buckle. "What's with you, Delta? You don't even like Carducci. I would have thought you'd be glad to be rid of him."

Liking or not liking Tony hadn't occurred to Delta. He was her partner. Period. There were unwritten, unspoken codes of honor cops adhered to among themselves. For better or worse, and all that jazz, really meant something on the streets. Miles had shown her that good cops were secure with their partner's strengths and willing to work out the weaknesses. No one was perfect—not Miles, not her, not Carducci.

For better or worse.

"You busted me to TP, sir, because you believed I could make a good cop out of him. And now, even before I get a chance to do so, you want to dump him like he was carrying the plague. Well, pardon me for saying it: you might give up that easily, but I don't, and I just want it to go on the record that I think you're making a mistake by letting him go. Carducci has so much untapped potential and I think I'm just the one who can tap into it." Delta knew that, under normal circumstances, the captain would throw her out on her ear. But this wasn't one of those times. Because of the department's fondness for good press, she was holding all of the aces. He had to play out this hand.

Shaking his head, Henry opened the file on his desk and pretended to study the contents of the first page before refocusing on Delta's face. "You are an enigma to me, Stevens—as unpredictable as they come. I expected you to dance a good old Irish jig when I cut him loose. Instead, I get the fight of my life."

"When I came to this department, sir, I learned a great deal about partner loyalty. I don't know whether or not Carducci's 'handicap' can be resolved, but I'd like the chance to try. Don't take the bat out of my hands before I get to the plate."

Captain Henry grinned. "Somehow, I'm sure you'd manage to get a hit anyway." Rubbing his chin and returning his gaze to the file, Henry finally shook his head. "The chief won't hear of it, and frankly, neither will IA. The chief won't have this department looking stupid because we keep one of our finest on Training Patrol."

"Then don't."

A silence hung in the air as the captain deciphered Delta's cryptic words.

"Turn the tables in our favor. Tell the press that you've decided to keep me on TP so that I can teach other cops to do what I do. They'll eat it up. You want good press? That's the way to do it." Crack came the sound of the metamorphic bat.

A sudden glimmer came to Captain Henry's eyes. "Now, that's an interesting twist."

Delta leaned across the desk and rounded third. "Captain, don't base your decision on publicity or politics alone. We're talking about a man's career here. I'm willing to take a chance on him, to try to work with him. Why don't you give him the same courtesy." Delta paused a moment. "Do me this favor."

Locking eyes with Delta for a second more, Captain Henry then turned away and stared out the window. "I'm not one for politics, Delta. I'm just a cop who wants this department to be the best it can be. If it were up to me, I'd go with you on this one. As it is, I'll have to talk to the chief and see what he says. I can't make you any promises, but I'll see what I can do."

"So, can I keep Carducci in the meantime?"

Captain Henry pulled his moustache and shook his head slowly. "For the life of me, Delta Stevens, I'll never understand why. But yes, you keep him until I have a chance to run it by Walker. But please, keep him out of trouble until then."

Delta suppressed a grin. "Thank you, sir." Grabbing the knob on the door, Delta turned and let a little bit of the grin creep out. "You won't regret it."

"I already do."

"Really?"

Captain Henry shook his head and smiled. "In my days, Stevens, a man was willing to give his life for his partner. I just hope to hell that doesn't happen to you."

"Me, either. Carducci's a good cop, sir. You'll see."

"I hope so. Oh, and Stevens? I'm going to give you some leeway on your attitude here, and chalk it up to that wicked looking bump on your head. But if you ever talk like that to me again, I'll bounce you outta here so fast, it'll make your head spin. You read me?"

"Loud and clear." Swinging the door open, Delta let the rest of the grin spread across her face.

She had won. Just what, she wasn't quite sure.

35

Closing the door behind her, Delta felt victorious. It was one of the many meetings in a captain's office where she felt she had taken the initiative by the balls and squeezed a victory from it. She had stepped up to the plate and smashed a grand slam, and it felt good trotting home.

Glancing over at Carducci, he looked like someone had trotted over him. Sitting alone in the muster room, his head hanging down, Tony was a beaten man. He knew his career, his dream, was on the chopping block and that Delta held the cleaver. What he didn't know was that she had chosen not to use it.

"Hey there," she said, taking the seat next to him. "You're looking mighty glum."

"You don't have to beat around the bush for me, Delta. I know what's coming down. I may look it, but I'm not stupid."

Delta studied his rugged features. On the outside existed this manly man who appeared to be more full of himself than a teenage movie star. He was arrogant, mouthy, conceited, and obnoxious, a man who knew he was good looking and charming and who used those strengths to gain entry into women's hearts. Yet, inside, Delta knew he was just a little boy—a boy who wanted to be a policeman more than anything in the world. That boy was sitting before her now, expecting to be told that his dream was over.

Delta remembered that feeling well.

In the days following her elimination of the man who had been sent to murder her, Delta carried this exact posture as she waited for the noose to squeeze one last time around her own neck. It had been the worst feeling, the scariest feeling in the world, waiting and wondering if someone was going to take her dream away. And many, many people stepped forward on her behalf during the long Internal Affairs investigation into the shooting—people like her CHP pal, Bear, and other cops, who came to her rescue when she needed them most. They had spoken highly of Delta's competence, of her character, of her ability to get the job done. They had stuck by her then because that was the spirit of law enforcement: you were in it together, or you were sunk.

She had not sunk. And she wasn't about to let Tony sink, either.

Even if he did screw up, he deserved the same consideration her colleagues had given her. Directional capabilities or no, Delta was resigned not to turn her back on him. Miles hadn't when she messed up. Miles had told her that the spirit of the law was always more important than the letter of the law. The letter of the law was reserved for jerks on the street, people who asked for firmer justice. But the spirit of the law, that was something altogether different.

It was in that spirit that she sat before Tony now. "You scared?"

Not looking up, Tony nodded. "I blew it. Now, I have to pay. It sucks, but that's how it is."

"Is it?"

Looking at Delta out of the corner of his eye, Tony nodded. "I fucked up, Delta. I'm sorry. I'm just glad you and the kids are okay."

Laying her hand on his beefy shoulder, Delta held his gaze. "Look, you made a mistake. Yes, it could have been a costly one, but it wasn't. Carducci, you've just learned what the public still doesn't get. We play those odds every night we go out there. We make life and death decisions in the same fraction of a moment it takes someone to flip television channels. And sometimes, we make the wrong choices. Sometimes the cost of those choices is priceless, sometimes it isn't. I've killed a man, Carducci. In cold blood. I raised my gun and I blew him away. It took me less time than it takes to change the channel for me to decide what to do. I've live with that decision every since. Do I regret it? No. I regret that it came to that, but I don't regret the action. That's what you need to do. Regret that you made an error, but don't regret that you tried to help me out."

Tony straighted up a little and turned to fully face her. "How can you be so understanding, Delta? The guys are right. I nearly got you killed."

"Right. You forced me into that house. You made me stay in there when I felt like I was melting. Carducci, I made choices that placed me in that position. You didn't have anything to do with that. It just wasn't my time to go yet, that's all. And when it is, there will be nothing you or anyone else can do about it."

Tony cast his eyes down at the floor. "Too bad the others don't see things through your eyes."

"The others aren't you partner."

Tony glanced back up at her. "Yeah, well, not for long. There's nothing I can do to change what happended that night."

"You're right. There's nothing you can do. Fortunately, there is something I can do and I've done it. I've got a job to do. You coming or not?"

"What?" Tony's eyes flashed a tiny bit of hope at her.

"You still don't get it, do you?" Grinning, Delta rose and patted his shoulder. "If I teach you nothing else, Carducci, let me make sure this one thing gets through to you: above all else, *never* burn your partner. Never turn your back on him when he's down, never point the finger at him, and never, ever, throw him an anchor when the brass is on his ass. You got that?"

Suddenly, a look of enlightenment dawned on Tony's face. Jumping to his feet, he threw his arms around Delta and hugged her. "You mean, I still have a job?"

Pushing him away, Delta nodded. "On one condition."

"Anything."

"You knock off the macho-man horseshit when we're on duty. I don't care how you act when we're not working, but from now on, be real with me and not a one-dimensional caricature of what you think cops are about. I want to see the person Tony Carducci is, not the man. You can be a cop and a human being at the same time. I want to see that happen."

Tony nodded vigorously. "I can do that."

"Good. Now, the only other thing we have to worry about is working on teaching you north from south."

Tony nodded. The shimmer in his eyes made Delta smile. "Can I ask you one question first?"

"Depends."

"He was gonna can me, huh?"

Delta shrugged. "I don't really know. It's over now, and time to move on."

"You could have thrown me an anchor, Delta, and everyone in the city would have understood. Why didn't you?"

"You said one question."

"It's the last one, I swear."

Opening the muster door to a very quiet front office, Delta waited for Tony to join her. "I've seen that fire burning in your eyes Carducci. You want to be a cop so bad, you can't see anything else. Don't think I would have gone out on a limb for you if I hadn't seen how desperately you want that badge. I know what that feels like. Something tells me you're worth the chance."

"Am I that big a risk?"

Delta smiled. "No more questions."

Tony stopped and looked deep into Delta's eyes. It was a moment between partners that only other cops understood. It was a look that said they were, in fact, in this together.

"I owe you, Delta."

"The only thing you owe me is the assurance that down the road, when I need you most, you'll be there with your gun blazing and your courage sitting on top of your badge. Give me that, and I'll call us even."

Tony smiled. "You got it. Anything else?"

Delta grinned and started out the door. "Yeah. Leave the aftershave for your dates. It gives me a headache.

36

A voice came over the air announcing that Megan's flight was ready to start boarding elderly, disabled, and children flying alone first. Inhaling slowly, Delta steadied herself. She had promised herself that she wouldn't cry. She didn't want to send Megan off on a sad note, after all, this was an exciting time in Megan's life and Delta wanted to be excited with her.

Still, she could feel the tears push their way past her resolve and touch the edge of her eyes.

"I don't want to cry," Delta said softly, holding Megan's hand. "But I can't seem to help it."

Taking Delta's hands in hers, Megan held it tightly. "There's nothing wrong with crying, my love."

"I want to be happy and excited for you." Delta felt like the incredible shrinking woman. Wherever her usual strength was, it was long gone.

"Honey, this isn't goodbye. It's more like 'see you in a bit.'"

"It sure feels like goodbye." Delta hated herself for acting so wimpy but she couldn't seem to muster up the courage to let go. "If you don't come back, I'm coming after you. I swear to God, Megan, if you even think of leaving me, I'll be down there faster than you can shake a stick."

"Shh. I'm not leaving you, Delta."

The voice came on again and announced that the back rows of the plane were boarding. Every muscle in Delta's body stiffened. "Ten weeks. Ten weeks and you'll come home to me." It wasn't a question.

"Hopefully, with my head screwed on right. Trust me in this, Sweetheart. I know what I'm doing."

"And your internship is all arranged. I mean, you're not going down there without a plan."

Megan smiled patronizingly. "Yes, dear, everything has been arranged. I have a counselor at the university there who is meeting me at the airport. When I get all settled in, the first thing I'm going to do is call you."

"You're sure they have phones?"

This made Megan laugh. "Honey, they're not barbarians."

"But they are third world!"

Megan shook her head as she lifted Delta's hand to kiss it. "Only to us. They're a lot like Mexico. They have cars, phones, buses, even stores!"

Delta bowed her head. It would be different if Megan had chosen New York or London or Paris. Delta knew what those places were like. But Costa Rica? Megan might as well be flying to the moon.

"Delta Stevens, you'll be so busy righting the wrongs of the world you're not going to have time to miss me."

"Don't bet on it." Delta looked up into those blue eyes that loved her so much and forced a smile. "The one thing I'll look forward to at the end of a shift will be marking the calendar that another day has passed."

The announcement that the next rows of passengers should board crackled over the intercom.

"Well, I guess this is it." Standing up, Delta bit her lower lip to keep it from trembling. "Write when you have time."

Wrapping her long arms around Delta, Megan embraced her for a long time. "I'll call you as soon as I'm settled. I promise."

Pulling away, Delta impatiently wiped away the tear that escaped her eye. "I love you, Meg. You know that, don't you?"

Tracing Delta's face with her fingertips, Megan nodded. "Yes, I do. And don't you forget that. You keep loving me through this, Delta Stevens. You've faced worse situations and never lost faith. Don't you dare lose faith in me."

Delta shook her head. The next tears rolled down her cheeks and this time, she didn't bother trying to wipe them away. "I won't. I promise."

The intercom crackled again. It was time for the remaining passengers to board.

"I better get going."

The bustle, the noise, and the excitement silenced as they looked into each other's eyes. Thousands of miles would soon separate them; Delta could only hope the distance wouldn't create a void too big to cross. She knew she couldn't hold Megan back, but she wanted to. She wanted to cry out that Megan couldn't go. Stay here! Stay here and fight through this with me! But she knew it was useless. Megan needed to go as much as Delta needed to be on the streets.

"I love you so much," Delta said, taking Megan in her arms. "Please come back to me."

Hugging Delta back, Megan lightly kissed her cheek. "There isn't a question that I'm coming back to you. Delta, you and your love pulled me out of a very deep, very dark valley. I can't imagine loving someone else as much as I love you. And when I come home, I'll come back knowing who Megan Osbourne really is now. And no matter who that is, she'll love you to the depths of her soul."

"And you'll give me an answer about the union?"

Megan looked around the airport before kissing Delta on the lips. "The moment I step off the plane."

The final boarding call boomed over the intercom.

Megan bent over, picked up her carryon luggage and gave Delta a look that said 'here goes.'"

"Meg—"

"Shh. Delta Stevens, you've never doubted yourself before. Don't start now. You are and always will be the love of my life. Stay safe for me."

"I will. I swear."

"You'd better, because I want someone to come home to."

"I'll be here with bells on. Nothing else. Just bells."

Megan smiled warmly. "God, I love you." Embracing Delta one last time, Megan kissed her neck before pulling back. "No matter where I go, my love, I'll carry your love with me."

"I love you, Megan. Be careful."

"You, too." Blowing Delta a kiss, Megan started down the runway. Just before she turned the corner, she stopped, turned back toward Delta and waved. "Stay true to me, Delta Stevens."

Delta waved back and tried to keep the remaining tears from breaking the flood gates as she watched Megan disappear around the corner. A part of her waited to see if Megan might change her mind at the last minute, but a bigger part of her knew better. Megan was gone.

Walking over to the window and watching the planes taxi in and out, Delta's heart felt like someone had just taken out a Grand Canyon-sized chunk. She never realized how painful it would be to watch Megan leave, and she shuddered to think how painful it would feel if Megan ever left for good.

37

Leaning into the passenger seat, Delta toyed with the new clip-on radios they'd been assigned after muster. "At last, our department enters the twenty-first century."

Tony acted like he didn't hear. "You hear that the feds are closing in on the guys that burned you?"

Delta nodded as she folded her long legs into the car. "Yeah, but did you hear how they were able to get so close?"

"Nope. I just know what I heard from the guys."

Delta grinned. "Do you remember when Connie and you went into the hotel and dusted for prints?"

"Yeah."

"Do you remember Connie picking up a notepad?"

Tony thought for a moment before shaking his head. "I don't remember."

"Well, she did, and we sent it to the lab to get the notes from the previous pages lifted from it."

"I remember you mentioning it at Connie's house, but I had forgotten all about it. Were we able to pick something up?"

Delta grinned. "Were we ever. We came up with an address, a date, and a flight number."

"They're booking out of here, huh?"

"Tonight."

"Tonight? Are the feds gonna be able to stop them?"

"I hope so."

Tony turned on her. "What do you mean, 'hope?' Why don't we go after them ourselves?"

Sighing heavily, Delta stared out her window. "Because we would all lose our jobs if anyone found out how deeply we've been in this case. Do you have any idea how much information we've withheld from the Federal Bureau of Investigation? You wouldn't have to worry about saving your job, Carducci. It would be unsalvagable." Delta looked back at Tony. "While they've been waiting out the big gun, we've run circles around them. Don't think they wouldn't have our heads on paper plates if they suspected we've been holding out on them."

"So why not just give them the rest of the information and let them handle it?"

His naivete was disarming. "Carducci, let me spell this out for you in plain English. We've broken the law. We have withheld information pertinent to the investigation, we have obstructed justice, and worse yet, we've killed two suspects in the case. It wouldn't be wise for us to run to them showing them all of the evidence we have. Not if we value our freedom."

Tony whistled. "I hadn't even thought of that."

"I know. Which is why I'm telling you. What happened that night in the desert and the night the house was set on fire can never leak out. Only you, me, Sal's bunch, and Connie know the truth about those two nights and the events leading up to them. It's got to stay that way forever. You understand me?"

Tony nodded, a look of fear glazing over his eyes.

"Don't be scared, Carducci. If worse comes to worse, it's the perps' word against ours. Nothing need ever be revealed."

"What's the use of breaking the rules if we can't keep something awful from happening? They're still going to get away. "

Delta stared out the window a moment before returning her gaze to Tony. "Not exactly."

"You mean we *are* going after them?"

Delta nodded. "Not just us. The feds and everybody else are going to be on this one."

"But how? I thought you said—"

"Connie is a genius. Nothing gets by her. When we finally got the pad back from our pals at the lab, we knew we had to get the information to the feds and we had to force them to act on it."

"So what did you do?"

Delta's heart raced at the thought. This was one plan that had really come together. "When the press was getting all excited about me saving those kids, someone said something about the power of the press. That's when we realized that we could use that power to our advantage. Connie concocted a note, supposedly from one of the perps, saying that he wanted out but didn't know how to get immunity. Then she wrote that if the feds couldn't get him out before they got to the airport, he would go to the press and see if they couldn't help with the immunity."

Tony whistled again. "She forged this note and sent it to the FBI? And I thought I had balls of steel."

Delta grinned. "In the note, she wrote the address of their new hideout and the time they would be leaving. Both of which the lab was able to lift from the notepad in the hotel."

"Incredible. I'm totally impressed."

Delta nodded. "You should be. There's nobody better than Consuela Rivera. Anyway, tonight, the feds will have the house surrounded. With any luck, they'll bag a few bad guys and be able to save face."

"Is saving face that important?"

"In our government? It's everything. That's why it's so important for us to help them be successful. If they win, we win."

"And if they lose?"

"You don't want to know. More than likely, they'll be looking for a scapegoat. And...well, there is someone we all know and love who would make the perfect mark."

Tony stared out the window, but said nothing. Delta knew what was at stake, and there was no minimizing the importance of allowing the feds to make the bust. If she upstaged them again, she might as well just turn in her badge."

"When's this all going down?" Tony asked.

Delta looked at her watch. "Oh, in about half-an-hour."

Tony came out of his seat. "Half-an-hour? Are you kidding?"

"Relax, Carducci. Our only purpose tonight will be to act as perimeter."

"You mean we're really not going to do anything?"

Delta patted his arm. "Nope, I'm afraid we're going to have to watch this one from the sidelines. Let's see how the big boys do it."

Suddenly, the radio crackled and sputtered their number before Delta could respond to anymore questions.

"S1012, this is C1919, over."

C1919 was Captain Henry. Delta and Tony exchanged knowing looks. If the captain was on the street, it could only mean one thing: the feds were getting ready to make their move. Picking up the mike, Delta grabbed her Cross pen with her left hand. "This is S1012, over."

"S1012, we have a 10-96 and will need to establish a perimeter extending from Hemingway and Thirty-third to Longfellow and Nineteenth. Be advised that you and all other responding units are to maintain the perimeter. Do not, I repeat, do not enter the red zone unless advised to do so."

"S1012, copy." Delta glanced over at Tony, whose expression had changed. "A 10-96 is an undercover surveillance. Looks like the show's about to start."

The radio came to life again and Delta knew by the amount of radio activity that the raid on the porno perps was getting ready to go down.

"All units involved in maintaining perimeter—we are assisting in the capture of possible 1-87 suspects. Again, do not enter the red zone unless directed to do so. Suspects are armed and very dangerous. Leave this station clear for this traffic only. All other radio communication should be on channel one-four."

Delta mentally surveyed the stretch of area they were to maintain. "They've given us the direct route to the freeway access," she explained as Tony maneuvered the patrol car through a U-turn. "If they get by us, we're screwed."

"Then let's not let them get past us."

Delta nodded. "Agreed."

"You think the feds know what they're doing?"

"Hard to say. They're calling the shots. It's our job to keep the balls on the felt." Picking up the mike, Delta asked Henry to switch channels.

"What is it, Stevens?" came the captain's taut and impatient voice.

"I just wanted to know what street they believe the suspects to be on, sir."

"Didn't you hear my orders? You're not to go near there. You've been given a post and I expect you to man that post until called off. Do you understand?"

"I understand all of that, Captain," she replied with equal impatience. "It's just that if they're on Pope or Keats streets, those houses have—"

"Stevens, I believe we have everything covered."

"Yes, sir. S1012 out." Turning the channel back to one-nine, Delta exhaled loudly. "I hope they know what they're doing."

Tony looked over at Delta. "What do you mean?"

Delta pointed to a cluster of houses sitting on Keats. "That's a weird area over there. Those houses were built by some architect who tried something original. The houses are set one in front, one in back, with two driveways exiting on two different streets. McAvoy's been on that beat for two months now, and is having a hell of a time getting to calls on time. It's a very confusing stretch of houses. You can't tell the front from the back. No doubt, our perps picked it for that reason."

"Just like they picked the Super Seven?"

"Exactly. These guys haven't been caught because they think about things like escape routes."

"What makes this street a good escape route?"

"There are a group of houses on Keats whose houses have the same front and back. They have a garage door at both ends of the garage and a front door on either side of the house. Even the lighting is done so you can't tell the front from the back. The builders thought it was a great idea because of the nature of one way streets. This way, they can drive out either way without having to make U-turns around islands that are half a mile out of their way. Unless they've got both sides of every garage covered, our bad boys could come screaming out of one."

"I thought you got the address."

Delta shrugged. "We got two of the three numbers. The feds are going to have to cover the entire street. That's why they're using us as the perimeter."

"Sounds like some developer in the sixties was on acid when he thought it up."

Delta grinned. "True story. Anyway, I'm sure none of this is news to anybody. I just wanted to see if the captain would give me any specifics."

"So now what?"

Delta shrugged. "Now we maintain the perimeter like we were told to do."

Tony slowed the car. "Man, that sucks."

Delta grinned. A small part of her was glad she had saved him from meter maid school. He was itching to be a part of a forbidden bust, and this made her like him.

"Yeah, it does, but you and I are on a short leash, my compassless friend. If we get out of line this time and something big goes down, we're history."

"That's never stopped you before."

Delta turned fully toward Tony. "Are you trying to get fired? I mean, you heard the captain. Didn't that mean anything to you?"

Tony shrugged. "I just don't believe that you're okay with sitting on the sidelines during this one. Come on, Delta, they almost burned you and those kids alive, and you're willing to play waterboy to the fed's quarterback?"

Delta shrugged. Tony was looking better all the time. "We're not the least bit sidelined, Carducci. As a matter-of-fact, we're right in the thick of it."

"How? We're way out here in the boonies."

Staring across an open field directly behind Keats Street, Delta studied the layout of a beat she was all-too familiar with. "If they're on Keats, they'll take the back side of the driveway out and cross here." Pointing to the field, Delta watched Tony stare hard at the direction her finger was pointing.

"Why here?"

A frown suddenly appeared on Delta's face.

"What is it?"

"I don't know." Delta closed her eyes and listened to herself think for a moment. "It's too pat—too easy. These guys aren't going to be brought down that easily. So far, their plans have been professional and elaborate. There's something missing. There's something we've missed." Staring out over the field, Delta traced over every possible escape route open to the suspects. Something was up; with the perimeter, the houses, the feds, something was wrong and Delta couldn't put her finger on it. What she did know was that these guys weren't simply going to hand themselves over. No, they had something going for them and she hoped the feds knew what it was.

"These guys are going to jail for the rest of their lives," Delta offered. "If they know the feds are on to them, then they've got an awful lot of shit riding on their shoulders."

"You don't think we have the advantage of a surprise attack?"

"Hell no. After reading in the newspapers that a cop saved the kids, after realizing that their pals Dice and Martinez were never coming back, they have to know how close we are. And that's what bothers me about this whole thing. They know we're right behind them, so...."

Tony nodded. "They've either gotten sloppy—"

"Or the feds have done the one thing a cop should never do."

"Try to outguess the suspect?"

Delta shook her head. "Nope. Underestimated them. Our bad boys have a card up their sleeve, Carducci. I can feel it."

"You really think so?"

"Yep. And let's hope the feds know which card it is."

Delta and Tony continued to cruise the established perimeter for the next two hours, waiting for even the tiniest signal that would alert them to trouble. At the two-hour mark, Delta looked at her watch and sighed.

"Maybe it won't go down tonight," Tony offered.

Delta shook her head. "It has to. They've pulled too many cops off their regular beats for this. No, tonight is definitely the night."

Tony turned the patrol car up a street paralleling Hemingway. As he turned, Delta's beeper went off.

"What the hell was that?"

"My pager. Pull over to that phone booth over there."

As the car sided up to the curb, Delta hopped out and quickly phoned Connie.

"What's up?"

"Del, remember my friend on the force in the reservation?"

"Yeah. Why?"

"I just received a fax from him. There's a possibility your suspects have a little girl with them."

Immediately, a hot flash waved over Delta. There could be no doubt about it, this was the suspects' ace. Nodding, Delta pulled her notepad and pen from her pocket. "I'm listening."

"My buddy said she was taken more than two weeks ago and he said he's positive it was our guys who got her."

"She isn't one of the kids I pulled from the house?"

"Nope. This girl is still at large, but she was snatched the same way. It makes sense that they keep one alive."

"For a hostage."

"That and the fact that they're still in the process of filming."

Delta remembered back to the motel. Hadn't Rubin mentioned something about finishing up their next project? "You think she's with them now?"

"Without a doubt. She's their ticket to freedom. If we back them into a corner...well, they've already proven that killing kids isn't a problem for them."

"Do you think the feds know?"

"I spoke with Agent Garvey a few minutes ago to feel his position out. The feds think they've got them on the run."

"So, they're not aware of the possibility of a hostage?"

"I don't think so. If they were, they'd have a top negotiator out here."

Delta thought back to the commendation Captain Henry had received for talking down a hostage-taker. "Are there any SWAT members assigned to this?" Delta waited while Connie did whatever she was doing with Eddie.

"Not that I can tell."

"The captain's out here. You think he's their negotiator?"

"Could be. I think you should advise him of the situation. I know we'll have a great deal to answer for later on, but a child's life, Del—"

"Is worth it. I'll see what I can do. Keep your ear to the radio, Chief. And, thanks."

"Be careful, Storm."

"Will do."

Returning to the car, Delta filled Tony in on her conversation with Connie.

When she was finished, Tony pulled the car back onto the street. "So, you gonna tell the feds?"

Delta nodded. She didn't see that she had any other choice. If the feds knew and weren't telling anyone, they were risking a child's life. If they didn't know, they needed to so they could modify their plan of attack. "A hostage sets up a completely different set of strategies, Carducci. The way I see this, the feds don't know. If they did, the SWAT guys would be crawling all over the place." Putting the mike to her lips, Delta quietly said into the still radio, "This is S1012, be advised there's a possible 2-0-7 involved and we have a potential hostage situation." Delta waited for the captain's voice to come booming over. She didn't have to wait long.

"S1012, this is your captain," he said very loudly. "Go to one-eight immediately."

Flipping the dial, Delta waited for Captain Henry to bark at her some more.

"What in the blazes are you talking about, Stevens?"

"Captain, I've just received word that they may still have one of the kids with them. They might have the little girl with them to use as a shield."

"Where did you get this information, Stevens? According to Detective LaFrenz, there's no indication that there's a child in that house."

"I just spoke with one of the reservation cops, sir, and he believes the girl is still with them." Delta waited for a response.

"Stevens, why is it you seem to have information no one else is privy to?"

"It just makes sense, sir. They still need a kid to finish their current filming. Also, as a hostage negotiator, you, yourself must know that a hostage situation paints a completely different picture. I'd bet a month's salary she's in there and they're going to use her as a shield until they can get to LAX."

"Hold on."

Delta waited what felt like hours. When he finally came back on air, his tone was decidedly calmer. "I don't know who your source is, Stevens, but Agent LaFrenz assured me that there is no child in that house. You saved all the kids we have on file."

"Files are often incomplete, Captain. What if I'm right?"

"Then some agent's head in the Bureau is going to roll. Over and out."

"Captain?"

"What now?"

Delta could hear him sighing loudly. "For the record, I'm not wrong."

"Let's hope you are, Stevens. Out."

Delta glanced over at Tony and shrugged. Captain Henry would never understand women's intuition anymore than he'd understand her gut's innate ability to "know" things. It was this knowing that made her feel Elson's disturbing presence whenever he was near. It was this uncanny knowing that gave her the edge over a man sent to murder her in that warehouse. And it was this knowing which Delta felt earlier, a trickle of adrenaline, a twitch of doubt that made her *know* why the suspects appeared cornered, but weren't. With a hostage, it was the suspects who called all the shots. All of them. The feds hadn't done their homework properly in the first place and this was where it had gotten them.

"Now what?" Tony asked.

Delta shrugged. "Now we do just what the captain said. We hope."

"But the captain—"

"Has to play by their rules. This is the feds's game and he knows it. He's not even back-up quarterback on this one."

Tony shook his head. "I'm think I'm beginning to get it."

Delta turned to him. "Get what?"

"Why you break the rules. Sitting around waiting for some idiot to get done scratching his butt while he thinks about what to do is making me crazy."

Delta couldn't help but smile. "That's slightly oversimplified, but you're pretty close. We're just going to have to sit back and see how this one turns out."

"So that's it? We're really going to just sit here?"

Delta shrugged and stared out the window. "I'm afraid so. We sit and wait and hope no one blows a hole through an innocent little girl."

"I'd rather have a root canal without novocaine."

Delta nodded and felt her stomach come to life. "Me, too."

38

It took less than half-an-hour for the radio to jump to life after Delta had spoken to the captain.

"This is C1919." It was Captain Henry. "All units be advised we have a hostage situation. I repeat, we have a hostage situation. Allow the white van access to the freeway and any other on-ramps. There are no plates on the van, but it does have a peace sign in the back right window. I repeat—all perimeter units are to allow van freeway access. Do not attempt to stop the unit. Do not attempt to follow."

Delta turned to Tony and smiled. "He believed me."

"That means a lot to you, doesn't it?"

"No. What's important is saving that little girl's life. "

"And you think we can do that?"

Delta slowly turned toward Tony. "I think we have to."

"Which means we're in?"

Delta shook her head as a slight grin curled on her lips. "I've either taught you really well, or I've failed miserably. I can't decide which."

"You taught me to get the job done. We've got a kid's life in our hands and someone is telling us to let her be taken by people we know will kill her the moment they get to their destination."

"So just what is it you think we should do, Carducci?" Delta suppressed a grin. He really had learned something from her after all.

"Well, escorting these shitbags to the airport isn't an option. I'm not stupid, Delta. I know that if push comes to shove, you'll shove right back. Don't do anything differently because you have a rookie for a partner. Do what you would normally do."

A short grin appeared on his face. She had done a lot of questionable things in her career, but saving Tony Carducci's career wasn't one of them. "No, Carducci, you're not stupid, but you just might be as crazy as I am."

Tony's grin matched Delta's. "Then tell me, Oh, Legend, what's up that sleeve of yours."

"You sure you're willing to risk it? We blow it and your career is history."

Tony shrugged. "Maybe, but I'd have some great stories to tell my grandkids."

Tony Carducci had come a long way. And whether they made it out of this one without being demoted, or worse, she knew that she had taught him one very important lesson: do what was best.

"First, we have to cover our asses." Turning the radio back to channel one-eight, Delta then pulled the shotgun from its nest. "When the captain wants to know why we disobeyed his directive, we'll say we forgot to turn the radio back to open air after we talked to him."

Tony's eyes twinkled. "God, you're good."

"It's not great, but it'll have to do. Now, my guess is that they'll come busting out of the south driveway and onto the field as they make their way to the freeway. They've got to be heading for the airport, and it's possible they've already asked for a plane or a chopper."

"If they get to the airport—"

"She's dead. They'll believe they're close to freedom and view her as additional baggage. It happens all the time in hostage situations."

"Then why are they allowing them access to the airport?"

Delta shrugged. "I haven't a clue."

"Then we're on our own."

"Exactly." Delta lightly touched Tony's arm. "It's not too late to back out."

Tony smiled broadly. "Not a chance. I didn't become a cop to watch crimes. I became a cop to prevent them.

I'm willing if you are. It's time, Teacher, to show me what it's really like out here on a beat with you. Put your chalk down and show me why there are stories miles high about the Incredible Delta Stevens."

Pulling away from his riveting gaze, Delta shook her head. "You're insane."

"Yes, but so are you, so we're even. What's the plan?"

Before Delta could answer, a loud sound of something breaking reverberated through the night air, slicing the silence like a well-sharpened blade. Turning to see what it was, Delta saw a white van crash through wooden gates from one of the Keats Street houses, and screech down Stein Street.

"Go!"

Without hesitation, Tony pressed the gas pedal to the floor and the squad car screamed after them.

"Left on Tennyson, right on Poe, and that will cut them off before they get to the freeway!" Delta yelled, reaching to turn both their portable radios to channel one-eight.

"Then what?"

Good question, Delta thought. She hadn't time to formulate a plan. "Ram them if you have to."

"But—"

"I know—'never use a vehicle as a barricade.' Forget the academy shit! This is real life! Ever play chicken as a kid?"

Burning rubber as he maneuvered his first turn, Tony nodded. "All the time."

"Ever lose?"

"Nope."

"Ever chickened out?"

"Nope."

"Can you win one more time?"

Tony grinned stiffly. "You bet your ass."

"Then go down one more street, take the turn, pick up speed, and head right at them. Just don't get us killed!"

Nodding, Tony tightened his grip on the wheel. As he took the turns, leaving more tire on the pavement, Delta wondered if she was doing the right thing. After all, he was just a rookie. Suppose he did chicken out? Or worse yet, panic, and kill them all? What if...

Glancing over at Tony one last time before the headlights of the van would be glaring into their eyes, Delta thought about Miles. He had taken more than his fair share of chances with her when they were first partnered. Maybe all rookies needed someone to believe in them before they could believe in themselves. Maybe that's what being an FTO was all about—showing Carducci that she believed in him. And right now, she knew she had no choice but to have faith in Tony Carducci, because barreling toward them at a pace much faster than Delta would have imagined, were two very bright headlights.

Reaching her right hand through the open window, Delta turned her spotlight on and aimed it at the windshield of the oncoming van. It did not slow down, nor did it veer from its deadly path. It was perfectly clear; if they were going to go, they were going to take anyone who got in the way with them.

Closer and closer the speeding vehicle came, like a bullet from a gun with only one course in mind: straight through them.

"Stay with it, Carducci!" she yelled as the van closed the distance rapidly. Grabbing the dash, Delta held her breath and waited for the impact that would probably kill them all.

As the headlights bore down upon them like the fire of a dragon, Delta tensed, waiting for the collision. Had she gambled everything this time only to lose it all? Had she misplaced her faith and cost them their lives? Looking into the headlights coming straight at them, Delta didn't even have time to pray.

But then, as Tony clenched the wheel even tighter, the van abruptly cut away, missing the front of the squad car by less than two feet.

Delta turned her head in time to see it collide with a parked car before careening into the only light post on the block.

Two feet. Two feet more and they would have been pasted to the back of the screen of the car like flies on a flyswatter. Two measly feet.

In the most expert fashion, like a teenager accustomed to spinning doughnuts, Tony spun the patrol car 180 degrees and burned off the last of the tires' tread as he screeched to a halt behind the van. The front of the van was hugging the light pole and steam was hissing nastily from the broken radiator. Like a wounded animal, it chugged once more before stalling out. Dead.

Picking up the mike, Delta started to call in when the passenger side of the van opened and a man took off running through the dark field.

"Get him!" Delta ordered, pushing open her door. Tony jumped from the squad car and scooted around the back of it before taking off into the ebony field.

Staring at the van in front of her, Delta felt the cold, clammy hands of fear reach once again into the crevices of her soul. She had faced a van like this a lifetime ago. A different make, a different circumstance, a different lifetime, but the memory was still there, haunting and tormenting her with the remembrance of a time when the occupants of that van snuffed out the life of the best man she had ever known.

And now, as she faced similar double doors with reflector sheets in the window and a peace sign on the right side, Delta again felt the icy tentacle of fear's hand as it reached into her heart and ripped open the scars formed long ago.

As if it happened yesterday, she remembered the doors bursting open, she remembered the shiny gleam of the murderous shotgun barrel as it swung toward them, and she remembered, all too painfully, the body of her partner being thrown into the air before slamming violently to the ground.

Yes, she remembered. She also remembered feeling like a failure for not being able to prevent his death. It was the same burden she had carried after Helen died. The feeling that if she had only reacted quickly enough, she could have saved them both.

Reaching for the shotgun, Delta wondered if the albatross hanging heavily around her neck would kill her or set her free tonight.

"All right, you son of a bitch," Delta muttered, as she pulled the shotgun loose and leaned it against her seat. It was an act born out of a desperate fear of repeating the past. It was also an act she had to resist. Remembering there might be a little girl in the van, Delta pushed the shotgun back into place. To protect the girl from stray shots, Delta would have to use her revolver. Pulling her sidearm from her holster as one leg reached the pavement, Delta felt a twinge of fear. She'd been here before, and failed. This time, she swore as both feet hit the ground, she would not fail.

Stepping from the car, she squatted behind the open door and aimed her weapon through the side window at the van's back doors. As before, Delta heard her training sergeant's voice as he warned them why vans were the most dangerous vehicles to pull over.

"You can't see them, but they can see you," he'd said, demonstrating how vulnerable cops could be when approaching a van. Miles had been vulnerable when he was killed. Even with all of his training and experience, he had still been a victim.

Wrapping her hands tightly around her Magnum, Delta promised herself that she wasn't going to be anybody's victim. Not tonight. Not ever.

With her weapon positioned out the window and her body behind the door, she waited. Reaching for the car mike, Delta keyed it to stay open and did the same with the radio attached to the shoulder of her uniform.

Suddenly, without warning, the van's doors burst open.

Standing in the spotlight was the thin man. In front of him he held a little girl by her neck. In his right hand, he wielded a .44 Magnum which he pressed against her temple. The little girl's eyes were wide with terror. She did not struggle or move. Like a badge, she stayed pinned to his chest.

To their left stood Rubin. In his hands was a Colt .45 with a silencer. Both weapons looked huge and out of place, like the caterpillar and mushroom in *Alice in Wonderland*. Maybe it was because the child seemed too small. Maybe it was because the guns really were large. Either way, they had powerful weapons and one of them was pointed directly at her.

Delta shifted her gaze from Rubin to the thin man. Rubin had a thin line of blood running off his cracked forehead which dripped like a broken faucet onto his shoulder. When his eyes met hers, he actually grinned.

"Officer Stevens," Rubin said, through his maniacal grin. "So you did survive? We had wondered what had become of our compadres."

"Dead." Delta said curtly.

"I see. Odd that you should come back to haunt us like this."

Delta aimed her gun at Rubin.

"No, no, Officer. Move one hair and the kid's DOA, got it?"

"Got it." Delta replied, checking her aim. Lowering her voice to just above a whisper, she murmured into her shoulder radio. "Carducci, quietly come back to the car. Approach from the east side with your gun ready. No matter what you see, don't do anything until I tell you."

"Didn't those federal agents tell you to back off?" The thin man asked, waving his Magnum like a toy.

Delta didn't respond.

"I'm afraid you should have left well enough alone, Officer Stevens. You see, you might have been lucky in the desert, but I believe your luck just ran out. And since you've disabled our car, we're going to have to take yours. So, slowly step out from behind the door and toss your pea-shooter to the ground in front of you."

Swallowing hard, Delta whispered into the mike. "You take the one holding the girl. He's on my left. When you see me shrug my shoulders, take him out. Don't hesitate or I'm dead."

Slowly rising from her crouched position behind the door, Delta kept her eyes trained on Rubin. She knew the odds of surviving without her weapon were slim. If they were going to take her patrol car, they would most surely leave her bloody body behind.

"Come out from behind the door and toss your gun out in front of you. Make any sudden movements and the girl dies."

"You'll kill her anyway, Rubin," Delta said, slowly moving out from behind the door.

"Maybe, maybe not."

"Kill her and you're screwed."

"That's where you're wrong, Ms. Stevens. You're the one who's screwed. You've gotten in our way twice now, and I'm tired of you. It's time for this little game to end. Now throw your weapon on the ground."

Delta looked down at her .357. She remembered the lessons they learned in the academy about never surrendering their weapons. The Onion Field murders, where two cops gave up their weapons and one cop was shot and killed with his own weapon, was replayed in every academy. "Give up your gun and you give up the ghost," was a popular academy saying. Her sergeant, her FTO, her captain, Megan, Connie, Miles, and everyone else she knew was screaming in her head and in her heart not to give it up.

Her gut told her something different. She knew she had no choice. She had to trust that Carducci was lurking somewhere in the shadows awaiting the right time to strike, and she had to trust that she was doing the right thing by breaking the first—and most important—rule every cop ever learned.

If she insisted on keeping her weapon, they would probably kill the little girl. If she gave up her gun, they would most assuredly kill Delta. The choice was not an easy one, but the decision was already made. If only she could buy enough time, she might be able to maneuver around the odds that were very quickly stacking up against her. If only....

Kneeling down, Delta carefully slid her gun about ten feet from her with the barrel facing the van and the handle towards her. "Don't let me down, Carducci," Delta whispered, rising from the road and staring at the silencer Rubin was still waving madly about. Her heart was beating so loudly, it echoed in her head. Her top lip was wet with perspiration and her stomach felt as if it found a new home lodged in her throat. She had wagered more than she could afford to lose and now it was time to pay up.

"My partner has the keys," Delta explained, eyeing the gun held to the little girl's head. The hammer was cocked and his long, thin finger was coiled around the trigger. Glancing down at her .357, Delta wondered just how big a mistake she had made. Would she die on the street behind a van, just as Miles had? Would they now use her as the classic example of what happened when you disobeyed orders and gave up your gun? What would Connie say when they told her that Delta had voluntarily given up her weapon? Would she understand? Would she know what odds Delta had tried to play? And what would Megan say?

"I don't know how you managed to escape Dice and Martinez, but you won't get away from me," Rubin said, straightening his arm as if he wanted the barrel of his gun to actually touch Delta. Up in the van, they were actually about twenty-three feet away. To Delta, it seemed they were merely inches apart.

"Step out from behind the door, Officer Stevens. There's no more time to chat."

Delta moved out so that she was completely away from the door. Never in her life had she felt this vulnerable. No gun, no door, nothing between her and the grim specter of death.

"Let the girl go. Better yet, take me. You'll get much further with a cop as a hostage."

Rubin smiled widely. "Oh, you've proven to be much more trouble than you're worth." Rubin lowered the weapon slightly and glared hard at Delta. "I do so hate it when women let me down. Your ninth life over, Officer. It's time to meet your maker."

As though in slow motion, Delta shrugged as the barrel of the silencer swung deliberately toward her. As the silencer pointed right at her, she dove for her gun and heard a solitary shot resound through the air. Looking up as she wrapped her hands around the wooden grip of her gun, she saw a single bullet hole between the eyes of the thin man. As his lifeless body fell backwards, Delta lifted her gun inches from the ground, and took aim as Rubin shot at her. Stroking the trigger once, Delta fired one round through the top of his forehead, blowing most of the top of his skull off. As Rubin reeled backward, he dropped the .45. The only sound Delta heard after that was the clattering his gun made as it fell to the floor of the van.

Still gripping her weapon, Delta yelled for Tony. "Carducci!" Rolling from her stomach, she held the .357 toward the field, ready to shoot again. In an instant, Tony was at her side, gun drawn and smelling like it had just been fired.

"Check for more," Delta ordered, waving her Magnum at the van. Covering Tony as he finished checking the van, Delta leaned in and helped the little girl struggle to free herself from the grip of the dead man.

"No more," Tony reported, pushing his weapon back in his holster.

"What about the guy you chased?"

"He's cuffed to the jungle gym across the way." Tony leaned in and examined the bodies. "Both dead?"

Delta nodded as she stared in at the bodies. "Ninth life my ass, you slimy little fucker." Carefully putting her gun back in her holster, Delta hugged the little girl close to her. "You're going to be all right, sweetheart," Delta whispered, pushing her hair out of the little girl's face. The cherubic brown eyes that looked up into hers were not the same eyes that had haunted her all those nights. No, these eyes were alive—afraid, shocked, older, but alive. Delta hadn't been able to save Helen or Miles, but this time was different. This time, she had gambled it all and won. Her jackpot was the life of the little girl clinging to her neck.

God, it felt good to win.

"She okay?" Tony asked, lightly stroking the little girl's hair.

Delta shrugged. "Physically, maybe. The rest of her? Only time will tell."

After bundling the girl in a blanket and resting her in the back of the car, Delta joined Tony at the back of the van. "How are you doing?" she asked. Laying her hand on his shoulder, Delta gave it a light squeeze. She remembered the incredibly painful gouge in her soul the first time she was forced to kill another human being. She remembered the all-too-lucid acknowledgment of the powerful responsibility she held in her left hand. She now felt that black, dark spirit covering her like a blanket. No matter how many times others would rationalize it for her, killing another person took away a piece of her soul. It was a heavy badge her heart wore every day of her life, and now, she had another scar to remind her of just how dangerous her job was. It was a badge that Tony Carducci now shared with her.

Turning from the dead men, Tony shrugged. "I'll be fine. You?"

"Shaking in my shoes and shitting in my pants." Taking her mike from her shoulder, Delta called in briefly to explain where they were and what had happened. It would be mere seconds before the first of many officers would arrive to cordon off the crime scene. Delta looked around her and knew she had to come up with something quick. Not only had she ripped the bust away from the feds, she had killed any chances of using these guys to get the big fish.

Ah, but there was still one alive, wasn't there?

Maybe the feds would be happy with one little fish that might lead them to the big fish. Maybe. Her life was filled with maybes.

"I wasn't sure you heard me," she said to Carducci as she checked on the little girl. Delta hadn't noticed it before, but her hands trembled as she tucked the blanket around her.

Stepping up behind her, Tony looked in on the girl and nodded. "I heard you loud and clear. At first, I wasn't sure what was going on, but I caught on."

"Thank God for that."

"That was some risk you took, giving up your gun."

"First off, we're not going to tell anyone I gave up my gun."

"But—"

"Look, you and I know I had no choice. But the brass? They won't see it that way."

Tony nodded and let out a huge sigh. "I got it. CYA and all that." Slowly turning from her, Tony stared into the van. "They don't look real anymore."

Turning Tony so he faced her, Delta softened her tone of voice. "You had no choice but to kill him. It was him or me. You remember that down the road when the press, IA, and even you question your actions. He would have killed us all. You did what was best."

Tony listened intently and nodded again. His powerful shoulders quivered at her touch, and she knew it was taking everything he had not to collapse right there. Killing someone was never easy, no matter how macho one thought himself. There was always a stillness, a silence that followed, as though the universe were judging your actions. Delta knew that Tony was experiencing that silence.

Inhaling a shaky breath, Tony swallowed hard. "For a moment there, after I first heard your shrug signal, I got kind of scared. All of a sudden, you were trusting me with your life and I wasn't sure I was ready for that. I was really afraid that I'd let you down."

Delta reached up and gently touched his arm. "I trust you with my life every time we go out on the streets. This time was no different. If you can't trust your partner, you might as well pack it in."

"But how could you be so sure?"

Delta smiled warmly. Traces of fear and fatigue from overstimulation outlined his handsome face. He was suffering what her shrink called shot shock, a sort of depressed condition that follows a shooting. Tony didn't know it, but the worst part wasn't over yet. The worst part was the doubt, the guilt, the nightmares that would follow. The worst part was waking up one morning knowing that there were family members, friends, and colleagues of the deceased who would never see them again. The worst was wondering over and over what they could have done differently.

"I counted on your ability to shoot him right between the eyes. I know what you're capable of doing, remember? I've seen you shoot. *You* were the ace up my sleeve. I needed you to down him with a single shot. You came through, and frankly, that doesn't surprise me at all."

"Really? Even after all my screw ups?"

Pulling Tony away from the van, Delta heard the sirens and the screeching tires of the feds and police hurrying to join them. "There's a trait in you that can't be taught or learned, and that's loyalty. You showed that the day you busted Miller's chops. I knew you wouldn't let me down."

Tony bowed his head before gazing over at the van. "They look so...."

"Unreal? Death is like that. It never looks like it looks on TV or in the movies." Delta looked once more at the dead men. They looked more like wax figures than real people. Their arms and legs were sprawled in different directions, as if someone had deliberately placed them that way.

"Do you ever get used to it?" Tony asked, shuddering slightly.

"To what? Killing someone? Never. You do what you have to do to get home alive. Remember?"

Tony nodded. "Lesson number one."

"That's exactly what we did."

Tony stuffed his hands in his pockets and looked out into the field. "I was really nervous."

Delta nodded and rubbed his shoulder with her right hand. "Me, too."

For a moment, the two of them walked over to the opening of the van. In a weird twist of fate, she and Tony had become the final jury. In the blink of a moment, they made a decision no one else seemed willing to make. In the second that it took for them to squeeze the triggers, Delta was judge and jury for a man who would have snuffed her out like a waning candle. And though she knew there would be a final, numbing pain when it was all done, she did not regret for an instant squeezing that trigger.

Without thinking, Delta put her arm around Tony and pulled him to her. "You did great," she said, feeling the sudden surge of emotion she always felt when Death brushed his frozen kiss past her cheek.

"You were the one who took the chance. All I did was follow your directions."

Delta looked into Tony's eyes. His young boy's gaze had transformed into the deeper, more serious look of a man. "And do you realize that you did follow them? I told you east and there you were. If I would have thought about your disability, or should I say, former disability, I would have said the passenger side of the car. But I didn't need to, did I? Your timing was impeccable."

"Well, I had a good teacher. She once told me that timing was everything."

Delta smiled to herself. She really was a good teacher. Odd...she never would have thought....

"But I have to admit," Tony continued, "that I thought I was going to shit my pants when I came around the car and there you were, standing in front of a gun with yours laying on the ground. You must have been scared out of your mind."

"Scared doesn't begin to touch it. I've never given up my weapon before. I had to trust that you would be there. I had to trust that you finally knew east from west. I had to...well, I had to trust you."

Tony bowed his head and looked away. "Thanks."

"Tony, I wouldn't have been on the streets with you unless I trusted you."

"What?" Tony wheeled back around and stared hard at Delta.

"I said—"

"No, I know what you said. You called me Tony." Delta smiled.

"I guess this means I've earned my wings?"

Delta nodded. "And then some. Unfortunately, you might have earned them just in time for them to be snatched away." Pointing to the stream of cars coming toward them, Delta shrugged. "We may look like heroes now, Tony, but by the time the feds and Internal Affairs get through with us, we may be begging for positions at the pound."

Tony stood as erect and broad as he could. "Delta, no matter what anyone says, we were awesome tonight. We may have pissed everyone off for doing the job they didn't do, but that's just tough shit."

Delta grinned. "Yes, it is. Unfortunately, we may be the only two who see it that way." Delta paused and looked up at the first cop who hopped out of a patrol unit. It was Jan Bowers, her previous partner.

"Is there anything that can keep you out of trouble?" Jan asked, throwing her arms around Delta and hugging her tightly. After squeezing Delta so hard that Delta could hardly breathe, Jan pulled away and pointed a finger at Tony. "It's damn lucky for you that this woman is in one piece, Mister. Damn lucky."

Delta couldn't help but smile. "Luck had nothing to do with it, Jan. The kid can shoot."

Jan laced her arm through Delta's and drew closer. "Good for you both. When I heard who they had saddled you with, I...well, let's just say you haven't been far from my heart."

Delta pulled Tony to her and ruffled his hair. "I must live a charmed life. No matter what happens to me, I keep getting great partners."

Jan stopped and pointed in the direction of a stream of headlights. "Let's hope your charm hasn't rubbed off, Storm. You're going to need it."

As the first unmarked vehicle rolled in with a black and white following close behind, Delta inhaled deeply and gathered her wits. She was glad that both Tony and Jan were with her right now. She knew she would need all the support she could get. "Tony, no matter what, you never saw me give up my gun, okay?"

"Gotcha."

"And don't," Jan whispered, "under any circumstances, deviate from whatever story Delta weaves for you. Giving up your gun is bad business."

Tony nodded. "Right. Anything else?"

"Yeah. Let me do the talking. I'm a little too familiar with these kinds of scenes."

"You can have it."

When the captain jumped out of the squad car and made connection with the head federal agent, Delta stood firm and noticed how proudly Tony was standing. He was standing so close to her, their elbows touched.

"I thought you told your men not to get involved," the tall, paunchy federal agent demanded of Captain Henry as they stood in front of the unmarked vehicle. But before Captain Henry could reply, the federal agent was issuing orders, sending his men scurrying like mice into the field and around the van. As if on cue, the yellow "crime scene" tape went up, cutting everyone off from the area, except for those who were already standing in it.

"Officer Stevens," Captain Henry said slowly and evenly. Delta noticed something different about the way he spoke, but she couldn't put her finger on it. "Who killed these men?"

"We did, sir."

Captain Henry glanced in the van at the two dead men. "Both shot in the head. Nice shooting."

Delta nodded. "Yes, sir, it was."

Looking into the patrol car, the captain kneeled down to touch the little girl's head. She was fast asleep. "Killed two suspects and saved the girl?"

"Yes, sir." She didn't know what else to say.

"When I'm through with these fed boys, I'll expect both your reports on my desk by oh-nine hundred. Is that clear?"

Delta and Tony both nodded.

"Oh, and one more thing. I don't know yet how this van happened to crash, or why you chased after them without making radio contact in spite of my orders, or why we didn't hear from you until this whole ugly episode was over, but you can be assured of one thing."

Delta swallowed.

Walking up to Delta and getting within an inch of her face, Captain Henry scowled. "You two are in deep shit if you can't justify every single move you made prior to killing those two men. Do I make myself absolutely clear?"

Nodding, Delta replied before thinking. "Sir, does the end every justify the means?"

"What?" Henry barked.

"Does the end ever justify the means to you?"

Captain Henry opened his mouth to respond, but simply waved his answer away. "Oh-nine hundred and not a second later."

Watching him walk back into the thick of the investigation, Delta heaved a sigh of relief. After answering all of the questions the feds threw at them, Delta and Tony finally got in their car and watched silently as Child Protective Services took the girl away.

"We're going to be fine, Carducci. Just fine."

"How do you know?"

"Just watch. Henry is going to look pretty sweet when he stands in front of the press with the chief and explains how *his* department caught and killed child killers. *His* officers saved the life of another child. *His* officers are looking pretty damn good right about now, compared to the feds. *His* officers did what the big, bad boys in their suits and ties couldn't do. Imagine how that's going to look. You'll see. Everything is going to be just fine. Politics is at work here and we've made a lot of the right people look good. That goes a long way in this city."

"I hope you're right. Right now, I just feel like sleeping and hoping that when I wake up, it's all over."

"Trust me on this one. By morning, we'll be heroes. There's not a cop in this world, captain or otherwise, who's going to reprimand us for what we've done here. You can rest easy knowing that there will be a tomorrow for us and we'll still be wearing our badges."

Tony sat in the passenger seat and rubbed his face with both hands. For a long time, he just sat and said nothing. Finally, when he did speak, his voice was low and barely above a whisper. "Delta, would you think less of me if I told you I feel like crying?"

Patting Tony's shoulder, Delta leaned over and hugged him. "Quite the contrary, partner. Quite the contrary."

39

"Let me get this straight. After you and I spoke on channel one-eight, you *forgot* to switch back to open air?"

"That's right." As was the custom in their department on cases involving the death of a suspect, the captain was interviewing Tony and Delta separately before sending them both to Internal Affairs. Both interviews were intended to ascertain whether the shoot had been a righteous shooting or a tactical error on the part of the cops involved. And while there was no doubt that it was a righteous shooting, the fact that Delta had already killed one man made this investigation a bit more complicated.

"Why do I find that hard to believe?" The captain folded his hands and stared over the desk at Delta.

Delta shrugged innocently. "I don't know, sir. If I had heard your order, you can be sure we would not have tried to apprehend the suspect or endanger the life of that little girl."

Leaning across the desk, the captain's eyes narrowed. "I find that even harder to believe than this bullshit you're handing me about not turning your radio back. You knew there was a little girl in that van, yet you continued to pursue it."

"Yes, sir. We were simply covering our end of the perimeter."

Leaning back, Captain Henry shook his head. "I can see we're not going to get anywhere on this. I tried to shake your partner down but he insists that you simply forgot about the radio because you were busy teaching him something. I even threatened to bust his ass outta here if he didn't come clean about this whole damned mess, yet he maintains your sorry ass story about you both 'forgetting.' You have certainly covered your ass this time, Stevens."

Delta suppressed a smile. "I only reported things the way they happened, sir."

"Of course you did," he mocked. "And this here, where you say the van drove into a parked car? The suspect who escaped from the van says your vehicle attempted to ram them. Is this true?"

"No, sir. It isn't. Both Officer Carducci and I are aware that it is against department regulations to use a patrol vehicle as a barricade. Section nine-twenty three of—"

"For crying out loud, Stevens, don't give me that horeshit! I want to know why our suspect believes you tried to run them down?"

"I wouldn't know, sir. Perhaps in all of the confusion, he made a mistake. He is, after all, a criminal." Delta had to choke back the sarcasm.

Henry scribbled a note and then looked at Delta suspiciously. "A criminal? I see. So, you and Carducci draw on the two guys in the van and decide to take them out before they kill you or the little girl, is that right?"

"Yes, sir."

"Then tell me something. According to the coroner's report, the angle of the entry in the suspect you shot is such that it came from practically ground level. Can you explain that to me?"

"The report is pretty clear about that, sir. I dove to the ground for cover."

Captain Henry's moustache twitched. "For cover? You dove to the ground for cover? Just what kind of cover would the ground have lent you, and what was your partner doing while you were grovelling on the ground looking for a place to hide?"

"As it states in the report—"

"To hell with this report! I'm asking you to tell me what really happened!"

"Carducci fired as I dove to the ground."

"For cover," he added sarcastically.

"Yes, sir."

"And in less than a blink of the eye, you killed two armed suspects."

"Yes, sir."

"Do you realize that I could take this flimsy piece of work to IA and let them have a field day with all of the discrepancies? Who's going to believe that you dove to the ground for cover? Who would believe that the getaway vehicle just happened to crash? Tell me that. Delta, this whole report is a crock of shit."

Delta shrugged. "That's how it happened, sir, and I'm standing by it."

Henry sighed loudly and leaned back in his chair. For a long time, he just studied Delta. "That's what your partner said."

Delta didn't respond.

"Do you also realize how impossible it will be for anyone to reprimand you and your partner? Not only did you save another child's life, but you've destroyed a porno ring that has, until now, eluded every major law enforcement agency in this country."

Delta knew, but said nothing.

Leaning across the desk as far as his large frame would let him, Captain Henry lowered his voice. "I'm not going to admit saying this to you, Delta, so if it gets out of this room, I'll have you for breakfast."

Delta nodded. "My lips are sealed, sir."

"Personally, I don't give a rat's ass how you did what you did. I have a granddaughter the same age as that little girl they took hostage and it doesn't bother me one bit to know that scum like that won't waste the taxpayers' money on a trial. Personally, I'm proud to know that my cops can do anything better than even the most highly trained G-men."

"Thank you, sir."

"And professionally, you have made this department, the chief, and me, look exceedingly efficient. The phones have been ringing off the hook with 'atta boys.' To the rest of the universe, it was a job well done, even if, in my opinion, you disobeyed my orders. And I'll go to my death believing this whole report is one huge fabrication."

"Does that mean you're going to let IA know that you don't believe the report?" Delta held her breath as she waited for the answer.

"Hell no. The report stands as is. You and Carducci corroborate each other's report, you caught the scumbags and disposed of them. The media is loving it, the DA is loving it, and the public is eating it up. The only ones sour are the feds and I've shipped their asses out of here."

"I'm glad it all worked out, sir."

"Well, not all of it. Stevens, I'm afraid I misjudged you. I read a bunch of horseshit about you and let it obscure my vision. I apologize for that."

"I understand, sir. You have your job to do as well."

"Yes, I do. And as of this moment, it is my duty to take you off of TP duty, and you and your new partner will be on your beat as of day after tomorrow."

Delta sat up as if stuck by a pin. "New partner, sir? I was just getting used to Carducci."

"Good. Because he's your new man." Captain Henry rifled through more papers before closing the report. "As far as I'm concerned, you two deserve each other. But if you're going to be cutting everything so close, I'd rather not have to explain how a Training Patrol Officer continues to be in the heat of the moment. As of today, Carducci has graduated from TP, and so have you."

Delta jumped out of the chair and shook his hand. "Thank you, sir. You won't regret it."

Shaking his head, Captain Henry rose and moved to the door. "I'd better not. You'll forever be an enigma to me, Delta Stevens. First you hate him, then you fight for him, then you lie for him, and now you want him for your partner."

Smiling from ear to ear, Delta shrugged. "He's grown on me. What can I say?"

"Say that you'll try to stay out of trouble for awhile. I'm going to a seminar next week and I'd like to know you're not going to be in the papers while I'm gone."

"I think I can handle that, sir."

"Good." Opening the door, Captain Henry patted Delta on the back as she started through it. "Oh, and there's one more thing."

"Yes?"

"Sometimes, Officer Stevens, the end does justify the means. This is one of those times."

"Thank you, sir." Walking out of the office, Delta looked across the room at Tony, who was listening intently to one of Connie's stories. Delta could tell by the way Connie was waving her hands in the air that she was conning him. Stopping for a moment, Delta listened to the sounds of the station as phones rang, papers were shovelled, and filing cabinets squeaked shut. Suspects were being brought in handcuffed, detectives collaborated with cops, and the wheels of justice kept spinning along.

This was her life. It might be crazy, it might be dangerous, but it was the reason she got up every morning; it was the reason she lived with such passion. It was the one great love that kept her on the edge. Maybe Megan would never understand that, but that's the way it was.

That's the way it would always be. Delta Stevens was a cop. And she loved every second of it.

About the Author

Linda Kay Silva is now a Lecturer in the Education Department at Mills College in Oakland, California. She also teaches Business Communications and Contemporary Literature at Heald College in Concord, California. When she isn't teaching or writing, Linda Kay is "in the wind" on her 1993 Harley-Davidson. Linda is currently working on her first screenplay, as well as books four and five in the *Storm* series.

Paradigm Publishing Company, a woman owned press, was founded to publish works created within communities of diversity. These communities are empowering themselves and society by the creation of new paradigms which are inclusive of diversity. We are here to raise their voices.

Books Published by Paradigm Publishing:

Taken By Storm by Linda Kay Silva
(Lesbian Fiction/Mystery) ISBN 0-9628595-1-6 $8.95

A Delta Stevens police action novel, intertwining mystery, love, and personal insight. The first in a series.

". . . not to be missed!" — *East Bay Alternative*

Expenses by Penny S. Lorio (Lesbian Fiction/Romance) ISBN 0-9628595-0-8 $8.95

A novel that deals with the cost of living and the price of loving.

"I laughed, I cried, I wanted more!" — Marie Kuda, *Gay Chicago Magazine*

Tory's Tuesday by Linda Kay Silva (Lesbian Fiction) ISBN 0-9628595-3-2 $8.95

Linda Kay Silva's second novel is set in Bialystok, Poland during 1939 Nazi occupation. Marissa, a Pole, and Elsa, a Jew, are two lovers who struggle not only to stay together, but to stay alive in Auschwitz concentration camp during the horrors of World War II.

"*Tory's Tuesday* is a book that should be widely read — with tissues close at hand — and long remembered." — Andrea L.T. Peterson, *The Washington Blade*

Practicing Eternity by Carol Givens and L. Diane Fortier (Nonfiction/Healing/Lesbian and Women's Studies) ISBN 0-9628595-2-4 $10.95

The powerful, moving testament of partners in a long-term lesbian relationship in the face of Carol's diagnosis with cervical cancer. It is about women living, loving, dying together. It is about transformation of the self, relationships, and life.

1992 *Lambda Literary Awards* Finalist!

"*Practicing Eternity* is one of the most personal and moving stories I have read in years." —Margaret Wheat, *We The People*

Seasons of Erotic Love by Barbara Herrera (Lesbian Erotica) ISBN 0-9628595-4-0 $8.95

A soft and sensual collection of lesbian erotica with a social conscience. By taking us through the loving of an incest survivor, lesbian safe sex, loving a large woman, and more, Herrera leaves us empowered with the diversity in the lesbian community.

". . . the sex is juicy and in full supply." —Nedhara Landers, *Lambda Book Report*

Evidence of the Outer World by Janet Bohac (Women's Short Stories) ISBN 0-9628595-5-9 $8.95

Janet Bohac, whose writing has appeared in various literary publications, brings us a powerful collection of feminist and women centered fiction. By examining relationships in this symmetry of short stories, the author introduces us to Dory and a cast of characters who observe interaction with family, parent and child, men and women, and women and women.

". . . *Evidence of the Outer World* is about people waking up, and figuring out what to do with their lives...(and) reflects Bohac's fascination and concern with women's choices." —Ellen Kanner, *Arts & Entertainment*

"...compelling short stories. Bohac made me care. I was sorry that the book had to end." —Barbara Heath, Women's Studies Librarian, Wayne State University

The Dyke Detector (How to Tell the Real Lesbians from Ordinary People)
by Shelly Roberts/Illustrated by Yani Batteau
(Lesbian Humor) ISBN 0-9628595-6-7 $7.95

Lesbian humor at its finest: poking fun at our most intimate patterns and outrageous stereotypes with a little bit of laughter for everybody. This is side-splitting fun from syndicated columnist Shelly Roberts.

"What a riot! A must read for all lesbians. Brilliant!" — JoAnn Loulan

"...the funniest necessity since we used to wear green on Thursdays...the perfect handbook in the confusion of these post-modernist times." —Jewelle Gomez

Storm Shelter by Linda Kay Silva (Lesbian Mystery) ISBN 0-9628595-8-3 $10.95

Officer Delta Stevens is back in the sequel to *Taken By Storm*. Delta and Connie Rivera again join together and enter the complex world of computer games in order to solve the mystery before the murderer can strike again.

"A lesbian 'Silence of the Lambs.'" —Catherine McKenzie, *Queensland Pride*, Australia

"...a page turning, heart-pounding, tension-building murder mystery..." —Lambda Book Report

EMPATH by Michael Holloway (Gay Fiction/Sci-fi) ISBN 0-9628595-7-5 $10.95

A story of industrial politics, and how one man with supernatural abilities is thrust into this vortex to single-handedly eliminate the AIDS epidemic. This is a book about AIDS that has a **happy** ending and it will keep you on the edge of your seat!

". . . read[s] at a breakneck pace." —Robert Starner, *Lambda Book Report*

"...brilliantly written, fast paced and highly entertaining..." —Catherine McKenzie, *Queensland Pride*, Australia

Hey Mom, Guess What! 150 Ways to Tell Your Mother by Shelly Roberts/Illustrated by Melissa Sweeney (Lesbian/Gay Humor) ISBN 0-9628595-9-1 $8.95

The Dyke Detector does it again! This time best-selling humor author, Shelly Roberts, trains her razor-sharp wit on another favorite pastime for all gays and lesbians: coming out to Mom. Whether. When. Where. What. And how! When Roberts writes, we all laugh at ourselves.

"Don't call home without *Hey Mom, Guess What!* A fabulously funny book." —Karen Williams, Comic

"...a hilarious book...Roberts goes all out to make coming out make you laugh out loud." —*Update*

A Ship in the Harbor by Mary Heron Dyer (Lesbian Fiction) ISBN 1-882587-00-6 $8.95

A murder mystery unfolds within Oregon's recent climate of increasing homophobia and anti-choice fervor.

May 1994 Releases

Weathering the Storm by Linda Kay Silva
(Lesbian Mystery) ISBN 1-882587-02-2 $10.95

The third book of this renowned series. Officer Delta Steven's hasten's to save children abducted by a child pornography ring.

Golden Shores by Helynn Hoffa (Lesbian Romance/Mystery) ISBN 1-882587-01-4 $9.95

Set in the posh resort town of La Jolla against a backdrop of international intrigue.

Make News! Make Noise! (How to Get Publicity for Your Book) by Shelly Roberts, ISBN 1-882587-03-0 $5.95

Shelly Roberts shares her book marketing secrets with other authors.

Ordering Information

California residents add appropriate sales tax.

Postage and Handling—Domestic Orders: $2 for the first book/$.50 for each additional book. Foreign Orders: $2.50 for the first book/$1 for each additional book (surface mail).

Make check or money order, in U.S. currency, payable to: Paradigm Publishing Company, P.O. Box 3877, San Diego, CA 92163.